Gamers

CAMBRY VARNER

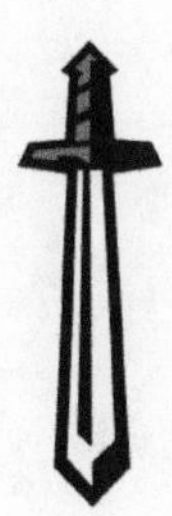

Published by Level Up in the United Kingdom in 2020

Cover illustration by Sippakorn Upama
Cover by Claire Wood

ISBN: 978-1-83919-048-3

www.levelup.pub

Dedicated to all the girls and women who wanted to:
Pull the Sword from the Stone,
Join the Fellowship of the Ring
Visit unexplored worlds
Save Gotham and Metropolis
Kill the Walking Dead
And found their adventure by picking up a controller.

Preface

"Sally? Are you online?"

"Just logged in."

"Cool! Main game and expansions installed? And updated?"

"Took a couple of hours, but yeah, everything is installed and updated."

"Great, go ahead and start the game. If you set up the subscription during installation, it should skip to the start game icon. Click it and let me know when you get to the character creation screen."

"Okay, it's loading up. How's Gina?"

"Saying I'm a bitch for trying to get you addicted to *Shadow's Deep*."

"Tell her I think she's right."

"Whatever, skank. On the character creation screen, yet?"

"Not yet. Tell me about this game. It's based off a tabletop game?"

"Pretty much. It follows the same rules with the software rolling the dice for you, but there are some differences because it's an online game. There yet, Sally?"

"Yes, I'm there now. What race should I be?"

"Depends. What class do you want to play as?"

"What are Rogues like in this game?"

"Pretty useful. They can pick locks, look for traps, sneak around, and backstab enemies. They don't have high health points, but they are very hard to hit and deal some serious critical damage."

"Alright, Rogue it is then. Which race?"

"Humans, elves, half-elves, halflings, or gnomes are all good for Rogues."

"I think I'll go with half-elf."

"Next should be your stats. Be sure to click the roll icon and then assign your stats. Since you're a Rogue, you'll want to put your highest number in Dex and your lowest in Strength."

"Okay, the stats and skills are self-explanatory. I can handle it from here."

"Okay Sally. Ask if you have any questions."

"What class are you?"

"I created a Cleric yesterday for tonight. Too bad a level fifteen Sorceress can't enter low level dungeons."

"Why did you want to become a mentor in the first place? Don't you get tired of answering the same questions over and over?"

"It helps out the *Shadow's Deep* community. A lot of new players get overwhelmed at first and quit playing before giving the game a chance. So, I answer questions and hold their hand through a first level dungeon and a few quests."

"Between playing and mentoring, that doesn't leave much time for your job. Don't you have articles to write?"

"They don't care what I do with my time as long as I turn in my material before deadline. Sometimes I'll take a break from *Shadow's Deep* to put my nose to the grindstone to pump out several articles to have on hand to send in. What about you? When are you going back to work?"

. . .

"Sally?"

"Sorry, I was reading some of the skills. I might go back next week."

"You've been saying that for nearly three weeks."

"I mean it each time. I promise I'll go back to work soon."

"Okay. Just don't wait too long."

"I finished with the character. What do I do now?"

"Alright, put on your headset and click start. It should spawn you near the Lair of Tears."

"Okay. See ya there."

Chapter 1

THE INCIDENT

It didn't hurt. There was no flash of light or cry of horns, or anything to indicate that her life would change forever after clicking start. Sally had been sitting in a soft leather chair in front of the computer monitor watching the loading icon spin and then she was standing in a field. The cool breeze of the ceiling fan changed to the warm touch of a bright afternoon sun. Oiled leather armor replaced the comfy sweatpants and t-shirt. Her feet, which had been bare on a hardwood floor now found themselves snugged in a pair of worn leather boots and placed upon the thick green grass.

Sally's eyes slowly adjusted to the brightness. The bedroom had been dimly lit during the early evening, with the monitor serving as the primary light source. Why the hell was she outside now in the afternoon?

She was surrounded by trees that stood like pillars of an ancient ruin. Birdsong echoed with the whisper of wind blowing through the leaves and foliage. A black mouth of a cave loomed before her, and in front of it was a woman in armor.

The woman was of average height but seemed taller in the ornate armor. Embossed on the polished chest plate was a bright sun with curling rays. The woman was richly bronze-skinned, and black hair framed her face beneath a white hood. What drew Sally's particular attention was the heavy iron mace being brandished in her direction.

"Who the fuck are you?" the woman demanded, jabbing the end of the mace towards Sally.

"Hey!" Sally backpedaled out of reach of the mace and wished she had a weapon herself, like a gun or a baseball bat. A sudden inclination dropped her right hand to her left hip and she drew a long thin sword from her belt. Holding the blade before her in one hand, Sally instinctively raised the other hand behind her for better balance. "You better back up before I put this through your eye and out the back of your goddamn head!"

"I would love to see you try, honey," the armored woman snarled.

"I will if you don't get out of here!" Sally cried.

"Screw you, skank!"

Sally blinked, stunned for several moments; then she called out, "Darcy?"

The woman's dark brows rose in complete surprise before she said, "Sally?"

They slowly lowered their weapons and then simultaneously raised them again, threateningly. Sally glowered at the woman who either was or wasn't Darcy. She sounded and spoke just like Darcy, but the woman's appearance was too harsh, with sharp facial cheekbones and small eyes.

"If you are Sally," the woman said slowly, "then what kind of party did I have for my fifth birthday?"

"I don't know because I didn't know you back then," Sally replied. "Our parents didn't get married until you were twelve."

"Oh-kay," Darcy said, still not lowering her weapon. "Let's try again. What game were you playing when our parents got married?"

"*Final Fantasy X*," Sally answered. "Look, I don't know why you're the one asking me these questions. You're the one claiming to be Darcy."

"Because I am!" The woman snapped. "And you don't look a thing like my step-sister!"

"What do you mean?"

"Have you seen yourself?"

Sally looked at her hands and stared in astonishment. They were standard hands with all ten fingers, but they weren't her hands. Hers had never looked so smooth and long. The nails ended in rounded tips and not the chewed nubs they had been before. She touched her face feeling her nose and eyes, but they did not feel familiar at all.

Her stepsister hooked her mace at her hip and stared at herself in the reflective surface of her shield. "Holy shit...holy shit...This isn't me..."

Sally, all threats forgotten, crossed the distance between them and peered into the shield's surface. "Oh God..."

The face staring back at her belonged in a fashion magazine or on an artist's canvas. A curtain of gleaming golden hair had replaced her mousy brown mop. And a porcelain face with bright blue eyes stared back at her in open shock: it was far from the face she had been accustomed to seeing in the bathroom mirror. Then Sally looked down at a body that couldn't be hers. For one thing, it weighed fifty pounds less, with a flat tummy and a trim ass that worked the leather pants like a maestro.

Placing her hands on her shapely hips, she said, "I guess I can slip into a size four now."

"Try a size one," Darcy said. "I think I'm a foot taller."

"Jesus, are we on drugs? We have to be on drugs."

"God, I don't know. The last thing I remember is logging onto *Shadow's Deep*."

"Me too." Sally ran a hand through hair that shouldn't be hers. She froze and then grabbed her ears. "Sweet Jesus, what's wrong with my ears?"

"Let me see!" Darcy seized her head with one gauntlet hand that bit into Sally's skin, making her wince, and swept aside the golden hair. "Shit, they're elf ears. You have elf ears!"

Sally wrenched herself from Darcy's hand. "But why? What's going on?"

Darcy's widening eyes stared at Sally, then down at herself, and the cave behind her. "Oh God…no, no, no, no, no."

"Darcy?"

"Shit," Darcy hissed, staring at the cave, then at the sun symbol on her chest, and then at Sally's attire. "Shit, this isn't possible. This can't be possible. We're in the game."

"What game?"

"*Shadow's Deep*!" Darcy yelled, rounding on her. "You told me you were making a half-elf rogue and now look at yourself! You're a half-elf wearing level one Rogue's outfit." She waved at Sally's clothing and then pointed at herself, "And I'm a third-level human Cleric, and that cave is the Lair of Tears."

"How do you know?" Sally peered at the cave, looking for a sign.

"Trust me. As many times as I created characters for this game, I'd recognize the tutorial dungeon."

"Is this like VR thing?" Sally said, feeling a little comforted that they had gotten some answers to their situation, but still lost and confused.

"Goddammit, you should know better than me that this isn't a VR game. Did you put a VR headset on your head when you started the game? *Shadow's Deep* isn't played like that." Darcy set her shield against her back. "And before you ask how we got inside the game, my answer is a big I don't fricking know."

"Okay," Sally said, feeling a bit miffed at being yelled at when she was just as much victim as Darcy. "So can you answer me this question? What do we do?"

"Let me think," Darcy said as she slid a finger up her nose where the glasses she usually toyed with when she was in deep thought were gone. She paused, evidently noticing the same issue. "It's going to be weird seeing without glasses."

Sally crossed her arms beneath her breasts, which were smaller and perkier than her real ones, and looked around. The forest was empty, almost silent, save for the crackling of branches in the wind and wildlife disturbing bushes. "Darcy, shouldn't there be other players?"

"What do you mean?" Darcy glanced at her, looking annoyed to have been tugged from her thoughts.

"Well, if this is the game, like you say, and this dungeon is where all the beginning characters start, then shouldn't there be more people coming and going? Why is it just us two?"

Darcy took in their solitary surroundings. It was empty save for the two of them. "I don't know. It might be only us."

"But why only us?"

"It's going to get old to hear myself say "I don't know" over and over," Darcy moaned, shaking her head. "Just don't ask me any more questions for the next five minutes, okay? I need to think."

As she waited for her half-sister's attention, Sally looked down at her new body. It was the body she always wanted, or any woman would want for that matter. She could fit herself into a black catsuit, like Kate Beckinsale in *Underworld*.

Darcy was mumbling to herself, as she did whenever she was puzzling over a problem, like she was studying in high school or writing up one of her RPG campaigns.

Setting her hands on her hips, Sally stared at the cave. If this place was part of the game, then would it make sense to behave as if they were in one? "Darcy, I think we need to go through the dungeon," Sally said.

Her Cleric sister lifted her head. "Why?"

"Think about it." Sally motioned at the opening of the cave. "When a game puts you in a dungeon, you must reach the end to advance."

"That's a good point," Darcy said, considering. "The Lair of Tears is only a first-level dungeon with a minor treasure chest at the end."

"Then it should be easy," Sally said. Then she considered all the games she had played before and remembered that they all had monsters and enemies to either avoid or fight. "Damn, we're going to have to fight our way through, aren't we?"

"Yeah, but I think we'll be alright. The monsters are low level, and I'm a third-level Cleric wearing heavy armor, and since you're a Rogue, they'll have a hard time hitting you." Darcy waved her mace at Sally and then expertly swung it in a short arc. "And I think we know how to fight with our weapons. Give your rapier a few practice swings and see."

Sally hadn't paid attention to how she was handling her weapon until now. Before today, she had never held anything more lethal than a kitchen knife. The rapier was light enough to hold in one hand; with a long, thin blade it had a white guard at the hilt. Instinctively, she drew her left hand back near her head as she raised the rapier with the right. Her offhand felt empty, as if she missed the grip of a second weapon. The blade whistled as she slashed the air, imagining the tip cutting through a carotid vein in the neck or slashing across a pair of eyes. Then she thrust forward, imagining the tip puncturing through the heart or between ribs into a lung. And down through the aorta vein in the thigh or groin.

Where was this knowledge coming from? It was as if she had been taking fencing lessons for years, which couldn't be further from the truth. The last time Sally had done anything of a sporting nature was the final year of high school PE.

She ducked back just as a mace swung inches from her nose. Taking another step away, she lowered her upper body in a defensive crouch, the rapier at the ready to return the attack. Of course, it was only Darcy, so she straightened and lowered the blade. "You were testing me, right?"

"Nah, I was trying to brain you," Darcy replied, weighing her mace. "I knew you would dodge it. You put your highest score in Dexterity, right?"

"Yes, like you told me too," Sally said, wanting to sheath her rapier, but keeping it drawn in case Darcy tried to test her again.

"What was your score?"

"An eighteen, but it went up to nineteen because I chose half-elf as my race." Wistfully, Sally thought back to sitting in front of her computer in her home.

"Yeah, Dex is a racial stat bonus for half-elves," Darcy said as she scanned Sally's appearance. "They also get plus two to Charisma. What's your Charisma score?"

"That's became my highest score after I chose half-elf. It started out as eighteen, then it became a twenty," Sally said. In most RPGs, Charisma served as a means of completing a quest or overcoming an obstacle without fighting. Sally enjoyed finding new lines of dialogue and taking advantage of any potential quest shortcuts to solving a challenge and gaining XP.

"Holy shit, you got two eighteens? How did you get those?" Darcy asked.

"I just clicked ROLL," Sally said with a shrug. There had been a warning on the character creation screen that she could only have a maximum of six characters per account, with stats that were assigned after just one roll for each. Sally had figured if she didn't like her initial Rogue, she could try again with one of the empty slots once she learned the game.

"So you got two eighteens on your first try? Talk about lucky." Darcy once again scanned Sally's appearance and nodded. "With a Charisma score of twenty, no wonder you look like a runway supermodel. Do you remember your other stats?"

"I know I put the lowest number in Strength, but that's all I can remember. I didn't think I'd have to memorize my character's info screen."

"That's alright. It shouldn't matter. Between the two of us, we can handle a tutorial dungeon," Darcy said.

Sally noticed a trace of fear in her own voice as she sheathed her sword, "So we're really going to do this?"

"Hey, it was your idea that we try the dungeon," Darcy replied as she dug through a backpack that Sally hadn't noticed before. "Check your gear, let's see what we have."

Noticing the weight on her own back for the first time, Sally shifted the bag off her shoulders and swung it around to inspect it. The backpack was made of durable cloth and leather with a bedroll tied to the bottom, and a coil of rope hooked on the back. The flap was secured by a small button, which she slipped free and looked inside. There was a small tinderbox, several packets of dried food that resembled beef jerky, actual torches, cutlery with a cup and plate, and a waterskin that resembled a canteen. Despite carrying a lot, there was plenty of space for more. There was, as well, something so small that she almost didn't see it. A thin corked vial was held in a small sleeve stitched into the side of the pack. The red liquid within it had a gleam to it that reminded her of metallic nail polish.

The bottle didn't have a label naming it a health potion, but it greatly resembled what Sally would expect one to look like. "I think I have a health potion." Sally looked up when she didn't hear a response from Darcy. "What's wrong?"

Darcy was also examining the contents of her backpack. On her face was a slight frown knitting her eyebrows together. Holding up her backpack's camping gear, she said, "You don't need these when you play the online version, but you do when you're playing tabletop. Weird that we would have these. Anyway, have an extra one." Darcy handed over a similar vial from her bag. "I have three of them, so that will be four health potions between us."

Sally tucked the potion into an empty sleeve next to the first one and closed the flap. "You know, this feels almost like a LARP."

Darcy moaned, "This is more than some weird costume shit."

Sally shouldered the bag, "What about when you and Gina do cosplay for conventions? Isn't that weird costume shit too?"

"Hey," Darcy said stiffly, "Cosplay is art, but enough about that, I'll take the lead, and you watch my back." Darcy lit a torch with a bit of flint and steel. "Being half-elf, you'll have low-light vision so you can see further in the dark than I can. Take the torch so I can use my shield, and you can use it as an offhand weapon if you need to."

***

Sally had always been a gamer since she first played Super Nintendo. It had been her cousin's console, and she had instantly fallen in love with it. After months of begging her mother for one, she was delighted one Christmas morning when she opened a gift to see the image of a Super Nintendo gleaming at her. From there, it had been the GameCube, Nintendo 64, and then the Xbox and Playstation consoles. After a summer of saving her allowance and a semester of good grades, she bought her first PC and kept it upgraded to play the latest game titles. She had played all of the Final Fantasy games, the *Myst* series, and numerous other RPG franchises that caught her eye.

Darcy was a different breed of gamer in preferring board games and tabletop RPGs; the more sociable forms of gaming. With her massive collection of rule books, campaign guides, maps and sourcebooks, Darcy had often played hostess to the games. There had been plenty of attempts by Darcy to get her involved, but Sally thought the games had too much math involved to be fun and that she would rather pop in a cartridge or disc and start playing without all the prep work of creating a character and learning rules. Also, console gaming was something she could do without having to endure the presence of others.

It had surprised Sally when Darcy took to playing *Shadow's Deep*, the latest and most popular MMORPG on the market. She had doubted that Darcy would figure out how to install the game, much less stick with it for so long. As each expansion for *Shadow's Deep* came out, however, Darcy was the first in line to pick up her pre-ordered copy during the GameStop midnight release. Sally had never been interested in online games, finding single-player games more relaxing and fun without the pressure of other people being involved. It wasn't until the previous week that Darcy finally convinced her to give *Shadow's Deep* a chance.

So here they were now, trudging through a tunnel and into a dungeon, wearing the bodies of adventurers in a fantasy world. Darcy stalked potential enemies with her mace and shield at the ready and Sally followed close behind her with the rapier and a torch to light the way.

"Seriously? You can't see the walls?" Sally whispered.

"I'm human. I don't have fancy low-light vision," Darcy replied, pausing for a moment to listen and then moving forward at a cautious pace.

Sally could see far beyond the edge of the torch's light, but the stone wasn't cast in a warm, orange glow. The walls appeared to her in grayscale like in an old TV movie. It was as though half her vision was color blind when the grayscale contrasted with the yellow flickering flames of the torchlight. This had to be what Darcy meant by low-light vision. It was eerie, almost surreal, like a bad dream.

"So, what can humans do in this game that other races can't?" Sally asked. As much as she wanted Darcy to pay attention to what was ahead, she was too nervous to stay silent for long.

"Non-human races have bonuses assigned to certain pre-determined stats, but humans can put their bonuses into any stat they want." Darcy pointed down the hall. "There should be a trap up ahead. Go ahead of me and look."

"I don't know anything about traps," Sally said, hearing a note of fear in her voice.

"Yes, you do," Darcy said impatiently. "Rogues have a bonus for finding traps. Just like with the sword, you'll know what to look for."

She hesitated, pretty sure she didn't want to tangle with any death traps.

Darcy, seeing her trepidation, gave an exasperated sigh, "Sally, I'm sorry but I don't have a ten-foot pole. You have low-light vision. You can see the trap before I can and I'm right behind you if anything goes wrong."

This statement offered little reassurance, but Sally knew that to proceed she had to go along with the search for the trap. Moving around Darcy with a light step, Sally held the torch high before her. Scanning the ground and holding her breath, she moved forward one step at a time. What was she supposed to be looking for? After she asked herself that, she saw it: a piece of string. It had once been strung across the floor, but something had cut it.

Kneeling, Sally carefully lifted the string and examined the end. Not cut, it was broken. The fibers weren't even as they would be if cut with a knife. The trap hadn't been disarmed: it had sprung before they got here. Looking up, sure enough, she saw that a scythe-like blade was embedded in the wall opposite to where it had been released. Someone had walked through here and broke the string, which had released the mechanism that held the scythe in place.

Where was all this information coming from? She was analyzing this string as if she was a CSI at a crime scene.

"Sally?" Darcy said, interrupting her thoughts. "What is it?"

A chill ran down Sally's spine as she realized the implication of her analysis. "It's a sprung trap and there's blood."

Using her low-light vision, Sally could see a trail of blood leading deeper into the cavern. She pointed it out to Darcy and said, "Do you think a monster could have sprung it?"

Darcy considered this for a moment. "It's possible, but I wouldn't think so. This trap is meant to teach new players about detecting and disarming traps."

"So, this means we're not the only ones."

"No, shit. Even I can see someone's been through here."

"No, I meant we're not the only players in here."

Darcy nodded. "You're right. C'mon, there shouldn't be any more traps before the next room so we can hurry. Whoever it is has been hurt."

While Darcy's armor clinked and rattled, Sally moved through the shadows as silently as a breeze. Before long, she could hear a screaming ahead. Evidently able to hear the howls too, Darcy dashed forward with her mace held high. Having been left behind, Sally hesitated, afraid to see the cause of the terrifying scream. Still, being left alone in the tunnel was just as scary and she ran into the next room a short distance behind Darcy.

The room was a mayhem of rats as big as terriers nipping at the heels of a tall woman. She was the source of screaming, which she did while frantically kicking rats off her legs and batting at them as they jumped on her waist. With admiration for the bravery of her half-sister, Sally saw Darcy took a moment to take in the situation, before wading in, swinging her mace in downward arcs. The mace clubbed a rat in mid-leap and then nailed another between the ears. For her part, Sally found herself standing at the door, too afraid to follow Darcy into battle.

The tall woman ran to a nearby wall and collapsed against it, wailing as a rat clung onto her arm and sank its sharp teeth into her skin. Galvanised, Sally ran forward and, without pause or doubt, deftly thrust the tip of the rapier into the rat's skull. It died before it could make a squeak of surprise and Sally had to shake the body off the sword.

Darcy was making short work of the other rats, which had turned their attention from the stranger to the Cleric raining pain and death on them. They couldn't bite through her metal boots, and she rewarded their efforts with kicks and stomps as if she were performing a crush video. Before too long, the ground was littered with dead rats, and Darcy was beaming in satisfaction.

Sheathing her sword, Sally bend down to get a better look at the woman. Upon first glance, Sally had thought the woman was wearing leather armor like her own, but now she could see it was animal hide, which hung around her waist like a kilt. More leather hide and metal were fashioned into a bra with a fur pelt draped over her shoulders. There was a wound across her shoulders, not from the rat, but caused by an overhead slash. It had to have come from the triggered trap in the hall.

"Are you alright?" Sally asked.

"Oh God, I want to go home," the woman moaned, covering her face with both hands.

"Where's home?" Sally asked, recognising a familiar accent.

"New York City," the woman sobbed. "My dorm room is C-twenty-three. Planet Earth. If that means anything."

"Actually, it does. We're from Florida."

Chapter 2

MEETINGS

The woman's name was Mi-cha Kim, it was Korean, but her American name, which she asked them to use, was Mina Kim and she had been a college student until she became a Barbarian, and found herself alone inside a dark dungeon.

"I was wandering down the hall blind until something cut me!" She sobbed as Darcy looked over her injury. "Then I ran in here, and all these rats started biting me!"

Sally was sitting beside Mina and knew she ought to be doing something to comfort her, but didn't know how to go about it. Taking her hand was too personal. Patting her shoulder and going "there, there" seemed patronizing. In any case, it was more prudent and helpful to get answers about their situation. "What's the last thing you remember?"

Mina sniffled. "Playing this stupid game. I was supposed to be doing a dungeon crawl with some game mentor and another player, but they were late, so went ahead by myself."

Darcy, who had been staring in deep thought at the injury, dropped down beside Mina. "Wait, what was your user name?"

"Kit-Kat two-o-two," Mina replied, wiping away a tear.

"I'm the mentor you were waiting for," Darcy said excitedly, then defensively, she added, "And I wasn't late. We said six-thirty, and it was only six-twenty when I logged in."

The Barbarian woman rolled her eyes. "I was in a hurry. I have a chem test to study for, and I needed to learn how to play this dumb game by Friday."

"So, nothing strange happened?" Sally said sharply, to get the conversation back on a topic she felt was more important. "No lights, no voice of God; the room didn't shake or anything?"

"Nothing," Mina assured her. "I was even texting my roommate and. then I was in this tunnel. I might have dropped my phone back there. Did you see it?"

"Nope, no cellphone," Darcy said, almost gleeful at a loss she deemed unimportant. "My glasses didn't make it and nothing of Sally's came through either.

"Oh, great," Mina muttered. "Maybe it's still in my dorm."

"Hold still, I want to try something," Darcy stood and closed her eyes in concentration. Then touching Mina's shoulder, she began murmuring in an archaic language.

A soft glow flowed from her fingertips and into Mina's skin. It spread, highlighting the web of blood veins beneath the skin and made the bones of her shoulders stand out in dark shapes. The flesh shifted and moulded back together, reknitting, and becoming whole and smooth. Where the rats had bitten strips out of her skin slowly filled in and became unmarked. The cut across her shoulders now looked days old, scabbed over, and no longer bleeding.

Mina sighed in relief and evident pleasure. "It feels like I've been injected with novocaine and morphine. What did you do?"

"I cast a heal spell," Darcy said, staring at her fingertips in utter amazement. "I just cast a goddamn spell."

"How did you know how to do it?" Sally asked, rising to get a better look at the healed injuries.

"I'm a Cleric. Clerics get healing spells," Darcy said, raising an eyebrow. "That's basic gaming one-o-one, Sally."

"I know that," Sally retorted. "But unless you've been keeping things from your family, you've never cast a spell in your life."

"It like you with the rapier. I wanted to cast a spell, and the knowledge came to me," Darcy said, very pleased with herself.

"That doesn't make any sense," Mina said, flexing her shoulders. She winced as the cut along her shoulders still ached.

"It's how the game works, and since we're inside the game." Darcy tapped the side of her head. "The knowledge is right up here. We just have to use it. Mina, are you well enough to keep going?"

Mina was quiet for a moment. "Yeah, I guess so, but you didn't heal all my health points. I'm down by three."

Darcy set her hands on her hips, both offended and suspicious, "How do you know how much health I've healed?"

"I can see it right here," Mina pointed at the empty space before her. "See? I'm at eleven of fourteen."

Sally looked at the space in front of Mina and saw nothing but empty air. Then with the gentleness of someone dealing with the disturbed, Darcy said, "Mina, there's nothing there."

Mina glanced at both of them, squinting large dark eyes as if she was having trouble seeing them. "You can't see it? It might be because it's my character screen."

"See what?" Darcy demanded. "Would you please make sense?"

Mina muttered something under her breath that was better left unheard. "Okay, close your eyes and think about your character screen, and you'll see what I mean."

Darcy gave Sally a sardonic look before closing her eyes. After several seconds, she opened them and nearly fell back against the wall, face displaying sudden shock. Her eyes flicked about, and she turned her head this way and that. "Oh, my God! I can see my character screen! Can you guys see this too?"

Sally tried it herself. Closing her eyes, she thought, I want to see my character screen.

When she opened her eyes, a new object was there! While most of the world had faded to a faint background, right in front of her was a block of bright gold writing: her character information. Sally's ability scores were listed along with her skills, equipment, health, and saving throws. Her health was at a full 9 points out of 9, which was reassuring, but also dismaying, in that the total was a lot less than Mina's.

Sally tried to touch the screen, but her hands passed through empty air. It was almost disorienting. Like staring at a 3D image in a movie theater. "How do I close out of it?"

"Just think 'close' or 'go away,'" Mina replied from behind the screen.

Sally thought close, and the screen blinked away letting her see clearly. She brought it up again and then dismissed it several times to ensure she could do it again at will.

Darcy was leaning against the wall, her lips moving as she read her stats. "Sally, I want to try something else. Give me back the health potion I gave you."

Taking the health potion from her backpack, Sally passed it to Darcy, who held it to her chest. After a few moments, she looked over with a pleased smile. "I had two health potions, and it updated to three once I took this one back. Look at your character screen and take this one back."

Sally summoned her character screen and looked at the list of her adventuring gear. On a line of its own was listed: 1 minor potion of health. Holding out a hand for the potion, she watched the line as Darcy handed over the vial. As soon as her fingers closed around the bottle, the line switched over to say 2 minor potions of healing.

"You're right. Mine updated, too," Sally said, feeling a sudden upsurge of elation.

Mina looked between them, confused and still afraid. "What does this mean for us?"

"It means there's a system in place with rules that follows game mechanics I'm familiar with," Darcy said. "We can use the rules to protect ourselves and maybe find a way home."

***

The useful trait of having low-light vision meant that Sally didn't need torchlight to write. Darcy had a leaf of papers, an ink pen, and a little jar of ink stored at the bottom of her backpack.

"Why do you have ink and paper?" Mina asked as she took a sheet from Darcy's upraised hand.

"Clerics are considered scholars in *Shadow's Deep*," Darcy explained, handing Sally a second sheet. "In the tabletop version, Clerics get paper and ink as part of their adventuring gear. I only have one pen though. Who wants to write their stats down first? Just the stats for right now, it'll take too long to write down everything: I can guess your approximate skill levels from your stats and class."

Since she had better vision in the dark, Sally was chosen to write hers first. Darcy said it would give her a better idea of where everyone was at with their abilities and skills so she could make tactical decisions for the next few rooms. And it would be easier to reach their character information from a piece of paper than have them constantly relaying what they saw on their character screens.

It was like a class assignment from middle school, she thought to herself as she penned her information.

Race: Half Elf
Level 1 Rogue
HP: 9 (9)
Armor Class: 16

Str:	10
Dex:	19
Con:	12
Int:	15
Wis:	14
Cha:	20

Skills:

Climb (Str/Dex)	4
Swim (Str)	0
Acrobatics (D)	4
Climb (Str/Dex)	4
Sneak (Dex)	6
Legerdemain (D)	6
Evaluate (Int)	2
Magic (Int)	2
Knowledge (Int)	2
Perception (Wis)	2
Ani Friend (Wis)	2
Healing (Wis)	2
Survival (Wis)	2
Intimidate (C/S)	5
Entertain (Cha)	5
Charm (Cha)	5
Deceit (Cha)	5

Abilities: Sneak Attack Bonus, Two-Weapon Fighting, Roguish Talent +3 to Locate Traps

Darcy looked over her sheet and nodded, apparently impressed. Sally couldn't help feeling a small measure of pleasure from the silent praise. It had only taken her moments to figure out how the scores worked to create the characters she wanted. If she had known she was going to become her character for real, however, then she would have made other changes such as putting the extra 18 into Constitution for more HP rather than into Cha.

It took a little longer for Mina to finish copying her character information, and when she handed it over to Darcy, she got the opposite reaction. Darcy stared at the parchment, then looked at Mina, and then looked back the parchment again. "What the hell is this?"

"What's wrong?" Mina said, taken aback. "I copied it exactly."

"How?" Darcy said, lifting her eyes from Mina's stats to the Barbarian woman. "How the hell did you get a measly sixteen in Strength? Are these…" Darcy's eyes narrowed dangerously, "are these default stats?"

Mina's face remained blank. "I don't know what that means."

"Did you click the 'roll' icon to get your stats?" Darcy said, hotly. "Or did you just click okay through character creation?"

Sally rose to her feet and peered over Darcy's shoulder at Mina's stats and grimaced. She may be a novice at this game, but even she could see that these stats were subpar compared to hers.

Race: Human
Level 1 Barbarian
HP: 11 (14)
Armor Class: 15

Str:	16
Dex:	15
Con:	14
Int:	12
Wis:	10
Cha:	8

Swim (Str)	3
Climb (D/S)	3
Acrobat (Dex)	1
Sneak (Dex)	1
Legerdemain (D)	1
Evaluate (Int)	0
Magic (Int)	0
Knowledge (Int)	0
Perception (Wis)	1
Ani Friend (Wis)	1
Healing (Wis)	1
Survival (Wis)	3
Intimidate (C/S)	5
Entertain (Cha)	-1
Charm (Cha)	-1

Deceit (Cha) -1

Abilities: Rage, Wrestler

"I was in a hurry," Mina said, throwing up her large hands in a sign of defeat. "I told you I had a chem test to study for."

"Default stats are gimped!" Darcy's voice rose with emotion. "You got stuck with basic crap scores when you could have gotten much better stats by rolling! Everyone knows that!"

Sally laid a hand on Darcy's shoulder to calm her before she went into a tirade. "There's nothing we can do about it now. Can we still finish this dungeon?"

"Yeah, we can," Darcy said, slowly deflating, letting the anger go. "With me here, the group dynamic is rounded out." She tucked the sheets into her bag and collected the torch from the sconce where they had put it before she passed out the sheets. "Alright, there are two more rooms ahead. Sally, you go first. Mina will go...wait, Mina, where is your weapon?"

"Over there," the barbarian woman pointed at a great ax lying on the floor yards away. It had double-sided crescent blades, with the handle looking like a roughly sanded tree branch. "I threw it at the rats."

"Why would you throw your only weapon!?" Darcy demanded scandalized.

"It was the only thing I had in my hands," Mina said pointedly.

"Don't throw your ax!" Clearly, Darcy could barely keep herself from screaming. Feeling sorry for Mina, Sally was glad to see her sister draw a deep breath and let it out slowly until she was able to control her voice. "Alright, Sally needs to go first to look for traps, Mina will go behind her, and I'll take up the rear."

"Waitaminute," the tall barbarian woman who was now shouldering her great ax. "Why can't I go last?"

Sally recognized the twitch that suddenly appeared beneath Darcy's eye. It was a twitch that occurred when she was about to go into a fury. It didn't happen often, but when it did, you remembered it.

"Because we'll need you to go in before Sally to fight the walking skeletons in the next room," Darcy explained in a stiff tone that begged for a drink or a cigarette.

"If Sally is going first anyway, why don't I give her my great ax, and she can go in fighting?" Mina asked, ignorant of the warning that Darcy's twitch brought.

Seeing Darcy's face go several shades of scarlet, Sally quickly spoke up, "Darcy, you're a mentor, remember? I don't know this stuff myself, so this is no different than answering questions in a forum."

Darcy nodded and visibly made the effort to calm down. "Alright, listen close. Sally is a Rogue and has less health points than you at only nine points. If she goes in alone, after one or two swings, she's dead. Your health is higher than hers, so you can take more damage before going down. And you deal more damage with your greatax."

"And no," she said just as Mina opened her mouth to speak. "Sally can't use your great ax because she's a Rogue. Rogues can only use simple weapons like rapiers, but Barbarians can use martial weapons like great axes. I need to go last so I can watch your back and heal you. And before you point out that I'm wearing armor, yes, my armor does protect me from taking damage, but my mace can't do as much damage as your ax. With that said, are there any more questions?"

Mina raised her hand with an expectant look.

Darcy drew a small breath, held it, and let it out slowly. "Yes?"

"Can't you top me off on health points? I only have eleven now, and if I have to fight off monsters, I rather do it with full health."

"If you had fewer health points, I would, but I think you can take a hit or two before I have to heal you."

"Couldn't you give me a potion instead?" Mina asked, voice up an octave, obviously stricken at the thought of getting hit "once or twice."

Narrowing her eyes, Darcy said, "I'm not giving you a potion to heal three measly hit points. You're just going to have to trust me to keep you standing. Now, if there isn't anything else up somebody's ass, then let's go."

Minutes later, Sally led the line, holding a torch to light the way for the humans. Mina followed almost close enough to violate her personal space, with Darcy marching at the rear. As much as Sally hated going first, she could understand Darcy's reasoning, as she was the only one with low-light vision and could see farther than the circle of light from the torch. A door loomed ahead, and without needing Darcy to remind her, Sally checked for traps.

With her relatively high Wisdom and Intelligence scores, along with two points she'd assigned to the skill during her character creation, Sally had a +5 bonus to the Perception roll for finding traps. When Darcy was convincing her to give *Shadow's Deep* a chance, she had explained the game's mechanics of dice rolls. The higher the number, the more the chance of success at whatever you were attempting to do. The imaginary dice roll was typically that of a twenty-sided dice, but there could be variations depending on magic items, spells and other contexts. The adjusted roll was compared to the difficulty of the challenge. Finding a trap in a tutorial dungeon was probably a challenge rated around 10. So a twenty-sided dice roll with a +6 bonus should yield a high enough number to be successful eighty percent of the time. All the same, it wasn't obvious what she should be searching for, when she had never used the skill before finding the string of the scythe trap. Sally looked for inconspicuous strings, hidden panels, tiny slits in the floor and ceiling, and found none. Then she tried the door. It was heavy and wooden with a large brass knob that was so rusted it barely reflected the torch's light.

"It's locked," she commented.

"Then pick it," Darcy barked from behind Mina.

"With that? My fingers?"

"With your thieves' tools."

Before Sally could utter, what thieves' tools? she knew where they were on her person. Just as Clerics got paper and ink pens, Rogues received a set of tools to pick locks. Sewn inside a hidden pocket on the inside of her leather jerkin was where the thieves' tools were kept. The pocket was small and narrow to keep the tools from slipping out, but they came freely when she plucked at them. They were thin, needle lockpicks of metal, a small mirror on a tooth-brush-like handle, tiny pair of scissors, and pliers. Tucking the lockpicks between her teeth, she slipped the other tools back into the hidden pocket and went to work. Without ever having done this before, she prodded at the tumblers and received a satisfying click of a released lock.

"Okay, I got it," she said, putting the lockpicks away.

"Alright, stand aside. Mina's going in next."

"I am?" Mina yelped in terror.

"Yes, you are," Darcy said severely. "We are not going through this again. If anything goes wrong, just Rage."

Sally sighed when she saw Mina's confused expression. "What do you mean Rage? Get mad?"

Darcy's face hardened, but she didn't fly into a diatribe. "We'll talk about it later. Sally, your rapier won't do much damage against skeletons, so hang back and give Mina support if she needs it. Use the torch like a club if you need to."

Mina stared at the door with quivering trepidation before she swung it open. At looked as though she was about to plunge in, however, at the last second she backpedalled and slammed backward into Darcy, who shrieked in fury and shoved Mina forward. This looked like it took Darcy some effort, what with the Barbarian being noticeably larger than she was, but anger and exasperation must have put some strength behind her shove. Sally watched as Mina stumbled through the doorway and Darcy plowed in behind her.

Following with the torch held high, Sally could see forms surging towards them from the darkness. Five skeletons wearing rotting rags charged at them with swords raised. They were like something out of a film, except they weren't CGI animation or claymation. Sally could smell the rot wafting off them and hear the chilling rattle of bones moving without flesh or tissue to cushion the joints. They converged on Mina, who began swinging her great ax in wild arcs, each one accompanied by a panicked shriek.

The greataxe caught one of the skeletons across the ribcage, taking off the arm carrying the sword. Darcy moved in and swung her mace at the head of another, completely shattering the skull in one blow. The bones fell in a pile at their feet in scattered shards. Sally stayed close behind Mina and Darcy, making sure the skeletons didn't try to come around behind them. Wailing, Mina kept swinging while Darcy cursed and smashed skulls left and right.

A skeleton finally noticed Sally and saw her as a potential target. Its eyeless sockets bored into her, nearly freezing her heart. She stabbed with the rapier, but the blade threaded harmlessly through the ribs of the undead. The metal rattled against the bones with a mad percussion that sent chills down her spine. Damn, her rapier only did piercing damage, and from how Darcy's mace was making short work of them, these creatures were susceptible to bludgeoning damage. The tip of the skeleton's sword barely missed her nose as it retaliated. Yelping, she dashed it across the temple with the torch, nearly scorching Mina's back.

"Hey!" Mina yelled, which turned into a shriek when a skeleton took advantage of her distraction and sliced her arm. "I need a heal spell!"

"Keep fighting!" Darcy groused, blocking an attack with her shield. "We almost got them!"

Sally thwacked the skeleton again across its ivory brow and ducked the return stroke. She had never moved so fast in her life; her reflexes were as quick as lightning. Whenever the sword came towards her, she moved out of its way. Sometimes the enemy sword was close enough that the blade stirred the air which she had occupied only a second ago.

Hit and dodge. Hit and dodge. Over and over, until its skull began to crack. The torch was hurting the skeleton, but the damage she was causing was low, probably due to her low strength or the improvised weapon. Eventually, the skeleton collapsed when its skull finally caved in. Looking around for the next opponent, Sally saw the room was empty save for the three of them. Darcy was breathing hard but looked nonetheless for wear. It was Mina who was looking at her bleeding arm in sheer misery. Blood was dripping off her fingers and dotting the ground.

Kicking away the remains of a skull, Darcy stepped over to Mina and laid a hand on her shoulder to cast a spell. Again, Sally watched with intrigue as the healing glow left Darcy's fingers and ebbed into Mina's wounded flesh. The flesh mended itself like some grotesque war video in reverse. Sighing in relief as the pain eased, Mina gingerly moved her arm and smiled when there was no pain.

"Sally, are you alright? I saw one go after you." Darcy said, checking Sally over.

"I'm fine," Sally held up both hands to show off her unharmed condition. "It couldn't land a hit on me."

"Okay. Mina, how are you on health?"

Mina checked. "I'm only two down from full."

"Good. We're doing great for a party of three." Darcy wiped the sweat off her brow and then adjusted her hood. "Just one more room, and we're at the end of the dungeon."

"Are all dungeons as straightforward as this?" Sally asked. "We've been going in one straight line."

"This is just a tutorial dungeon, remember? Most dungeons are mazes with traps, secret rooms, dead ends, and plenty of monsters. Some dungeons are so big they can take weeks to finish," Darcy replied as she checked her backpack. "We're going to take a break while we suss out what our next move is. The next room is going to have kobolds, and they have a leader that thinks he's Billy Badass because he can shoot magic missiles."

Mina timidly raised her head, an action which looked so out of place on the broad face of the powerfully built woman that Sally had to resist smiling. "What are kobolds?"

"Little lizard people with bad attitudes who have managed to slam two brain cells together to figure out how to swing sticks," Darcy said, settled her backpack on her shoulder.

Again, Mina raised her hand. "What are magic missiles?"

"You don't have to raise your hand," Darcy snapped, getting exasperated again. "We're not in a classroom."

"Sorry, a habit from college," Mina said sheepishly, her broad cheekbones turning pink. "But what are magic missiles?"

"Magic Missile is a low-level spell that shoots magical darts. They don't do much damage, but they never miss the target. They can whittle away your health if you aren't careful." Darcy explained launching into a lecture that Sally recognized from her years as a Game Master teaching new players the rules. "Mina, you'll go in first and draw the magic missiles your way."

Mina looked as if Darcy declared they were going to chop her foot off. "Seriously?"

"Yes, seriously," Darcy said sternly. "I'll be there to heal you if you need it. If it gets dicey, you can Rage."

"You mentioned that earlier," Mina said. "What is that?"

"It's a special ability for Barbarians. It temporarily increases their Strength and Constitution by four."

"So getting angry will make me stronger and healthier?" Mina sounded very doubtful.

"Yeah, you know, you get pissed off, and you want to beat the shit out of someone," Darcy said. "You never felt that way before?"

"I've been angry, but I never wanted to hurt anyone because of it," Mina said, cringing at the thought.

"Really? I think there's an issue with my blood sugar if I don't feel like that at least once or twice a day." Darcy shrugged and continued, "Sally, you'll hang back until the fighting starts. Then creep in and take out Billy Badass while we distract him. You should kill him in one hit."

Sally's brows rose. "You want me to do that by myself?"

"Yes, being a Rogue, you can deal extra damage with surprise attacks and Sneak is a Dexterity and Intelligence skill. With your nineteen Dex, it should be very high for a beginner."

Sally summoned her character screen and looked at the list of skills. Sure enough, among her skills, Sneak had the highest bonus. "Yeah, I've plus seven."

"See? You got this," Darcy said with an affirmative nod. "The challenge rating is likely to be ten. Alright, are we ready?"

Mina said, "No."

Sally shrugged, "I guess so."

Pretending that she had a more eager team, Darcy pointed at the door with her club and spoke with enthusiasm, "Let's go."

***

I can't do this.

It was amazing how often she could think these words in the handful of minutes it took for them to get to the next room and for Darcy to propel Mina through it. There was a frightened scream quickly followed by hisses and snarls and the whoosh of a great ax being swung and Darcy cursing as she bashed heads with her mace.

Sally was tempted, oh so tempted, just to stand back and wait for the fighting to finish and deal with Darcy's outrage afterward. Yet, hearing Mina's cry of pain moved her to action. Bending low, she walked through the door in a crouch she could never have sustained for long in her old body. As it was with finding the trap and Legerdemain, the knowledge of moving without sound and staying in the shadows came to her instinctively.

Short lizard people wearing ragged clothes surrounded Mina and Darcy and jabbed at them with long spears. On the far side of the room was a lone lizard, a kobold, prancing about waving its claws as if it was doing a cheer for his team. With each wave and hiss, a glowing blue arrow shot from its claws. The first arrow penetrated Mina's shoulder, and then a second barely missed Darcy's right eye but left behind a thin red line along her cheekbone. Both of them were suffering from dozens of gashes and bleeding tears in their clothing.

Sally pushed back her fears and dashed along the wall, well out of sight of the attacking kobolds, not even Mina or Darcy took notice of her, although they were probably wondering where she was and when she would act. Her rapier made not one sound as she drew it from the sheath. Once she flanked him, with no hesitation or second thought, Sally streaked forward and shoved the blade hard between the ribs of the spell-caster. The tip emerged from the chest in a fountain of dark blood.

The kobold jerked and twisted on the spit, more blood dribbling through the neat hole in its chest. The metal had pierced its left lung and blood spurting up the throat kept it from rasping out a warning to its fellows. It died on Sally's rapier before she pushed it off the blade. So far, the kobolds had not noticed their fallen leader, and if Darcy or Mina saw, they were smart enough not to stop fighting.

Before she had time to hesitate or reflect on what had just happened, Sally went into action. Striding forward and lunging, she thrust the rapier through the back of a kobold who was furiously jabbing a spear at Darcy's shield. The enemy soldier managed to let out a bloody croak that made the others finally take notice of her. Their confusion was enough to give Darcy and Mina the advantage. The great ax swung, slinging black blood, and the mace rose and fell. Sally pulled back the rapier and claimed another kobold life before the battle was over: all the lizard people lay dead at their feet.

The three of them panted together and Sally tried not to look at the twisted bodies. They weren't human, but they had worn clothes and used weapons, which were several grades above being animals. Mina turned away and began vomiting, which set Sally's stomach on edge. Had this body eaten anything? She didn't think so and that, believe it or not, made her hungry.

Darcy's face was pale and covered in sweat. She drew a short breath to collect herself and said, "There's a treasure chest over there. We might as well see what's inside."

For the first time, Sally noticed the wooden chest sitting on a raised stone. It looked like a generic treasure chest from any RPG, with a wooden frame and metal keyhole.

"Is that what they were protecting?" Mina gasped. She was blinking at the chest with teary eyes. "Oh God, we killed them so we can rob them."

Darcy shot Mina a stern look. "No, kobolds are evil creatures. Trust me; whatever they have, they took from someone they killed and they were going to kill and eat us if we didn't kill them first."

Her words didn't ease the brunt of seeing the dead creatures on the ground. Sally turned away from the sight but paused to ask, "Is the chest trapped or locked?"

"Neither," Darcy sounded relieved to be moving onto another subject. "There's not much in there. Mina, how's your health? Do you need a heal spell?"

Sally approached the chest and raised the lid. She was almost expecting a ceremonious chime to play as the lid rose. No music played, nor did the interior of the chest glow, but inside was a pouch of coins, a health potion, and a dagger. Sally picked up the blade and held it in her left hand. It felt natural, and she liked the weight of it, sensing that it would serve her well, which was odd as she was right-handed.

On a hunch, she summoned her character screen and checked the section where her combat skills were listed, and first was Two-Weapon Fighting. Did that mean what she thought it meant? Drawing her rapier with her right hand, she held it in a pose with the dagger raised near her head in the left. Now this felt better than before, this was what was missing earlier. She regretted not having the dagger for the earlier battles. In holding the two blades, Sally experienced an unusual sense of power, as if she could strike at will and never receive any blows in retaliation.

A sigh of relief from a freshly healed Mina broke her concentration on her character sheet. Upon collecting herself, Sally sheathed the rapier and tucked the dagger into her belt, claiming it for herself, and gathered the coin pouch and potion. After giving the chest's interior another glance to make sure she hadn't missed anything, she handed the items to Darcy, who looked at them.

"Yep, just like usual," Darcy said with a satisfied nod. "Five gold pieces, a potion, and a dagger. Let me hold onto the money; Sally, you keep the dagger; and Mina, you can have this health potion."

The Barbarian grimaced as if she couldn't stand to look at the offered potion. "I'm not going to need it if we're going home, right?"

Darcy chewed her lower lip. "Yeah, maybe, we'll see what happens when we leave the dungeon. There's a door over there that should lead out."

Without a word, the three of them went to the door, which opened freely, and walked through a long tunnel until they saw the ring of light at the end. Though the sight of natural light was a pleasant sight after being so long in the dark, dread filled their stomachs as they stepped out into the open air of the forest. The afternoon sun greeted them with slanted rays of light beaming through the canopy.

Mina moaned, dropping her ax. It fell on the grass while she covered her face with both hands. "We're still here."

Chapter 3

SPRING BELL VILLAGE

After a short trek from the cave, they found a small clearing to rest. Mina sulked with her ax by her side while Darcy was thinking hard with her arms crossed. Unable to sit still, Sally was standing and staring morosely at the trees surrounding them. Again and again, the questions swarmed their brains: Why were they there? How did they get there? And how did they get back home?

Darcy was the first one to break the silence, "We can't stay here."

"No shit," Mina snapped. "I want to go home."

"No, I meant we can't stay out here in the forest. Sally and I have never been camping."

"Neither have I!" Mina wailed. "I hate the outdoors! It's going to take forever to get a fire going with wood still wet from last night's rain!"

Staring at her, Darcy asked, "How do you know it rained here last night?"

Mina moaned, exasperated, "Because the grass is really green and the soil is still soft and cold."

"But if you hate the outdoors so much," Sally ventured, "then how do you know about the grass and soil?"

Mina stared dumbfounded with a blank gaze. "I…I don't know. I don't recall watching it on the Discovery channel."

"It's because of your survival skill," Darcy explained. "Barbarians are automatically trained in survival because they live in nomadic tribes. Check your survival skill; what bonus do you have?"

After a moment of consulting her character screen, Mina said, "Plus three."

"See?" Darcy said waving her hand. "That's enough to make you an outdoorswoman. You should know how to find edible berries and roots, and even hunt. I think hunting rabbits has a difficulty of seven, so you've a good chance of success."

Mina looked disgusted. "Gross."

"Then we'll have to go to the village," Darcy sighed.

"What village?" Sally said.

"Spring Bell Village," Darcy said, rising to her feet in a clink of armor. The sound made Sally look up alarmed at first, she was still unused to the fact her half-sister was wearing metal. "It's the first village players visit after finishing the Lair of Tears. We can spend the night at the inn."

Sally nodded in agreement. Since completing the dungeon didn't send them home as they had hoped, then the next best thing was to find a place to stay while they recovered and figured out what to do next. "Do you know the way?"

"I think so. It's disorienting as I'm used to seeing everything as animated computer graphics on a monitor, but I remember you have to take a right when you leave the cave." Darcy pointed in a direction that didn't seem to lead anywhere but to more trees as far as Sally could see.

Mina took a quick look at the sun. "That's west…God, how do I know that?"

"It's weird, isn't it?" Sally said, remembering the alien familiarity she had with the rapier and thieves' tools. "It's like the knowledge just comes to you when you need it."

"It's the same way with spells," Darcy supplemented. "It's really eerie. Like remembering a dream you had last week."

They continue talking as they followed Darcy. Now and again, she'd stop to get her bearings. They were undoubtedly deep within a forest as there were no ranger signs, paths, or even litter to mark that humans had been here. No airplanes flew overhead nor was there the distant sound of traffic or machinery. It was both peaceful and creepy at the same time.

"And everything is based on how many points we put in our skills? How does that work?" Mina asked as she stepped over a log that both Darcy and Sally had some difficulty climbing over.

"The online version is based on the tabletop game," Darcy explained, launching into GM lecture mode. "But it's basically the same system. Behind the scenes the game rolls a twenty-sided dice and you add your skill points to the result. The higher the number, the more likely you are to succeed at a task. Like fighting or picking a lock."

So there was a giant dice out there deciding their fate? As funny as that sounded, the idea unnerved Sally. She couldn't help looking up to see if there were a giant die spinning above their heads.

"What happens if you fail?" Mina asked with a bit of worry in her voice.

"It depends on what you're trying to do. If it's to know something, you draw a blank and don't know anything. If you're trying to attack, you miss. If you try to climb a tree, you fall." Darcy said pausing for a moment to study a tall tree. "Damn, this tree is taller in real life than I would've thought. Anyway, that's why it's important when you level up to put your extra points in skills you will use often. Sally, being a Rogue, will put hers into Sneak and Critical Attack. I'm a Cleric, so I put mine in Healing and various spellcasting skills. Same with our starting allocations."

Then Darcy's eyes narrowed at Mina. "Unlike someone we know, who went default and therefore got all her skill points assigned for her by the game."

"I was in a hurry," Mina said, drawing back defensively. "And I didn't understand what anything meant, so I chose an already made character."

Astounded, Darcy's eyes bugged. "Did you click your way through character creation and take the first default character?"

Thinking back to when she was browsing the character generation menu, Sally recalled that the classes had been listed in alphabetical order beginning with the Barbarian class at the top. And the race was automatically human unless changed to a different one. And now she realized that Mina had the same appearance as the default female barbarian avatar: black hair tied back from the face; strong cheeks and forehead; and a muscular but feminine build.

Darcy must have noticed the same thing. "You clicked on the first character at the top of the screen. You didn't even take the time to read what each class could do. That's why you don't know anything about Rage."

"Oh, alright!" Mina snapped, kicking a stick hard enough to send it flying into a bush, scaring away whatever woodland critters were hiding there. "I was in a hurry because I need to learn how to play by tomorrow. I didn't know I was going to get trapped in the game! If I did, then rolling stats or going default would be a moot point, because I'd never have bought the damn game in the first place."

Sally couldn't see any sense in arguing with that as she had to agree. If she had known the same, she never would have bothered with *Shadow's Deep* in the first place. Perhaps Darcy realized it too as she gave Mina a hard look, but said nothing and resumed leading them out of the forest.

***

The village had an appearance that matched how Sally imagined a medieval village would look. Small wooden cottages stood in lackadaisical rows and the people went about their chores, while little children played and older ones helped their parents; several geese strutted across a yard. Some people stopped to stare as the three adventurers walked between the houses; one mother called her children and hauled them inside by the arms despite their protests. Two old men, smoking pipes over what looked like a game of checkers, paused their game to watch as they passed.

Being stared at was awkward enough in real life and it was even more so in this strange world. Sally wished Darcy would stop gawking back at everything. For the third time, she nearly bumped into Darcy's back, her sister having stopped to gape at a house. "Hey, keep walking."

"Oh my God," Darcy whispered in utter amazement. "I can't tell you how many times I've been through here. Look, over there is the baker's house. He sent me on so many fetch quests, and all I got was a stupid piece of cake that only healed ten health points."

"Then either go say 'hi' or keep walking," Sally groused, averting her eyes from a man leading a mule who was staring at them in open astonishment.

"I bet that cake would taste delicious now," Darcy said in wonderment.

Sally prodded her along with a poke in the shoulder which Darcy didn't feel for the heavy armor. So she tapped her on the hooded head instead. "Go!"

"Sister Korra!" called a voice so close it startled the three of them.

Sally swung around to see a woman approaching them, carrying a bundle of cloth between two weathered hands. She was plump, with a rounded bosom and swaying, broad hips that made the hem of her dress sweep the path with each step. Tagging along behind her was a sullen little boy wearing dirty clothes with smudges on his face as if he had just taken a tumble on a dirt pile. He regarded them with bright blue eyes that seemed to glow against the soiled face.

"I've been calling since you passed my house!" The woman said, breathing heavily, beads of sweat rolling down ruddy cheeks. "I made this to thank you for finding my boy. I don't know what I would have done if he became some kobold's dinner."

She held out the bundle towards Darcy who took a startled step back; bewilderment etched on her face. The woman tilted her head in confusion, mingled with concern. "Sister Korra, are you alright? Don't you remember me?"

Slowly, recognition dawned in Darcy's eyes followed by amazement. "Mrs. Farnell? You gave me a quest to find your little boy. I found him in a kobold cave about to be roasted alive."

The woman's face brightened with a friendly smile. "Yes! And I'll ever be in your debt for the kindness you've shown my family. I was baking when I saw you walking by the window, and I have brought you bread fresh from my oven and have my son here to thank you himself."

Darcy held up both hands to halt the gratitude. "Please, don't. It's alright."

Sally begged to differ. The baked bread smelled delicious, and her stomach was reminding her that she hadn't eaten anything since a pizza she had ordered for while the game installed. I want the bread, Darcy, she mentally sent.

The woman handed the bundle to Darcy. "Please, take it. Cedric, thank the woman for saving your life."

The boy scowled at Darcy, as though more annoyed about an interrupted playtime with his friends than grateful. Sally guessed, however, that Darcy, who had very little to do with children and whose typical experience with kids involved her cussing them out during an online match, was just as unhappy with the situation as he was. Cedric grunted a word of gratitude and looked plaintively at his mother for release.

"Go on, you wee scamp and mind you're home in time to help your sisters with the chores." The words were barely out of Mrs. Farnell's mouth before her son took off like a convict freed from a chain gang. With the sigh of exasperation that all mothers express towards their impudent children, Mrs. Farnell continued, "Please, enjoy the bread and may Shantra look after you and your…friends." She gave Sally and Mina an odd look before hurrying away.

Darcy stared at the retreating woman in wonder. "She looks wider than her animated counterpart. Must be the art style."

Sally and her stomach were more interested in the bread. Steam rolled off the cloth covering the hot bread and unable to resist Sally plucked it from Darcy's fingers and unwrapped it. The delicious smell of fresh baked bread wafted up into her face as the rich brown loaf greeted her. She tore off a pinch and popped it into her mouth and moaned in delight, "I'm orgasming in my mouth right now."

"Are you seriously going to eat that?" Mina's lip curled in disgust.

"Why? It's good," Sally said, popping another bite into her mouth.

"You do realize that they had no concept of sanitation back in medieval times?" Mina leaned away from the bread as if it was something pulled from a toilet. "They didn't know anything about germs or bacteria. She might have coughed in her hands, changed her baby's diapers, and picked her nose before kneading the dough without having once washed her hands."

Spitting the bread piece out as her stomach twisted, Sally handed the loaf back to Darcy wishing she had some mouthwash. The Cleric merely tucked the bread into her backpack, silently, without any reaction to Mina's words and Sally recognized the signs of Darcy being in deep thought. She became like this while planning a campaign or figuring how much money she had blown over a weekend.

Darcy began marching with an urgency she hadn't demonstrated before, so suddenly both Sally and Mina had to jog to catch up. The Cleric's armor rattled and creaked in protest at her fast movements while Sally and Mina moved silently in their leathers and hide armor. They must have looked quite the sight among the villagers who wore only basic peasant clothing, nor was anyone else wearing armor or carrying weapons.

"It's this way," Darcy said, more to herself than to them, as she rounded a corner.

The houses gave way to a clearing at the edge of the village that opened out to a broader road, well worn by wagon wheels and the feet of travellers. Along a bend in the road, an inn stood with a weather-beaten sign swinging from the eaves. On it were words almost faded and smoothed by wind and rain: Spring Bell Inn.

It was a two-story building with several chimneys smoking from a thatched roof. Sally could see movement through the lit windows and could catch the scents of tobacco and food wafting from the building. Her stomach growled, reminding her she was still hungry and a bit of bread had done little to satisfy this. Even with Mina's warning about the lack of food safety in this setting still haunting her, Sally could not quell her hunger.

To her disappointment, instead of heading for the inn Darcy went to a smithy at the other side of the road. Horses were grazing inside a corral and a few of them raised their heads to whinny a greeting as Darcy approached the blacksmith. He was short with thick arms and chest squeezed within a leather apron and he was bent over an anvil knocking a horseshoe with a hammer until he noticed them approaching. Raising his head and wiping a hand across his sweltering brow, he watched with suspicious eye until his gaze landed on Darcy. Like Mrs. Farnell, his face brightened into a broad smile, one that revealed missing teeth.

"Sister Korra!" He greeted setting aside the horseshoe and hammer. Fetching up a dirty cloth, he began wiping his hands clean as he approached Darcy. "What can I do you for?"

Darcy's lips tighten for a moment before speaking, "Did I help you with anything yesterday?"

"Of course." The man bobbed his head in an eager nod. "My new tools would have been lost if you hadn't protected the delivery wagon from bandits."

Darcy nodded as if she were expecting this. "And afterward you sold me a new sword and shield."

The man's eyebrows rose in mirth and confusion. "Ah, no, Sister, I have nothing like that for sell. You'll find nothing sharper here than a kitchen knife, I'm afraid." He waved a hand at a table laden with metal farming tools and horseshoes. "I've never handled a sword in my life."

Darcy's face relaxed into puzzlement, then tighten into deep thought again. "So you never sold any weapons before? Ever?"

"If you count cooking knives as weapons," the man said as he fixed Darcy with a worried look which was slowly deepening into suspicion. "Are you having fun with me, Sister?"

"Uh, no, I'm not..." Darcy stumbled over her words, shaken from her train of thought.

Oh no, Sally thought. He's going to think Darcy has either lost her mind or making fun of him. Either way, I don't think we're going to get any freshly baked bread from him.

Then a thought bloomed into an idea that burned fierce enough to burn away any misgivings and doubt. Sally stepped forward, taking Darcy gently by the arm and smiled at the blacksmith. "I'm sorry, but the Sister suffered a serious blow to the head earlier, and she's been confused ever since. We really should get her to the inn so that she can recover in comfort."

The man's face revealed a flux of emotions. First, it was a flutter of anger, then dawning understanding and concern for Darcy. "I see. Yes, she should have a lie down until her wits return. I can call for the miller's wife to tend to her."

"Please, don't bother, she's alright, just a touch bit confused is all. C'mon Dar—Sister Korra." Sally lea Darcy away by the arm while giving the blacksmith a wave. Once they were well out of hearing, she whispered, "What are you doing? You almost pissed that guy off."

"Yeah, wouldn't want to do that," Darcy whispered back. "His backstory mentioned his bad temper." Then she fixed Sally with a quizzical look. "When did you become a fast talker? You played him like a fiddle."

"I...I don't know. I knew he was getting agitated and you were fumbling your words," Sally shrugged. "I just knew I had to step in and say something and the words just came to me."

A wide grin stretched across Darcy's face. "Your awesome Charisma. That's what it is. Just like with everything else."

"Can we please get inside somewhere? People have been staring at us," Mina interjected, glancing around furtively. "And it's getting dark."

"Yeah, let's go," Darcy said suddenly taken by energy. With long strides, she led them to the front of the inn and pushed open the door with the confidence of someone returning home from an errand.

There was an immediate hush as they entered. It was the early evening hours, and many of the farmers and villagers were having a drink before returning home. Sally lowered her eyes, refusing to make any eye contact with them and Mina must have felt the same, as she looked at the ceiling as if something very interesting was floating over their heads. It was Darcy who chose a table isolated from the other customers and, just like when she was outside in the streets, she stared around in wonder.

The inn's interior was roomy with a roaring fire crackling in a massive fireplace with rows of tables sitting in its light. A barmaid walked among the tables bringing drinks and food and casually chatting and flirting with the men, while a heavyset man stood behind the bar swabbing out a mug while talking with a customer tottering on a stool.

Sally didn't realize how tired she was until she sat down. Everything they had endured since the Incident had been done on an empty stomach and had drained all her energy reserves. Sharing the same condition, Mina covered her mouth and gave a long jaw-popping yawn. "God, I could sleep and never wake up."

"Something's not right about this," Darcy said, pushing back her hood. Long dark hair fell loose from its confines and down her shoulders. It was quite different from Darcy's usual bob of curls.

"I think that became apparent when we found ourselves trapped in a game," Sally said dryly.

"That's not what I'm talking about," Darcy said, rolling her eyes. "In the game, the blacksmith sold low-level weapons. He remembers me doing his quest, but he doesn't remember selling me a weapon?"

Sally considered it for a moment. "Blacksmiths in any games I've played usually upgrade or sell weapons and armor."

"It's not like that in real medieval times," Mina said, shifting her greataxe off her back and propping it against the table. Rolling her shoulders in relief, she continued, "Village blacksmiths made farm equipment and horseshoes. If you wanted weapons and armor, you needed a blacksmith that worked with the army or at a castle."

"That is true," Darcy said, touching her chin in a thoughtful gesture. "How do you know that?"

"I watched a short commentary on medieval life for some credit in history class," said Mina.

"So everything is as I remember it from before," Darcy said in a contemplative manner. "Except for the blacksmith..."

"Sister Korra, hello, good to have you back!" A barmaid appeared at their table, startling them. She was a pretty girl with a splash of freckles across her nose and hair drawn back in a burgundy braid. "What can I get for you?"

"Uh, three ales and three bowls of stew," Darcy said offhandedly.

"It'll be ready in a pip," the girl assured them before dashing away.

Once she was gone, Sally leaned towards Darcy and whispered, "Why do they keep calling you Sister Korra?"

"That's the name of the Cleric I made yesterday," Darcy said, touching her chestplate. "'Sister Korra' did low level quests to get to level three. They don't know either of you because you only just made your characters today."

Mina thoughtfully rubbed her chin. "So if the game people remember everything you did yesterday then someone or something was watching you play."

Darcy shrugged. "Or maybe they accessed my game save file. It would have a record of all the quests I've completed."

"That makes sense," Sally said, glancing around the inn. There were a few patrons staring openly at them. Uncomfortable, she looked away and kept her eyes on the table. "What I don't understand is why it's only us three? If *Shadow's Deep* is so popular, then where are the other players?"

Darcy tapped a metal finger on the tabletop. "That's a good question. There should be dozens of first level characters running around the village, but it's just us three. Why only us?"

"We share a time zone," Mina pointed out. "Maybe it's whomever happened to be on eastern time whenever this 'thing' happened."

"There would still be a lot of players," Darcy said. "There's got to be another reason."

"Here we are," the girl said, bringing a large tray laden with three full mugs and three steaming bowls. She laid out the meals with expert precision while balancing the tray on an open palm. "It'll be ten silver, Sister."

Darcy opened a pouch tied to her belt and produced a gold coin. "Here, take this."

The girl took the coin with an appreciative smile and left them to their meals. Sally looked down at her stew where bits of meat and vegetables swam together in a thick broth. Hunger refused to let her think about the unsanitary habits of the middle ages, and she dug in. Darcy pulled the bread out of her backpack and broke it into several pieces on the cloth and let it sit in the middle for them to share. The bread dipped in the broth was divine and Sally, careless about table manners, bent over her bowl and ate with gusto.

Mina regarded the stew suspiciously. "Didn't they have anything else other than stew?"

"I don't know," Darcy quipped. "Why didn't you ask for something else instead of sitting there like a bump on my ass?"

Mina's face darkened, but she snatched up her spoon and began eating, shovelling spoonfuls of stew into her mouth. After chewing a mouthful, she stated, "This could use some more salt."

Though Sally preferred sweet tea or soda with a meal, the ale was better than she expected. It had a fruity and nutty taste that was pleasant. With food in her stomach, Sally found she was able to think clearly.

"We need to try to find other players," she said, pushing back her bowl. "I find it hard to believe that we're the only ones this is happening to. I bet if we asked around, the villagers might have stories of other players helping them or we can at least put the word out somehow that we're looking for 'other travellers.'"

Darcy nodded. "That's a good idea. We'll sleep here tonight and start asking around first thing in the morning."

Mina pointed at something in front of her face. "What does this mean?"

"I can't see what you're pointing at," Darcy said gently, but Sally could hear the struggle in her voice to remain amiable.

"This bar right at the top of the character screen," Mina said.

Summoning her character screen, Sally look at the top to see what Mina was talking about. "Wow…is that an…experience bar?"

It certainly was an experience bar, about less than a quarter full of glittery gold. Above the gold was the number 60 and at the other end was 300.

"I'm at sixty of three hundred experience points," Sally muttered in wonder. "Where did the sixty points come from?"

"You were automatically awarded fifty points for completing the Lair of Tears," Darcy said.

"Shouldn't it be per combat?" Sally asked. "We fought the rats, skeletons, and kobolds."

"It's like that outside of a dungeon, but inside, you only get XP once you reach the end." Darcy studied her character screen. "I didn't get any because I already finished it once before. Nope, I'm still at two-hundred and thirty of two thousand seven hundred, so no XP for 'Sister Korra.'"

"What happens when you fill the bar?" Mina asked.

Darcy raised an eyebrow. "You level up! You get more health, skill points, unlock new skills…c'mon, this is gaming one-o-one."

“I know at least that much about games!” Mina said, her cheeks turning pink. “I mean would the same happen to us in this world?”

“I would think so,” Darcy replied. “So far this world has been playing by the game’s rules so I wouldn’t expect anything different, unless something happens that proves otherwise.”

With their meals finished, fatigued set in and each of them began yawning in turn. After everything that had happened, Sally was looking forward to a warm bed, though she’d rather it was her own bed in the really world.

Finally, the serving girl reappeared at their table. “Anything else? Pie perhaps?”

“Pie sounds great, but we need rooms. How much for three?”

The girl’s smile faltered at the edges. “Three rooms?”

“Yeah, one for each of us,” Darcy said expectantly.

“Oh.” The girl’s smile faded a bit more. “I…I don’t think we have three rooms available.”

“That’s fine, we can bunk up in one or two,” Darcy said, opening her coin pouch.

The girl’s smile was gone to be replaced with an apologetic grimace. “We can’t…oh drat it all, you’ll need to speak with Pete.”

“Smiley Pete?” Darcy said, craning her head towards the big man behind the bar.

“No, he’s Sensible Pete, the Innkeeper,” the girl said regretfully and quickly collected their bowls and mugs.

“Is something wrong?” Mina asked.

“You’ll have to speak with Pete,” the girl said without looking at them. She dashed away before they could ask any more questions.

“That was weird,” Sally commented. “Why are you calling the innkeeper Smiley?”

“That’s just a nickname the fans gave him because in-game he has this stupid grin on his face,” Darcy said as she glanced across the room towards the innkeeper who looked less than pleased to be doing his job, not really earning the Smiley Pete nickname.

Darcy rose from her chair. “I’m going to find out what’s going on about the rooms.”

Once Darcy left, Sally glanced around the tavern and noticed a lot of hostile eyes fixed on their table. Men were craning their heads to look at them, and even one of the barmaids was turning her head in their direction as she passed between tables collecting empty mugs and plates. Sally now had the sinking suspicion that the question about getting rooms wasn't about whether they had any, but whether they would rent them any rooms.

"Shit," Sally whispered, wondering what the hell they were going to do if they couldn't get rooms. Wasn't Sister Korra respected in this town?

Sally noticed Mina staring over her head and twisted around in her seat to see what the taller woman was looking at. Darcy was standing at the bar talking with the innkeeper with her coin pouch in hand. The innkeeper shook his head, and Darcy reached into her pouch and held up several gold coins to prove they could afford the rooms. Again, the innkeeper shook his head and said something that made Darcy's brows furrow. Then Smiley Pete pointed at their table and said some more words and Darcy's eyes widened and then narrowed; she seemed infuriated.

"Looks like trouble," Mina murmured in trepidation.

"Maybe I should go over there…" Sally said, knowing that once Darcy got pissed, insults and curse words would spew from her mouth like water from a broken fountain.

"No, stay here." Mina touched her arm before she could stand. "He might think you're trying to gang up on him if you join in."

Sally had to admit to herself that she preferred not to get involved. She wasn't good around people, and hated any conflict or confrontation outside of a video game, movie, or TV show.

The innkeeper jabbed a finger at the door with a few loud words that drew the attention of the men nearest the bar. Darcy shoved her coin pouch onto her belt and stalked back to their table. She dropped into her seat seething, her eyes blazing with indignation.

"I'd ask for a damn drink, but I don't want to put another cent in that asshole's pocket," Darcy growled.

"What's wrong? What happened over there?" Mina asked, looking towards the bar where the man was wiping down the table as if someone had spat on it. "And what's his problem with us?"

"He doesn't have a problem with you or with me," Darcy said dryly. "He has a problem with Sally."

Sally's blue eyes went wide. "What did I do?"

"Nothing," Darcy sighed, her fury extinguishing into remorse. "Except you chose half-elf for your race." She leaned back in her chair, looking exhausted. "It's my fault. I forgot this area of the game has a racism problem against non-humans. The only reason he let you come in here and eat with us was that you were with me, but he says giving you a room would be crossing a line. His words were, "nobody is gonna sleep in a bed after a bloody pointy."

Mina frowned, confused. "So they refuse service if you pick a non-human character in the game?"

Darcy looked very tired, and rubbed the bridge of her nose. "They'd still sell you stuff and let you sleep in the inn, but they would make rude remarks like, 'don't get dirt on the linens, dwarf' or 'better watch how you swing that, elf, or you'll break your twig arms,' stuff like that. I guess in this world they can and will refuse you service if they don't like you." Then she gave a nasty glare at the innkeeper who resumed his distasteful task of cleaning mugs. "Except he was supposed to use the lines, 'All with good coin are welcomed here,' the kindest man in the village, but in this life, he's an asshole."

Sally sat in silence, completely taken aback. She thought back to when they first arrived at the village, the long stares from the villagers, the odd look from Mrs. Farnell, and how they were being gawked at by the other inn's patrons. It wasn't the whole group they had been staring at; it had been her. She was so stunned; she didn't know what to think or feel. Sally had always found the presence of others uncomfortable, but she had never before been rejected outright.

"So what do we do now?" Mina said, with a note of panic in her voice. "We can't sleep out in the woods."

"Stinky Pete," Darcy said, "and I will forever refer to Smiley Pete as Stinky Pete from this day hence, said he wouldn't mind her sleeping in the stable. I told him that if she has to sleep in the stable, then all three of us were going to sleep in the stable."

Mina opened her mouth to protest, but must have seen something in Sally's face, because instead of a complaint, she muttered, "Sounds good to me. I bet the beds have lice anyway."

Chapter 4

NAOMi

Sally tried not to let her feelings be hurt, telling herself over and over as they walked to the stables behind the inn that it didn't matter. This dumb world was just some dumb game her dumb sister talked her into playing. And the dumb world had dumb villagers and an asshole innkeeper. God, she hoped the placed burned down around Stinky Pete's head.

Darcy pushed open the barn doors, and the smell of dry hay and horses wafted over them. Suddenly, Sally became so angry and miserable, she didn't know whether she wanted to throw herself on the hay weeping or go back and knock out every one of Stinky Pete's teeth.

"It's not worth fretting over," Darcy said laying a metal gloved hand on her shoulder.

"If I had known that being a half-elf was such a sin around here I wouldn't have chosen it as a race," Sally muttered.

"If I had known I was going to be trapped in this game I never would have played it," Mina commented dourly.

"Sally, listen, don't get yourself in a funk over it." Darcy's face was grim with eyes carrying both concern and pleading. "You can't go hide away in your apartment and play video games until you feel better. I need you with me, okay?"

Sally wanted to be angry with her stepsister, wanted to scream in her face and even hit her, but that would be childish, and Darcy was right. She nodded, "Alright, I'm with you. I'll be alright."

They found a clean stall with fresh hay and spread out their bedrolls. Though Sally was tired, it seemed that none of them were able to fall asleep quickly.

It took Darcy a while to figure out how to remove her armor and set it aside in a neat stack in the corner, Sally offered to help but Darcy wanted to get the hang of it for herself. Once free of it, Darcy stretched her limbs and twisted at the waist to pop her back, while stating that moving in armor was like wearing a trash can. A white tabard with a sun crest embroidered on the front almost gleamed silver in the dim light of the stables. It was thin and hung down the front and back between her legs.

Then Darcy began examining and feeling her own hard muscles beneath a brown skin. Her long hair lay over her shoulders like dark curtains. And she wasn't the only one examining her body.

Sally noticed that Mina was staring at her bodybuilder body. She was still feminine, despite broad, rock-solid shoulders. And judging by how she kept staring and cupping her chest, her current breasts were bigger than those of her old body.

For her part, Sally was flexing, finding her new limber body much more mobile and agile compared to her previous one. Not since her prepubescent years did she have a flat stomach and trim hips. When Sally hit her teenage years, the pounds went straight to her hips and thighs. She had gone through years of failed diets and workout routines where weight was lost, but then regained.

Darcy looked over at her as she did stretches. "Sally, remember that restaurant where we waited for two hours to get our food?"

"Yeah. You wouldn't let me leave a tip."

"Right, but remember how tables that were seated after us were getting served first," Darcy sat down on her bedroll and pulled off her boots. Her feet were covered in hosen, long knee-length socks that itch.

"It took the waiter a long time to get our food."

"No, it was because he was racist. He didn't want to serve a black girl."

Was that right? Sally paused her exercises. The waiter hadn't smiled when he seated them and he had spoken very curtly. It was nearly thirty minutes before he returned with their drinks and took their orders. Sally had thought it was because the restaurant was so busy or the waiter was new and having trouble, so she had remained patient and polite while Darcy, who was usually impatient and vocal, sat silently glaring at the waiter whenever he passed their table. He never came by to apologize for the wait nor to refill their drinks. The ice cubes in their glasses became water by the time their food arrived.

Several times, Sally had suggested getting up and going somewhere else, but Darcy told her they weren't leaving. When the waiter finally brought their food, Sally had thanked him, but Darcy angrily ordered him to refill their drinks right now, or she was going to complain to a manager. The waiter's face turned bright red, and he promptly refilled their glasses and kept them full until they finished eating. Sally's mother, having once been a waitress, taught her to always leave a tip, no matter how bad the service. When Sally laid a five-dollar bill on the table, Darcy scooped it up and shoved it back into Sally's hand, and told her to keep it.

Why hadn't she noticed it back then? Was she so self-absorbed that she didn't see her own sister being abused? "I'm sorry I didn't realize that was happening."

"Being a white girl in the US, you're not really experienced with shit like that," Darcy said, picking straw from the bottom of her hosen socks.

Sally snorted, "Try being a fat girl in the US."

"Or an Asian in college," Mina added. "When I get the top grades in class people think it's because I'm Asian, that I'm super smart. They don't think it's because I put in the work and studied while they went out partying and drinking."

"And now look at yourselves," Darcy said, holding out her arms in a presentation. "Sally's a supermodel, Mina looks like she ate a steroid-pumped quarterback, and my hair is straight, but at least I'm still black."

"And a holy savior of the people," Sally said, rolling her eyes.

***

Darcy was delighted to see Sally was in the humor for mockery. Knowing her half-sister well, Darcy felt that before long she would enter a depression slump. But they didn't have the luxury of being able to spend time moping. They needed to figure out how to get home and be alert for any dangers in this world. She knew this world better than her own bedroom and was quite aware of its many dangers. The Lair of Tears was only a tutorial dungeon and didn't light a candle compared to the real risks out there.

The village was supposed to be a safe zone where players could buy items and receive quests, but Darcy had the ill-feeling that this was no longer the case. Things were different, as proven by the blacksmith not selling weapons and the innkeeper's blatant racism. It was like going into your home and finding the furniture had been rearranged. And laid with traps. She was confident she could guide Sally and Mina in this world but doubted she could keep them safe. Sally had great stats and therefore great skills for a new build. But Level 1 was still only Level 1. Those stats meant very little unless she could survive and realise their potential. And Mina, while being easy on the eye, was liable to wreck Darcy's head with her inability to adapt to the game.

An urge to yawn broke into her thoughts, and Darcy gave in to the fatigue. For now, they needed rest to be ready to take on whatever the morning would bring. Hopefully, somewhere there were others from the real world who had a better idea of what was happening and whom they would find soon.

***

Sally managed to get a couple of hours of sleep, but it was hard to get comfortable. The straw kept scratching her arms, and the woolen bedroll itched. Being thin made it easier to curl up in a ball, but even that unusual position unnerved her and kept sleep at bay.

When she woke up again, it was due to the pressure in her bladder. The ale she drank was ready to make its reappearance. Oddly enough, there was plenty of light in the stables. Sally could see clearly as if an overhead light was on, but there were no sources of light. Then she remembered having low-light vision which would make it easier to go to the…

"Well, damn," she whispered, realizing the chances of there being a bathroom around here were slim to none. There might be an outhouse or a latrine, but seeing how the innkeeper didn't want her sleeping in one of his beds, then he might not want her to use the same toilet as his customers.

Darcy slept alongside one wall of the stall, and Mina was propped against the opposite side with arms crossed over her stomach. Moving slowly, Sally rose without disturbing them. There was no whisper of straw being disturbed or her boots scuffing the dirt as Sally left the stall and went outside. It was eerie being able to see so well outside, just as when she sneaked around the kobolds. She could see everything clearly, as if it were a bright sunny day instead of the middle of the night.

The thought of sneaking into the inn and using their indoor toilet came to her. Being a Rogue, she could pick the locks and be in and out before anyone knew she was there. Why should she squat outside when she could just as well use the toilet in the inn?

No, she couldn't do that, the more sane part of her psyche pointed out. The innkeeper would go crazy.

But why not? A rebellious, angry part declared. His racism still hurt, and she would certainly get the last "word" on that.

Before she could talk herself out of it, she was already taking her thieves' tools out of her hidden pocket and heading towards the inn. The lock was a breeze to pick; she barely stuck the lockpick into the keyhole before it clicked open. The large room was empty, as all the customers had gone home for the day or perhaps were upstairs asleep. Without a creak from the floorboards, Sally explored the downstairs part of the building.

As tempting it was to tamper with the barrels of ale behind the bar (like poking little holes low down and letting them leak overnight), Sally decided against it. Knowing how much of a racist he was, Smiley Pete would lay the blame on her, and he would be right to do so. No, better not give in to temptation and just find the bathroom. Her bladder wasn't used to having to wait so long.

Eventually, she found a chamber pot in a closet in the kitchen. She grimaced, imagining the cook taking a bathroom break right in the middle of the kitchen and then going right back to cooking. Mina must never know. After relieving herself, she slid the chamber pot back into the closet with her leavings inside. Let them clean up after her.

Rinsing her hands in cold dishwater in a basin, she heard voices. At first, it was just a murmur she could barely hear and then the creak of heavy footsteps on wooden stairs. She ducked down beneath a table and listened intently. The voices became louder as the footsteps left the stairs and moved across the main hall.

"The three of them should be sleeping in the stable," a man's thick voice said.

"All three are travelers? Have they been in the village long?" another voice asked. This one was raspy, as if the man had been smoking since high school.

"The Cleric, Sister Korra, was seen around the village yesterday, but no one has seen her companions before today—a tribeswoman and an elf."

They were talking about Sally and her friends! If it were possible to sink into the floor and hide, Sally would have. She held her breath, fearful she would give herself away just by breathing too loudly.

"If they're asleep, then we can take them away without a fuss, and you can say they left before the dawn."

"And my pay?"

"You'll get it tomorrow."

Sally stayed very still until the men left the main room, their footsteps pounding in her ears. One headed upstairs, and the other went outside; she could hear his feet scraping the stone steps. Even when the footsteps faded away, Sally was still too afraid to move. What if they came back? What if they heard her and came after her?

A voice inside her head ordered her to go warn Darcy and Mina, but terror immobilized her. Never before had she known such fear. No one had ever wanted to physically hurt her and now she understood how the girls in the horror films felt when they hid from the killer.

Darcy needs you! Get your ass out there and help her, the voice in her head screamed.

Yet, she still couldn't or wouldn't move. She couldn't imagine life outside of that medieval kitchen which had become her safe place. If she stayed here until morning, then…what? What the hell was she going to do by herself in this world without Darcy?

Get up, get up, get up!

Slowly, she rose and nearly ducked back down again when she remembered she had left her rapier dagger behind in the stables. Who needed weapons to use a bathroom? How the hell was she to defend herself and help Darcy and Mina without a weapon?

Waitaminute. I'm in a kitchen full of knives!

And sure enough, there was a rack of knives on the wall. Sally picked one up and weighed it before putting it back and taking another one. She didn't understand why it mattered how the knife felt in her hand, but it did. If the knife didn't weigh just right, then she couldn't handle it correctly, especially if she threw it. Threw it? She knew how to throw knives?

Sally selected three knives that felt right, not perfect, but they would have to do and left the kitchen. With a hammering heart, she went through the main hall and a side door that had been left ajar. Sally opened it with just enough space to slip through, staying close to the wall and using the shadows as camouflage.

She could hear other people creeping across the grass. Their feet scuffed the surface and crunched the soil which was oddly loud to her. Did elves have good hearing alongside low-light vision? They must have, as she could hear the men's footsteps as if she was right next to them.

Listening to the sounds of her enemies was unsettling as she expected them to hear her as well as she could hear them. Thus far, no one had shouted or started chasing her, so she must be in the clear. Shapes were moving around the stables. Edging closer, she could see that several men surrounded the stables. They wore red bandanas across the bottom half of their faces and leathers with knives and daggers at their belts, or else they held weapons in their hands.

She counted nearly seven, but there might be more on the other side where she couldn't see. It would be impossible to take on all these men by herself with only three kitchen knives, but if she could wake up the others, then the three of them could manage together or at least fight their way through to escape.

If she shouted now, the men would realize her presence and come after her. So she had to get inside the stable before her enemies. Bending almost double, Sally crouched as low as she could while still being able to move. Her body was limber enough for this to be very close to the ground, as if she had spent years doing yoga and eating fat-free yogurt instead of sitting in front of a TV playing video games and snacking on Chips Ahoy.

Eyeing the back of a man who was standing guard while others stalked the stables, Sally crept forward with the intent of knocking him out with the hilt of a knife (again, this was the knowledge that just came out of nowhere). This, she felt was a good plan, until she heard a sharp snap beneath her boot. Looking down, Sally saw the broken twig and stared at it in horror, knowing full well that twig hadn't been there a second ago.

She could hear Darcy declaring that she had rolled a 1 on the die.

"Someone there?" A voice barked.

"Shit," Sally hissed ducking back towards the inn, deeply regretting this foolish streak of bravery on her part.

"You!" Her heart leaped, thinking they had spotted her. Instead, the voice ordered, "Go find out who's out there. If it's one of the women, grab her and bring her along."

"Dammit," she breathed.

She could lose him in the forest; the dark shadows would give her plenty of places to hide. There was, however, an open space about a football field length between the tavern and the edge of the forest. With the moon shining bright, they would catch sight her before she made it across. Just as she decided to head back inside the inn, the front door of the building swung open, and a man trudged out wearing the same leathers and the same bandana across his mouth as the others.

"The other one isn't inside," he called as he left the door for the stables.

"Keep your gob shut and your peepers open," a chastising voice hissed. "She's somewhere around here."

Oh, God. They were looking for her already? How did they know she had been inside the inn?

With all thought of warning Mina and Darcy gone and every instinct of self-preservation firing up as never before, Sally clenched a knife in hand and moved towards the back of the tavern. Maybe there was a cellar or a backdoor she could use to get inside. Since the attackers had already looked inside the tavern, it would be the best hiding place until they left.

As luck would have it, there was a window just around the corner. It was dark, and Sally pressed her nose to the glass. The room beyond looked empty and deserted. If she could open the window, she could slip inside and hide until the men left.

As her hands pressed against the sill, a voice said, "I wouldn't go inside. There are bad guys hiding in there."

Sally's heart leaped to her throat, and she frantically looked around but saw no one. Even with her low-light vision, she couldn't see the source of the voice. Had it been her imagination or her paranoia?

"Up here."

Sally looked up.

A girl was sitting on the roof, wearing what looked like white pajamas with no shoes. Her hair was dragged back into two bushy pigtails that looked like two matted balls of cotton. She sat gaily with her legs slightly swinging as if she should be sitting on the edge of a bridge and tossing flower petals into the water.

"Who are you?" Sally hissed, afraid to raise her voice any higher than a whisper.

"Naomi," the girl said and then pointed. "There's a bad guy behind you."

Sally whipped around in time to see a man sneaking up behind her. With a short cry, she brought up her knife in time to block his dagger, but barely. His blade slid across hers and then downwards towards her knee. She danced back, slamming her back into the wall next to the window and the dagger found nothing but air. He lunged forward with an open hand to catch her throat. Sally saw the move, and in reflex thrust the knife through his open palm.

The man moaned, stumbling backward, grasping his impaled hand. Sally let go of the knife and grabbed a second one from her belt. Her attacker's eyes blazed so hotly she could have seen them without her low-light vision. He turned towards the stables, and she didn't have to see his mouth to know he was about to shout for help.

Before any sound emerged from the man, Naomi landed on his back, wrapped her arms around his neck and choked off his shout. He wrenched his body from side to side to dislodge her, but she braced her feet on his hips, raised a fist no bigger than a coffee mug, and delivered a blow to his temple. The man collapsed on the ground as if he had been shot. The girl bounced to her feet as if she were wearing a jetpack.

"C'mon, we can get away in the woods." Naomi grabbed Sally's arm and pulled her along towards the field.

"Wait, there are others…" With the girl's help, maybe she could help Darcy and Mina after all.

"It's too late. The Cut Throats already got 'em, but I know where they're going." The girl pulled her arm insistently. "I'll help you get them back, but right now we gotta book it."

Book it? Stunned, Sally let Naomi pull her away from the tavern, and they both took off across the clearing. There were shouts behind them which spur them to run faster. Naomi sped ahead, her legs churning into a blur, and she ran with an unnatural speed that left Sally behind.

"Wait!" Sally hissed.

"Hurry!"

"Slow down!"

Too late. Naomi zipped between two trees, nearly rebounding off them like a pinball between bumpers. Sally scooted between the boles and ducked low, taking full advantage of her sneaking skill and low-light sight. Behind her, she could hear men shouting and boots thumping on the grass.

Without thought or hesitation, she began scaling a tree. Her hands and feet finding handholds and steps with ease. She laid flat along a branch, looking down at the heads of men breaking through the foliage.

Holding her breath, she watched and waited as the men slashed the bushes to scare her out of hiding.

"There were two of them. I saw two of them!" said a man with a head so bald it gleamed in the darkness.

"There's nothing for it. They pulled a runner. At least we have the two in the stables so the Boss should be happy."

"He won't be if they don't have it."

"Well, that'll be their problem, won't it?"

The men drifted through the trees and out of sight. When Sally couldn't hear their footfalls any more, she released the breath she had been holding and sagged on the branch. Her heart was still pounding hard in her chest, and she could hear the blood rushing through her ears.

"Hey, they're gone," someone whispered right next to her ear.

Sally nearly fell but caught herself by locking her legs around the branch and hugging it with both arms. Looking up, she saw Naomi hanging upside down from a higher branch with her legs folded over the limb like a gymnast.

Sally managed to get herself into a sitting position on the branch. Once balanced, she was able to focus on the most important thing on her mind. "Tell me. Are you from the—the real world?"

"The place with McDonald's, Twitter, iPads, and Google? Yeah," Naomi said, still hanging upside down.

The relief of finally meeting another person from the real world made Sally almost light headed. "Do you know why we're trapped in the game?"

"I was about to ask you the same thing," Naomi said. "I was logging onto *Shadow's Deep*, and then I was in the tavern."

"You started in the tavern?" Sally asked.

"It's where I logged off yesterday. I did a pretty tough quest, so I went to the inn to heal my character," Naomi righted herself on the tree branch and had a thoughtful look on her face. "I think I came to this world sleeping because I woke up in bed as if I had been sleeping all night."

"We started at the Lair of Tears." It made sense that players would start where their characters were when they last logged off within the game. Darcy would have logged off with her Cleric at the Lair of Tears where new players like Sally and Mina began. Since Naomi was having her character rest in the inn to restore health, then she appeared sleeping in bed.

Naomi lowered herself onto the same branch as Sally with a dancer's grace, barely making the tree limbs waver under her weight. Squatting on the branch, balanced on the balls of her feet like a small stone gargoyle, she regarded Sally with light blue eyes. "You're level one?"

"Believe it or not, this is actually my first time playing," Sally sighed. Logging into the game may have been hours since, but now it seemed like many days ago.

"Really? Are the others level one too?"

"Mina is, but Darcy is level three. What level are you?"

"Five."

Sally's eyes narrowed suspiciously. "If you're so high level, then why couldn't you save my sister and Mina?"

Naomi chortled. "Level five isn't high level, and the Cut Throats bandits are levels six and up and there were a lot of "em. I could have taken one or two by myself, but the rest would have turned me into hamburger meat. You must be a new player if you don't know who they are."

"Cut Throats?" Sally was again experiencing that overwhelming feeling that she was way out of her depth.

"They're the main bad guys in this area," Naomi said. She laid a finger across her chin in thought. "The weird thing is that they have never came into the village before. You only saw them in quests or random encounters in the forest."

Sally knew how that went with RPG villages, which were usually safe zones. The villagers would gripe about monsters, bandits, or a dragon causing problems, but you never actually see the danger come to the village unless it was scripted by the game.

"You said you knew where they were taking my friends."

"Yeah, to their hideout in the forest." Naomi hitched a thumb over her shoulder in the direction the men had departed.

"Let's go rouse the villagers and..."

Naomi shook her head. "Sorry, that's not how the game works."

"What do you mean? The villagers can help us."

Naomi snorted. "It was the innkeeper that sold you out to the Cut Throats. I heard him talking with the Cut Throat outside my room. And the villagers won't help outsiders who hang out with an elf, even a half-elf."

Sally's lips tighten in a near grimace as she didn't need that bit of hurt brought back. Swallowing it back, she said, "Then what do we do?"

"We go save them," Naomi said almost bouncing on the branch in a jovial mood,

"You already said that you can't handle them alone."

"We can together."

Sally opened her mouth to unleash a hundred reasons why that was a terrible and suicidal idea, but the only words that came out were, "We can't."

Electricity sparked in Naomi's eyes, and for the first time, the girl knelt perfectly still on the branch. Then in a steely tone, she said, "Yes, we can. Can't is not in my vocabulary. You can stay in this tree if you want. I won't be here telling you you can't, because I'll be saving your friends. You can come with me if you want."

With that said, Naomi dropped from the branch. Sally watched in open mouth astonishment. Not because the girl was spiraling to her death, but how gracefully she fell. No, it wasn't exactly falling. It was gliding downward as if she had an invisible parachute slowing her descent. She landed on her bare feet with less effort than a dismounting gymnast.

It wasn't as graceful, but Sally climbed down the tree with smooth expert movements until she was on the ground with Naomi. "Wait, I'm coming too."

***

The night air was cold against her face as Sally trekked along behind Naomi, who moved at a brisk walk. She was actually jogging, but she kept stopping to let Sally catch up to her. Every once in a while, Naomi would suddenly perform a cartwheel or flip over an obstacle like a large stone or log. One time her heel nearly caught Sally on the chin when she somersaulted.

Exhausted from trying to catch up to Naomi, Sally motioned her to stop and the girl did so reluctantly, shifting from one foot to the other as if she had to pee. Being still at last, Sally got a chance to get a good look at the girl, who couldn't have been any older than fifteen or sixteen. Her hair was very pale blonde, almost as white as her clothing which looked like durable linen pajamas and it hung off her slight frame in wrinkles.

"What's your class? I don't recognize it."

"I'm a Monk."

Sally blinked in utter confusion. "Like Shaolin or Kung Fu monks? I thought this was a western medieval world. Why would they include an eastern base class?"

Naomi shrugged. "Dunno. My brother and I love martial arts films, so I chose Monk as my class."

"Alright," Sally was eager to learn what she could from Naomi, "so you woke up in the tavern and then what happened?"

"I was freaked out, but I was hungry too, so I ordered something to eat. Then I overheard the innkeeper complaining about a Cleric getting mad at him for not letting her half-elf friend sleep in one of the rooms." A smile spread across Naomi's round face. "I thought you guys might be players too, but I wanted to be sure before I said anything. I was gonna follow you around tomorrow to see if you acted like players."

"That's similar to our plan," Sally said. It was painful to remember that Darcy and Mina helped came up with that same idea and it made her realize how deeply she missed and worried for them.

Naomi continued recapping her story. Unable to sleep, she had climbed through the window and onto the roof to stargaze and look over at the barn where Sally slept. The sounds of footsteps inside her room had caught her attention. Taking great care not to be seen, Naomi peeked over the eaves and through the window to see the innkeeper and a man dressed like a Cut Throat rummaging through the room and her backpack.

"What were they looking for?" Sally asked. "Money?"

Naomi shook her head. "I don't think so. They were mad that I wasn't in the room so I think they were after me too."

"Do you think they know we're...players?"

Naomi considered this a moment. "No, I don't think that's it. I don't think they know this a game. They all act like normal people."

That, to Sally, was one of the ways that this world was horrifying. In a typical game, NPCs acted according to a script that wouldn't change too much, whatever the players' actions. In this version, it seemed that the NPCs actions were based upon their own nature or motivations, which was proving to be very lethal with bandits coming into villages and taverns, which were usually safe zones in RPGs, and racist innkeepers betraying their own patrons. These were symptoms of a game gone wrong.

If the Cut Throats weren't after them for being players, then why come after them at all? A sudden thought prompted Sally to ask, "Naomi, did you play the game yesterday?"

"Yeah, I play almost every day," Naomi nodded hard enough to make her pigtails bob.

"Did you do anything in the game yesterday? Anything significant?"

Naomi rubbed the back of her head. "I dunno. I did some quests. Why?"

"Because my stepsister Darcy created her Cleric yesterday and did quests to level up," Sally explained, almost in an urgent manner. Maybe if they understood what the Cut Throats were after, then it would perhaps give them a clue on how to get Darcy and Mina back. "All the villagers that gave her quests remember her. They've been calling her by her character's in-game name, Sister Korra. What did you do yesterday?"

Naomi shifted from foot to foot as she thought. "Nothing really. I just did some grinding. I killed some wild boars, bears, and wolves..."

"Be glad there are no park rangers out here," Sally muttered.

"I also killed a few Cut Throats," Naomi raised her shoulders in a shrug. "Maybe they want revenge or...oh, shoot. I think I know what they want."

Sally restrained herself from seizing Naomi by the shoulders as if to shake the information out of her. "What?"

"It was a random drop. I swear, I didn't take it on purpose, but it was loot!" Naomi opened the front of her gi, showing off a white undershirt and drew out a leather packet sealed with a circle of red wax. Upon closer inspection, the wax had a seal of a hawk with spread wings grasping a struggling serpent in its talons.

Sally broke the seal and opened the bundle. Inside were several folded pieces of paper which she opened and tried to read. The handwriting was tiny and the words were squeezed together as if whoever wrote it wanted to write a novel on a single page. She was able to make out a word here and there, but none of it came together to mean anything. They were written in elegant calligraphy, but it was so curly and full of flourishes that it was impossible to decipher.

Naomi was squinting at a second note and shrugged. "Sorry, I don't know what it means."

"I don't know either. If they're after these letters, then we can make a deal with the Cut Throats and get Mina and Darcy back."

"We can't do that! It's a quest item!" Naomi snatched the packet and the pages from Sally's hands so fast that her hands were a blur and held them to her chest as if they were her baby instead of pieces of paper. "We can't let the bad guys get these."

"Why not? We can't even read them!" Sally cried with her hands curled if she might try to take them back.

"They must be really important if they're willing to kidnap people to get them back so that's all the more reason why they shouldn't get them!" Naomi shoved the packet back into her gi and tied it with the finality of chaining a gate. "I don't think the Cut Throats are going to keep their end of any deal we make with them anyway. We're better off fighting them."

"How?" Sally cried utter bewilderment. "All I have is two kitchen knives."

"That's why we're out here!" Naomi held out her arms to indicate the forest around them. "We need to find their scouts, kill them, and take their weapons as loot. You'll have a decent weapon, and we can find out where the hideout is."

Sally's jaw dropped. She tried to speak, but her tongue failed her. After closing her mouth, she swallowed and then swallowed again. Slowly, with all the will she possessed, she asked, "You don't know where their hideout is?"

"Nope," Naomi said, digging a finger in her ear so nonchalantly, one would think she was attending a boring lesson. "I hadn't gotten far enough in the Cut Throats questline to get to the hideout."

"But you said you knew where they were taking Mina and Darcy." It was all she could do to keep from throttling the girl.

"Yeah," Naomi inspected the tip of her finger and flicked off whatever nastiness she found in her ear. "Because where else would they take them?"

"So why are we out here if you don't know where the hideout is?"

"Because this is where I encountered Cut Throats in the game yesterday," the girl said, finally getting exasperated from the line of questioning. Though, not as much as Sally is for having to ask them. "We just have to keep walking, and they'll jump out and attack us eventually."

"Oh my God!" Sally yelled, finally losing her composure. "We've been out here for hours, and I'm tired, scared as hell, and my sister is being held captive by people calling themselves the Cut Throats for Christ's sake! You've wasted time looking for crooks that probably not even out here!"

"Oh, but we are, Miss Elf."

Sally whipped around. Three men were standing behind her. All of them wearing the same red bandanas across their mouths and noses and in their hands were daggers and swords which glinted maliciously in the moonlight.

Chapter 5
CUT THROATS

Darcy's favorite part of the day was the hour before waking. All bad things were forgotten, and the world was a comfortable blanket wrapped around her.

"Darcy…Darcy!" A voice penetrated the blissful languor.

Darcy rolled onto her side, curling up in her bedroll, and tried to ignore the persistent voice. "Make it go away, Gina."

"No, it's 'M'-ina," the voice said, sounding out the "m" sound. "Get up. There are men outside."

Darcy unwillingly left the land of sleep behind and found herself eye to eye with an Amazonian bronze giantess. A cry stuck in her throat as the events of the past day crashed down on her. Clearing her throat, she listened. "I don't hear anything."

"Trust me; they're there. I woke up, and I heard someone walking around outside."

"It might be one of the stable boys checking on the horses."

"There aren't any horses in here!" Mina hissed, her eyes wide with fear. "And Sally's gone."

Darcy looked down at the empty bedroll beside her which was void of a half-elf Rogue. "Where the hell did she go?"

"I don't know!" Mina cried in a near panic. "She was already gone when I woke up!"

"We have to find her!" Darcy said, rising to her feet.

"We got to hide!" Mina protested, remaining crouched in the stall. "They're out there!"

Before Darcy could retort, she heard the large stable doors creak open. She ducked down and thought herself foolish for giving into Mina's paranoia. It was probably Sally coming back. Yet, something told her that it wasn't Sally. A stone settled in her stomach as her feelings of dread gave weight to Mina's fears.

"Mina, get your ax," Darcy hissed reaching for her armor.

Once she touched the chest plate, she withdrew her hand. No, it was too heavy to put on without making too much noise and that would take too long. Going without the chest armour would lower her Armor Class from 17 to 12, but there was no help for it.

"Mina, you're gonna have to take the lead. As soon as they get close, take their heads off with your ax, and we'll run out the back. I'll stay close behind and heal you if you need it."

She noticed that Mina wasn't holding her ax. She was hugging her knees, shaking, with brown eyes as large as silver dollars. "Darcy..."

"Mina, get your ax..."

"I can't..."

"It's right there!"

"I can't move. God, I'm so scared. I can't move."

Darcy fought with the diatribe that threatened to explode from her. A twitch started in her right eye, but she managed to keep herself under control. Not because she was considerate of Mina's mental state or feelings, but because blowing up right now would give away their position. It was both trying and antagonizing to keep calm when all she wanted to do was throttle the wretch.

Something about Mina caught her eye and Darcy's fury abated. The Barbarian wasn't trying to be difficult to be contrary, she was actually frozen with terror. She was nearing the point where the fight or flight instinct would take over. If Mina ran, it would give them away just as surely as Darcy shouting would. And if she fought, like Darcy wanted, it would sloppy, without thinking or strategy which would be dangerous and counterintuitive to any plans for escaping with their lives. She needed to bring Mina away from that edge and being angry with her wouldn't help with that.

"I know you're scared. I am too," Darcy said gently. "We can save ourselves, but I need your help. If I could, I would take the point, but I don't have your health points or Strength. It has to be you, but you won't be alone. I'll be right there beside you healing you, okay?"

Mina remained frozen for several heartbeats before she slowly reached across for her ax. "Okay, I'm alright. I...I can do this."

"Good." For a brief second, Darcy checked her character screen and eyed her +7 in Perception. Had her previous, real-world experience let her see how close Mina had come to panicking and to choose the right words to calm her? Or had being in the game helped? Darcy felt that there was no way she could have played it so cool in the real world. The game was affecting her just like Sally.

Darcy picked up her mace, both hands squeezing around the knotted handle. "Alright, we wait until they're at the stall and then we beat their asses and run."

Mina nodded with tight lips. Darcy waited, hoping the Barbarian had her fear under control, and listened to boots crunching on dry straw and dirt. Mina went still, tensed, exuding terror in waves. Darcy made a note to stay low in case Mina's attack went wide. It wouldn't be good to have her head lopped off by her own fighter. That is, if the barbarian woman took any action at all when the right time came.

Darcy chanced a peek from around the edge of the stall. There were three men, all of them wearing familiar bandanas across the lower half of their faces: Cut Throats. She stared in awe, struck by the thought that they looked like professional cosplayers at a convention. Darcy drew back and held up a hand at Mina and raised three fingers.

Mina narrowed her eyes perplexed. She mouthed, to the count of three?

Darcy shook her head. She shook three fingers at her and mouthed, three men.

Mina looked more confused. Women?

Darcy shook her head, baring her teeth as she mouth again, three men!

Again, it didn't click for Mina. She shook her head, and her mouth open in a "what?"

Darcy bit her lip to keep from screaming. She thrust one finger, then two fingers, and then three fingers in Mina's face. Then she mouthed: One. Two. Three. Motherfuckers. Out there. Then she waved her hand towards the doors.

Mina gave her an offended look. Darcy was about to hit her when a voice came from overhead.

"Well, ain't this a tantalizing conversation."

They looked up to see a man leering at them from over the top of the stall. "If you ladies would just come out, we have some questions..."

He never got to finish that sentence as Darcy smashed the side of his head with her mace. With a grunt, he slumped out of sight. Both Darcy and Mina barreled from the stall, nearly knocking down one of the men who had hidden around the corner.

Mina yelped as a knife slashed her arm, and in response, perhaps by reflex, she floored the offender with a solid punch across the nose. Darcy's opponent fared much better when he grasped the wrist of her hand that held the mace. In return, she grabbed the hand that held his knife. Her back thudded against a wooden post, and the dagger came dangerously close to her eye. Wrenching her head away, she twisted, almost breaking the grapple, but he shoved her hard enough against the post which knocked the wind from her.

Just as her strength would have given out, and the dagger would have found its mark in her face, Mina grabbed the Cut Throat from behind. She flung him away from Darcy as she would a raggedy scarecrow. His body arced through the air until he landed on a pile of feed bags and tools. He lay stunned, giving them precious seconds to flee.

Darcy grabbed Mina's arm. "Out the back! Hurry!"

The doors ahead were closed. Mina grabbed each one and threw them apart as if she were opening shower curtains. The doors nearly hit the men waiting outside.

Darcy realized, too late, they were running into a trap. The men inside the stables were sent in to flush them out into the waiting crowd of Cut Throats. Darcy counted nearly a dozen men with weapons and dangerous glints in their eyes. Their best bet was to fight their way through and run. She gripped the mace and realized she had foolishly left the shield behind.

Mina uttered a belated warning cry as a net fell over them, bearing Darcy to the ground. The heavy metal sewn into the net weighed her down, making it impossible to maneuver under it. Mina managed to remain on her feet, but the net prevented her from doing anything more than that. Then the men descended upon them. A cudgel smacked Mina across the back, and she fell when the back of her leg was kicked. Darcy curled into a ball against the kicks and punches that rained down upon her.

So this is what an asskicking feels like, Darcy thought sourly as a boot heel ground into her shoulder. Then she began to panic, fearing the men intended to beat them to death.

A sudden shout stopped the beating, and the men pulled the net away. Darcy was too hurt and sore from the beating to struggle as hands hauled her up and tied her wrists behind her back. Darcy was bleeding from the nose and mouth, and Mina's right eye was turning red and would be swollen shut soon.

A bald man was looking between them with dark eyes as hard as pieces of flint. "Did they have it in their bags?"

"No sir," a voice behind them said.

"Search them."

Hands pawed through their pockets and clothes with rough disregard for their injuries or modesty. Whatever it was they were after; they didn't find it.

"They don't have it, sir," another brute muttered.

"Damn. Boss won't like that one bit," the bald man said coldly. "Especially after we lost the elf too."

Darcy closed her eyes in utter relief. Sally was safe and away from these bastards. But where was she? No, right now she had to focus on getting the two of them out of captivity. Shoving down the waves of panic threatening to send her to into tearful hysterics, Darcy thought more quickly than she believed herself capable of.

C'mon, think, dammit. You know this world better than your own apartment. You know this game better than your own life. If this happened in-game, what would you do? The better question is, what can I do?

She summoned her character screen and looked at her status. Her health was down by 10 from the beating, which brought her to 17. Darcy frantically studied her character sheet and moaned at herself for her stupidity. She had put her highest score into her Wisdom for spellcasting. If her hands had been freed, she would have slapped herself. How could she have forgotten that she could have cast other spells to that of Heal? A Fear spell might have made these men run away in terror, or a Commanding Will spell could have forced one of them to attack the others. With her hands tied, she couldn't cast any spells now.

Stop focusing on what your characters can't do, and focus on what they can do. That's what Darcy had lectured during her tabletop sessions when players facing a tough situation complained about the skills their characters lacked. So, taking her own advice, Darcy eyed her highest ability score, which was an 18 in Wisdom. Wisdom factored into her spells' magical ability and put points into her Perception (+7). The former had let her see Mina's state of mind and how to help her find courage: but how could it help her now?

A tiny bead of sweat was rolling down the bald man's temple. His breathing was short and quick and he kept glancing at them furtively, as if hoping what he sought would suddenly appear in their place. Darcy noticed all of this with near a tunnel vision focus and realized that the leader of these Cut Throats was afraid to return to his superior empty-handed.

"What should we do with these two, sir?" one of the men asked.

"Do away with them. They're useless to us…"

Mina moaned in terror, but Darcy swallowed hers back. "No, sir, you don't want to do that."

Both men looked at her with bemusement as if surprised by her ability to speak. The bald man sneered, "And why is that, dearie?"

"I'm Sister Korra, a Cleric of the Lady of Shantra. Killing one of Her clerics will rain down pain and death upon you." Her voice rose in vehemence, but she quickly dampened it to continue more calmly, "And the temple will pay handsomely to see my companion and I returned safely."

The bald man spat on the grass and fixed her with a sharp look. "A Cleric of Shantra, huh? And why, pray tell, would a cleric of such an esteemed order be traipsing these backwoods with a half-breed and a heathen?"

"They're converts," Darcy snapped arrogantly. Her heart was racing. Her Charisma score wasn't particularly high at 12, granting only a +1 in most social-related skills, but maybe game-mechanic would allow her Knowledge of Religion skill to come into play. "They saw the Holy Light of Shantra and wished to pledge themselves to Her service. Attacking a cleric comes with dire consequences, but if you let us go, I'll pray for forgiveness on your behalf."

The bald man gave her a contemptuous glare. "Oh, you'll pray on my behalf, eh? We'd rather have the money. Get the horses. We're taking these two with us. The Boss will decide what to do with them."

Darcy maintained her straight back posture even though she wanted to fall weeping in gratitude. Mina was goggling at her, but Darcy refused to make eye contact, lest she lose her self-righteous mien. She had saved them for the moment, but their salvation was very fragile right now, and any sign of weakness on her part could shatter it.

Horses were led out from the forest and both Darcy and Mina were hauled up onto the back of a formidable destrier. They were tied together at the waist with Darcy at the front and Mina behind her. With the barbarian woman being nearly two heads taller, this made Darcy feel like a kid riding with an adult.

While the men mounted up, Mina hissed, "What the hell was that?"

"What do you think?" Darcy whispered, keeping her face forward. "I had to give them a reason not to kill us. The Order of Shantra is a religious military group that even the Cut Throats don't want to cross. Thank God, I chose Shantra as my character's deity."

"What happens when the Order of Shantra says they don't know a Korra?"

"Maybe we'll have escaped before that happens." Darcy scanned the trees, hoping to see a blonde figure watching. "Sally's out there somewhere."

"Will she come to save us?"

"What can she do alone with these assholes by herself? She doesn't know the game rules, and she's only level one," Dary said. "I want her to stay somewhere safe until we get out of here and find her."

"Can we get out of this?" Mina looked fearfully at the men.

"I think so, but listen, we don't have much time. When you get the chance, break the ropes."

"With what?"

"With wishful thinking," Dary hissed. "No, with your Strength. You're a Barbarian, one of the stronger classes and you have a Strength of plus three. It might be enough for you to break the ropes if your character rolls high enough."

"I don't think I can…"

"If you can't break the ropes, then Rage, it'll boost your Strength bonus from plus to plus seven."

"You-you want me to try now?"

"No, not with all these bastards watching us. I'll tell you when the time is right."

***

Sally couldn't move. It was like her insides and bones had been replaced with unmovable rock. Her mind was screaming at her to run, attack, or shout for help, but her body wouldn't obey. Never before had she experienced such paralyzation. This immobility was more than shock and fear, and the Cut Throats were surrounding her with daggers gleaming almost wetly in the moonlight.

With a cocked fist, Naomi shot past her like a comet. The punch sank into the man's solar plexus with the force of an angry bull. With a low, airless groan, the man doubled over, and Naomi's other fist met his chin in an uppercut, throwing him off his feet. The other two men stared in astonishment to see their leader felled by a girl barely half his weight.

Again, Sally tried to move, but couldn't. What was wrong? Had a dart dipped in paralyzing poison hit her like in the movies? She could only watch mutely as Naomi took on the other men by herself.

The second man attacked and the blade sliced through empty air as Naomi spun away. The third man tried to grab her, his fingertips dotting her sleeve, but the girl did an elegant flip backward, her foot connecting with his chin mid arc, sending him stumbling back with a bloody jaw.

And just like that, whatever was holding Darcy place was gone. The second man was going for Naomi's exposed back. Without hesitation, Sally shoved a knife into the man's back, between the ribs, and thrust upward. Hot blood seeped over her fingers. With a choked squawk, her opponent went limp, falling back against her. She shoved him off the knife in time to see Naomi grappling with the last man. Her legs were wrapped around his waist and hooked at the ankles. She wrenched his head back with both arms around his neck and chest.

Immediately, Sally shoved the knife deep into the exposed chest of the bandit, piercing his heart. The man's eyes rolled up in his head; death claiming him instantly. The body hit the grass with barely a sound. It wasn't until Sally could hear her own breathing that she noticed the sticky blood congealing on her hands. It reminded her of elementary school when she would smear Elmer's glue on her hands just so she could peel it off after it dried. Then the detail of the recent violence came back to her and just like Mina had done after the fight with the kobolds, Sally threw up on the grass.

God, she hated this body that made her do things she would never have done in the real world. She had acted without thought, killing the men as casually as she would draw breath or blinking. When she recovered, she noticed Naomi digging through the pockets and belts of the dead men.

"Stop that!" Sally barked rounding on her. "What the hell are you doing?"

"Looting!" Naomi announced filching several coins from an inner pocket. "What's wrong?"

"I just killed them!" Sally cried, shocked by the girl's nonchalant attitude.

"So? They were gonna kill us," Naomi said as she palmed the coins and stood. "What did you think they were gonna do to us? Ask us for directions?"

Sally looked down at her hands, covered in sticky blood and almost wiped them on her legs, but stopped herself before she soiled the cloth. She needed soap and hot water, and even then she doubted she could wash it all off. Her hands would always be covered in blood.

Naomi held out two Cut Throat weapons for her. "Here. Now you have a sword and a dagger. And we get XP for this encounter too."

Sally summoned her character screen and sure enough the bar had changed with 87 of 300 at the top. How was the XP distributed? Was it per Cut Throat or for the entire encounter? She wished Darcy was here to answer her questions.

"This one is alive. He's just knocked out." Naomi pointed at the man she was rendered unconscious. "He can tell us where the hideout is."

"Oh, so he's just gonna tell us, the people who killed his friends?" Sally said, bitterly.

"We'll beat it out of him," Naomi said exasperated. "Why are you making this so hard?"

"Why are you taking this so…so casually? We just killed two guys, and you're talking about torturing another."

"To save your friends!" Naomi cried, standing up on the torso of one of the dead men, so she was almost nose to nose with the taller Sally. "If I could push a button or click my heels three times and "poof" they're rescued, I would! But this is the only way to save them. So I'm sorry that your moral sensibilities are offended by all the blood and violence, but

I'm going to ask you to be a big girl and shelve it until we get your friends back, okay?"

Sally closed her eyes, pinched the skin between them, and swallowed back the torrent of anger she wanted to unleash. Naomi was telling the truth, and Sally hated her for it. "Alright. Let's do what we need to do to save Darcy and Mina."

Naomi stared hard at her, clearly unconvinced and Sally glowered back before bending down to undo the dead man's sword belt. It shouldn't be so easy to steal from the dead, but there was no resistance as she pulled the belt free. She put it around her waist and thrust her sword into the sheath and slid the fallen dagger into the belt on the other side. The kitchen knives were dropped on the ground and forgotten.

Satisfied, Naomi stepped off the dead man and hauled the unconscious Cut Throat to a tree and tied his hands behind his back with the other dead man's belt.

"So how do we do this?" Sally said, feeling a little sick to her stomach, but she was swallowing it back, thinking only of Darcy and Mina.

"Wake him up, of course!" Naomi declared. Before Sally could stop her, she gave the man a resounding slap across the face. When the man didn't stir, she delivered another one that made Sally flinch.

"Dammit! You're going to end up killing him!" Sally caught Naomi's wrist just as she was winding up for a third slap.

"Look, it's working," Naomi said, pointing with her free hand at the stirring criminal.

"Oh, bloody 'ell," the man muttered rolling his jaw. "What did you birdies do? Stomp me face in while I slept?" It took him seconds to realize the state of his hands behind his back, and he glared at him, made all the more heated by his red cheeks from being slapped. "'Ell 'appened to the others?"

"Dead!" Naomi declared, shaking her hand loose from Sally's grip. "And you're gonna wish you were too if you don't tell us where your hideout is!"

The man spat foully, the spittle almost landed on Naomi's foot and guffawed. "Go ahead. I'm used to gettin' beat bloody. Me pa used to tear open the skin on me back with his damn belt and me mam would sprinkle salt in the wounds to make the lesson stick."

Naomi's face fell, and she gave Sally an uncertain look. "I kinda don't wanna hurt him any more now."

Sally lowered her face into a palm and moaned into it. "Dear God, it was your idea."

"Yeah, but was before I knew he had such a sad backstory."

Sally took matters into her own hands and collected a second belt from the other dead body and looped it between her hands.

Naomi gasped, "Oh no! Don't use his childhood trauma to torture him!"

"Shut up," Sally snapped.

She booted the Cut Throat in the chest, and she secured the belt around his legs tightly. She moved quickly before he got the idea of kicking at her, then she hauled up the prisoner by the collar. His unwashed odor wafted into her face, making her wince in disgust and even his breath was foul with teeth in desperate need of dental work.

He sneered at her. "Wot? Are you gonna give me a kiss? Sorry, slags don't catch me fancy."

"You're going to tell us where your hideout is," Sally began with steel behind her eyes. "Where you keep prisoners, and how to sneak in and out of that place."

"Why should I do that?" he snarled, gritting yellow teeth.

"Because you want us to come back," Sally said in a calm voice. The words were coming to her, drawing from her +5 Charisma bonus. "We're going to leave you here with two dead bodies covered in blood. You lived out here in the woods, so you know that wolves, bears, insects, and monsters all love fresh meat."

The Cut Throat's sneer fell back into a pained grimace. Taking satisfaction in that, Sally continued, "And you know what else? You can scream as loud as you want, but no one is going to come. You're out here all alone in an area that I'm certain no one save for your gang knows about, and I doubt they'll find you before the wolves do. First, they'll go for the easier meals, the two dead men over there, but they won't last long. The best you can hope for is a big bear will come along and bite your throat out clean, but I don't think you'll be that lucky.

"Wolves will come in a pack, and to start with the alphas will eat, tearing into your flesh, ripping back your clothing to expose more meat. That'll attract the flies and insects who'll crawl inside you and start on their share. Maybe they'll rip into something vital, and you'll die quick, but I don't think so. No, they'll want the meaty parts first. Your arms, your legs, and belly, leaving the organs inside to keep you alive long enough for the Omegas to have their turn."

The Cut Throat's face had gone white, making the bruises on his face stand out in stark contrast. "You're mad."

"No, I'm worried about my friends," Sally dug her fingertips into his shoulder and squeezed hard. "I'm willing to do anything to save them, even if that means leaving you here to get eaten alive."

The man looked between them, his eyes bright and wide like a caught wild animal. Naomi stepped forward and knelt beside Sally. "I give you my word that once we rescue them, we'll come back and release you. You can trust me because I took the Vow of Truth."

That seemed to be enough for the man though Sally didn't know what the Vow of Truth meant. He started talking.

MCRANDO

Darcy had always wondered what it was like to ride a horse. She assumed it was like riding a motorcycle but from a greater height. In reality, it was like sitting on a swaying bench which chafed her thighs and made her back hurt. Coupled from her lacerations from the beating, she was in pure misery. And, ironically, while Darcy had the power to ease her pain with a Heal spell, her bound hands prevented it. Mina's bellyaching didn't make matters better either.

"How much longer before we get there?" Mina whined.

"Don't be in a hurry to get there," Darcy hissed. "We don't know what they're gonna do to us when we arrive."

"I thought they were going to hold us hostage."

"Yeah, but their boss might have other ideas. Don't say anything and let me do the talking."

For the last hour, Darcy had been eyeing her character screen trying to form plans for all the scenarios they might face. Their best hope involved Mina having a chance to break the ropes. Though she was familiar with the Cut Throats in-game, Darcy had no idea of what they would be like in this world. The Cut Throats were low-level enemies for new players to cut their teeth on in early encounters. They dropped only low-level loot and questline items that would lead the players who followed it to the Cut Throat's hideout. This zone functioned as the first real dungeon crawl after the Lair of Tears. The boss of the dungeon was the Cut Throat's leader, McRando, a level 8 Rogue.

Facing McRando wouldn't be possible for a level 3 Cleric without her armor and a level 1 Barbarian coward who didn't know how to Rage.

Their best bet was to wait and hope that they would be tossed in a cell together, so they would have a chance to escape.

The horses broke through a copse of trees into a glade. The open sky allowed enough moonlight to see clearly, but Darcy still couldn't determine where they were. The men quickened their pace, not from fear, but as though eager to reach their destination. She had to peer hard to realize that on the other side of the glade was the Cut Throat's hideout.

Darcy recalled from the *Shadow's Deep* Wiki page that the bandits' headquarters had been a hunting lodge for some local duke or count a few centuries back. The noble abandoned it to an infestation of goblins, and the Cut Throats cleared them out around ten years ago and made the manor their base of operations. The reason it stayed hidden for so long was that the forest had sought to take the building back by growing thick vines and foliage over the wood and stone. It provided the perfect camouflage from any kingsmen or travelers, at least for those the Cut Throats didn't capture or kill.

Men opened a second story windows and hailed them. The wide double doors, entirely hidden by a mesh of leaves and vines, were pushed open by four men, two on each door. The Cut Throats took Darcy and Mina inside, horses and all. Hooves thumped on the old wooden floors, long since scarred and filthy from many boots and hooves coming and going over the years. The Cut Throats led the horses into what had once been a parlor where the furnishings had all been removed or stolen.

Despite her fear, Darcy couldn't help staring in wonder at the interior of the hideout. She had run through this dungeon so many times that she knew the layout by heart. It was as if a rich fan had built it with lifelike detail. There was a long table covered in loot and food with three golden candelabras casting a dull yellow glow over the whole room. And there was the side door that led to the rooms the Cut Throats used as a barracks.

Darcy and Mina were hauled off the horse and would have hit the ground if the Cut Throats hadn't gripped them so hard. Their legs wobbled from riding the horse for so long that they needed time to be accustomed to solid ground again, but the Cut Throats weren't patient enough for that and dragged them staggering down the hall. Men jeered at them, some making crude comments and deadly threats.

Clenching her teeth, Darcy refused to let them see her fear, but sadly Mina had no such qualms. Whimpering, she cowered behind Darcy, eyes full of tears, suddenly flinching when a brutish man with a jagged scar across his face lunged at her. The men roared in laughter until they were silent by a sharp cry of "Shush it!"

Looming at the end of the hall was a large man. He stood over six feet, and his black vest and shirt barely contained the thick muscular frame which seemed to fill the hall. One side of his face was swatch in a crimson cloth where a right eye had once been, and the other eye was black as polished onyx. White teeth beneath a beak like nose were bright in stark contrast to his black beard.

He regarded the bald man with a disdainful glare. "Who are these wenches? Did they have the package?"

The bald man hesitated, clearly unhappy to be the bearer of ill tidings. "They didn't have it, sir."

The single black eye switched to them and then back to his underling. "Then why in all the hells are you here and not out there getting my letters!"

Letters? Darcy raised her head and quickly lowered to keep them from seeing her reaction. It couldn't be the letters she was thinking of, could it? If it was, then it made sense why the Cut Throats took the risk of kidnapping them from the village. And that could mean they were in even more danger...and not just from the Cut Throats.

"I have men searching the forest as we speak, sir," the bald man said quickly, almost soothingly to the bigger man. "Whoever took them won't get far, I assure you."

"And what am I supposed to do with these birdies, Sikes? One looks mean enough to bite a man's prick in half, and the other could fight a bear and mother his cubs too."

It was debatable to which of them he was speaking about, but Darcy still prickled at the insinuation, whichever one it was. Mina was too scared to react with anything other than a sniffle.

"This one," the bald man, Sikes, tapped Darcy on the shoulder, "is singing about being from the Order of Shantra."

"And is she?" McRando demanded.

"Seems this matches her tune," Sikes said motioning to a Cut Throat who held up a shield with the Order's emblem of a sun embossed on the surface.

"Why is a member of such an esteemed order out this far from the cities?"

"Let's see if she sings the same song for you as she did for me," Sikes turned to Darcy and gave her a hard glare.

Darcy hoped she would meet or beat the Knowledge of Religion roll that had led her to convince Sikes she was an ordinary cleric, but she had the feeling it would be tough to fool the higher level and more intelligent McRando. She opened her mouth to speak, but he cut her off. "Stop. This one sang a song, but I'm interested in what the tall one has to sing. You, wild woman, tell me what you and the little one were doing out in this part of the world."

If Darcy could have cursed without giving them away, she would have. Barbarians had low Charisma scores, especially the default builds, and Mina didn't know this world at all. Casting a despairing looking over her shoulder Darcy saw that Mina was sweating profusely, her brown skin turning an ashen shade.

"S-s-sir?" Mina stammered. "I-I don't kn-know..."

"She's not that bright!" Darcy interposed. "I found her in the far off lands of Yirn. She can't read or write, and she barely speaks clearly."

"Shut your mouth, or I'll put a fist in it," McRando snapped with a flash of teeth. "Start your story, bear woman."

So now Darcy knew to whom he was referring earlier.

Mina was frantic, looking between McRando and Darcy, who could only peer back with wide eyes, trying to communicate with her companion what she desperately needed to know to conjoin their stories.

"We're on a pilgrimage," Mina started at last, with evident hesitation. "I'm converting."

With a look of contempt McRando was leaning into Mina, staring at her with his one eye as if he could tell that she was really a small Asian girl and not this Amazonian warrior. "Why would a woman of the plains want to leave her hunting grounds to join the strict and proper Shantras? Did you shame your tribe?"

"Yes! Yes, I—uh, I killed someone!"

Darcy gave a slight nod of encouragement; Mina was doing well.

"Murder? I don't know many of your people, but from what I hear, murder is a minor offense among your tribes. Who did you kill?"

At a loss, Mina said, "My husband for cheating on me with another woman."

McRando's eye narrowed. "That's quite strange for a tribe woman to be jealous of another woman. Do the tribes not practice polygamy?"

Mina moaned, obviously giving up and resigning herself to the fate of being murdered by bandits in a fictional world. "I don't know…"

"The first truth I heard from your mouth yet," McRando growled looking between them; his face becoming more and more unhappy with what he saw.

"She speaks well for someone of the tribe," Sikes commented, staring at Mina with a skeptical glare. "Most of them use broken Common or point and grunt."

"You caught that too, eh?" McRando said. His one-eyed gaze took in Mina from her leather boots, hide armor, tanned skin, and muscular arms. "I've seen very few tribesmen, but none of them ever showed so much fear as this one does. They were proud, never betraying any emotion save for fury at any slight, real or imagined, or distaste for civilized folks like me."

Sikes gave a chuckle that ended abruptly when McRando looked across at him.

Then the Cut Throat's leader turned to Darcy and her heat beat faster under the gaze of that skeptical eye.

"You're not much different. That's the armor and shield of the Order of Shantra, but something's not right. She doesn't have the …" He looked at the bald man then shook his head. "Discipline. Calm. You know, that kind of control they have."

Her back stiffening, Darcy found herself trying to stand straighter and more poised, but it was no use. McRando clearly had a high Perception skill.

"She's bad-tempered too. I wonder how could she have gotten her hands on the Order of Shantra armor without being hanged?

"Was it just the two of them?" McRando suddenly demanded, turning a dark eye on his underling.

"Pete says there were three with this group," Sikes said and then lowered his eyes. "An elf, sir, but she ran away with the stranger staying in the inn."

"Shame, shame," McRando said sadly, emphasizing both word. "Elves fetch a high price downriver. Bring her back alive if you find her and kill the stranger once you have the letters. As for these two, throw them into a cell. They're hiding something, and I aim to find out what it is."

***

"We should rest," Naomi said after coming to a sudden halt.

Having been running to keep up with the girl's fast gait, Sally almost barreled into her. Bending double, Sally panted through her open mouth, gulping air while her legs burned. Despite how tired she was now, she was impressed by how far and how fast she had run. It had to have been at least fifteen miles or more. Jogging around the block once had been tiresome in her old body. If she had tried running such a long stretch back then, she'd be in the hospital.

"Alright, we can take five minutes," Sally managed to say once she caught her breath.

"I'm gonna need about an hour," Naomi declared dropping onto the grass into a relaxed position. Both hands cushioned her head and one foot balanced on a knee.

"We don't have an hour!" Sally cried.

They had come to a small clearing where there was a break in the branches allowing moonlight to spill across them. Naomi looked up at the moon and said, "The river's thirty minutes away, and there are three or four hours before the sun comes up. By then, we'll be in the caverns, and we won't need the cover of night to hide us."

The Cut Throat told them about an underground river the gang used to smuggle supplies and stolen items in and out of the hideout. The cave was well hidden behind a waterfall and guarded by two or three guards.

"But what about Darcy and Mina?"

"They'll be fine," Naomi said with a wave of one hand. "The Cut Throats went to a lot of trouble taking them captive. If they were going to kill them, they would have done it back at the stables. And the Cut Throats sell people into slavery, so they might keep them alive for that."

It was so strange listening to Naomi speak. She looked like a teenager, but spoke like an adult who've seen and done it all. It made Sally feel like the kid in this partnership. "Why an hour? Why not just take five or ten minutes and be on our way?"

Naomi sighed and rolled her eyes. "Because I need to get my ki points back."

"Oh God," Sally moaned. This was yet another characteristic of the game she had no idea about since she was a damn newb. "Forgive me for asking this, but what are ki points?"

"It's a Monk's special ability," Naomi explained, wagging the foot on her knee. "It's like magic, but instead of spells, I do special attacks. When I knocked out that guy with one punch and fought those guys that tried to jump us, I was using ki points. I'm low right now, but I'll get them all back if I rest for an hour. Anything can go wrong once we're in the caverns and I want to have all my ki ready when it does."

Sally lowered herself into a crossed-legged sit beside Naomi. "You don't think we're going to succeed?"

Naomi's foot stopped wagging and after a moment of silence, she said, "I think we can, but it's going to be dangerous with just level five me and level one you. I wish we could do encounters until you level up a couple of times, but I don't think we have that kind of time."

As much as she didn't want to say this, Sally felt it had to be said. "I know this is going to be really dangerous and I appreciate your help, but you don't have to come with me if you don't want to."

"No, I want to. And I have to," Naomi tilted her head to face her. "I'm Chaotic-Good. If someone is in trouble, then I have to save them."

Sally wasn't sure what Naomi was talking about, but she had a feeling it was more stuff from the game. "If I had known that this was going to happen when I logged onto the game, I never would have bought the damn thing. I only started playing because Darcy kept bugging me to do so."

"Darcy? That's your sister, right?"

"Yeah, my stepsister, but we're pretty close. It's not like what you see in movies or TV shows where the stepsisters are each other's throats." Sally hugged her legs to her chest (another feat she couldn't pull off in her old body) and planted her chin on her knees. "We're both gamers. I was into consoles and PC games while she was into MMOs and tabletop RPGs. She once ran a campaign that lasted nearly two years in high school. Every weekend she and her friends would gather into her game room and would play all day. Like from seven in the morning to past midnight!"

"You ever joined them?" Naomi had rolled onto her side, listening with interest so intent that it made Sally uncomfortable.

"No, I'm not a sociable person."

Sometimes Sally heard Darcy and her friends laughing down the hall and wondered what was so funny. She thought about going to join them, but never could get the courage to do it.

"I'm the same way," Naomi said, interrupting her thoughts. "I stay in my room a lot after school. Sometimes, when my brother has time, he takes me to the park."

Sally grimaced at the thought of going to the park. Why go outside when you had TV, internet, and videogames? "I didn't really go outside much. Definitely not to parks."

"I never had much use for the park either," Naomi replied. "He thought it made me happy to go, so I went to make him happy. Do you have any rations? I'm a little hungry."

Since Naomi mentioned it, Sally realized that she too was feeling peckish. "All my rations were in my backpack. Sorry."

"What's your Survival skill?"

"It's a plus two."

"That might be good enough. Can you look for some berries or roots for us to eat."

Sally shook her head. "I'm a city girl. I wouldn't last an hour in the wilderness unless I had a stocked mobile home and wi-fi. I wouldn't know what to look for."

"But your character will," Naomi said, rolling onto her stomach with her chin on folded hands. "Stop thinking about what you couldn't do before and start thinking about what you can do now. Haven't you noticed that you know and understand things that you didn't before coming to this world?"

Thinking about how Darcy knew how to cast spells and how Sally became an expert with the rapier, she looked at her other skills. Sneak was at a generous +6, while Acrobatics was at +4. Sally knew that sneaking worked, so decided to try some tumbling to get a feel for how to use a skill she wasn't familiar with in real life.

Stretching out her arms, Sally tipped to her side and performed a perfect cartwheel. Excited, and to see if she could, she stood on her hands with legs together and toes pointed towards the sky. She maintained this position for nearly a minute before gracefully righting herself. Before the Incident, she couldn't have pulled off anything more dexterous than rolling over in bed.

"I'll be right back!" Sally said, feeling a burst of confidence and dashed into the woods at a speed that amazed her.

She could see the trees clearly to avoid running into them, and the roots stood out against the dark grass, so she didn't trip on them. For the first time since this crazy nightmare started, she was having fun. It was the same excitement she experienced when starting up a brand-new game on the weekend with ordered pizza and soda on the way. Just for the joy of it, she did a forward flip over a log and then cartwheeled between two trees with entwining branches. Maybe there was a good side to being in this world, after all.

Then she realized that Darcy and Mina likely weren't having any fun being held captive by bandits who call themselves Cut Throats. Okay, playtime was over. The least she could do was find some berries while they waited for Naomi's ki to recharge, but it was easier said than done. Despite having low-light vision, she couldn't find anything safe for consumption. Blueberries were clinging to a vine, but tell-tale white specks on the leaves told her intuition that they weren't safe to eat.

At last she realized that she had found what she was looking for: berries with dark sinks as large as walnuts. Her character's intuition was that they were not dangerous, so she popped one in her mouth and moaned as the sweetness spread across her tongue. Yes, this would do nicely. Gathering all the ripe fruit that she could into her pockets and the crook of one arm, Sally reckoned she had more than enough to feed Naomi and herself.

A twig snapped.

In an instant, Sally was on her feet with the dagger in hand, scanning the trees around her. The sound came from the west, but nothing was there. Or at least as far as her low-light vision would let her see.

She felt eyes on her, like the clothes on her body. "Hello?"

Silence. It hung in the air, permeating the darkness around her. She listened for any movement, another twig snapping, the rustle of bushes, or the creak of a branch. But there was nothing.

It was not the Cut Throats. She didn't know how, but Sally knew it was not them. All the hairs on the back of her neck stood up and she swallowed. "Hey? Hello?" Sally called again. "Answer me if you can hear me! Don't hide and jump out at me like a slasher from a movie."

No response. Only the weight of unseen eyes on her. Without losing her grip on the dagger, she began walking. "Alright, I'm going. Sorry for bothering you. Goodbye. Sayonara. Adios."

She kept walking, forcing herself not to run. Isn't that what happened in horror movies? You start running, and the monster begins chasing you? Or you run right into the slasher and he's waiting with huge machete or chainsaw?

Gradually, she felt the chill of being watched leave her. She took another long look around but saw only darkness and forest.

She hurried away, and it was a struggle not to run.

***

Eyes zeroed in on the spot between the shoulder blades of the retreating half-elf. Fingers pulled the string taut until it the bow that held it creaked. The tip of a white arrow gleamed in the moonlight.

A tongue touched an upper lip in a thoughtful motion. One beat, two beats, one more and the half-elf would be out of range.

A third beat passed and the white arrow lowered, and the string relaxed.

You get to live one more day. A gift from me to you. Use it wisely, hon.

Chapter 7

ESCAPING AND TRESPASSING

The manner in which Sally returned, often turning to look behind her, alerted Naomi that something was wrong.

"Are you being chased?" her companion asked.

"No, I—Jesus, I don't know," Sally said, as she swept the area with her eyes. "I think someone's out there, and it's not Cut Throats."

"Were you attacked?" Naomi's body looked tense as if she was readying herself to take action if needed.

"No, but someone was watching me."

"How do you know it was a person? It might have been an animal."

"No, it…It was a person." Sally couldn't put her feeling into words as it wasn't exactly like being watched. It was as if she was being studied like a rat in a maze. "How much longer do you need to rest?"

"Twenty minutes, and I'll be good to go." Naomi popped a berry into her mouth. "Hmm! These Gumdrop Berries are delicious! Try some!"

"How do you know they're called Gumdrop Berries?" Sally ate another berry and then understood why. It tasted and had the texture of sweet flavored gum.

"You have to collect these for a quest, but I didn't know they tasted this good," Naomi said, helping herself to another.

Eating the berries with Naomi made her calmer, and Sally began to wonder if there actually had been a watcher. Perhaps it was something her frightened mind and adrenaline conjured up. What she needed to do was concentrate on saving Darcy and Mina.

As soon as the berries were gone, she looked around. "Done resting? We should get going."

"One sec," Naomi blinked. Her eyes focused on a character screen Sally couldn't see. "Yep, all eleven ki points are back. Let's go."

***

"Please, God, don't let them kill me," Darcy could hear Mina whispering.

The Cut Throats had taken Darcy and Mina through a set of heavy doors lined with brass and down stone steps into what had once been a large cellar. A wall had been knocked out to make space for cells. They shoved the two of them inside, wrists still tied, and slammed the door shut with an ear-piercing clang. Once the Cut Throats guards had left, Darcy tried to peer around for a way out through the bars and cursed herself for being human. It was dark, with a distant torch down the hall serving as the only light source and Sally, with her low-light vision, would have been able to see clearly. Hell, being a Rogue she might have been able to maneuver these ropes off her.

"Shut up," Darcy grunted as she looked down the long hall outside of their cell. With her hands still tied, Darcy was prevented from casting spells, but hopefully, that wouldn't be the case for long. "Mina, you need to break the ropes."

"I'm trying! I've been trying!" Mina wailed, almost falling over from where she sat against the wall.

If she started rolling on the floor like a weeping toddler, Darcy might break the ropes on her own to throttle her. "Then you have to Rage and break the ropes. Get angry! Get pissed off!"

"I'm too scared," Mina cried.

"I'm scared too! I'm scared you're going to get me killed because you won't get it together!" Darcy kicked the bars, which gave a metal thunk in protest. "I never thought I would end up getting killed like this, because of a crybaby!"

Trembling, Mina bowed her head low and sobbed. It was pathetic to see a large, muscular woman break down, and Darcy felt the stirrings of guilt needling her. She didn't want to feel guilty as she believed her words and emotions were justified. Yet, her Wisdom score was forcing her to see that Mina was in the middle of a breakdown and shouting and berating her was only going to make it worse.

Kneeling on the floor beside Mina, she said, "Look, stop crying, alright? I'm sorry. I—I don't handle frustration well. Sally keeps telling me that one day I'm going to run my mouth off at the wrong person and get my ass kicked."

The barbarian sniffled, breathing hard, and Darcy wished she had a tissue or at least had her hands free to wipe away the tears.

"I don't know how to Rage," Mina sniffed, "I have never been in a fight in my life. I don't like confrontation."

Darcy sighed, thinking of other classes Mina would have been better suited for. "You should have created a Bard and stayed in the back with the Cleric to buff and debuff."

"What's buff and debuff?"

Once again, and not for the last time, Darcy wished her hands were free so she could bury her face into them. "Buff strengthens the party and debuff weakens the enemy. Haven't you ever played games before?"

"Well, yeah!" Mina said, almost offended. "I've played *Monopoly*, *Sorry*, *Life*, and *Clue* on family nights."

Now it was Darcy's turn to be offended. "Those are kiddie board games! I meant real games on PC or console."

Mina blinked. "We never owned a gaming console, and our computers were for homework and school assignments only."

Was this girl from another planet or some bizarre mutant from the underworld? "Not even a Vita? Or a Switch? What about tablets?"

Mina shook her head. "Mom and Dad limited our time on the iPad, and we only used it to watch movies and kids' Youtube."

"Oh, sweet Jesus in the Manger. Are you serious? You've never gamed?" This was inconceivable. How was it possible to live a wholesome life without video games in it? "What about tabletop RPGs?"

"What are those?"

With her mind blown, Darcy sagged against the wall. All her life she had played games. Like Sally, Darcy had upgraded consoles as they were released. They had gone through the early Nintendo phase and invested in both Xbox and PS4, along with upgrading a PC. While Sally stuck to her consoles, however, and played single-player games, Darcy had focused on tabletop RPGs and branched into MMOs when she was introduced to them by a cousin. Games had been her social outlet and her core focus outside of school and family. Imagining her life without games was impossible.

Then that brought up another question. "Why were you so interested in playing *Shadow's Deep* if you aren't gamer?"

The barbarian woman sighed and inclined her head. "You're going to laugh at me."

"I won't," Darcy promised. "C'mon, tell me. I really want to know."

Mina shifted, trying to get comfortable, which was hard with only her feet and legs free. "Alright. There's this boy..."

"Oh God, please, say no more." Darcy rolled her eyes. "You're one of those..."

Mina's brows rose. "One of what?"

"Girls who only play games to hang out with a boyfriend or get a guy to notice them. Let me guess. You met a boy who's really into *Shadow's Deep*. You thought if you got into it too, he'd notice you. Am I right?"

Mina glowered but stayed silent. If Darcy didn't know there was a coward behind that scowl, she would have been scared. The Barbarian woman looked mad enough to tear heads off. Darcy was about to apologize but then froze, an idea forming.

She twisted her lips into a smug smile. "And I bet you lied to him. You told him that you played the game too." Then a realization came to Darcy and her eyebrows rose high. "And that's why you were in such a hurry to learn how to play, isn't it? Because you want to impress him right away."

"Shut up," Mina said, her face turning bright red. "I really wanted to play..."

"But with him!" Darcy said, rising onto her knees. She couldn't tower over Mina, the Barbarian was too tall, but she was able to bring herself eye level. "God, I hate girls who play games to get guys! It makes us female gamers look bad! Do you know how many times I've been asked if I played games to find dates? Or if I'm a lesbian. I am a lesbian, but I shouldn't be labeled as one because I'm a girl who likes games. And it's because of girls like you!"

"Stop yelling at me!" Mina's teeth nearly glowed white as she bared them. She pivoted her body to face Darcy, her broad body almost bursting with fury.

"I'm not yelling. I'm telling the truth," Darcy said evenly. "But you wouldn't know that because you are a liar!"

"Don't call me that!" Mina snapped.

"Are you mad!?" Darcy yelled.

"Yes!"

"Then Rage, goddamn you! Rage and break the ropes!"

Mina's eyes darkened from both fury and fear and she opened her mouth wide enough to stretch her lips across her teeth and let out a strangled cry. Arms and chest growing taut, her muscles bulged, straining the hide armor. Then her arms were thrown upward with a torn rope around one wrist. Darcy's cry of joy turned into a strangled gasp as Mina's large hands closed around her throat and began throttling her.

***

With her low-light vision seeing further than Naomi's human eyes could, it fell to Sally to keep a watch on their surroundings. In case the Cut Throats patrolled the river, the plan was to go upstream for half a mile along the bank before moving into the adjacent foliage until they got to the waterfall.

When they finally found the river, Sally was surprised by how deep it was. The water was about as wide as she could throw a knife and deep enough to cover her; they might need to swim at some point, but they wouldn't get in the water just yet.

"You might need to scout ahead of me," Naomi explained. "Your Sneak skill is higher than mine."

Sally didn't like the idea of going it alone. "Let's just stick together in case we come across something unexpected. Isn't your Sneak as good as mine?"

"Yeah, but you're the one with the Sneak Attack. You can do a lot more damage ambushing them than me."

"I rather not attack them by myself," Sally said dryly. "They'll kick my ass before I can touch one of them."

"No, they won't. Not if you surprise them," Naomi said with an impish grin. "If you surprise an enemy, you get a free action round while they are stunned. They can't move until after you take a turn. And since you're a Rogue, you'll automatically do bonus damage."

Sally blinked, thinking back to the bizarre moments she was paralyzed when the Cut Throats surprised her. "What happens if we get surprised?"

"The same thing. We can't move until after all the enemies have their turn, which would be pretty bad for us, I guess," Naomi admitted.

Despite accepting the theory that her ambushing an enemy might work, Sally insisted they not split up and with Naomi behind her, went upstream with watchful eyes and pricked ears. Twigs and low-hanging branches—which were silently brushed aside—tugged at their clothes. Fortunately, there did not seem to be any Cut Throats in this area and nor did they see any boats. Yet, Sally didn't relax her guard until they arrived at the waterfall. The water fell from twenty feet in an opaque curtain of constantly moving water that would hide any cave.

It was easy enough to run to their destination, but to actually arrive was terrifying for Sally. Many times she was tempted to let Naomi go it alone, but knew she would never forgive herself for turning back.

I can do this. It's no different than dealing with skeletons and kobolds. And I have a level five player with me. We can handle this together.

They were close enough to the waterfall that the roar of water would hide any sound they made. Crouching low behind rocks, Sally peered over the top of the stones.

"I can go ahead and see if the cave's there," Naomi said, eyeing the waterfall.

A new worry pricked Sally's heart. "You think he was lying? After everything I told him?"

"I don't think so, but you can never be too careful. He might have forgotten some details," Naomi scooted around the rock. "Be back in a sec."

She was off like a shot, darting along the bank and traversing through the water with barely a sound. Ducking under the surface, she became a pale shadow passing beneath the water like ghost, until she finally disappeared altogether. A minute passed, then two minutes. Sally counted the seconds in her head and couldn't decide if she should wait longer or go in after Naomi. Before Sally could make up her mind, the girl burst through the surface, startling her.

Naomi paddled to the bank and shook the water from her hair like a dog before giving Sally a toothy grin and a thumbs up, "The guy wasn't lying. There are docks inside with a pier and wooden walkways. There's a couple of guards, but we can take "em."

Sally swallowed back a wave of fear. They were able to fight off the Cut Throats in woods, but she still feared fighting more of them. "Can we sneak past them?"

"We could, but it'll be safer to take them out so we won't have to worry about them later." Naomi shivered; her wet gi was dripping. "It's warmer inside too."

"You didn't see Darcy and Mina?"

"I would have told you if I did," Naomi said with a roll of her eyes. "No, I didn't see them, but they wouldn't keep them so close to an escape route. How's your Athletic skill?"

Sally checked her character screen. "It's a zero."

"Ouch, being level one stinks, but your Sneak is high so that we can manage." Naomi went back into the water and stopped once it was chest high. "Stay close to me, or if you need to, you can hold onto me."

The water seeped through her soft leather boots sending shivers up and down Sally's spine as she waded into the water. Her boots kept getting sucked into the mud and she was envious of Naomi's going barefoot: the Monk didn't have to worry about ruining any footwear.

The water didn't get any warmer deeper in. It was so odd to be submerged in water while fully clothed. Sally flexed her arms and legs and found they could move easily without being constricted by her clothing. The leather didn't weigh her down nor (as she made an experiment with breaststroke) did it slow her.

Naomi paddled next to her. "Stick close to me and do not go up for air until I give you a signal." In a demonstration, she thrust both thumbs upward. "Ready?"

"No, but let's go anyway."

They each took a deep breath and went under. Sally instinctively closed her eyes to protect her contacts, then remembered she was no longer wearing them in this body. Opening her eyes, she could see clearly underwater, as if she were wearing goggles. Maybe the low-light vision also gave her a sharp image underwater.

Naomi was motioning for her to follow and started scissor kicking towards the waterfall. The Monk swam so fast that Sally struggled to keep up as they passed under the waterfall and into the cave. It took no time at all for her eyes to adjust to the darkness, and she could see the wooden columns of the pier and walkways. Ahead, Naomi was kicking hard, a white shadow that was easy to follow in the dark water. Sally's lungs were beginning to burn for want of air, and she all she could hear was her heart pounding, but she did not dare surface until Naomi gave her the all-clear to do so.

Finally, Naomi stopped and pointed towards something almost too dark to see. It was the shadow beneath the pier, a safe place to get air and remain hidden. Sally's lungs were ready to burst by the time they were beneath it. Once her head had broken the surface, it was a struggle not to gasp loudly, but she gulped down air as quietly as she could.

Naomi was right about it being warmer inside the tunnel than outside. The sound of water bobbing against the columns and the distant echoes of dripping water mingled with the sound of burning wood. Opposite the pier, a campfire glowed hotly between two sitting men. Sally could hear them speaking, but they were too far away to understand what they were saying over the dripping water.

Naomi didn't seem to have needed air as much as Sally had as she barely looked out of breath. "They're over there getting drunk, so this will be easy."

Sally didn't share Naomi's opinion but kept her comment to herself. "What do we do?"

"You wait here while I throw rocks at them."

"What?"

"It'll be a surprise round if I get the drop on them. I can KO one with a rock to the skull, and then I'll nail the other one on my next turn. That way, we don't have to fight them."

Anything that would keep her out of a fight sounded good to Sally, but she doubted this plan would work. "What happens if you miss?"

"Then you'll have to help me."

It was a weak plan with very little chance of success. Naomi was a higher level than Sally, and maybe she could knock out two men by throwing rocks at them, but the doubt refused to go away, and Sally's mind began working quickly. Remembering the kobolds, she looked around and spotted a ladder at the edge of the pier. It was on the opposite side of the men, and it was dark enough that Sally felt confident they couldn't see her.

"Alright, I'll go around behind them," Sally said, her voice didn't shake or reveal any trace of the fear she was feeling.

Naomi's eyes widen. "I meant you could throw rocks at them too. Your Dex should be high enough to land a hit."

"If one of them gets away, they'll run for help, and we'll never find Darcy or Mina if that happens." Sally was surprised to hear the conviction in her voice. And she was confident in her plan as it formed in her head. "There has to be a way further into the hideout. I'm going to find it and block their escape. Give me ten minutes before you attack. Try your best to knock out the first one with a rock, and if you can't get the second one, let him run to me, and I'll take care of him."

"Are you sure?" Naomi asked. "You sounded hesitant earlier."

Sally tightened her lips, then nodded. "I'm sure."

God, can I do this? She thought over and over as she climbed the ladder. The men were dangerous and likely had weapons and if she messed up, they would hurt or kill her. Or Naomi could get hurt or killed despite being level 5 and it would be on Sally because this was her plan...but it was a better plan that Naomi just throwing rocks.

Going into Sneak was as natural an act for her as breathing or blinking. The wood did not creak beneath her weight, and the water falling from her clothes and hair made no dripping noise. From the edge of the platform, she could see the men sitting on opposite sides of the fire, taking turns with a demijohn. The light was so bright it cast the shadows of the stalagmites onto the wall like the needle-sharp teeth of a monster. Scanning the area, she saw a tunnel that led off from the main cavern that had to be the entrance of the hideout. Unfortunately, it was too close to the men for comfort.

There was no way she could sneak around them without being seen in the firelight, which would cast her shadow across the wall like a projector. She didn't need the game to tell her that, so what should she do now?

Another idea formed, and she could only hope that Naomi would pick up on it without being told. It was risky but carried more weight than merely throwing rocks at the Cut Throats. Gathering her courage, Sally offered up a small prayer and then put her plan into motion.

Raising a hand to cup her voice, she sang out in a low spooky voice better suited in a haunted funhouse. "Creepy voice over here."

Both men jumped to their feet and drew their weapons, a rapier and a cudgel. Keeping to the shadows, Sally edged away, her eyes never leaving them as they looked around. Naomi hadn't acted yet, so maybe she had caught onto the new plan?

"Who's over there?" The one with brandishing a cudgel demanded. He was an ugly round man with more fat than muscle and he spoke with a mouth missing several teeth.

The man with the rapier was younger with a leaner frame. He held the rapier with a loose grip that revealed that he didn't know how to properly wield it. "Better come out now. It'll go harder for you if we have to find you."

Sally couldn't stop herself from responding. "You couldn't find your ass with both hands and a map."

There was a pause, then both men turn rigid with fury. The larger man tapped his cudgel in his palm, and the younger man rattled the rapier. He stepped forward as if to plunge into the shadows after her. "You want to come out in the light and say that, bitch?"

"I'm sure you can hear me just as well in the dark," Sally replied. Her heart pounded so hard it wouldn't have surprised her if it leaped from her chest. Never before had she felt so brazen and she wasn't afraid at all! No, that was wrong. She was scared, but the fear was pushed to the side by her excitement and confidence. They couldn't see her, and if they did come after her, she could protect herself.

For her plan to work, she had to get them to separate. The younger man looked the most likely candidate. "Is it true what they say about men with thin swords? Their dicks may be small, but at least they're thicker than their swords?"

The young man's face went so pale that Sally was certain her insult was unintentionally valid. His face darkened so dangerously that there was no doubt he wouldn't hesitate to put the rapier through her heart and he surged forward, his boots thundering on the wooden planks. With a speed she could never attain in her old body. Sally ran backward off the edge of the walkway and caught it as she fell. Her feet dangled several above the water, but no sound was made, and she still wasn't seen. He spun around above her, almost swinging his sword in the darkness to catch her.

"Come out here, you sodding wench!" he cried through gnashing teeth. "Let's see how clever you are after I cut out your tongue! Though I may put it to good use before I do!"

Sally's eyes grew wide, shocked, and offended. *Had this asshole just threatened to orally rape me?* If there had been any qualms about killing him before, they were gone now.

From where she hung, she could see the older man looking amused at the other's plight, but still too cautious about joining in the hunt. Good.

A large object flew from the edge of the water and collided with the side of his skull. The man went down with only a faint grunt, and Naomi appeared at the edge of the firelight. The younger man was so engrossed in his hunt that he didn't notice his partner had fallen.

With one hand, Sally drew her dagger and tucked it between her teeth. The metal tasted cold and bitter, with the edges almost biting into the corner of her lips. She ignored it, watching for the right moment and that wasn't long in coming. The man finally turned around and saw Naomi pushing through the water to come ashore. He shouted several foul curses and began hurrying towards her, believing her to be the quarry he hunted.

Sally moved in a blur of motion; she climbed onto the pier, took the dagger from her mouth, before seizing him from behind, and plunging the blade into his chest several times. The bandit jolted from each stab, lifting her off her feet as he spasm and choked, maybe trying to curse or threaten her for the last time. Then he slid to the floor in a lifeless heap.

A tremor of guilt rose in her heart but was quickly extinguished. Sally didn't have time to feel sorry about killing him, especially since she was sure he would have hurt and killed her if he had the chance. She took the rapier from where it had fallen from his hand and discarded her own short sword. The rapier felt more familiar in her hand than any sword. Then she pulled the dagger from his chest and cleaned it on the edge of his shirt.

She noticed her hands were shaking. Sitting back, she stared at them. They weren't her hands, but they were reflecting her feelings. And what her feelings exactly? Her fear was gone, the confidence still there, burning bright like the sun, but what was making her hands shake? Happy that she was still alive? That she wasn't the one dead? No. It was excitement...she was having fun.

Sally had taken no pleasure in killing the man. A part of her would always hate killing, but there would be no more hesitation in doing so. Not as long as it was done in self-defense. No, her plan had worked. A plan that she thought up and amended midway and put into motion had come to fruition and she was taking pleasure in that. It was like playing a game and coming up with the solution or method to killing a boss, accomplishing a goal, or solving a puzzle, but so much more than that now.

Coming to her senses, Sally hurried to meet Naomi, who was already looking through the unconscious man's pockets. Moving closer to the fire, Sally realized she was cold when the heat washed over her, warming her and feeling wonderful. "What did you find?"

"A few coins and this!" Naomi held up a small bottle in which he popped the cork off and sniffed the contents. Her face twisted in a wince. "Ugh, it's booze!"

"Shame it isn't a health potion," Sally said, grateful that neither of them had taken any damage. "Let's go find Darcy and Mina."

"What about this guy?" Naomi pointed at the fallen man.

"Tear off his sleeves and bind his wrists and ankles with them. As long as he's not a danger to us, there's no sense in killing him."

It only took Naomi a few minutes to bind the man, and the two of them then set off into the tunnel. Behind Sally, the fire continued to cast the shadows of the stalagmites into quivering shows. It gave the appearance of a salivating monster.

***

An owl had been his only companion since the wretched women left him trussed up like some nobleman's man supper. It repeated the question of "who?" "who?" "who?" until he felt he could snap his bindings and kill the creature with his bare hands. No, no, he needed to save his fury for when he found those wenches.

It would be hours before the sun rose, and the man had no intention of waiting until then. He struggled against the ropes, twisting this way and that to loosen the knots. Then he spied the knives on the ground and recognized them as the same ones that had killed his comrade. Stupid, stupid wench had given him a means of escape. Once free, he would run to the hideout and warn the Boss. Then there will be a reckoning on those birdies, oh yes, there would be a reckoning.

Rolling towards the knives, he nearly cut himself on them and it took several tries to grasp a hilt and angle it against the leather. It was slow going as the belt was thick, but he was determined. He cut himself several times which caused him great pain, but it fueled his fury and motivation to be free. This would be nothing compared to what he'd do to the girl and that half-elf bitch. Once McRando learned what they had done to one of his own men, it wouldn't matter how much they were offering for elves downriver. McRando would cut her open from throat to crotch and feed her guts to the boars.

A cold shiver ran down his back as if someone had stepped on his grave. He stopped, his eyes looking around wildly and listened for anything approaching. Nothing. No hungry animal stalked towards him from the trees and nor did he hear any growls or slavering maws.

He was safe. Wait, what happened to the owl? It was no longer hooting.

A pair of white boots appeared before him. Where did they come from? He had heard nothing!

Before he could raise his head, one of the boots pushed it down into the earth, pinning it there with enough weight to almost crack his skull. The knife fell from his spasming fingers. It was the half-elf bitch! She came back to finish the job!

No, it wasn't her. He remembered the half-elf had brown leather boots commonly seen in this area. This person wore boots of silvery leather with white steel toes. Who was this?

The heel ground into his temple, and he moaned. "St-stop!"

"I'm having too much fun to stop."

The foot slammed on his skull, hard. His vision darkened at the edges, and nausea swam through him. It was all he could do to keep from puking. Lying down, he risked choking on the vomit. "What do you want?"

"Oh, I don't want anything. Just curious. Did a half-elf woman tie you up like this?"

"Yes…are you with her?"

"No."

"Are you going to untie me?"

"No."

He nearly bit his tongue as he shouted, "Then what do you intend to do with me!?"

Pain burst through his back and chest. Something sharp had penetrated his back and pierced his lung from above. He hissed, eyes going wide, and he struggled for breath. Another arrow pierced the other lung on an exact level with the first, filling his lungs with blood. He didn't die quickly.

His killer watched him expire and listened to his desperate croaks. The body spasmed one last time before going still. The killer shouldered the ivory bow and left the corpse while singing. If Sally or Darcy had heard it, they would have recognized the song as Mark Collie's *In Time.*

***

When Darcy woke up, her throat felt raw as if she had swallowed dry sand. Her vision was blurry, and after batting her eyes several times, the world came into focus. She tried to sit up, but her hands were still bound behind her and her head felt as if the bones in her skull was sliding around.

"Mina…?"

“I-I’m here,” said a strained voice. “I’m sorry…I’m so sorry! I don’t know what came over me!”

“Help me up.”

Strong hands raised her as she weighed no more than a rag doll. They held her steady until she was able to sit up on her own. Darcy was pleased to see that Mina was free, and it hadn’t been some hallucination taking hold before she had been plunged into unconsciousness.

“Are you okay?” Mina bleated.

“I’ll be better if my hands were untied,” Darcy muttered, then noticed Mina’s bloodied lip. “What happened?”

Mina’s throat bobbed as she swallowed back a sob. “These two men came in and pulled me off of you, and I started hitting them.”

Near the open cell door were two men on the floor sprawled like broken dolls. They were still alive but badly beaten. One had blooming bruises across the side of his face, and the other had an arm twisted at an odd angle. Mina choked on a sob as she untied Darcy’s hands and apologized over and over as her thick fingers fumbled with the knots.

Once her hands were free, Darcy touched her neck, wishing she had a mirror to see the damage. She could, however, see it as a numerical value. Summoning the character screen revealed she had lost three hit points, and then she checked her spells.

“Mina, how’s your health?”

“I’m a bit sore, but I’ll be alright,” Mina said, grimacing as she tried not to look at the men.

“I meant your health points. How many have you lost?”

Mina wiped her nose on the back of her hand like a kid and checked. “About twelve.”

Even in Rage mode a level 1 barbarian would have trouble fighting two enemies unarmed. Darcy laid a hand on Mina’s shoulder and concentrated. The healing spell flowed from her fingertips and into Mina’s flesh as it had before in the Lair of Tears. A bruise forming on Mina’s shoulder faded away and the swollen corner of her mouth reduced in size until it was gone. The barbarian woman gingerly prodded the spot with her tongue and found no pain.

Then she looked away, refusing to meet Darcy’s eyes. “I tried to kill you.”

Darcy took Mina by the arms and had to use extra force to turn the larger woman around. "It's alright. You got us free. Let's focus on getting out of here."

The guards had dropped their clubs during the beating, and Darcy picked them up and handed one to Mina. "We should both be proficient in simple weapons. Try not to throw this, okay?"

Mina took the weapon in both hands and muttered, "I'm not going to throw it. Except maybe at your head."

Darcy perked up, feeling almost proud. "See! That's the spiteful spirit."

Chapter 8

TOM

McRando was not a happy man. Too many strange things were happening in his forest, and he didn't like it. The damn letters were lost, and his men had yet to find them. It was a shame the blighter that lost the letters was already dead, or McRando would have made his hide into a pair of shoes. Then there was a lone half-elf in the area, but the damn ingrates had lost her and brought him two strange women who didn't even have the letters. Worthless.

Well, that last thought wasn't true. They were both handsome women who could still line his pockets with coin. There was, however, something queer about them. Being the bastard son of a dockside whore in Alexandria had exposed McRando to all manners of cultures and foreigners, but he had never seen the likes of these two. Their mannerisms contradicted their appearance, like poor actors in elaborate costumes.

He rubbed his bearded chin in thought. Were they spies? Spies could have discovered knowledge about the letters and so would steal them, but if they were professionals their lies would have been far more rehearsed and plausible.

Members of a rival gang? No, his men wouldn't have caught them so easily if that was true.

He thought of more possibilities, but none of them seem likely, and it disturbed him. McRando's intuition had never let him down. It had protected him from the many dangers of a childhood in the slums. It had led him to taking leadership of a gang and had kept him out of the hands of the city watch. When he was shanghaied onto a pirate vessel, he served as a cabin boy until he engineered a mutiny and took over the ship, naming himself captain. When the King's warships finally caught up to them, he survived and, along with a handful of his most loyal crewmen, followed this river to find the hidden cavern and the villa, which became a haven for his Cut Throats. He had been here for nearly twenty years, and here he was determined to stay for another twenty, if the gods didn't smite him first. Even if that were to happen, he would still survive.

McRando had always been able to anticipate his enemies' moves and circumvent them thanks to his intuition, which he trusted more than he ever had his own mother. And his intuition was plaguing him about the women, but he didn't know what he ought to do about them. Killing them would end the matter, but if they knew about the letters or, worse, about the man in the cells below…No, better to keep them alive and find out what they knew. If his men could find the half-elf and if she had the letters and answers, then all the better.

There was another problem. Someone was out there killing his men. When the letters had failed to arrive, he had sent men to look for the courier and when those men didn't come back, he sent more men after them. They found the bodies riddled with white, elven arrows and had gotten it into their foolish heads that the elves from Saige had come north to reclaim their lost land, but McRando knew better.

On the edge of the desk was a white arrow his men had brought back. Picking it up he twirled the shaft between his fingers. McRando had seen such arrows as treasures stolen from museums or forgotten tombs. The arrowhead gleamed like moonlight and the white shaft, though wood, was as hard as steel and smooth as glass. The leaf blade arrowhead was still sharp, he merely tapped the tip with an index finger, and blood welled up from the tiny wound. These were masterwork arrows, a craft lost to the elves for many centuries; yet this one was newly crafted.

The Cut Throats weren't the most skilled of fighters, but they knew these woods well and had ambushed many an unwary traveler. It would take a great deal of skill to put one over on them. At first, McRando believed this killer must have been the person who had taken the letters, but the gang member who had been robbed of the letters had been pummeled to death, not perforated by arrows. The killings had continued, and it was not only his men who were the victims.

A scout had brought word that a caravan leaving from Everguard had been attacked, with all the participants—merchants, free riders, guards, and mercenaries—dead. Their bodies were riddled with white arrows, many having died where they stood or as they fled. Among the deceased had been dignitaries from far off lands and from across the sea. Some of those found murdered were in their elaborate vardos, where they had hidden in cowardly fashion as their guards died defending them.

Most astounding of all, the one aspect to the ambush on the caravan that brought a chill to McRando's dark heart, was that nothing had been taken. The cargo was untouched: no pockets turned out; no jewelry cut from fingers or necks; and no children or women kidnapped.

McRando was not a man to turn down an easy profit, but even he knew the danger this could bring the gang. When word of the slaughter reached the capital city, the kingsguard would come to investigate. McRando ordered his men not to touch the caravan, not one bauble or coin was to be taken, as suspicion for the act would otherwise fall on the Cut Throats, and until the true killer was found and hanged they would be made to pay. For in the eyes of the guards the Cut Throats were as low as rats.

McRando wasn't worried that the king's men might find the villa, no one had found it in all this time, but the king could increase security along the roads and rivers, preventing their smuggling operation from turning a profit. He might have to send word to Riker to not expect any cargo until this mess was sorted.

There was too much mischief happening in his forest, and none of it was his own. And his intuition told him that there was more to come. No, McRando was not a happy man at all.

***

The tunnel brought them to a hole in a wall that branched out into a stone hallway with sconces providing light, and the dust on the floors muffled their footsteps. The torches offered very little warmth, but Sally barely noticed the temperature.

Since their Sneak skills were high, they took turns scouting a hall; Sally leading until she found a spot with a good view and then motioning Naomi to come along and take over. It was Sally's idea that if one of them was seen, then the other could ambush the attackers. They communicated through simple hand signals to prevent any whisper giving them away.

Every room they came across, they checked whether someone was present. First, Naomi would listen with her higher Perception (+5) for any noise. If she heard anything, they moved on, but if there were no sound, Sally would check the door for traps and pick it if it was locked.

So far, they had only found empty rooms with supplies, stolen loot, and beds. They didn't dare take the time to search the rooms for anything useful as sometimes a Cut Throat would come by. When that happened, they ducked inside the room and hid until he passed.

"This is getting us nowhere," Sally whispered after the footsteps of a Cut Throat faded out of hearing. "I say we grab one and make him tell us where they are."

"They may miss him or find him tied up," Naomi pointed out. "And they'll know we're here."

"And they won't find that out when they discover the men we left by the pier?" Sally was desperate to locate Darcy, and each empty room they came across made her fear more and more that she had been taken elsewhere or was dead. No, she didn't dare give that inconceivable notion another thought. Darcy was alive and she would find her alive. That was the only way this could end.

"The men at the campfire were getting drunk," Naomi said in a calm voice that contrasted with Sally's agitation. "If they were seriously guarding the place, they would have been alert or patrolling. I don't think the dock gets much protection since the cave is well hidden. It'll take a while before anyone checks on them, if they even bother to do so."

"This is still taking too long," Sally muttered.

"We've only been looking for ten minutes. We haven't gone far because we've been taking it slow to stay hidden."

Has it only been ten minutes? It felt longer with her nerves and fear making each second crawl by. The world would not right itself until her sister was found.

Naomi checked the next hallway and froze at the end of it. Flattening herself against the wall, Sally gripped the dagger close to her chest. The Monk made a halting motion and then slowly backpedaled to her and held a finger to her lips as she pointed to the room they had just vacated. They ducked inside the room and eased the door closed.

Naomi said, "Around the corner, I saw two guards standing in front of a door."

"Did you see Darcy?" Sally blurted.

The girl shot her a fixed look. "Sorry, Sally, but seeing through solid walls isn't a Monk ability."

"I mean, they could have Darcy and Mina behind that door."

"I will agree that there's a reason the Cut Throats are guarding that room, but that doesn't mean your friends are inside," Naomi said diplomatically. "Attacking those guards is a big risk for something that isn't a sure thing."

"It's them," Sally said, taking Naomi by the shoulders, her fingers biting into the gi's fabric. "I know it's them. Please, we have to take the chance."

Naomi shrugged off her hands. "Ow, alright, alright. Calm down. We need to come up with a plan first."

"I already have one. We make sure there's no one else along that hall, then we surprise them. I take one, and you take the other. We do it fast before they have a chance to run or yell for help. Use a ki point if you have to."

"Sounds good to me. I'll take the one furthest away."

Creeping back out, Naomi paused at the end of the hallway, gave Sally a nod, then the short girl in the white gi sprinted forward. Sally tried her best to keep up. Ducking the swing of the cudgel of the first guard, Naomi was past and launching herself onto the second with a flurry of blows to his face that bore him down to the floor.

Encouraged, Sally crashed into the first guard, jabbing an arm across his throat to cut off a shout and catching his wrist and twisting it hard until he dropped his cudgel. The man punched her in the side with his free hand, making her flinch, which was the opportunity he needed.

Shoving Sally, he pulled away, but she caught him again. With an arm hooked across his throat, she hauled him back, again stifling any yell for help. "Naomi, help me!" she hissed as she struggled with the Cut Throat.

"In a second!" Naomi grunted from where she was still wrestling with the Cut Throat beneath her. She grabbed his head with both hands and smashed it onto the floor. When his body went slack, she leaped off him and went to help Sally.

A roundhouse kick ended the man's struggles. Sally set him down against the wall, panting and angry with herself for almost failing. If she had sneak attack bonuses, then she should have managed this man when she caught him by surprise. Perhaps she should have used her dagger to kill him instead of choking him. No, killing him wasn't necessary and it shouldn't be the solution to every problem.

"Someone's definitely in there," Naomi said with an ear to the door.

Sally snapped out of her deep thoughts and pulled her thieves tools from her pocket. "Stand back."

Her heart was pounding in exuberance at having found Darcy, her imagination running ahead from the rescue to the thought that they could finally leave this dangerous place. The lock was a bit trickier than the ones she had picked before. It took a few tries before she managed to tame the tumblers.

As soon as the lock gave in, she opened the door. "Darcy?"

The room was lit by a single candle on a table where a man was sitting. His dark hair was unkempt, hanging loosely about his temples and he wore a torn white shirt and homespun breeches. A half-eaten meal was on the table before him and he held a spoon paused before his mouth. Lowering it, he studied her, bright blue eyes bright like bits of glass. "I've waited long enough."

Sally scanned the room but saw there was no one else in this room: no Darcy or Mina.

"Dammit," Sally hissed. She struck the doorjamb with the flat of her hand in frustration. It was as Naomi had warned; they had taken a risk for nothing.

"That isn't a greeting I would expect from a rescuer." It was hard to tell if the man was annoyed or surprised.

There was a long chain from the center of the room connected to a fetter around his ankle which rattled across the floor as he pushed back the chair and stood. Sally felt an irrational resentment for this man rise in her gut. How dare he be here expecting her to rescue him when she meant to save Darcy!

"I didn't come here to save you," Sally said coldly.

His eyebrows rose, and his mouth dropped open in utter astonishment. Recovering quickly, he looked bemused, "Then pray tell, why are you here if not to rescue me?"

Sally ignored his question and asked her own. "Have you seen two women? A tall Barbarian and a dark skin Cleric? They would be prisoners too."

"You're the first woman I've seen in weeks," the prisoner replied. His eyes stayed on her face with such an intensity that it made her uncomfortable and angry.

She lowered her eyes and cursed at how they had wasted their time and effort for nothing.

Naomi squeezed pass Sally to get a better look at the chained man. "Who are you?"

The man's eyebrows rose as he took in Naomi's appearance. Sally couldn't fault his reaction upon seeing the short, barefoot girl with tangled pigtails wearing a gi. He opened his mouth to reply, then closed it. Sally noticed him nervously licked his lips before speaking, "You can call me Tom."

"And why are you here, Tom?" Naomi asked, standing on her toes to see him better without getting closer.

There was a brief pause before he said, "I'm the son of a merchant. These bandits attacked our caravan and took me for ransom. If you free me, my father will reward you handsomely."

His eyes were cast to the left as he spoke, and he scratched the edge of his jaw. There was a tiny bead of sweat forming on his brow. All of this stood out as if Sally were watching him through a microscope.

He's lying. I don't know how, but I know he's lying to us.

"Sure, we'll help you! Sally can pick the lock around your foot," Naomi said, giving the man a thumbs up.

It was all Sally could do to keep from bobbing her on the head. Instead, she caught Naomi by the arm and hissed in her ear, "He's hiding something."

Naomi wrung her arm free. "So?"

"We don't know anything about him." Sally shot the man a glance. He was fiddling with the spoon as if to entertain himself while they spoke politely, but he was listening to every word they said.

"We do know he's a prisoner here so he can't be a Cut Throat," Naomi said gently as if reassuring a child. "And remember, I'm Chaotic-Good. If I see an unlawfully imprisoned person, I have to help them."

Sally pinched the bridge of her nose, as Naomi's prattle was grating on her nerves. "We can't sneak around while dragging him along. We have a hard enough time defending ourselves, much less a third wheel."

"I'm not sure what you mean by calling me a 'third wheel,' but I assure you I can defend myself," Tom said, dropping his spoon on the table in a dismissive manner. "I know how to wield a sword, and I'm willing to help you find your friends before we flee this place."

"See?" Naomi held out her hands towards him as if he had offered a solution to a quagmire of a puzzle. "That settles it."

It did make sense, Sally wouldn't deny that, but something about the man bothered her. He was lying about his identity; but did it really matter? Naomi had a point about his not being a Cut Throat, and he was offering help, which they dearly needed. Caving, she slipped the thieves tools from her pocket and approached the man.

In the candlelight, she could see him clearly. He was much taller than she, standing little over six feet. His body seemed stable, strong, and long of bone. Dark, unruly hair hung in his eyes and down to his shoulders, almost blending in with his matching beard. Blue eyes gleamed like polished stones, and they watched her come closer in a way she didn't find comfortable.

"Put your foot on the table," Sally ordered, wanting to be done with this as soon as possible.

He obliged, and the chain slithered across the floor as the motion pulled on the slack. It took only a few moments, and the manacle fell from his ankle and thumped onto the table. He moaned in relief as he rubbed and scratched the reddened skin. "You have no idea how long I've had this itch."

"Scratch it on your own time. Let's go." That came out ruder than she intended, but she couldn't help it.

"Right then. We can't keep your dear friends waiting," he said with a sardonic twist in his mouth.

Sally clenched her jaw to keep from saying sorry as she would have in the real world whenever she unintentionally offended someone. Sometimes she came across as rude when really she was anxious. To avoid this, she generally stayed away from unfamiliar people. Unfortunately, since arriving in this world, she had been thrown into the company of several bizarre strangers.

Naomi bounded over to him, holding one of the guard's fallen clubs. "Think you can use this?"

Tom lifted the club and weighed it and gave it a few experimental swings. "Yes, this shall do until we find something with a steel edge."

"We haven't introduced ourselves," Naomi said, looking as if she were about to clap her hands in delight. "My name is Naomi Burnes. And she's Sally…I don't know her last name. Sally, what's your last name?"

Sally was hesitant to give out her full name, but then it was not like Tom could look her up on Facebook. Actually, she didn't even have a

Facebook or a Twitter account, never seeing the need to report her every action to the internet.

"Sally Davis," she said, trying to sound pleasant and not as sullen as she was feeling.

Then, cheerfully, as if she were describing a school field trip, Naomi proceeded to tell him about the Cut Throats having kidnapped Darcy and Mina and how Sally and her had found the hideout.

Sally couldn't help but take some pleasure in his shocked expression when Naomi described their battles. "You took on armed men with just your bare hands?"

"Well, Sally helped me a few times."

"You weren't hurt?" Tom asked with a touch of concern in his voice. "Or afraid?"

Naomi shook her head so hard the pigtails swished like loose ribbons. "No way! It was fun!"

"I must say," Tom said, "it is refreshing to meet a young lady that has other interests than finding a husband."

Why were they treating this man like they'd met him at a picnic or a party? Sally thought as she followed them into the hall. *What we're doing is dangerous. We could get killed.*

At the thought, a chill went down her spine and she grasped Naomi by the shoulder, "What happens when you die?"

Naomi turned around, stunned. "What?"

Tom looked at Sally with raised brows. "That's a bit of an odd question to ask right now."

Shit. Tom wouldn't understand what they're talking about as he was only an NPC. Ignoring him, she focused on Naomi, trying to get her meaning across with eyes and words, "What happens to you when you die…here?"

Naomi's eyes widen. "Oh! Well, you…"

Sally raised a hand to stop her. "Wait, come over here and speak with me. Tom, can you keep watch outside in the hall? This won't take long."

"Should you be having a theological discussion right now?" Tom asked, completely taken aback.

"It won't take long," Sally repeated without giving him a second glance.

They strode several yards away, almost to the opposite end of the hall. Bending close to Naomi, she whispered, "Quietly. What happens in the game when you die?"

"You start over in the nearest graveyard," Naomi whispered, looking thoughtful. "Your stuff gets left behind for anyone to grab, though."

"Do you think we'll resurrect in a graveyard?" Sally asked, feeling a cold weight on her stomach.

Naomi visibly swallowed, as Sally's fear finally seemed to have spread to her. "I don't know. We could ask Tom."

Sally sharply shook her head. "Don't ask him anything. He's an NPC that thinks this world is real. You can't tell him that it isn't or he'll think you're crazy."

Naomi pursed her lips and furrowed her brows. "I don't think I can do that. I took the Vow of Truth."

"What the hell is the Vow of Truth?" Sally hissed. "Are you Catholic?"

"No, we're Presbyterian. The Vow of Truth is a Monk thing. I get extra ki points as long as I tell the truth."

Sally blinked and said, "Why? What happens when you lie?"

"I lose all my ki points. I won't get them back until a Cleric casts an Atonement spell on me, and I don't tell another lie for a whole month."

"That's pretty strict for an online game." Sally didn't want to think about how they would have fared without Naomi's ki giving her an edge in battle. "It's not a lie if you don't tell him."

"Yeah, but isn't a lie of omission is still a lie?" Naomi tugged one of her pigtails in uncertainty.

Sally thought fast, and the words sprang to her lips, rolling off her tongue like unfurling silk, perhaps thanks to her high Charisma score. "The last time I stepped on a scale, it was over two hundred and fifty."

"Really? Okay, I'm sorry?" Naomi said, bemused. "What does that have to do with what we're talking about?"

"Exactly!" Sally pointed out. "You didn't need to know that, so I didn't bother telling you. Just like Tom doesn't need to know he's an NPC in a game world. If he outright asks you about it, fine, you can tell him, but until that topic is brought up, he doesn't need to know, and you don't have to tell him."

Naomi wrinkled her nose in thought, then she brightened. "Okay, I guess that makes sense."

Feeling as if she had dodged a bullet, Sally wasn't willing to let anymore of Naomi's morals cause her any more grief. "Are there anymore vows you've taken that are going to cause me problems later?"

"Just the Vow of Poverty."

"What does that entail?" What other stupid rules did Naomi have to follow? And where were these Vows coming from?

"The total value of all my possessions cannot cost more than ten gold pieces. That's why I left my shoes behind at the inn."

"And the game lets you have these vows?"

"Not before, not when you sat in front of the computer. When I woke up in the inn, though, my character screen offered me the vows on the second page."

Sally raised an eyebrow. "What second page?"

"The second page on the character screen," Naomi said. She noticed Sally's confusion and became puzzled herself. "You've only been looking at the first page this whole time?"

It took Sally a moment of thought before she smacked her forehead. How could she have been so stupid? RPGs tended to have more than one menu for character info such as equipment, special abilities, and skills. "How…How do you get to the second page?"

"You swipe it. Like this." Naomi raised a single finger and passed it before her as if she was using a tablet.

And she and Darcy considered themselves techies. Of course, when they were kids, the concept of tablets and advanced handheld devices were in science fiction movies. The most sophisticated devices you could own in your home were old computers and 32-bit consoles. Yet, Naomi grew up with tablets and touchscreens so it made sense she would quickly catch onto something as simple as swiping a screen to see more content.

Sally brought up her character screen and raised a finger towards it. Then in a sudden moment of intuition, she held her finger over the word Charisma in the list of abilities. A heartbeat later, the word highlighted in blue and a small box filled with gold lettering formed above it.

> This score reflects a character's ability to influence others; physical attractiveness; etiquette; and wordplay. Charisma is used for the skills: Charm, Deceit, Entertain, and Intimidate.

Sucking in a quick breath, Sally brought her finger to the next word above it: Wisdom. Again, the skill highlighted in a soft blue outline and another box appeared.

> This score reflects how characters perceive the world around them, from finding items to sensing danger, or having insight into the emotions of others. Wisdom is used for the skills: Perception, Animal Friendship, and Healing.

Well, that was informative and helpful. It functioned just like a tutorial or aid in games. Giving her wrist a flick, Sally swiped to the second screen. It was a continuation of the first page that included a panel for additional equipment that couldn't fit on the first page. **Spells/Abilities** was printed in bold gold letters at the top and beneath it were the words Sneak Attack and beneath that, Two-Weapon Fighting. Sally highlighted the first, and again the words glowed blue, and another box appeared.

> The Rogue Special Ability: On a successful attack on an unaware opponent or an opponent that cannot defend itself, you automatically deal critical damage. You can use this ability with either a melee or ranged attack.

That explained how she was able to instantly kill those guys in the woods and that man on the pier, but what about the guard in the hall? He seemed pretty surprised when she attacked him. Why didn't she succeed?

> Two-Weapon Fighting: You can fight with a weapon in each hand without penalty as long as the weapon in the offhand is light.

So that was where her talent for fighting with rapier and dagger came from.

Swiping to a third page, Sally was taken aback to see a single list with small compact lettering. At the top were the words Skill Check Log. The letters were too small to read, but now understanding the character screen functioned like a touchscreen, she raised a hand and spread her thumb and forefinger apart. The screen zoomed in, and she could read the text clearly.

Sneak Check: 15, Success!

Sneak Check: 17, Success!

Sneak Check: 14, Success!

She tried to highlight a line, but there was no glow or no informative boxes. Then she scrolled to the top and read the top line.

Grapple Check: 13, Success!

Grapple Check: 8, Failure!

Sally rubbed her chin, thinking. Grapple? Wasn't that when you grabbed someone?

Wait! She hadn't attacked the guard but tried to grab him. He nearly broke free when she failed the check, but since she succeeded in the second check, she was able to catch him again.

She began scrolling down, and sure enough, there were the results of her encounter with the man in the cavern.

Attack Check (rapier): 17, Success! CRITICAL HIT!

Sneak Check: 18, Success!

Climb Check: 15, Success!

Sneak Check: 16, Success!

Climb Check: 13, Success!

Swim Check: 13 Success!

Survival Check: 14 Success!

Encounter Won! 37 XP Awarded!

The mystery behind this log became clearer as she read. It was a log of all their skill checks and experience points gained with the latest ones at the top. She scrolled to the very bottom, even zooming out so it would scroll faster. At the bottom, two words in bold font stated: **Game Start**.

This log must have begun the moment they appeared in this world. Scrolling lower only caused the log to bounce on the bottom, no matter how much she flicked her finger up. Then she read each skill check and thought back to fighting the rats, checking and dismantling the trap, the skeletons, and sneaking behind the kobolds and performing a critical hit on their leader. There was one that stood out.

Sneak Check: 7, Failure!

That was the only Sneak check that was marked as failed. When was that?

Her mind's eye brought up the image of the twig she had stepped on that brought the Cut Throats down on her. Had it been there before the check was made, or did it appear because she failed it?

This log will blow Darcy's mind when she sees it…oh shit, I forgot about Darcy!

She dismissed the character screen, and when it disappeared, she was peering into blue eyes inches from her own. She yelped and swung at the figure, but her hand was caught in both of Tom's.

"I'm sorry! I didn't mean to frighten you, but I was curious about what you were looking at with those beautiful eyes."

Sally was in no mood to be placated with compliments. Snatching her hand back, she gave him a scathing look. "Where's Naomi?"

"Right here!" Naomi was shutting the door and pushed on it to make sure it was locked. "We locked the guards up in the cell while you were busy. Tom said there's a second level above us where Darcy and Mina might be."

Sally fixed Tom with a searching look. Was he telling the truth, or was he trying to lead them into a trap?

As if reading her mind, he held up both hands, showing his palms. "I want away from this place as soon as possible, but I know I'll never make it out on my own. Allow me to return the favor of rescuing me, even if I am not the one you intended to save."

His eyes weren't looking away from hers, instead they were focused on her face and eyes. The game, via her Perception check (+2), told her he was telling the truth, but was her roll high enough to be sure of this, or low enough that she'd failed and in fact he was fooling her? Unfortunately, as a quick look confirmed, her log never listed Perception checks.

There was no other way around it. Sally sighed, "Alright, lead the way."

Chapter 9

WOLFE

"God, I'm so sorry, Darcy," Mina whimpered for the hundredth time during their long trek down the hall.

"Stop apologizing and keep quiet," Darcy hissed crouching against the wall. "Our Sneak skills are low enough without you apologizing every ten seconds."

"I can't help it," Mina said as she stepped over the prone figure of the man she clocked over the head with a fist. "I swear I didn't mean to cough! I was holding my breath so I wouldn't make any noise at all!"

With a sharp motion, Darcy cut her off and peered around the corner. It was clear for now, but they had to move fast. Someone was bound to notice the trail of unconscious and bloody men they were leaving in their wake. It wasn't Mina's fault; Barbarian was not a Dex based class, and Sneak was not one of their class skills. It was fortunate that she was strong enough to render the bandits harmless before any of them had raised the alarm.

If Sally was here, she could scout ahead to make sure the way was clear. Thinking about her reminded Darcy of how deeply worried she was: Sally was by herself in this crazy game world and had no idea of how it functioned. And worst of all, elves and half-elves were a hated minority in this area. She needed to find Sally and make sure she was safe.

The first time they had come across a guard, Darcy had acted instantly, smacking him across the jaw with the club. When he spun and hit the wall, stunned by the blow, Mina pinned him to the stone with one hand like a needle through an insect specimen.

Darcy thrust the end of the club beneath his jaw until he was staring at the ceiling. "How do we get out of here?"

"You'll never make it out of here alive," he grunted. "McRando is going to make boots out of your skins!"

Mina grimaced. "Ew!"

"Shut up!" Darcy snapped and thrust the club into his gut. "You better tell us what we want to know, or I'll shove this sideways up your ass!"

The Cut Throat spat at her. "Such a nasty mouth for a cleric. The rugs McRando wipes his boots are cleaner than your tongue."

I'm failing my Intimidation check; my Charisma and Strength aren't high enough.

The man was glaring at her and his mouth was working as if preparing another wad of spit.

Maybe I need to try Charm instead? I have a +2 in that.

"Hey, we'll let you go if you tell us how to get out of here?" she said sweetly and had to stop herself from batting her eyes.

The man was unimpressed. "McRando will use my tongue to polish his boots if I help you!"

"This McRando guy must like his boots," Mina commented.

Darcy shook her head, giving up. "Knock him out, Mina."

"How?" The barbarian woman looked between the Cut Throat and Darcy.

"Just smack his head against the wall until he passes out."

The man's eyes widened as he looked at Mina: a mountain of untapped strength.

Shaking her head, Mina looked from the man to Darcy, "I don't want to hurt him."

"You beat the hell out of those guys that attacked you in the cell!" Darcy groaned. It was a struggle not to smack her forehead.

"They were hitting me with clubs!"

"Never mind, I'll do it." Then Darcy bopped the bandit over the head with her mace, and he went slack, held up only by Mina's hand.

The next guard they came across heard them when Darcy, who spotted him around a corner, backpedaled into Mina. Her heel came down onto the larger woman's foot, and she yelped. When the man came around to investigate, Mina and Darcy grabbed him. This one put up more of a fight, but between the two of them, they managed to disarm and pin him to the floor.

"Is this roughhousing?" Mina asked as she easily pinned the man's arms to his side. "I have never done it before. It's almost fun." She was trying to lighten to mood, like someone who had wronged another and who hoped that if you could get the other person to smile or laugh, then it was no big deal.

"No, this is not roughhousing, and it's not fun!" Darcy was struggling to get the man's legs under control as he tried to kick her. In frustration, looked up at Mina, "Make him tell me if there's a key to the caverns."

"O-okay. Uh, sir, is there a key to ahh—a cavern?"

"Blow it out yer arse, bitch!"

Mina's mouth dropped open in hurt shock. "Hey..."

Darcy grunted as their prisoner managed to land a solid kick at her midsection. "Dammit, Mina, scare him! You should have a decent Intimidate skill."

"Oh, uh, a-alright," Mina said in uncertainty and looked down at the Cut Throat as if he was a vicious cat refusing to get into a pet carrier to go to the vet.

Then a change came over her as Mina's eyes became sharp flints, and her mouth tightened into a toothsome glare. Her body seemed to be expanding, looming over the Cut Throat like a landslide. Her voice, several octaves deeper, said in a gravelly tone. "If you don't tell me where that key is, I'm going to grab you by the ankles and spin you around until you throw up."

It wasn't the wording so much as her fearsome demeanor that loosened his tongue. "There are only two keys to down below. The Boss has one, and Wolfe has the other."

"Dammit!" Darcy muttered. "Knock him out, Mina. We gotta talk."

Mina gave the man an apologetic look before she grasped his skull and smacked it on the floor. Once he was out cold, they both rose together. Darcy rubbed her bruised stomach and checked her health points which were still full, so she hadn't lost any from being kicked. "We have to head down."

"But we came in from upstairs," Mina said, almost panicking.

"There are too many Cut Throats up top. Going down, there is a secret entrance behind a waterfall that leads outside. However, there's a thick door blocking the way, and we don't have the key."

"Can't we pick the lock?" Mina shuffled her feet, her hands fidgeting.

"We're not Rogues, and we don't have thieves' tools," Darcy explained, shaking her head. "I'm hoping we can force the door open or wait until someone opens the door and knock them out and go through. We just have to be careful not to run into Wolfe, who's down in the lower levels."

"And who is Wolfe? Another Cut Throat?"

"Yes and no. He's a level five werewolf."

***

"I'm sorry, I can't get it opened," Sally muttered in defeat when the pick nearly snapped when she tried to force the tumblers. She slipped them away into her pocket and looked at the lock in distress.

True to his word, Tom led them to the way upstairs, but they still had to avoid the guards along the way. They had dodged one by dashing into an empty room and waiting until he passed. Sally had been leaning against the wall with her ear pressed to the door to hear the footfalls fade away. She didn't realize that Tom was close behind her, listening at the door too with his body close enough for the front of his shirt to brush her back.

Had Tom intentionally invaded her personal space? She couldn't tell if he was purposely walking so close beside her in the halls that his shoulders touched hers when they took a turn together, or lightly touching her elbow whenever they hid inside a room and crouched down. It was nothing that she could rightfully protest at or take offense to.

Was he trying to flirt with her? Or was he being a pervert? She didn't have any experience with flirting other than what she saw on TV, and why would he want to flirt while they were in so much danger? Naomi was more friendly with him, so why wasn't he interested in her?

That's because Naomi looks like a frumpy ragamuffin, and I look like a runway model. If he knew what I really looked like, he wouldn't give me a second thought.

It certainly didn't help that she was stuck with him on one side of a locked door. Sally gave it another push, and it steadfastly wouldn't budge. "Shit."

Tom pursed his lips in a displeased line. "They must have already had it open when they brought me down. I would have heard such a large door open and close so there must be a key."

"But where?" she said. "Naomi hasn't found one on any of the guards."

The Monk had dutifully looted the guards and found only a handful of copper coins among all of them. Tom had taken the boots from one of the men so he wouldn't have to continue barefoot and had advised Naomi to help herself to a pair, but the Monk had declined stating that she ran faster barefoot.

"A guard around here must have the key," Tom said, I suggest we stop sneaking around and smash some heads together until we find it."

Naomi practically hopped and clapped her hands. "Yes! That sounds like a good idea!"

"There's a lot of them, so we'll have to take them out a few at a time," Sally cautioned. "We'll get overwhelmed if we're not careful. I'll scout ahead to look for guards since my Sneak skill is high and I have good hearing."

It wasn't much of a plan, but it was the best she could think up. Plus, it would give her space from Tom without coming across as rude. Naomi could handle herself if he tried to betray them and with her keen elf hearing, Sally would be able to hear anything happening behind and in front of her.

With no idea of the layout of the dungeon nor where a key might be, as was typical for a dungeon crawl, they would have to explore each room and take out any enemy they came across. If Tom wasn't exaggerating his fighting prowess, then they had a decent chance to survive and gain the key.

The person in her thoughts gave Sally a sardonic grin. "I'm being given orders by a half-elf woman?"

Remembering the prejudice from the tavern, her eyes narrowed as she said in a searing tone, "If you have a problem with that, you can leave. I'll even point you in the direction of the exit."

Tom held up both hands, showing he meant no harm. "Forgive me. I didn't mean to come across as an elf hater. I am unaccustomed to be given orders so casually, but I am willing to—no, honored to aid you in rescuing your friends."

He spoke with such sincerity that Sally was taken aback and experienced some guilt over her outburst. She shook off the feeling, like a jacket that had become too warm. The fact that Tom was hiding something from them should not be ignored, but she couldn't do anything about it—not until after she found Darcy. Her sister would know what to do about Tom.

"You can come with us," Sally said, using a tone to indicate that if he did anything that slowed them down or endangered them, it wouldn't go well for him.

He actually gave her a quick bow with a joyful smile in response. "I am your servant."

She went ahead down the hall and paused at a crossway to listen. No sounds of Cut Throats patrolling reached her ears. Listening, she checked each door as she went. For a floor with so many doors, one would think there would be more Cut Throats down here. Not that she was complaining as it made things easier, but if something was too good to be true...

It was slow going, and she checked behind several times to make sure Naomi and Tom were following at a safe distance. When she did so, Naomi gave her an OK signal, and Tom winked at her. This gesture annoyed her so much that Sally almost missed the voices of men talking ahead. Bending low, she sidled towards a large door at the end of a long hall. The closer she drew, the clearer she could hear them.

"Bloody "ell! Everyone? All dead?"

"Dead where they stood. Freeriders, merchants, women, children, everyone. It happened again this morning, before sunrise. Took out the poor saps on watch and went from tent to tent, killing folk in their sleep, as happy as you please."

"Blimey. Nothing taken?"

Sally heard a note of fear in the questioner's voice.

"The merchants all dead with their gold rings still on their fat fingers. How many blokes do ye think took part in it?"

Sally counted three voices and thought that it would be three on three, but if they got a surprise round they could easily manage. She was about to return to brief the others when she heard a thick snarling voice mutter, "One."

"Only one, sir?"

"One and one alone killed that many people. Bloodlust was in the air and it's the first time I've smelled such, other than my own."

What were they talking about? No, that wasn't important right here. She could faintly hear the splash of liquid and the thud of cups on a wooden surface. It should be simple enough to wait until they were drunk and then surprise them.

As she was moving away, there was a deep grunt followed by a spine-tingling hiss. "Someone's at the door."

Sally held her breath, heart pounding in her chest as her pulse throbbed in her neck.

Through the door, she heard a low snort and then a bass growl mutter, "It's a stranger. Female. Elven, but human too…It's her! The half-elf wench that eluded Sikes last night!"

"Shit!" Sally took off at a full sprint down the hall just as she heard several boots hitting the floor.

The door banged open as she turned a corner, already calling for Naomi and Tom. Not daring to risk looking behind her, Sally could nevertheless sense the men gaining at her heels. Long fingers prodded at her shoulder, not quite able to snag her shirt, but within seconds her pursuer would catch her.

Then Sally did something completely crazy and risky: she dropped into a roll. Taken entirely by surprise, her pursuer tripped over her and went skidding across the stone floor. She came up, drawing her both the rapier and the dagger in a single motion. In mid-rise, she shoved the blade between the ribs of a second man and spun at the hip. The rapier cut the air in a long arc. If she had been faster, she would have cut the throat of the third man, but he tilted backward at the last second. The rapier's tip flashed through the place where his throat had been.

In response, he swung a morning star that barely missed her head. A few strands of hair were caught on the sphere's teeth and pulled free from her scalp. From behind him, Sally saw Naomi dash from out of the room she and Tom had hidden, waiting for the right moment. With the speed and ferocity of a train, Naomi charged towards Sally's opponent and Tom ran behind her, his amiable smile gone and in its place was a warrior's determination.

The injured Cut Throat clutched his wound with one hand and thrust his sword at Sally, trying to catch her stomach. She barely parried it with the rapier before shoving him against the wall aggravating his injury further. Before she could finish him with the dagger, a ragged growl blew hot breath across her neck.

The injured man's hard-lined face gave her a foul smirk. "Say hello to Lieutenant Wolfe, elf girl."

Sally turned to face an eight-foot werewolf, which was looming over her. Dark fur bristled as layers of muscles shifted and bones cracked beneath it. From large spread hands, darker talons sprouted, breaking through the fingertips. It was the man who she had tripped earlier, now transformed: the remains of his tattered clothing clung to him. Saliva dripped from the needle-sharp incisors while a red tongue lolled over them.

"Put down the sword, girly, and Lieutenant Wolfe won't bite your head off..." the Cut Throat's threat ended when Naomi's fist connected with his jaw.

"Got him!" Naomi whooped and then froze when she saw the werewolf. "Oh, wow!"

Throwing herself at Naomi, Sally carried them both out of the way as Wolfe lunged. The two of them hit the floor as one and both scrambled away from snapping teeth. Naomi crawled between the legs of Tom and the last bandit, which whom he was still engaged. That battle was in the Cut Throat's favor as he fought with a steel sword and Tom had only a club, which was getting notched as he blocked each blow.

Sally tried to follow Naomi between the fighting men, but a hand of gnarled fingers gripped tight around her ankle and pulled her backwards across the stone. Her hands pawed at the surface, trying to gain purchase, but the only thing she could grab was the lower leg of one of the fighting men. She couldn't tell if it was Tom or the other man she was holding onto as they were both wearing the same type of boots. The werewolf bodily lifted her off the floor, she anchored herself to the owner of the boot who almost lost his balance but maintained the battle with his foe.

Perhaps it was the Cut Throat's foot, as the werewolf, who could have easily drawn both her and the man towards him, stopped pulling. The monster maintained its painful grip on her, and she felt her ankle bruising under its thick hand.

Behind Tom and the Cut Throat, Naomi had pulled the boots off the fallen man to pelt them at the werewolf. The first one missed, but to Sally's delight the second smacked it between the eyes. Uttering an ugly growl, amber eyes flashed in deadly rage at the small girl, but it was clear that Naomi wouldn't stop. She had reached inside her gi, producing rocks she had collected from the cavern, which she began to throw.

One flickered between the fighting men to nail Wolfe's black nose, causing a small spray of blood. The monstrosity hissed, eyes narrowing, gaze leaving Sally and zeroing in on Naomi. Wriggling free, Sally felt relief as her leg slipped from his grasp, followed by anxiety for her friend as the werewolf lunged forward, bowling over both the fighting men. Shockingly, Naomi had been snapped up in his vast maw.

Sally could only watch as razor sharp teeth plunged through the gi, and blood soaked the white cloth. Naomi didn't make any noise, but her wide eyes revealed the terror and pain she was in. Then the werewolf shook her like a dog would a child's toy, back hunched from the effort of it. And like a doll, Naomi's arms and legs flopped as though boneless and blood splattered across the floor and walls.

A wordless scream tore from Sally's throat as she launched herself from the floor. Evidently dazed, Tom was sat against wall against which he'd been thrown, while his opponent lay in a limp heap on the floor, rendered unconscious from crashing against the opposite wall. At the hip of the Cut Throat was the pommel of a dagger, which Sally grabbed without slowing her stride. Drawing her other dagger, she leaped with both daggers raised. She landed across the werewolf's hairy back and both daggers bit into the hide right between the shoulder blades.

The creature roared, opening its mouth wide, and the girl spilled from the bloody jaws. Naomi landed in an unmoving heap on the floor, the white material of her gi now crimson. Sally alternated between daggers, pulling one free and thrusting it back into flesh and then the other. Clenching with her knees, she rode the werewolf as he spun in place, trying to dislodge her.

"Die! Die! Die! Just die!" Her screams were lost in the furious and agonizing howls of the monster.

There was little blood on the werewolf's back as the injuries healed almost as quickly as she made them. The wounds closed and sealed themselves before her eyes. Wolfe threw himself against the wall, catching her leg between his flank and the stone. The leather protected her skin from being scraped, but the weight fractured the bones. Sally had never experienced such pain before. It stoked her fear, but fury as well.

She had to kill the werewolf before he twisted around and caught her. His throat: she should have been stabbing him in the throat. It was beyond her reach now, and climbing was impossible with her leg trapped. She resumed stabbing the flank with one dagger in the hope of getting him to move from the wall, but he only growled at her, knowing he had her pinned. A large hand roamed behind him, seeking her other leg. Once he had a good grip on her, he would break that leg, and that would be the end of it.

But he had forgotten about Tom.

Having collected the sword from the fallen Cut Throat, Tom ran it through Wolfe's exposed flank. It sank into his flesh so fast that the monster didn't even seem to have noticed the blow until, with a stream of blood, Tom pulled the blade out. Wolfe's scream then rang in Sally's ears, and he wrenched to and fro, his black talons carving slashes into the walls. With her leg free, she now had her chance. Pulling herself up by a pelt that was long enough for her to grasp, Sally hung on as Wolfe whipped about in an effort to snare Tom in his talons. Tom backed away, warding off these wild attacks with the sword.

Sally hauled herself up the spine, ignoring the agony screaming in her leg and knee. Her torso was along his heaving shoulders when she drew back her dagger and shoved it into the beast's neck with all her might. It cut off Wolfe's snarls, turning them into wet hisses as his windpipe was punctured.

He flung himself backward against the wall, and Sally found the grip of her one hand in his fur was not enough. Suddenly, she was falling. The wind was knocked out of her when she hit the floor, preventing a scream that she mouthed when she landed on her injured leg. Wolfe fled down the hall, loping on hands and feet like a natural wolf. Immediately, Tom dropped his sword and bent over Naomi's body, where Sally could see her blood on his pants and boots.

Sally struggled to stand, but white-hot pain seared through her leg. Oh, this wasn't going to heal anytime soon. This required a week in the hospital, a cast, weeks of hobbling around on a crutch, and physical therapy to regain full mobility. And in this world, there was no hospital with any modern healthcare. She'd be lucky if they knew how to splint it so as to ensure the leg would heal correctly, without giving her a limp for the rest of her life. And that was only if they managed to get her out of here alive.

Then the pain was gone. As if someone had switched off the pain receptors in her brain. At first, she thought she was going into shock, then she realized could easily move her leg which now felt fine, healthy, whole as if it had never been injured in the first place. Even more so, she felt rejuvenated, like new energy was coursing through her veins. Her limbs had been sore from holding onto Wolfe, but now she felt as if she could run for miles without breaking a sweat.

Her vision suddenly went dark, the wall and floor fading to black. Bright golden letters flared to life and gleamed before her eyes with a solid shimmer.

YOU HAVE LEVELED UP!

She blinked at it several times, nearly blinded by the light. "What?"

More words appeared beneath the Level Up announcement, which was scrolling upwards.

Would you like to continue leveling up in the Rogue Class? Yes/No?

What? What was this? She didn't have time, Naomi was hurt and needed her.

Without giving it any thought, she muttered, "Yes…?"

The word **Yes** highlighted blue, and the rest faded away to give way to more gold lettering.

You have attained the 2nd Level in Rogue. You have gained the Rogue's Evasion ability. You can easily dodge magical, non-magical traps, and area effects while suffering little to no damage. Wearing medium to heavy armor will negate this ability.

Just like in the game, we level up and get new abilities and skills.

And sure enough, the words faded and gave way to a list of skills gleaming at her. Bold letters formed before it, closer to her face as if it were a 3D image.

Award your skill points. One for one for Class Skills. Two for one in non-Class skills. The number of new points cannot exceed your new current level. Choose thoughtfully and carefully as this cannot be undone and no more points will be awarded until your next level.

The words faded and she was left with the skill list. Below it was a pool of ten points that glowed a bright, highlighted blue.

"Please, I don't have time for this," Sally begged. "Naomi is dying…"

Whatever operated this…System—she now dubbed it—either couldn't hear her or didn't care. The skill list gleamed persistently at her, giving her no choice.

Her class skills each had small star beside them: Climb, Acrobatics, Evaluate, Charm, Deceit, Sneak, Legerdemain, Perception, and

Intimidate. If she had read the instructions correctly, then it would take one skill point to boost each of these by one. Any others would take two of her skill points to go up by one. It made sense to award all her points to her class skills and be done with it.

No, stop, think! That was would Darcy would tell her. Even if Naomi died, as tragic as that would be, she would still be trapped in this world and she had a chance to make herself stronger in skills that would boost her odds of surviving. Rushing through this could lead to regrets later.

Sally looked at the skills, all of them, with a critical eye. Sneak was a no brainer as she had used that the most. So two points went to it. She tapped the word Sneak twice and the skill list updated: the +6 flipped to a +8.

Okay, Perception made sense, so she could see trouble coming. Two points into that. The +2 went to a +4.

Recalling her spurt of antics in the forest, she considered putting two points into Climb, but paused when Swim caught her eye. It had been a struggle to swim after Naomi and likely she had a 0 in that. It would cost two points to raise that by 1 and four to raise it by 2. After a moment's thought, she tapped Swim, likely they would need to leave the way they had entered the hideout. The 0 switched to +1 and she was down to four remaining points.

Maybe it would be wiser to spread them out among her other Class skills: Charm (+6), Deceit (+6), Climb (+5), and Legerdemain (+7). She tapped each skill and as they updated to reflect her choices, she thought to herself that she might come to regret them. But that would come later.

When the skill list disappeared. Sally pushed herself from the wall and hurried to Naomi. The girl was very pale, lips almost white, and eyes closed. Tom was supporting her head with an arm while pressing his hand across her stomach to stop the bleeding. How long had she been allocating skill points while Naomi bled out?

His eyes widened when he saw Sally approaching. "I thought you were injured."

"I'm fine, but Naomi..." Tears sprung to Sally's eyes as she took in Naomi's state. "God, she can't be dead."

Would Naomi disappear and reappear in a graveyard? Or would she die and leave behind a corpse? Guilt filled her to the point that Sally believed she could burst. They had been overconfident and careless and Naomi was paying the price for it.

She didn't hear Tom calling her name until he touched her shoulder and shouted at her. "Sally! She's still alive, but barely that."

"Then we have to get her to a doctor or a hospital."

Tom's face hardened in a grim mask. "The nearest hospice is a five-day journey by horse. Her best chance is if there is a healer in Spring Bell, but I don't believe we can get her there in time."

Inside her heart, Sally felt an intense determination. "Darcy is a Cleric who can cast healing spells."

She began to rise, but Tom grabbed her wrist. "You don't know where she is, and that thing is still out there, and it almost killed you too." His eyes flitted to her now solid leg and then back to her face. "What happens if you come across it or get attacked by Cut Throats?"

"I can handle myself," Sally said, checking her character screen. Her HP had gone up from 9 to 18. "I'll be back with Darcy. Keep Naomi safe until then."

***

They found the door exactly where Darcy remembered it from the game. As she feared, it was locked tight. Becoming a bit more confident in her new body's strength, Mina tried to force it open, but the door wouldn't budge nor creak from her efforts.

"Sorry, you can't force it open, even if you use Rage. The dungeon is designed to make the players fight a werewolf for a key to advance to this level." Darcy half-heartedly hit the door with her mace, which made a hollow thunk.

"So, what do we do now?" Mina said, almost sagging against the door.

"Well, we could go up and try to leave the way we came." That was impossible with their low Sneak skills giving them away at every turn. There was the option of fighting their way out, but it just as useless as sneaking. There were too many Cut Throats, and there was McRando who was the second and final boss of this dungeon. Though Darcy had spells, she only had six of them left. Mina was strong enough to handle two or three bandits, but any more would overwhelm her and she certainly couldn't fight McRando on her own.

No, their best option was to wait until someone came along and opened the door for them. Then they could knock that person out and then head downward. The only question was whether that happened before or after the men they assaulted woke up and sounded the alarm. This would be a bad place to get trapped.

"Do you hear something?" Mina pressed her ear to the door. "There's something on the other side."

Darcy could hear it too. Her eyes went wide as she recognized it as someone struggling to jam a key inside a lock. "Mina, back away from the door!"

Mina barely cleared the way before the door was swung open with enormous force, and a snarling werewolf with blood-matted fur glared bloody hatred at them. A dagger was sticking out of the side of his damaged neck. He bared his teeth, lips twitching from the force of his growl and his ears folded back to its skull.

Mina froze in utter terror, but the Cleric raised a hand. A cold calm came over Darcy, and she knew what to do. Her lips moved, forming words she had never spoken before and pointed with two fingers towards the werewolf. The air around them streaked and danced as tiny branches of power gathered and convalesce into a small ball at her fingertips. She cupped her hand before her, gathering the ball of energy into her palm. The power radiated through her arm, almost painful, but also wonderful. Her hair rose off her shoulders, waving from the wind generated by the magic Darcy had summoned and she zeroed in on the werewolf and threw the ball at it.

The ball burst and white lightning, so bright as to be blinding, arced through the air in zagged branches. It struck the beast in the chest, and he began to howl in pain as electrical currents set all its nerves aflame. The smell of burning flesh and fur hit her nose, and Darcy cringed as the power evaporated, leaving behind a smoking figure whose fur was darker than it was before the spell.

"Mina! Attack it! Now!" Darcy cried, remembering that the spell, Divine Lightning, granted a bonus to the next attack against the target.

Spurred into action, Mina raised the sword she had stolen from a Cut Throat, and brought it down across the beast's forearm. The severed limb spun through the air before it flopped on the floor, inches from Darcy's feet. The resulting scream was incredibly loud. Darcy worried that it could be heard throughout the complex, bringing McRando and his full gang down upon them.

"K-k-keelll yuuuuu," the werewolf rasped through his canines. "Make yuuuu ssssssuffffferrrrrr."

And this is where he kills us. Darcy thought miserably. We hurt him, but not enough to kill him. I don't have time to cast another spell before he's on us.

The werewolf lowered himself in a ball of fury to pounce, but halted, his amber eyes widening. The tip of a blade burst from his chest, skewering his heart. He swayed on his feet, blood dripping from his maw, and collapsed on the floor. Black fur receded into flesh that rippled like water. Long limbs shortened, and the muscular frame shrunk until what remained was a naked man with a dagger in his throat and right arm chopped off below the elbow. Darcy recognized him as Lieutenant Wolfe's human form, with chestnut hair and gray eyes, which remained open in death.

A beautiful half-elf was standing in the doorway, holding a bloody rapier. She stared uncomprehendingly at them. Darcy, however, knew at once it was her half-sister, but saw that she was different, stronger somehow.

"Sally!" Mina cried, breaking into action first. She swept up the half-elf woman in a huge bear hug, lifting her off the floor as she would a child. "You found us!"

Sally grunted as the hug squeeze the air out of her lungs, but she hugged Mina back, clearly just as happy to see her again. When she was released onto her feet, she turned to Darcy, and both sisters embraced tightly.

"I was so worried about you," Darcy said, feeling tears forming in her eyes. "I was afraid you were alone in this crazy world."

"I—I wasn't alone," Sally's voice cracked as she spoke. Darcy was alive, and they were reunited and all the fears and worries she had carried all this time was gone, and the relief was almost overwhelming, making her feel exhausted. She wanted to collapse on the floor and sleep for years, but they had to hurry.

"Darcy, you were right," Sally drew back, clutching Darcy's arms tightly. "There are others trapped in the game too. I met one of them. Her name is Naomi, and she helped me get here, but the werewolf hurt her pretty bad."

Darcy wiped away a tear and said, "Lead the way."

As the two sisters hurried through the now broken door, they failed to notice that Mina was staring wide at something only she could see.

Chapter 10
BATTLE

"They're in the tunnels!" McRando bellowed.

Sweat stood out on Sike's brow. He could feel a bead sliding along his temple and down his jaw. It was never safe for anyone when McRando was in this state. The large man gnashed his teeth, and his eyes blazed like hot embers. The only man whose temper matched McRando was Lieutenant Wolfe, and he was now dead. Upon hearing a piercing scream from below, men were sent to investigate and they returned with the word the werewolf was killed, and the prisoners had escaped.

"Sir, I'll take a score of men down below and bring them back."

"No!" McRando jabbed a thick finger at Sikes's face. It was so close it nearly poked his left eye. "You'll take a score of men around to the waterfall and block their escape while I take the rest down below to root the buggers out myself."

"Yes sir," Sikes said and quickly departed to carry out the orders, not wishing to be around an enraged McRando any longer than necessary.

The Cut Throat boss began shouting orders and summoning men as he donned his cutlass and stormed from the office. The wenches had been helped. There was no way the two of them had killed Wolfe alone. Someone else had found the secret cave and had come in that way. Whoever was on guard duty at the cave would find themselves covered in honey and bound near a bed of ants before the day's end.

Losing Wolfe was a grievous blow to the gang. Wolfe had been a lieutenant in the Farron army until he had contracted lycanthropy from a rogue werewolf. Were-people were shunned, thus he was forced out of the army to eke out a living in the wilds. When McRando had found Wolfe, he had seen someone of great value: a strong right-hand man with leadership skills. Surprisingly, Wolfe had been the closest thing to a friend that McRando ever had in his long years as a bandit. Oh, how he would make these wenches pay for what they had done to Wolfe and for humiliating the Cut Throats. They would serve as a lesson for all who would dare to cross him.

***

The hallway was empty when Sally led both Darcy and Mina back to where she had left Naomi and Tom. The only sign they had been there were the bloodstains on the floor and walls and the dead or unconscious Cut Throats.

"Tom, where are you? Where's Naomi?" Sally cried, feeling that panic was about to overtake her. Had Tom decided to risk Naomi's life and take her to the village, or had the Cut Throats had found and taken them both?

"Here!" A side door opened, and Tom's head poked out and came out when he saw her. He was shirtless, showing off a lean torso and pale skin. "I didn't want to be out in the open, so I brought her inside. She's still alive, but she hasn't much time."

"I found Darcy," Sally cried, towing Darcy along by the hand.

With Tom holding the door for them, they hurried inside, to what had once been an old workroom. Naomi was prone on a table, deathly white, with Tom's shirt wrapped around her waist. It was already soaked through with blood. Sally touched Naomi's face and was shocked by how cold she felt. How could she still be alive after losing so much blood?

Darcy drew back the cloth and grimaced as more blood flowed from open wounds, but swallowed back her horror to summon up the necessary magic. The magic pooled in her hand, and when she laid it across Naomi's chest, it flowed from the palm and into the girl's body. Before their eyes, flesh webbed and knitted together forming smooth skin with no marks or any sign of damage. Naomi's face flushed as color and warmth returned to her cheeks and her lip began to darken.

Slowly, Naomi's eyelashes fluttered, and her eyes opened. Sally nearly whooped for joy as Naomi turned her head, first to Sally and then to Darcy and whispered so softly, "Did we save them?"

Sally nodded, tears rolling down her face. "Yeah, we saved them. This is Darcy, my sister."

"Hi, Darcy," Naomi said with a weak smile. "Nice to meet you."

"Yeah, same here," Darcy returned the smile. "How do you feel?"

"Sore, but it's getting better. I think I can walk."

"Rest a few minutes before you try," Darcy warned. "Let me know if you're still sore, and I'll cast another healing spell before we leave." She turned to Sally with a questioning look. "You came in through the waterfall, right?"

"Yeah, and the way back should be clear. We took care of the guards, but there might be more." It was comforting to have Darcy back in control again and a weight was lifted off her shoulders that she didn't realize was there before. Sally looked around and found Tom watching them near the door. "Tom, can you go make sure the way out is clear of Cut Throats?"

"Yes, of course," Tom said. He turned to Darcy and Mina and gave them a gentlemanly bow. "It's a pleasure to meet you both at last."

Once the door closed behind him, Sally sighed, relieved to have a chance to speak freely. "We've been careful of what we say around him since he's an NPC."

Mina shrugged. "He seems nice."

"He's alright, I guess," Sally said, crossing her arms. From the corner of her eye, she saw Darcy's staring in open mouth awe at the door where Tom was a moment ago. "What is it?"

"That...that guy just now." Darcy pointed with a quivering finger. "Did you find him locked up in a room?"

"Yeah," Sally said, concerned by Darcy's reaction. "We were looking for you, but found him instead. He said his name was Tom. Do you know who he is?"

Darcy nodded, slowly recovering from her shock. "His name is Prince Alexander Tomas Dragoran."

Sally blinked. "He's a prince?"

"Yeah! He's the third prince of the Farron Kingdom." Darcy wrung her hands together and began pacing from the edge of the table towards the door. "He's a major NPC in *Shadow's Deep*. He got captured by Cut Throats on his way back from negotiating a peace treaty with the Saige Republic and rescuing him is a bonus side quest for this dungeon."

Naomi was pushing herself up to sit cross-legged. Her skin tone had returned to its natural color, and though there were still dark circles beneath her eyes, she looked quite happy. "I knew rescuing him was a good idea."

Reeling from the revelation, Sally leaned against the table. A prince? Was that what he was hiding from them? His comments about girls Naomi's age being interested in balls and of being unused to receiving orders made sense now. "So, what happens after you rescue him?"

"He becomes a temporary follower and helps you clear the dungeon," Darcy said.

"Well, it seems he's been doing that," Mina said with a shrug. "Does this mean he's following the game's protocol or just doing what seems natural for a prisoner?"

"I don't think so," Sally said, considering everything they had seen since arriving at the village. The NPCs had all acted as though human, from their prejudices to their greed. No, the people they met were real, or, at least, as good as the real thing. "If the people were following a program, then Smiley Pete wouldn't have been such a jerk about me, and the Cut Throats would never have come into the village to kidnap people. Those are things would never have happened if they were following the game's script.

"Darcy, what happens to the Cut Throats after the players clear the dungeon?"

Darcy touched her chin in thought. "In the game, the Cut Throats never really go away. Once you clear the dungeon, the prince proclaims the party the heroes and that Spring Bell is safe from the Cut Throats, but the dungeon resets for the next group of players."

"But do you encounter them again after this dungeon?" Sally asked though she suspected she knew the answer.

"Only as random encounters in the forests in this area," Darcy said tiredly. "However, I have the feeling that it's going to play out differently in this world. McRando, he's the Cut Throats' boss, the guy who thought we had the stolen letters."

"Letters? Oh! I have them right here." Naomi reached into her tattered gi and pulled out a leather packet containing the desired letters. It was wet and covered in blood, but the contents within were still intact. "I got these while I was playing the game the day before. It was a drop from a random encounter with the Cut Throats."

Sally had forgotten entirely about the letters until now. "That's right! Just like when you were leveling up as Sister Korra. Everything that Naomi did before this craziness happened has stuck."

Darcy turned her gaze to Naomi as if only now realizing she was a fellow player and stalked over to her. "Were you playing the game when you appeared in this world?"

"Yep! Just like you guys."

The corners of Darcy's mouth twitched before she took the letters from Naomi's hand and opened the packet. She flipped through the pages and squinted at the writing. "These are written in code."

"Can you read it?" Mina asked, peering over Darcy's shoulder at the unfolded page.

"No, but I don't need to. I already know what they say. They're correspondences between corrupt officials whom the Cut Throats were acting as couriers for. Is there a candle in here? We need to burn these."

"Why?" Naomi burst out, aghast at having what she deemed as loot destroyed.

"Because they're dangerous! Look at what happened when the Cut Throats only thought we had them." Darcy began looking around for a lit candle or a torch until she got an idea. Dropping the packet on the floor, she pointed a finger at it. A word of arcana left her lips and the parcel and its contents was ablaze, much to Naomi's dismay.

"Hey! That was a quest item!" She would have bounded off the table to stop the burning if Sally hadn't caught her. The girl was almost in tears as she cried, "You can't do that...what about the quest?"

"Trust me when I tell you that we want nothing to do with that quest." Darcy ground out the flames with her heel until the letters were nothing more than ash. "It's far too advanced for our levels. Two first level characters, a third level Cleric and whatever level you are, which isn't high enough as you have no idea what kind of quest these letters will lead us into."

"One level two," Sally quietly corrected as she consoled a weepy Naomi. From Darcy's bemused look, she said, "I leveled up a while ago."

"You leveled up?" Darcy said, turning to see her. "How?"

"When the werewolf injured Naomi, I managed to hurt him enough that he ran away. After that, a screen popped up saying I leveled up." Sally leveled a hard gaze at Darcy. "And that's not all. We can switch to other pages on our character screens. You only have to swipe left or right. Check it out."

Darcy's eyes went wide as she brought up her character screen. Her finger waved back and forth as she switched screens. "Holy shit..."

"Um, I leveled up too," Mina said, sheepishly raising her hand. "Everything went black and all these gold words told me I had leveled up."

"The same thing happened to me!" Sally said, almost excited at the shared experienced. "It told me I got Rogue's Evasion. It's supposed to help me evade traps and damage?"

"Yeah," Darcy said, deep in thought. "If a trap goes off or there's an area affect, like a fireball or acid spray, without surprising you, you take half damage on a failed save or no damage at all on a successful save."

"What does Sense Danger do?" Mina asked. For the first time since Sally and Darcy met her, she seemed actually excited. "It says I have a bonus to perceiving danger and it's harder to surprise me."

"It gives you a bonus to Perception whenever someone or something is trying to sneak up on you," Darcy said offhandedly, as if speaking on autopilot. "What your XP numbers now?"

"Four hundred and thirty-seven," Sally said. "That's fifty for finishing the Lair of Tears and Naomi and I fought some Cut Throats on the way here so that added thirty-seven. Then I guess I earned three hundred and fifty for chasing off the werewolf."

"I'm at four hundred, so I guess it's just the Lair of Tears for me and the werewolf," Mina said, then screwed up her face in confusion. "Why didn't we get any experience points for all the Cut Throats we fought on the way down here?"

"Yeah, Naomi and I took out two guarding the waterfall cave, but I looked at the log and didn't see where I got any for that," Sally said, checking the log again just to be certain.

It had updated to reflect the new level.

LEVEL UP!!!

350 XP for Successful Boss Fight: Lieutenant Wolfe!

Sneak Check: Failed!

"Because we're in a dungeon," Darcy explained. She was rubbing her chin in her usual habit of deep thinking and was pacing back and forth. "The rules for earning XP are different because they didn't want players camping in dungeons to grind rare drops and XP. So you don't gain any XP until you accomplish a dungeon goal, in this case fighting Wolfe. When Sally and Naomi forced him to flee, they won the encounter and got XP for it. When he attacked us at the door, Mina and I fought him in a separate encounter. Sally may have been the one to deal the killing blow, but she had already been awarded for beating him so it was divided between Mina and me."

The game—the System—followed the rules, but it kept throwing everything off. It was harder for Darcy to get a bead on what would happen next or the best way to handle this world. Ultimately, it came down to one thing they were certain of. If there was a System in place controlling everything, then someone or something created it and made those changes to *Shadow's Deep*.

There was a thumping at the door, and Prince Alexander Tomas Dragoran burst through the door and slammed it shut behind him. "The Cut Throats are coming. All of them. From below and above. We can't get out without running into a score of them."

They all reacted in different ways: Mina wailed and dropped to the floor covering her face, Naomi brought up her fists with a happy hop, Sally felt tired, and Darcy's eyes burned with determination.

"We can do this," she said. "It won't be easy, but we're better off now than we were separated. Mina, get off the floor and help pri—Tom—blockade the door. Sally, check for any secret passages out of this room. Naomi, how is your health? Do you need another healing spell?"

Working together, Tom and Mina overturn the table Naomi had laid on and pushed it against the door. Naomi declared she could use another cure spell only if there was one to spare, but taking no chances Darcy cast one on her anyway. Now she only had three spells left.

Eyeing the room and mentally taking in what she saw, Darcy pictured it on an overhead map like the one she had used for countless encounters and many campaigns and modules. Except this time it would be life or death.

Sally searched the walls, knowing what to look for, but not finding it. There were no hidden doors behind furniture or nearly invisible seams of a panel. The room was sealed with the door being the entry and exit. She went to Darcy shaking her head, "Sorry. No way out of here other than the door."

"Good," Darcy said staring at the door with a tactical eye. "I didn't think there was one, but I wanted to be sure."

"Good? How is that good? We can't get out of here," Sally pointed out with a wave of a hand. "We're trapped."

"True, but it also means they can't attack us from behind nor surround us," Darcy said, satisfied, almost mad, gleam in her eye. "They may have the numbers, but we have the advantage. We know they're coming and which way they'll come in. And we already dealt with Lieutenant Wolfe, so we only have McRando and some Cut Throats to deal with."

Sally swallowed, fear filling her chest and stomach like cotton, thick and suffocating. "How?"

Darcy ignored her and motioned for the others together. Pointing at a group of barrels sitting forgotten in the corner of the room, she said, "Gather the barrels and set them on both sides of the door with just a little bit of space between them. No more than three side by side."

Tom looked at Darcy with his brow furrowed, "What are you planning?"

"We're going to bottleneck the doorway. Only a few of them can come in at a time; that way, we don't get overwhelmed. Hurry, they'll be here any second."

Between the five of them, they managed to set up the barrels as Darcy ordered. Naomi perched on the edge of one looking like a kid at a fair while the others looked grimly to Darcy. None of them could see how setting up the barrels could help them, but Darcy's felt full of energy.

As if on cue, she pointed at the barrels. "That is our kill zone. Mina and Tom, you two are going to fight side by side at the end of the barrels, opposite the door. When they kick in the door, let them come to you. I'll be standing right behind you casting Divine Flame and healing you."

Sally chewed her lip and asked, "Wouldn't Divine Flame burn a spell?"

"It's a cantrip so I can cast as many of those a day as I need to. My remaining three spells are for healing serious injuries, so don't turn to me for healing if you get nicked." She shot a hard look at Mina, who was trembling and pale. "Sally and Naomi will be behind the barrels. Since they are smaller and more dexterous, they can surprise attack the bandits as they come in and keep them from going through the barrels. The Cut Throats will have to deal with attacks from the front and side while getting hit with fire from overhead. If we kill enough of them, they'll have to deal with rough terrain as they walk over the bodies."

As if a deliberate signal, Sally heard a crash outside, down the hall. She held her breath and listened to the distant echo of boots on stone. Sally and Darcy reached out and held the other's hand for a moment.

"Sally, I'm sorry," Darcy said, surprising the half-elf. "I got you into this."

"No, it's not your fault. You didn't know this would happen," Sally said, shaking her head and flinched when the crashing became loud

"If we survive this, I'll see to it that we make it home," Darcy promised.

***

First the doorknob was tried and upon finding it locked heavy boots began hammering on the door. Sally was kneeling behind a barrel with gritted teeth. A part of her had hoped the bandits would move onto the next room, but another part knew battle was inevitable.

There were shouts from outside, soon joined by more voices. Mina was trembling, but she clutched the hilt of the sword with both hands in a white-knuckle grip. A trickle of sweat rolled down between the prince's eyes as he focused on the door with the grimness of a knight going to war. Darcy fletched her hands open and shut as she waited with the cantrip at the ready. Sally took slow, deep breaths through her nose, finding her thoughts surprisingly calm. Only Naomi seemed giddy with excitement at the incoming onslaught.

Within seconds, the door burst open, banging the table aside to make way for two men with swords. They spotted Tom and Mina and charged with the confidence of being backed by many. They didn't realize until it was too late, that there were more than two opponents present. Sally and Naomi attacked, fists flying and rapier slicing the air. They were down before they reached Mina and Tom, but more were coming through as the first fell.

Tom met blade with blade while Mina was able to hold her own. Darcy pointed with two fingers and shouted a word of power that sent a plume of radiant fire at an unlucky Cut Throat. Sally ducked behind the barrels each time a Cut Throat focused on her and if he persisted in trying to get at her, he was punished for his efforts with a blow from behind by

Naomi. And when a Cut Throat went for Naomi, Sally shoved her rapier between his ribs from behind. More men came in only to be surprised by the force waiting for them on the other side.

Soon five men were dead, then eight, then ten, and then Sally lost count. Just as Darcy predicted, the numerous dead and wounded made it difficult for the men coming into the room to keep their balance making it easier to catch them unawares.

We're doing it. Sally thought as she pierced the side of an unsuspecting Cut Throat with the tip of her rapier. *We could actually win this. We could come out of this alive.*

Then McRando made his appearance.

"I don't care if you have to drown them in your filthy blood! You kill those bastards or I'll make boots out of the lot of you!" A roar thundered through the doorway. "Get out of the way and I'll show you how it's done!"

A tall, powerful man with a thick beard burst into the room, knocking aside the men who were scrambling to get out of the way. Half of his face was covered in a red cloth, hiding a missing eye while his remaining eye burned with absolute fury. He paused at the door, with an expression of disgust, as though he could not believe such a rabble could have killed his right-hand man and made a mockery of his gang.

Naomi leapt over the barrel at him, going on the attack. He caught her wrist as easily as he would a tossed beachball and just like a ball, threw her across the room. The small girl spiraled through the air until she smashed against the far wall and landed on the floor, unmoving. Darcy turned away to tend to the fallen Monk while Tom surged forward swinging his sword which was blocked by McRando's cutlass. The blades sang together as steel kissed steel.

"Should have stayed in your room, Prince," McRando growled over the locked blades.

"Go to the Abyss," Tom snarled back.

The swords hissed as they parted with a spray of sparks and then met again in clash of metal. Sally waited, breathing through her nose and biting her lip hard enough to bleed. Any second the metallic clanging would be replaced with the wet sound of flesh being sliced. From where she hid, she saw Darcy casting a healing spell on Naomi and Mina backing away, sweating in terror.

Tom was able to stand against McRando, but he shouldn't have to do it alone. When metal clashed again, she moved. From between the barrels, she brought her knife around to sink it into McRando's right kidney only to have her hand caught in a meaty fist.

"You thought I couldn't see you there, elf bitch?" McRando snarled at her, holding Tom's sword at bay with ease. Tom was looked at her in concern, distracted, and that was all the bandit boss needed. With a mighty thrust, he shoved Tom away and swung his sword downward towards Sally.

For several terrifying seconds, Sally knew she was going to die. She couldn't move, couldn't react, but could only wait for the blade to render her in half.

Bright light burst across McRando's face. He threw back his head at the last second, but the Divine Flame cantrip still put his beard on fire. Darcy had two fingers pointed at McRando from where she knelt beside Naomi. He howled, thrashing his face to and fro to put out the flames crawling along his beard. Sally raked the rapier across his leg, cutting through his pants leg and flesh.

He cursed and released her and Sally rolled away and didn't bother to try hiding again; his one eye could see her despite her Sneak skill. The least she could do now was back up Tom.

"Mina!" Darcy yelled. "Get in there and help!"

"I can't!" Mina whimpered backing up near her. "I'm not a fighter! I was studying to be a doctor!"

"Rage! Help Tom and Sally or he's going to kill all of us. You boy-crazy loser!"

Color surged to her face, turning it bright red, and before the fear could take back control, Mina was evidently able to seize her anger.

Get angry. Be angry. Swallow it and feed it at the same time.

Her embarrassment ignited into fury and an image of her attacking Darcy with the sword trembling in her hands came, but she squashed it down. No, Darcy was not the object of her anger, no, her true transgressor was the man who had caused them to be kidnapped and put them in this situation to be scared, attacked, and humiliated.

With a shriek that would outmatch a bear with a nail in its paw, she lunged at McRando, swinging the sword overhead. He blocked it, but his arms strained to keep his metal between his face and her sword. He stepped back, letting the sword slide off, only to be nicked by the glancing blow of a rapier.

Shocked by the ferocity of the Barbarian, McRando found there was no time to react or strike back at her, as the prince had returned to the melee.

Blades flew through the hair like panicked birds. McRando artfully blocked, parried, and dodged, but felt that luck would run out for him eventually. Soon his clothing was bloody from the numerous shallow cuts where blows found their mark. And he had to be on guard for the sudden hot burst of fire that more than once had scorched his face.

Though he was a strong fighter in his own right, he knew he couldn't hold out forever against three combatants and a magic-user. Retreat now, and he would bring a reckoning upon these fools that would make the gods weep. With a solid punch to the barbarian woman's solar plexus, he spun and kicked the prince's feet from beneath him. Leaping around, he had barely taken a step towards the door when a presence blocked him.

The damn elf woman. No matter, he was the stronger fighter. She was small and weak; he could rip her apart with a swipe of the cutlass. When she tried to block it, her thin rapier would break in two, and her pretty head would roll on the floor.

The sword cut the air, but not her. She ducked down beneath the blade and thrust upward. The tip penetrated through cloak and flesh, sinking into McRando's abdomen. Agony lance through his torso and he drew back, sliding his gut off her rapier. He touched his front and his hand came back bloody.

The bitch had almost gutted him, and she still wasn't moving out of the way. He swung at her, each swipe of the sword going wild, the pain throwing off his arm.

Why didn't I let him run away? The fight would have been over.

With both dagger and rapier forming a V, Sally blocked his attack and realized the answer.

If we let him escape, we'll have to watch our backs forever. I saw the hate in his eyes. I know he'll keep coming after us until we're dead. One way or another, we have to end this now.

Tom rose from the floor and rammed into McRando from behind.

McRando gave a roar. "I might be going down, but I'll take one of you into the Abyss with me!"

As much as he would like to cut the bitch in half, killing the prince would be more satisfying. The political fallout when his body was found in a thieves' hideout would cause a war. McRando knew he must strike hard and true, fell the prince with one blow, so the cleric had no time to heal him.

He turned at the waist, aiming for the prince's exposed flank. Steel bit into flesh and Tom cried in pain, stepping back, blood rushing down his side. The wound was deep, but not fatal, for the bandit leader had forgotten the barbarian woman, who pulled Tom back at the last second and caused the blade to miss the vital organs. Worse, McRando had turned his back to a rogue.

The sharp metal thrust into his body so fast that it was almost painless. Every muscle twitched and blood filled McRando's mouth. Then the rapier was pulled from his back and the bandit boss dropped to his knees, dropping his sword. This was the end, he knew, the inevitable end for those who led the life he had. Yet, he wasn't quite ready to leave this life quietly.

"You have no idea what ye've done," he muttered darkly, looking at them all. The cleric was tending to the prince's wound, using one of her final healing spells to stop the bleeding. The barbarian woman was panting, coming off her Rage, and the monk girl was sitting on the floor, still dizzy from a concussion. He saved his last gaze for the half-elf rogue staring down at him, her rapier still covered in his blood. "Ye've no idea what is waiting for you when Riker finds out what ye've done. When he does, you'll wish I had sold you down the river."

"Considered me sold on this," Sally said raising her rapier and ending it once and for all.

Chapter 11
THE STRANGER

Sally was numb, shocked that it was over, and they had made it out alive. Running feet disappeared down the halls, but it was the sound of fleeing men, not reinforcements coming to attack. The large body of the bandit leader continued to bleed, blood webbing in the cracks of the stone floor. Sally moved away from the blood nearing her boots and felt the sweat clinging to her body, making her feel cold and clammy.

After Darcy's healing spell, Tom now sported a swollen mark along his side. He was sitting on the floor beside Naomi, who was given the same order: sit still. The Monk was pouting that she had missed the final fight, and the prince was comforting her by putting an arm around her shoulders. Having settled Naomi and Tom to her satisfaction, Darcy was checking on Mina.

The battle had happened so fast, and with the adrenaline pumping, Sally hadn't noticed McRando cutting her right upper arm nor the bruise forming on her cheek where a Cut Throat had landed a punch. Thankfully, the bandits saw it prudent to carry bandages, so Darcy had what she needed to tend to their injuries without using her last spell.

Mina seemed close to passing out, with arms covered in blood. Her face hadn't lost any color though, as Naomi's and Tom's had after being injured. She was swaying on her feet until Sally came up to her and said, "You did good. You saved us."

"I—I did?" Mina said, looking almost tearful.

"Yeah, you landed the blows he couldn't block, and you saved Tom."

Mina raised a hand to wipe the sweat off her face, but paused when she saw it was covered in blood. With a pained expression, she said, "How much longer do you think we'll be in this room?"

"Not long, I think. Everyone is getting their bearings. It was a pretty hard fight."

"I think I need to step outside. I'm about to throw up." Mina was looking a little green.

"Okay, but just outside, alright? We don't know if some Cut Throats might want to even the score."

"Alright." Mina looked so tired, Sally could imagine her falling asleep on the cold stone floor.

Thankfully, it wasn't long before they were ready to leave. Naomi stayed close to Tom, evening supporting him despite being a foot shorter than him, but, jovially, he let her. Darcy was just as eager to leave, but as a precaution, she had Sally scout ahead and made sure the way was clear. It didn't take Sally long to report back there were no Cut Throats in sight and that it was safe to leave.

But Naomi shook her head, "No, we gotta loot this place." This earned her looks from everyone, but she resolutely went on. "After you kill the boss, you get loot and treasure. I already searched his pockets and found a few gold coins and his sword."

For the first time, they noticed she was dragging a cutlass behind her in her free hand. "I thought maybe Mina could use it? It does more damage than a shortsword."

"No way!" Mina snapped, startling them with her intensity. "I don't want it."

Darcy interposed herself, "Naomi, drop the sword. We'll go looking through the hideout and find Mina's greataxe, and maybe find the rest of our things."

Tom made a derisive snort. "I'm all for searching the bandit's stores, but I doubt there's anything of value left behind. The Cut Throats would have already raided the coffers before fleeing," then he saw Naomi's eager face, and he sighed with resignation, "but they may have overlooked something."

"I'll lead the way," Darcy said, pinching the bridge of her nose, feeling fatigued. *What time was it now? How long ago had it been when they woke up in the stables?* "Stay close, and be careful. I only have one spell left until tomorrow."

No one hindered them as they went up to the ground level and then further up to the second story of the villa. The building layout was precisely as Darcy remembered, so it didn't take long before they found McRando's chambers and office, which, as Tom had predicted, was already scoured of valuables. It would seem that Cut Throats had worked fast when they were abandoning their hideout: drawers had been emptied, chests and trunks broken open and turned out, and even the clothing had been ripped from a wardrobe and the silk sheets taken from the bed. The only items untouched were the books on the shelves and the maps tacked open on the wall.

Darcy looked over a ledger left opened on the desk while the others poked around. Naomi was clearly disappointed at how little was left in the ransacked office and bedroom and pouted on the upset bed swinging her legs back and forth.

"For someone who's taken a Vow of Poverty," Sally said, eyeing her critically, "You're really hung up on finding loot."

"That's part of the game!" Naomi said, throwing up her hands.

Sally pressed a finger over her lips and pointed at Tom, who was flipping through opened letters stashed away in a broken box. He showed no interest in them, nor did he seem to have heard Naomi.

"Be careful of what you say," Sally said in a low whisper. "Go help Mina find her greataxe, and you might find something worthwhile."

Naomi hopped to her feet with a slight roll of her eyes. "Okay, mom."

Sally was tempted to make a rude sign at her back but thought better of it. She had almost lost Naomi twice, and she appreciated the girl's presence too much to take it for granted now. She was just a kid; in fact, how old was the girl? She looked like she was fourteen or fifteen, but she acted younger. Then again, sometimes, she acted older. Was that her real self or part of her character stats? Naomi didn't seem to have any anything to say about her body, the way Darcy and Sally often remarked on theirs.

With nothing better to do, Sally went to see what Tom was doing. After all, Darcy was too busy mumbling to herself as she looked over the maps; some she had taken down and folded up. It was best to leave Darcy to her own devices when she was this deep in thought.

"What are you busy with?" She asked the prince.

Looking up at her, Tom let the letters fall into a slant inside the box and set it down on the table in a dismissive manner. "I suspect there is a reason behind my imprisonment beyond that of a ransom. My father is a powerful man and has many enemies who may want to hold his son for leverage."

Sally clenched her jaw to keep from pointing out that his father was the king, so of course, he would have enemies. "Have you found anything?"

"No, and I don't believe I will. Such letters would have been destroyed."

Immediately, Sally thought of the letters Darcy had burned. Had the answer Tom was looking for been among them? It was better not to know. "What are you going to do now?"

"I don't know. It rather depends on your plans. I don't fancy traveling alone in these woods, not with desperate bandits about."

"I don't know what we're going to do," Sally said. "Not until Darcy tells us. She's familiar with this area."

"You're a traveler? Are you from Saige?"

"No, we're from…much further away," Sally said carefully. She didn't know enough about this world to come up with a plausible explanation for their group.

"You said that Darcy is your step-sister. I take it your human parent married hers?" Tom sounded polite, curious rather than troubled.

"Yes, our parents married," Sally said, feeling uncomfortable by his sudden interest in her background.

"You're very close for a cleric of Shantra and a half-elf," Tom commented, his eyes never leaving her face.

Sally was now very uncomfortable. Why was he fishing for information? She didn't understand what drew his interest or what he found unusual about the two of them, but the less said, the better. Responding with a shrug, she said, "We're family, and that's all that matters to us."

As if sensing she was putting an end to this line of discussion, he nodded, "I understand. I am quite envious of your close relationship with her."

"Oh, that asshole!" Darcy shouted, startling them both.

Tom could barely hide his mirthful smile. "She has quite a mouth for a cleric."

"Ah, you should listen to her when she's really mad," Sally said with an amused smile. "It's like she's trying to summon demons."

"Sally! Get over here and look at this! At this!" Darcy thumped a page in the ledger several times with an index finger as if she was condemning a sinner. "Look at who was getting paid each time the Cut Throats attacked travelers!"

Sally hurried to the desk and looked at the pages. It was a language she had never seen before, like crooked letters, but to her amazement, she understood the writing. She recognized the consonants and vowels as if they were written in the English alphabet, but they were different symbols representing the sounds of language and numbers. Focusing on what Darcy was pointing out, she read the strange print.

"Innkeeper?" Sally read out loud. "Wait, you don't mean Smiley Pete?"

"Look at this!" Darcy waved a hand at a lower shelf where small bottles were sitting undisturbed. Each bottle had a rolled-up message curled inside it. Darcy picked one up and pulled out the cork and tapped the note into her hand to be unrolled it. Then she read, "Two travelers carrying gold. Taking the north road."

Sally's eyes widened at the indication. "No…you don't think that…"

As if to prove her point, Darcy uncorked another bottle and read, "Caravan carrying silks and spices taking the west road." And then another bottle message read, "Merchant and two mercenaries taking the east road."

Tom's face went very dark and cold. "I believe that if you keep looking, you will find one that says a party of four taking the kingsroad northward."

Sally glanced at Tom, feeling a heavy weight in her stomach. "What happened to the others?"

"They killed the guards, and seeing no need to keep my valet alive, they killed him too," Tom said morosely with clenched fists. "What I don't understand is how they were able to set up such a well-planned ambush. We arrived at the inn late that night and left early the following morning. We were attacked only a few miles north of the village."

"It's easy with these," Darcy held up the bottles. "North of the village is a stream that feeds into the river. Most travelers will stop at the inn to eat and rest. There Stinky Pete can see if they're worth robbing and can walk his greedy ass with a message in a bottle and drop it in the stream where it'll find its way to these caverns. Every time the Cut Throats rob travelers based on his tip, McRando sends him a reward."

Tom turned his furious gaze to the ledger. "Then he's just as bad as the Cut Throats. We will use this as proof to bring the man to justice."

Sally noticed Darcy's face stiffened before she pulled a few sheets of paper from the ledger and folded them. "The Cut Throats are gone. Tell the authorities of what happened, and they can make sure it stays that way. As for the innkeeper, you let me handle him. Trust me. He's going to regret making deals with bandits by the time we're done with him."

Sally wondered what Darcy was talking about, but decided to wait until later once they were out of earshot of Tom to ask. It was so hard to speak with him around as she had to watch every word she said, and sometimes she saw him looking inquisitively at her as if he wanted to ask her a question, but had decided against it.

He's no fool. He knows something isn't right about us. He's curious but smart enough not to ask because he knows we'll lie or not give him the whole truth. The sooner we part ways, the better.

Naomi and Mina returned, bearing Mina's greataxe and Darcy's armor and mace. It was safe to assume that their backpacks were claimed by fleeing Cut Throats, but overall that was a small loss they could live with. With the maps, they could easily find their way back to the village.

"Do we really want to go back?" Sally said, remembering the reception she received yesterday. Then, somewhat guilty, she remembered the bandit they had left tied up. Her promise had been to free him.

Soon, they were strolling through the front doors of the villa, the same Mina and Darcy had entered bound on horseback many hours ago, but now it was late morning with a clear blue sky. It was the sort of day that back home would send people to the beach or even to do yard work. Not that Sally, who had spent her childhood in apartments without yards, had spent a day like that. Nor on a trip to a beach.

"Let's go," Darcy declared, leading the way. "When we get to the inn, let me do the talking. You alright, Naomi?"

"I'm fine. I don't feel dizzy anymore," Naomi replied, almost skipping along ahead of them. "I'm a little hungry, though. I haven't eaten anything since last night."

"Just try to hold on. You'll have plenty to eat soon."

Sally was content to let the others converse while she fell in behind Darcy. It felt odd not to feel afraid. Fear had been a constant ever since she opened her eyes and found herself in this world and this body. Now it was gone for the time being, and she could relax. At least until the next crisis. They were still in this world with no idea of how to get home.

Were they dead, and was this world hell or purgatory? Maybe it was heaven? Aliens? Or some crazy gas that had been filtered into her apartment, giving her hallucinations?

"You were brave," Tom said, interrupting her thoughts.

Sally blinked, startled, and uncertain of what to say. "Thanks?"

"You were amazing fighting the werewolf and McRando. Where did you train?"

Oh great, he was trying to fish for more information again. "Here and there. I sorta taught myself…" That was partly true. She came into this world already knowing how to use a rapier because she chose the Rogue class.

"You have great skills for someone self-taught," Tom commented almost ruefully. "I trained many hours every day with steel, but I don't think my talent matches the skill you have with the rapier. Have you done mercenary work?"

Sally shook her head. "No, never."

"Do you intend to seek work as one?"

Disturbed by how he was oddly persistent about their intentions, Sally hid it with an offhand shrugged, "I have no idea what we're going to do after today. That will be up to Darcy, I guess."

After continuing in silence for several minutes, Tom said, "If you need work, my family's home can always use more guards. I lost two of them when I was captured."

"That's kind of you," Sally replied. "I'll talk to Darcy about it." At first, she had no intention of doing anything of the sort, but then thought better of it. As much as it sickened her to think of it, there was no telling how long they would be trapped in this world. If it was to be for a long time, then they would need some way to support themselves.

***

Sikes was lucky to get a horse when he did. It was the last one in the stables, and it had been necessary to kill a man to get it. Hooves cut the turf as the animal galloped through a hidden path known only to the gang and he slapped its rump to get it moving faster.

It had only been a matter of time before McRando fell from power. Yet, Sikes had imagined that when that day came, he would be in a better position to take over the gang, or at least become Wolfe's right-hand man.

Now his daydream was shattered, the fools fleeing like rats from a sinking ship when they should have killed the interlopers and avenged their fallen boss.

The women were loose ends he would cut off later. For now, he needed to recoup the losses and get the gang back together and find a new lair. The prince would most certainly have his father's men scour the villa if not outright destroy it. The Cut Throats would have to eke out an existence on new territory elsewhere.

Fortunately, he had the means to start anew: a chest full of gold hung from one side of the saddle, and a second chest of precious gems was on the other. With these, he could form his own gang far away. Maybe as far as the capital city or further to the eastern islands.

Perhaps if Sikes had been paying attention to his surroundings instead of his prospects, he would have noticed the sudden stillness in the forest. Maybe he would have seen the nervous quiver in the horse's flanks, or even caught a glimpse of silver in the canopy.

A streak of white flitted between the trees, and the horse screamed. Before Sikes could realize what was happening, another arrow hit the horse's other fetlock. It reared up and bucked, throwing him off. The wind was knocked out of him, but he recovered quickly in time to roll out of the way as the horse collapsed with a third white arrow in its throat. Its eyes rolled almost beseechingly at him.

Sikes crouched behind it for cover and scanned the trees. The first shot came from the west and then the second from the east. He was surrounded, but by who? It was much too soon for the kingsmen to begin hunting for them; moreover, they would have demanded his surrender before firing. And he knew of no rival gang that used white arrows.

His blood turned cold as he remembered the caravans and travelers who were all killed by the same arrows. And not one item of value was taken or disturbed. He drew his sword, despite knowing it would be useless against a well-aimed arrow. His only chance was to run under cover of foliage and flee, but he couldn't leave the chests. They were the key to his future; without them, he might as well be dead.

An arrow hit the now dead horse's flank, inches from his face. He crouched so low he was nearly kissing the ground. Another arrow darted next to his knee and then another near his left arm. What were they playing at? They weren't making any demands. Were they missing on purpose? If they could hit the fetlocks of a galloping horse, then perforating him with arrows would present no challenge.

A cold revelation came to him, chilling him to his very core.

"Oh Gods," he muttered. For the first time since he was some street urchin in the streets of Everguard, he felt untold terror. They were trying to get him to run so they could hunt him like a frightened hare. He was never a praying man, though he had heard plenty from the lips of the countless people he had robbed or murdered. The gods never had much use for them, nor he for them, but now he was praying to every deity he knew of for deliverance.

"C'mon now," a voice called from the branches of the highest tree. "You're not making this any fun."

He had never heard such a strange accent before, and he had heard plenty. The words were spoken in a long drawl. Not Farron nor Saige.

"Tell ya what," the voice said in a sing-song tone. "What if I give ya a ten second head start? Scouts Honor, I won't fire until I count to ten."

Could he trust the strange speaker? Did he dare risk playing this crude game?

"I'm gonna start now. One…two…" the voice said in a merry way he had heard children used in play. "Three…"

Before the voice reached four, Sikes was already sprinting between boles and through the foliage. He couldn't hear the counting over the crash of bushes and his own thundering heart. A part of him burned from the humiliation of being forced into playing this game, but he could hide until one of the archers showed themselves, and then he would make them pay. He knew how to hide, how to wait for the perfect moment to strike.

Sikes threw himself onto the ground and rolled into a thicket, pulling branches over him. His breath was stirring the grass until he forced himself to take long, slow breaths. Slowly, he drew a dagger from his belt. The sword would be too cumbersome and give away his hiding place. They would come looking for him, and they would not find him, but he would see them first.

Sikes didn't have to wait long.

The voice carried in the wind, "Olly, Olly oxen free! Yoohoo! Anyone there? Hmmm, I wonder where he went…" the voice was mocking, like that of a child at play who knew where his friends were hidden. Sikes' gaze switched from right to left, looking and looking, but not seeing the voice's source. "Gee whiz, I think he got away. Aw shucks, I better give up and go home before it gets dark."

Where are you? Sikes gripped the dagger's hilt so tightly, his hand quivered from the effort. *Stop playing games. Come out where I can slit your throat.*

There was silence. The only sound was his shallow breathing and the gentle crackle of tree branches moving in the breeze. He swallowed carefully, blinking grit from his eyes.

All of a sudden there was a fire spread around him, the dry brambles of the thicket acting as tinder. Sikes yelped, rolling as fire clung to his sleeves. Scrambling from the thicket, he batted away the flames and saw what remained of a burning arrow. Instead of white, it was bright red with a black head and feathers and it was disintegrating as the flames ate it. It was a fire arrow: an arrow imbued with the essence of fire to burst into flames upon impact. Quite expensive on the black market and banned by most kingdoms.

An arrow sank into his shoulder, and Sikes barely had time to scream before a second arrow struck his other shoulder, nearly wrenching him around from the force of impact. Dropping to his knees, Sikes scrambled for the fallen dagger. His hand was mere inches from it before it was pinned to the ground, an arrow sprouting from it like a tree. His screams and curses rang through the forest, filling the silence with his pain. Collecting himself and mustering his grit, he grabbed the arrow and tried to pull it free, but it was many inches deep in the earth, and it hurt too much to struggle with.

"Hey, dumbass," the voice said from above him. He raised a tear streaked face to the figure sitting on a thick branch high above. The man was clouded in shadow, but he could see white boots dangling before him. "You didn't stop to think I wouldn't have explored my hunting ground first? That I didn't know about this oh so convenient hiding place, you think you found? Bitch, please."

His teeth chattered as he realized he was going to die. Sikes always knew he would meet his end at the hands of another eventually, but not like this. Not being toyed with like a wounded bird. "Get it over with! Kill me, damn you!"

The man crossed his legs and bent down with an arm propped on a knee and a hand cupping a chin. "I could kill you. I mean, I really ought to since I went through all this trouble, but for some reason, I'm not really Jonesing for it anymore."

Sikes hissed through his teeth, both through fear and agony. "What then?"

He couldn't see a face, but he could see the rough outline of a toothy grin. "Oh, I'll think of something. Until then, you get to live for a while longer. Do you need a health potion?"

Sweat was rolling into his eyes, which he blinked away. It was cold and clung to his skin like slime. "What?"

"Do. You. Want. A. Health. Potion?" The figure said slowly, as if speaking to a backward person. And there was an impatient edge in the voice with a streak of malice.

Sikes felt that his fate was still spinning in the air, and he could still die this day if he didn't make the right choice. "Yes…please?"

A red vial spun through the air and landed within easy reach of his uninjured hand. With the tips of his fingers, he rolled it close enough to grab but didn't dare drink it with the arrows still in his body. The skin would heal around the shaft and making it impossible to remove without causing more damage than the initial injury. He managed to remove the arrows from his shoulders first. The blood soaked his shirt and ran down his arms, but the arrow in his hand refused to be extracted. Breaking the shaft proved impossible; the mastercrafted material was as durable as metal.

He didn't dare ask his attacker turned benefactor for help. What if pleading for more aid tipped the balance against him? Intuition, almost as keen as McRando's notorious ability, told him that his fate had yet to be decided. He was being watched and his worth judged.

Taking two deep breaths, Sikes gritted his teeth, and with one hand around his wrist, he pushed his impaled hand up the shaft. Wood caused friction within the open flesh and darkness edged his vision, but he continued until it was pulled free of the feathers. The length of the shaft was covered in his blood, and seeing it made him nauseous. He allowed himself to vomit now so he could keep the health potion down. With shaking and bleeding hands, he managed to uncork the vial with his teeth and bring the red liquid to his lips. It was high quality, thick like syrup. Already the pain was ebbing away, and the hole in his hand filled in with pink flesh.

He enjoyed the pain relief so much, he didn't realize the figure had left its perch on the branch until he saw white boots plodding towards him. He looked up and got his first clear view of his attacker.

"You're a..."

"Problem?" The attacker asked, voice dripping with poison. "Do we have a problem? Please, tell me we do, because I like solving problems." A long ivory bow with a sharp tip pricked the skin beneath his chin, tipping his head upward to look into a face as pale as snow and framed by hair as black as night.

He shook his head, the bow tip drawing blood as it scratched his skin from his movement. "No. There's no problem."

"Good. Get your ass up and go get those chests." The bow tip was withdrawn, as in an afterthought, an inquiry was made, "What's your name?"

"Sikes," he said, still not feeling safe enough to stand. The dice still hadn't landed yet.

"Yikes, Sikes, buy some kites," There was a laugh at a joke he didn't understand. "I think we're going to get along just fine."

And just like that, the dice landed in his favor. He wouldn't die this day, but he had a new master now. And this one was far more dangerous and crafty than McRando had ever been.

Chapter 12

THE PYRE

It was Naomi and not Sally who spoke up for the Cut Throat they had left tied up in the forest. The young girl became adamant they fulfil their promise and free him before returning to Spring Bell. Sally would rather that Naomi had forgotten about the man until morning at least, as she was tired, sore, hungry, and just wanted to lie down and sleep for a year or two. Another night in the forest would serve him right.

Then again, she didn't really want to be responsible for some guy getting eaten alive by a wolf or bear, even if he was a Cut Throat. Especially since, as Naomi was quick to point out, they did promise they would release him if he told them how to get into the hideout.

So they took a detour westward with Naomi leading the way. In her excitement, she'd run ahead till they couldn't see her, and when they caught up they would see her jogging in place, urging them to hurry. Despite her youthful energy, the others went at their own pace, all of them tired from lack of sleep and the hard fight. All of their bellies were growling and there was much talk of food, save from Tom, who had eaten more recently than any of them.

Upon coming across the dead man, Sally lost her appetite. Already, ants were taking their share, along with a fox that hurried off into the underbrush at their arrival. Naomi was standing so strikingly still it was a marvel for the usually active girl. Mina quickly put her hands on the Monk's shoulders and told her to look away, but Naomi wouldn't move from where she stood, staring with wide somber eyes at the white arrows sticking like a flagpole from the man's back.

"Who would kill a bound man like this?" Tom asked, horrified.

"Could it have been his own men?" Mina said, looking around as if the killer would step out from behind a tree.

"No, it wasn't them," Darcy said so strongly it drew all eyes. She noticed them staring at her, and she supplemented, "The Cut Throats don't use arrows like these."

Naomi burst into tears, covering her face with both hands and sobbing into them. Instantly, both Tom and Sally went to her, consoling her together.

"Hey, hey, it's okay," Sally said, touching Naomi's hair and looking into her tearful face. "It's not our fault."

"But we promised him..." Naomi whimpered. "I promised we would set him free..."

"And we kept that promise. We came back."

Tom laid a hand on Naomi's thin shoulders. "There's no way you could have known someone would do this before you returned."

Naomi seemed to calm down, but she still sniffled. "We should bury him."

All of them cringed at the notion of spending hours digging a hole and burying a man when they were already exhausted and hungry. Thankfully, Tom offered a better solution, "Cremating him would be better. It's a more common practice in Farron."

Gathering firewood seemed less taxing job than digging a hole with their bare hands.

While Sally and Tom consoled Naomi, Darcy sidled next to Mina and said, "Mina, can you take Tom and find wood to burn? I need to talk with Naomi and Sally in private."

"What do I know about firewood?" Mina said, rubbing the back of her head. Darcy gave her a good hard look until it clicked for her. "Oh yeah, my Survival skill. That gone up by the way. I put two points into it so it's a plus five now."

"Good, good," Darcy said, pleased that Mina seemed to finally be getting her head into the game. "Where did you put the other points?"

"Into Sneak. It's a plus two now."

Darcy felt her grin fade. "Wait, what? Why?"

"Because I was so bad at it before," Mina replied, looking uncertain having seen Darcy's reaction. "Should I not have?"

"Uh, no, it's okay. It's just that I would have put them into a Barbarian Class skill, like Swim or Climb so you can boost them up by two. You sorta burned two points by increasing a skill you were already low in by one point." Normally, Darcy wouldn't reproach a player for their choices, but that was back in the real world when the game was just a game. Here there were lives on the line. Still, Mina could have done far worse. "Look, don't worry about it. It never hurts to increase your Sneak skill and I'll come up with a plan for how we need to develop our characters the next time we level up."

Mina seemed reassured and nodded. "That's not a bad idea. I still don't know anything about this game and I got questions. The System asked me if I wanted to continue leveling into Barbarian. I said no and it offered to let me multiclass into Fighter or Rogue."

Darcy's eyebrows rose. "But you stayed a Barbarian?"

"Because neither seemed any better," Mina said, sadly shaking her head. "No offense to Sally, but Rogue doesn't seem any safer than Barbarian or Fighter."

"What do you mean by a safe class?" Darcy asked, having a sinking suspicion about where this was going.

"I don't want to be a front-line fighter any more. I want to be a Cleric like you."

Yep, there it was. Darcy sighed into her hand before saying, "We'll talk about that later. Right now, I really need to check something out about Naomi and I don't want Tom around when I do."

"Sure, how long do you need?"

"About twenty minutes should do. I hope," Mina said, looking over at Naomi. The girl had calmed down and was rubbing her tear-streaked face on her sleeves. Tom was speaking gently to her while Sally patted her shoulder. It was odd to see Sally being so sociable, but they had gone through a lot. "Watch what you say around Tom. He thinks this is the real world, and there's no reason to have him think otherwise.

Once Mina and Tom left and well on their way, Darcy called Naomi over. The girl had been gathering sticks and laying them out in a long oval for the funeral pyre. She wasn't her usual jubilant self, more subdued, but there was still a bounce in her step as she came up to Darcy.

"Naomi, hey, I need you to check your logs and tell me if you failed or passed a Constitution check." Darcy looked at Naomi with such intensity that the girl was taken aback. Even Sally noticed Darcy's firm gaze and knew it didn't mean good news.

"Sure, one second." After a few moments of finger wagging, she said, "I failed a Constitution save with a six."

Sally noticed Darcy flinching at the news. "What's wrong?"

"Did you fail the Constitution save during the werewolf attack?" Darcy asked grievously.

"I think so..."

"Damn, you have lycanthropy," Darcy said, sighing.

Sally put a hand on Naomi's shoulder and squeezed it. "Are you sure?"

"Yeah. It's not an issue in the MMO version, but in the tabletop version, if you get bit by a were animal, you have to make a Constitution save. Pass it, then nothing happens other than being hurt from the bite, but if you fail it, you contracted the curse too."

"Oh god, no," Sally breathed in horror. "Wh-what can we do?"

"It's not the end of the world," Darcy said, holding up her hands. "We'll have a cleric remove the curse."

"But aren't you a cleric?"

"I am, but I can't learn Remove Curse until I hit fifth level," Darcy said. "Don't worry; there are high level clerics at the temples in Everguard. They may charge us, but they can help her."

"So, um, at the full moon, I'll turn into a werewolf?" Naomi asked quietly.

"No, we're going to keep that from happening," Sally said, reassuringly. "We'll go to Everguard and get you cured, okay?"

"But will I really turn into a werewolf?" Naomi asked, a bit louder than before.

"Yes, but as Sally said, we're not going to let that happened," Darcy said firmly. "So don't worry about it..."

"Can we wait until after I transform once and then cure me?"

Both Darcy and Sally looked at each other, nonplussed. Hopeful as a child begging for a treat, Naomi continued, "I mean, you'll have to chain me up or put me in a cage, so I don't go out killing anyone, but it would be awesome to be a werewolf."

"We are not going to let that happened," Darcy said, her voice transitioning from misplaced reassurance to outright chastisement. "We're going to Everguard and get the curse removed, and don't you dare mention that you have lycanthropy to anyone. Sally had it bad enough being a half-elf, they wanted to kick her out of an inn. With you, they'll get the torches and pitchforks."

***

Before long, Mina and Tom returned with firewood. They untied the dead man's wrists and crossed his arms crossed over the chest. Even his hair was combed from his face by Naomi's fingers. Sally couldn't help seeing the irony: they had left behind dozens of dead men in the tunnels with no thought, yet here they were sending the one they hadn't killed off with honors.

Naomi insisted that Darcy, being a cleric, say a few words before they burned him. And being unable to decline without making Tom curious, Darcy made the best attempt she could, given she was coming from a non-religious family.

"Dear Heavenly Lor-Shantra, Hallowed be Thy Name," Darcy began with her head bowed. "Ashes to ashes, dust to dust, on Earth as it is in Heaven. Dear Shantra, please take this man into your Holy Embrace, for he died here, and we know not his name. Amen."

All of them said amen together, followed shortly by Tom who glanced at Darcy and then at Sally, but said nothing and stood near Naomi with a hand on her shoulder as she began crying again. Even Mina seemed downcast by the funeral with her head bowed and eyes lowered. While the corpse burned, Sally sidled next to Darcy, who was holding one of the arrows and spinning it between her fingers. Ever since they found the body, she had been staring at the arrows in grim silence.

"What's wrong?"

Darcy held the arrow up for Sally to have a closer look. "These are mastercraft arrows. The most powerful arrows you can get in this game."

Taking the arrow from Darcy's hand, Sally studied it. It felt light as air but solid like stone or metal. The tip was quite sharp, pricking Sally's finger when she tested the point.

As Sally sucked on her fingertip, Darcy gravely said, "You can only buy those in high level areas, and they're so expensive that it's cheaper to get the materials and craft them yourself."

Sally raised her head from her finger as Darcy's implication dawned on her. "Another player?"

Darcy drew a deep breath and slowly let it out through her nose. "I don't know. Nothing is as it should be. When it was just a game, the innkeeper never had any dealings with bandits. He'd stand behind the bar smiling and sell items and rent rooms to players, regardless of race. The

Cut Throats don't kidnap you to get back letters and you only saw them in the forest outside of the village. It's the same world I know, but I still don't recognize it."

Sally recalled the previous night when she felt the cold presence of another person watching her. Was it the same person who had killed this man? Was it a player that believed they were still playing the game? Or an out of place NPC with dangerous weapons? If it was a player, it should be someone they could talk to and reason with. Yet, the sight of the dead man, still bound tight with arrows sticking out of his back was too gruesome to ignore. It was no accident, nor was it any form of self-defense. It was murder.

Looking over at the others, who were still watching the fire burn, Darcy said in a low voice, "Don't repeat to them what I just told you. They have enough to worry about already."

"Sure, the arrows are just between you and me." When no one was watching, Darcy tossed the mastercraft arrow into the fire, and Sally did the same. They glowed with intense heat before turning black and breaking apart in the embers.

***

While the body continued to burn, Mina maneuvered to stand beside Darcy. Sally had gone to stand next to Naomi who was beginning to look crestfallen again, her excitement over the possibility of becoming a werewolf dissipating.

"Can we talk now?" Mina asked.

"Sure, but speak softly," Darcy replied with a cautious glance towards Tom who was standing near Sally.

While Sally comforted Naomi, he raised a hand as if he wanted to touch the half-elf's shoulder, but thought better of it and lowered it to his side. Darcy looked between the two of them and mentally sighed. This would not end well for either of them.

"You don't want to be a Barbarian anymore," Darcy said, turning her attention back to Darcy.

"Yeah, I want to change classes," Mina said, looking at her large hands. "I'm no good at fighting."

"You helped out back there with the Cut Throats," Darcy said, recalling how Mina stood her ground despite her own fear against score of Cut Throats. "You managed to stand toe to toe with McRando."

"I know, but I still don't want to be a Barbarian," Mina said, leaning forward seriously. "I'd rather stay in the back where it's safer."

"Well, the reason why it seems safer in the back because there's a fighter in the front keeping the nasties from getting to me." Darcy explained. "Every decent party needs a front-line fighter to deal and take damage for the others. I know it's not ideal for you, but you were really kicking ass back there."

"I was…I wasn't myself when I Raged," Mina looked away, fear and shame tightening her face.

"That's the Barbarian's special ability. It makes them stronger and does a lot more damage."

"You keep saying damage, but what you really mean is hurting people."

Oh, so that was what this was about. Darcy rubbed her mouth and chin as she carefully chose her words. "They would have killed us."

"My family hates violence. Dad goes to gun control rallies, Mom runs a free clinic, and my brother joined the Doctors Without Borders. And I'm in this world, mowing down people with a sword and axe." Mina looked down at her hands, which were large, with thick fingers from years (that she had never actually experienced) of handling weapons.

"So, what should we have done?" Darcy said a little heatedly. It was a struggle not to raise her voice and draw the others' attention. "I'm not big on killing people either, but what else should we have done? Let them slit our throats? Stand by while they sold Sally into slavery and locked Tom up again?"

"I—I don't know." Mina lowered her eyes, and her hands closed into fists nearly the size of footballs.

"We didn't ask for that fight." Darcy's anger rose, but she swallowed it back to speak calmly. "They were the ones who kidnapped us, and their pet werewolf nearly killed Naomi. We didn't kill a convent of nuns, but bandits that called themselves the Cut Throats, dammit."

"I know that! But it still doesn't feel good that I did that." Mina rejoined.

Darcy pinched the bridge of her nose and swallowed back all the mean things she wanted to say, but knew wouldn't help anything. Then she said in a gentle tone, "Mina, if this were a tabletop or MMO, I would say do whatever you want, but it's life or death now. I don't know how long we're going to be trapped in this world or…" As much as she didn't want to say the words out loud, she continued, "or if we're ever going home."

Mina's throat visibly bobbed as she swallowed. They both stood in silence as the horrible notion of never returning home weighed on them. Darcy brushed aside the thought, though it lingered at the back of her mind as she continued. "To survive, we have to be a strong party, and that means fulfilling our class roles. I do the healing and spell casting, Sally sneaks around and lands critical attacks on enemies, Naomi can distract and confuse the enemy, and you have to be at the front taking the hits and dealing the most damage."

Mina sighed, deflating, and it was a pitiful sight for an Amazonian warrioress. Out of sympathy Darcy laid a hand on Mina's shoulder and met her eyes, "But that doesn't mean we can't make some changes that can suit your personal needs and benefit the party too. We can look at some options for the next time you level up."

Mina perked up and even smiled a little. "Thanks."

"And I need to apologize for what I said to you in the cell and later during the fight with McRando."

Mina shrugged. "It's okay. It did the trick and made me Rage."

"Still, I wanted to say I'm sorry," Darcy insisted. "I shouldn't have used your issues to trigger you."

Mina shifted uneasily on her feet, and a pink blush spread across her olive cheeks. "You were right. I got myself into this situation because I wanted to impress a guy."

Darcy looked away, feeling ashamed. "When we go home, you'll have a story for him."

Chapter 13

THE INN

By the time they returned to Spring Bell village, Sally was tired, sore, and very hungry. Yet Darcy strode through the village as if she were leading a victorious army. People paused to stare at the strange ensemble following the Cleric. A bouncing girl in white tattered clothing; a red-faced barbarian woman who slumped her shoulders as if trying to hide; a nervous half-elf woman, and a tall, bearded man who walked with the grace of a nobleman.

Darcy used more force than necessary to throw open the doors of the inn and they banged against the inside walls. A startled Smiley Pete dropped the mug he had been cleaning. It hit the floor with a solid clunk and rolled out of sight as if fleeing the Cleric's wrath.

The barman opened his mouth to roar at such aggressive mishandling of his building when he recognized Darcy and the others who walked in behind her.

The Cleric gave him a scathing look, the Monk scowled, the half-elf glared, and the Barbarian looked sullenly at him. But the most venomous eyes were those of the man, who looked as if he would rather cut off Pete's head than look at him.

Recovering himself, Pete narrowed his eyes, brow wrinkling as his chins quivered. "What the bloody hell is this?"

"You know what this is," Darcy replied evenly. "This is karma biting you in the ass. You're going to provide us rooms and meals. You're going to have our clothes washed and mended. You're going to replace our lost backpacks and bedrolls with new ones. Then you're going to give us each a week's worth of rations and camping supplies. And you're going to do all of this for free."

Pete's mouth flapped open, wholly flabbergasted and speechless. It took several tries to speak, his lips trembling in fury when he finally said, "Like bloody hell I will!"

"Like bloody hell you better!" Darcy returned, slapping the page from the ledger on the counter.

Pete arched an eyebrow and looked down at the page.

Never before had Sally seen someone go from beet red to white as a ghost so quickly. He looked sick as all the color bled from his face and his lips no longer quivered from hot rage, but cold terror.

"What do you want?" he said, his eyes focused on Darcy.

"What I already said," Darcy said heatedly. "Hot meals, hot baths, and hell, hot beds too. Our clothes are to be washed and mended. If it can't be mended as good as new, then replace them with brand new ones. It's the least you can do since you're responsible for..."

"Yes, yes, alright," he said hastily, motioning for her to keep it down while casting a nervous look at some patrons who were peering curiously at them. "If I give you what you want, then you keep it hushed?"

Darcy nodded. "Tomorrow, if we're happy with everything, I'll hand this paper over to you, and you can burn it or wipe your ass, whatever you want to do with it."

Then the half-elf leaned forward, bringing her nose almost close to his own. "We want dinner waiting for us by the time we're done bathing. And we want the best rooms you have with clean beds."

Nothing made Pete's blood boil than being ordered about in his own inn by a half-breed wretch. He almost—almost—spat in her face and ordered them out of his inn. When word got around that he had served a non-human in his inn, then there would go his business. If his deal with the Cut Throats became public, however, the villagers would string him up and leave his corpse to feed the crows.

"Very well," he said through his gritted teeth.

***

The floor of the bathroom was polished wood with a single drain in the center surrounded by three brass tubs, which were currently filled with hot water. Each of the adventurers had received a cake of soap and a washcloth and their clothes were collected by a serving girl who eyed Naomi's ruined and bloody garments with shocked apprehension.

After undressing, yet again Sally marveled at her new body. Everything was so small and thin. Her arms were tight and toned, her legs didn't brush together when she walked, and when she sat in the tub, she was amazed by how little space she took up. A second person might actually fit in with her, which was proven when Naomi unceremoniously jumped in with her, causing a huge splash that spread water across the floor.

"Jesus Christ!" Sally cried when Naomi, who had submerged, broke the surface, blinking water from her eyes. "What the hell?"

"Sorry, but there are only three tubs!" Naomi said, lying back against the side of the tub.

Mina was already soaping up her arms and shoulders. "She wanted to get in with me, but there's no room in my tub."

Sally groaned and scooted back, giving more space to Naomi. "Sit still and don't splash."

Darcy was standing by the door, listening. With a self-assured nod, she let the towel slip from her torso and claimed the last tub. Her body was thicker than Sally's slim frame, but more muscular, solid, and athletic, "Alright, we're alone. We can talk freely. Naomi: tell us what happened when you appeared in this world."

"It's like I already told Sally," Naomi sighed. "I was at my computer playing *Shadow's Deep*."

"At what time were you playing?"

"I don't know…"

"Was it morning or night?"

"Afternoon."

Darcy lowered herself in the tub, both wincing and sighing in relief as the hot water eased the ache in her bones. Once she was settled with her toes wriggling beneath the water, she asked, "Where do you live?"

"Phoenix, Arizona."

The skin between Darcy's eyebrows knitted. "Was it sometime after four when you logged on?"

Naomi considered it a moment and nodded, "Yeah. I think so. I finished my school work, so Mom said I could play *Shadow's Deep*.

"Alright, we have a connection now."

"And what's that?" Mina asked, leaning over the edge of the tub, which sloshed water onto the floor.

"We got transported at the same time. Six-twenty in Eastern time and likely four-twenty in Mountain time. So whatever happened, it happened to us all at the same time."

"Alright," Sally said, picking up the soap and rubbed it between her hands to build up a lather. "So why isn't the village crawling with other players? We can't be the only ones."

"They might not be advertising themselves," Mina suggested. "We were pretty freaked out when we appeared here, so they might be hiding."

"I don't know about that," Sally said. "When we came back to the village, I was looking around and all I saw were villagers and no one that looked like an adventurer or a player. No fancy clothes or weapons. Or anyone that wasn't human."

"There's got to be another connection other than the time." Darcy moaned, sinking into the water if she would drown herself out of frustration.

Mina was quiet for several moments, then she said. "What about the server? Remember, you told me to choose the Aslan Twenty-Five server when I logged in."

Naomi raised her head, recognizing the name. "Yeah, that's the server with my character profile."

"Forgive my ignorance, but what is a server?" Sally asked.

Darcy rubbed her brow and sighed. "I keep forgetting you don't know much about MMOs. Think of a server as a copy of the game. *Shadow's Deep* has over seven million players, but if you put them all into one server, it would crash the game. So they split the players onto hundreds of different servers so everyone can play at the same time."

Then Darcy sat up, as a revelation dawned on her. "As more players subscribe, the techs create more servers to ease the queue times. And they would restrict the number of players on a new server to make sure there are no problems before it becomes fully accessible."

As Darcy spoke, the connection was making sense now with the time and now the server. Were there other players in the same predicament as them?

"How many players can a server hold?" asked Sally

"About a hundred thousand, but in newer servers, we're looking around a thousand online at any given time," Darcy said, wrinkling her brow in thought. "The Aslan Twenty-Five server was only a few weeks old, so there shouldn't have been that many people logged into it. It's the reason why I chose it as a place to teach new players. The assholes and trolls tend to stick to bigger servers where there are more people to harass."

Mina's sloshed water over her shoulders, rinsing the soap from them, her face was set in a thoughtful demeanor. "That's still a lot of players. We should have seen others by now."

Darcy shook her head. "Not necessarily. *Shadow's Deep* is pretty big, especially with all the expansions that extend the world map. Think of a country as big as Asia, with only a thousand people. How often do you think they run into each other? Then narrow that down by the number of players who were playing at the same time as the Incident, then there might be only a few hundred people, if that."

Sally was scrubbing her arms and shoulders while listening. The soap released a fragrant smell that was soothing, clearing her head, and the warm water eased out all the aches in her legs and feet. If the conversation wasn't so meaningful, she would have fallen asleep in the tub.

Darcy was thinking out loud, speaking more to herself than to them, but they listened intently as if she were. "Our best bet to find other players in this area of the world is Everguard. We can get Naomi cured of lycanthropy while we're there."

Mina was scrubbing the bottom of one foot. "What's Everguard like?"

"It's a pretty big seaside city that serves as a trade hub for the continent. Players can use the auction house and the bank…" Darcy surged up so fast from the water that Sally thought she fell out of the tub. "Holy shit…holy shit…we have to go to Everguard…we have to."

"We know," Sally said slowly. "To get a Naomi cured of her lycanthropy and find other players."

"Because yesterday," Darcy said with eyes beaming brightly. "I transferred a hundred thousand gold from one of my previous characters into a bank in Everguard for my Cleric to buy equipment. If everything I did in Spring Bell village stands, then that money should still be in the bank under Sister Korra's name."

***

Smiley Pete must have taken Sally's warning seriously, as fresh clothes and a hot meal were waiting for each of them when they finished their baths. They chose a table far away from the other patrons and ate with gusto without speaking. It wasn't that they were afraid of being overheard if they talked, but because they were so hungry and the food so good that they were more focused on filling their bellies than anything else.

A hundred thousand gold would definitely help them out in this world, thought Sally. Between them, they had five gold coins that Naomi looted from fallen Cut Throats, and they had gotten this food, baths, and rooms for the night through blackmail. Plus, if Everguard was a hub of trade and banking, then there had to be other players there. Would finding them answer any of her questions about how this had happened and how to get home?

A man appeared at their table and sat down between Sally and Naomi. They stopped eating and stared as the man began helping himself to the meal. It took them nearly a minute to recognize Tom or Prince Alexander Tomas Draggoran. He had shaved his beard, revealing a handsome face with high boned aristocratic features. His hair was tied back from his face in a short tail still damp from the bath, and his new clothes were a linen shirt and dark trousers. Back at the hideout, Tom hadn't been a bad looking man, but now that he was cleaned up, he was a fetching sight indeed.

He noticed the stares. "Forgive me, was I intruding?"

"No! No! It just took us a minute to recognize you without the beard," Darcy said quickly. "Mina, get him a drink and Naomi, scoot over and give him more room..."

"Please, don't make any special effort for me," Tom said, halting them with open hands. "You know who I am, don't you?"

Darcy bit her lower lip. "Well, there was a reason why they put you in a cell guarded by two guards."

Sally picked at a piece of meat on her plate. "And McRando did call you a prince before he died."

"It was not my wish to hide my true identity from you, but I could not be certain if I could trust you at first," he said, casting a glance at Sally and then at Naomi. "For all I knew, you would have kept me as your own prisoner for ransom or to use as a hostage against my father."

"It's alright," Naomi said reassuringly. "We still like you."

He smiled at the girl and even ruffled her hair. "You remind me so much of my sister, Maureen. She would have been your age if she had lived."

So surprised that she dropped her spoon, Darcy said, "You had a sister? I didn't know that Farron had a princess."

"She was only my half-sister, a child by my father's mistress, so she didn't warrant the title of Princess. She lived with me at my mother's estate until she died of the Poxy when she was nine." The prince's face softened in a manner Sally hadn't seen from him before. "She is one of the reasons why I undertook a diplomatic mission to Saige. Maureen was a half-elf."

"Oh, I see." Understanding had dawned on Darcy's face, but Sally knew her own face would be showing confusion.

"I want to ease the discrimination against non-humans in Farron. The first step towards that is brokering a peace treaty with Saige and opening diplomatic ties. Maureen might have lived a happier life if my country wasn't so intolerant of her."

Sally realized he was genuinely regretful for his sister's hard life. Was this her empathizing with him or was this her +4 in Perception? "I'm sorry for your loss. And I hate that you got kidnapped before you could make it to Saige."

"The Cut Throats kidnapped me on my way back from Saige," the prince said with a small smile. "I met with the Council, and they seemed agreeable on the idea of a peace treaty. That's why I must return to the Capital as soon as possible before my father suspects foul play on Saige's part. There will be no peace if the Kingdom of Farron accuses the Republic of Saige of kidnapping me."

"How do you intend to return?" Darcy asked, taking more interest in the conversation now that she had eaten. She pushed aside her clean plate and refilled her cup.

"I shall have to go to Everguard. I have an uncle from my mother's side that operates a trading company. He can arrange safe passage for me to the Capital."

"Why not go with a trade caravan? You could hide your identity and be a guard." Darcy asked.

"Unfortunately, the caravans have stopped," The prince said in a low voice. "While you were bathing, I've been talking with the other patrons. They say there are fiends attacking caravans."

Mina shrugged, "We already took care of the Cut Throats, so it should be safer to travel."

The prince shook his head, "No, it was not them. All the travelers were killed, but none of the cargo nor valuables were taken. Nothing. And they were all killed with white arrows, like the ones that killed that poor soul in the forest."

Sally" felt her stomach flip, and she looked at Darcy, whose mouth was set in a grim line. The colour of her face was fading to a pale brown, but she maintained eye contact with the prince. "It must have been the same fiends who killed the bandit in the forest then."

Sally glanced at Mina, who had noticed Darcy's reaction, but was ignorant of the implication and Naomi was too engaged with eating a pastry to pay any attention. Good, that way they wouldn't blurt out the sinking suspicion that Sally had about the source of the white arrows and the "fiends." Then an unbidden memory rose of her standing frightened in the woods with an armful of berries and a knife. Now she intuited who was watching her that night and how close she had come to being killed.

"Is something wrong?" The prince said, breaking into her cold thoughts. "You seem stricken."

"No, I'm fine. I'm just shocked by how someone could do that," she said and tried to change the subject. "It's a shame about the caravans. How do you intend to get to Everguard?"

"He can come with us!" Naomi cried, jumping into the conversation. "We're going to Everguard too."

It was all Sally could do to maintain a calm demeanor and not wince, but Darcy was nodding, "That's a good idea, Naomi. We're leaving tomorrow morning. You should come with us."

Tom's face brightened with a smile. "Yes, I would like that. I enjoy our time together, and sharing the road with you will be safer. All I ask is that you continue to call me Tom. It'll be safer if my identity is kept a secret."

"Good idea," Darcy said, pushing her plate away and rising. "I'm going to give Stinky Pete a list of what we need for tomorrow. Sally, I'll meet you upstairs in our room."

"Sure," Sally set down her cup and rose. "I was about to turn in early anyway. I think the less seen, the better."

A hand touched her wrist before she could step away from the table. "Sally," Tom said quietly, "I was hoping you would speak with me a moment."

Sally looked back at Darcy, who was looking between them with large eyes. "Turning in early is a good idea. Alright, everyone, let's go to bed."

"But I'm still eating," Naomi whined despite Mina lifting her from the table.

"We'll take it to go then," Mina said as she easily tucked Naomi into her armpit and grabbed the plate of pastries in her other hand. The Monk waved goodbye as she was carried upstairs and Mina looked back at Sally with an expression the Rogue couldn't read.

"I'll see you later," Darcy said before departing.

Sally sat down, nervous about whatever it was that Tom needed to talk about. Maybe Darcy should have remained to take part in this discussion. "What's wrong?"

"Nothing's wrong, or, I hope everything is well." He reached for a bottle of mulled wine and filled an empty cup. It was offered it to her, and she accepted it. "There's something that has been bothering me. Ever since I met you."

Sally knitted her eyebrows. "And what's that?"

"I know your sister is not truly a cleric of Shantra," Tom said, chilling Sally's blood. "She doesn't know how to give last rites, and she has gone for hours without praising Shantra's name, a feat I have never seen anyone of the order accomplish before."

She had a feeling that Darcy's half-assed prayer over the funeral would rouse Tom's suspicions. Thinking quickly, she said, "She hasn't been a cleric very long." That was technically true.

"If she's an acolyte, then why is she without her mentor so far away from a Shantra temple? I won't deny she has divine magic, I saw it for myself, but her manner is quite strange for a cleric. And she is not the only one with a strangeness about her."

Sally set the cup down, losing her taste for mulled wine. "If you don't want to travel with us..."

"I do, I've become quite fond of you all." His eyes peered into hers, and she swallowed despite her throat feeling tight. "But there's something so strange about all of you. The way you speak, act and even think. You barely reacted when you learned I was a prince, and I hear you whispering when you think I won't notice or hear."

"Maybe it's better if you don't travel with us after all..." She didn't know what else she could say to deter his reasoning.

"Do you not want me to travel with you?" There was a trace of hurt behind his eyes that made her feel guilty. "Or are you deflecting my questions?"

"I don't understand why you want to travel with us since you don't trust us." Maybe she was deflecting the question as she wasn't good with confrontations like this. Sally would much rather be upstairs right now with Darcy and not having this discussion where she felt out of her depth. Darcy would know what to tell Tom and how to ease his suspicions as she knew this world and this NPC far better.

Now he was the one offended. "We fought a werewolf, the Cut Throats, and their leader together, and you believe I don't trust you? My dear, I trust you with my life, but it is you who do not trust me."

"It's not a matter of trust. You...you wouldn't understand, you wouldn't want to understand if I told you."

"I can try. Are you foreigners from a land across the sea?"

"Think whatever you like," Sally said, standing up, determined to leave whether this conversation was finished or not. "I'm going upstairs. If you trust us enough to travel with us, then please trust us enough to understand that while you may feel comfortable sharing your personal history with us, we would rather keep our personal history to ourselves. Goodnight."

Her wrist was caught as she turned away and she had to fight down a reflexive desire to swing around with a punch. Instead, she stood still and ground her teeth.

"You're right. I was prying into your affairs, and that was not my intention. Please, stay, let's not part with crossed words."

He sounded so remorseful that she relented. A little. She would still rather be upstairs, but she turned around. "Alright, I'm not mad anymore. I'll stay for a few minutes, but let's talk about something else, okay?"

"O-kay? You use such strange vernacular. What does it mean?"

She sat down again, a bit more relaxed and lenient. "It's a different way of saying yes or something is acceptable. What does vernacular means?"

A small tugged at the corner of his lips. "It means words used by people from a specific area or region."

"Oh. Have you ever been to Everguard?" It was better to move the topic onto safer ground and gain some information too.

"Once, when I was a boy," Tom said, collecting a second cup and pouring mulled wine for himself. "I accompanied my mother to visit her brother, the uncle I spoke of earlier. It was my first time leaving the Capital, and I must have been six or seven back then, so it was quite an adventure for me. I didn't see much of Everguard as I was kept safely away in my uncle's manor. What I did see was the wealthier side of the city; they call it the Golden Quarter. It was well protected by the city watch. Perhaps that's even more the case now since Everguard has become rife with crime in recent years."

The mulled wine had a spicy taste that pinched Sally's nose. It rolled over her tongue and made her feel warm inside. "How bad is it?"

Tom took a long pull from his cup and licked his lips, as if unaccustomed to no longer having a moustache and beard. "There has always been crime in Everguard as there would be in any large city, but recently a gang has become quite daring. They've raided warehouses, robbed noble houses, and even attacked a nobleman's carriage in broad daylight. Not much is known about them except for the name of their leader. Riker."

Sally's felt the mulled wine turned to ice in her stomach. Riker. That name sounded very familiar. Where she heard it before?

Tom was looking into his cup, his fingers flexing slightly around it. As if hearing her thoughts, he added, "It's the same name that McRando mentioned before he died."

Ye've no idea what is waiting for you when Riker finds out what ye've done. When he finds out, you'll wish I had sold you down the river.

"Oh shit…" Sally moaned. They were going to Everguard where this Riker was operating. They already brought down one crime boss, and now they were about to go into the territory of another. "Then, we shouldn't go Everguard if Riker is there."

"I wouldn't let the last words of a murdering thief dissuade us from going where we must," Tom said, draining his cup and set it down and pushed it away with a gentle touch of his fingers. "We have no reason to believe his words were anything more than the final curses of his violent life. And we won't be the only travelers going to Everguard. It's the largest trading port on the western coast where thousands of people make their home. As long as we don't march into the city declaring ourselves as the killers of McRando of the Cut Throats, I doubt they will raise so much as a hair at our arrival."

"But still…" Sally sighed, finding little comfort in his words. "There's avoiding trouble, and there's walking right into the lion's den."

"It amazes me how quickly you can go from bravery to fear so quickly. And the opposite is true as well. As if you can't make up your mind of what you want to be. Or maybe, you don't know yet what you are."

Sally raised her eyes as his hand caressed her cheek, fingers pushing through her hair. It was like a weak electrical current brushing her skin. Then his face drew close to hers and she flinched, uncertain if she liked what she felt or not.

Tom withdrew his hand and looked away. "Forgive me. The wine has addled my head. It was not my intention to approach you like this."

"It's—uh—okay," Sally said, feeling the heat rise to her face.

"When you say okay, do you mean…?" There was a hope behind his eyes that almost made her panic.

"I meant that I'm not angry or offended," she said quickly.

"Is there someone else?"

"No, but that doesn't mean—I—I really need to go before Darcy starts to worry."

"Goodnight, Sally. I look forward to our journey together."

She felt his eyes on her as she walked upstairs. It was a struggle not to flee up the steps, and she didn't dare look back.

***

Darcy was sitting cross-legged on a bed, only wearing a tabard looking over a map spread open across her knees. She looked up as Sally came inside. "So, what did he want to talk about?"

Sally made sure the door was shut and locked before she said, "He tried to kiss me."

Darcy gasped, her mouth dropping open. It was a familiar sight on a different face. "Oh, my God? Did he? I can name ten fangirls that would give up their left arms to be in your shoes."

Annoyed, Sally stalked to the opposite bed. The room was large enough for two beds and a short set of drawers and a table between them. She sat down on the bed, fixing Darcy with a hard look. "Did you know he was going to do that?"

"Sally, he likes you," Darcy said pointedly.

She blinked. "But he likes Naomi."

Darcy snorted and shook her head. "Naomi's just a kid and reminds him of his kid sister. You're the one he's been making eyes at. You didn't get the clue when he asked you to hang out with him? Alone?"

"He's the one with the clue," Sally retorted. "He knows you're not really a cleric, and I had to explain what the word 'okay' means."

She shucked off her boots and undressed for bed. God, even after the bath, her feet were still sore. Sitting down on the edge of the bed, she rubbed one foot with the ankle balanced on her knee. A feat in her old body that would have required some maneuvering. "He thinks we're foreigners."

Darcy shrugged. "That's probably for the best. Does he still want to travel with us tomorrow?"

"He almost begged me to let him come along with us," Sally said as she rubbed her other foot. They were feeling better now, but she wasn't looking forward to them being stiff in the morning. "Why do you want him to come along anyway?"

"Because we're going to need all the help we can get. Having a prince owing us a favor won't be a bad thing, especially if the gold I deposited isn't there. And the trip to Everguard will be dangerous," Darcy replied, laying out the map and pointing at a spot. "We're here in Spring Bell village, and Everguard is way over here." She drew a finger in a long line across the parchment to a large mark next to the blue water. "It's roughly a five-day journey by foot in areas that are higher level than we are. Players aren't supposed to get to Everguard until level ten. Since Mina isn't confident as a Barbarian, we can certainly use a high-level fighter with a solid head on his shoulders."

"What are you going to do about Mina? She did alright against the Cut Throats, but even I can tell she has problems with this world."

Darcy closed the map and put it away into a bag next to her bed. "She doesn't want to be the tank for the group anymore."

"Being the tank is a dangerous job that she didn't sign up for," Sally said, settling into her bed, stifling a yawn.

"We're in the same predicament too, but if we're going to survive in this world, then we've each got to contribute to the group's dynamic. You caught on pretty quick, and Naomi loves this, but Mina needs to get her head straight." Darcy picked up a piece of parchment and stylus and stepped off the bed to offer them to Sally. "I know you're tired, but if you can just jot down a copy of your character screen, so I have an idea where your strengths and weaknesses lie. I already had Mina and Naomi do theirs during your date."

"It wasn't a date," Sally said hotly, before reluctantly leaving her warm bed to take the parchment and stylus. She sat up, yawned into the back of her hand, and began scribbling her stats. "How does the overall group look?"

"Well, both Naomi and I have the highest Wisdom scores believe it or not. Mina is our strongest player, even with her subpar scores. If she had let the game roll her stats, then she might have some decent scores, and she would have better options for multiclassing."

"I take it that she doesn't have many options to do so?" Sally said, raising her eyes from the parchment.

"Her only two options were Rogue and Fighter. She'd be better off going with Fighter, but she wants to use healing spells," Darcy pinched the bridge of her nose, sighing. "But her Wisdom score is too low and she'll need to level up a few more times before she can increase any of her ability scores. Unless...well, there's Paladin."

"Paladin? That's like a knight or something?"

"A holy knight, but you have to be Lawful-Good to be one. Since Mina chose a default Barbarian, then her alignment is Chaotic-Neutral and the game won't allow her to choose Paladin."

"Explain these alignments. I heard of them in memes, but I'm not sure what they are."

Darcy set her elbow on a knee and propped her head on her hand. "It doesn't matter in the online game, but tabletop it helps define how players roleplay a character. And there are items in the game that only players of certain alignments can use."

"Can Mina change her alignment so she can become a Paladin?"

"I don't know. It's not something you can change by just leveling up. It depends on the Game Master, or in this case, the System, whether her alignment changes based upon her actions."

Finishing with copying her character stats, Sally handed the parchment to Darcy who looked them over with a nod. "You got good stats and you were smart to boost your Sneak skill." She paused. "I would have put the points you spent on Swim into Charm or Perception instead."

"I thought I'd have to swim out the way we came," Sally said with a shrug.

"That's the challenge with raising skills," Darcy explained. "You want to raise the skills that will be useful later on, but then you end up not having to use them. Like bumping up Climb because you think you're going to a mountainous area, but you end up in a marshland where Swim would be more useful."

"I take it you have opinions on how we should level our characters from now on?"

"Yeah," Darcy said with a "that's obvious" tone. "As for you, keep boosting your Sneak skill. I don't need to tell you how useful that is. And I know you haven't been using it, but Charm and Perception are good skills, especially in Everguard. At level three, your Sneak Attack will do more damage and you'll get a plus one to finding traps."

"What about Mina and Naomi?"

"Honestly, I'm not sure," Darcy said, stretching out on the bed, fatigue finally claiming her. "Barbarian and Monk are the two classes I'm not that familiar with as I tend to play spell casters or Rogues and I don't have the game books with me to consult. Since Naomi's level five, it'll be awhile before she levels up and Mina is going to go with whatever will keep her safer so I suggested she stick to Climb and Swim so she doesn't fall from tall heights and drown."

Earlier Sally had checked her experience points and saw that she had only gained 180 from the encounter with the Cut Throats and McRando. As did Mina and the others. Darcy explained that XP was divided between participating party members. It still seemed a little low since it was supposed to be a boss fight, but Sally wasn't one to complain about coming out of that mess alive.

Now she needed sleep, but she remembered there was something else she needed to share with Darcy. "There's another thing: Tom told me about people in a caravan being killed. All of them with white arrows."

Darcy look at the ceiling soberly and nodded, "I heard about that too from the serving girl, and it has me worried."

"Is it other players?" Sally's question hung in the air between them like a guillotine blade.

Darcy's voice carried an imperceptive tremor. "Maybe. And if it is, then they're high level. They would have to be able to make mastercraft arrows and kill off an entire caravan of people. That's why I want Tom to come along with us: he can fight and will be another pair of eyes on the road. If anything should happen, we're better off with him than without."

Sally considered this for a moment then said, "It's worse if it's players, isn't it?"

Darcy drew a breath and released it through her nose. "Yeah. Way worse."

Sally wasn't familiar with multiplayer games. Still, she had heard enough to know about griefers and trolls who purposely ruined the game for others by camping near spawn points to gun down emerging players or harass other players through chat or mic. What would those trolls do if they found themselves in a game world come to life? Sally had figured trolls were cowards who used the anonymity of the internet to make people's lives miserable.

What if the players—and Sally hope to god that it wasn't players—were people who still saw this as a game where anything goes. Instead of worrying about finding a way home, they saw this as a means to cut loose, to fulfil dark fantasies of death and power.

Fear squeezed her heart, and Sally asked, "Will we be safe in Everguard?"

Darcy nodded firmly. "Yes. Everguard is full of high-level guards, and I'm sure there's plenty of other high-level NPCs who won't fancy being killed."

Sally fidgeted with the blankets, seeing some comfort in the walls of a medieval city filled with guards. It was better than traveling out in the woods. "Shouldn't we tell someone? Not Naomi or Mina, of course, but the law or Tom?"

"No way," Darcy said. "They'll suspect we have something to do with it, and then what can we tell them? This is just a hunch, and things aren't exactly happening as it does in the game. This could be some high level boss hiding out in the forest having himself a good time attacking caravans. If it is players, then how do we describe them? We don't know what race or class they are."

"If that is what you think is best," Sally said despite her own misgivings about it. Then another worry came to mind. "Darcy, do you know who Riker is?"

"Yeah, but don't worry about him. We're going to steer clear of him in Everguard. As long as we don't trigger his questline, we'll be fine."

"McRando said something about Riker coming after us for killing him."

Darcy shook her head, "In the game, McRando and Riker had nothing to do with each other."

"Like Stinky Pete and the Cut Throats?"

Sighing, Darcy said, "Riker is the leader of the Thieves' Guild in Everguard. You encounter him when you take an investigative quest from the city watch. As long as we don't get involved with the quest, we shouldn't run into him."

"So, we shouldn't worry about him at all?"

"There's no need to worry about him until we get to Everguard. Right now, we need to focus on the trip," Darcy said, promptly closing the topic of Riker and studying the map. "It's a five-day journey, so we should get to Everguard with two days to spare before the full moon. We'll go to the bank, get the money, and go straight to a temple. After that'll figure out what we're going to do next."

With that said, they both settled down to an uneasy sleep. Darcy put the papers away on a shelf and blew out the candle. In the dark, there were several long moments of silence until it was broken.

"Sally?"

"Yes?"

"Thanks for coming to save me. And Mina too. I don't think I thanked you for that."

"You would have done the same for me."

"Yeah, I would have."

There was another long moment of silence.

"Darcy?"

"Yes?"

"Will it be weird if I sleep with you tonight?"

"No, come on over."

There was silence again, and this one lasted many hours.

Chapter 14

DEPARTURE

The sun was just beginning to rise when Darcy gently shook her awake. Sally yawned, wishing she could take a morning shower to fully wake up.

"Is there any coffee?"

"Yeah," Darcy said, adjusting the armor in place at her shoulder. "Stinky Pete wants us out of here as soon as possible, so he had breakfast prepared early. Don't take too long. We need to be on our way as soon as we can."

With the promise of fresh coffee and food, it took Sally very little time to dress and head down. As Darcy said, a table laden with food was waiting, and the welcoming scent of coffee touched her nose as she approached. The others were already seated and partaking of the food.

Darcy was sitting next to Tom and studying the map with him. After downing a cup of coffee, Sally made herself eat despite not being a breakfast person. They had a long journey to make with a time limit, and the more ground they covered today, the better. Naomi was talking animatedly with Mina, almost spraying bread crumbs as she spoke with her mouth full. The Barbarian listened with a slight smile, maybe the first genuine smile Sally had seen on the swarthy face since they met. Naomi was excited about the journey claiming it would be like the *Lord of the Rings*.

Stinky Pete was watching them from behind the bar with foul expression. Sally believed that if he had owned a gun, he would shoot them all, starting with Darcy or her. It was best to finish eating quickly and be on their way. As if perceiving the same thing, Darcy rolled up the map and ate the last few bites of her sausage.

"Eat up, guys. We're leaving in ten minutes." Then she and Tom rose together and went to the bar.

Seeing Darcy coming towards him, Pete squared his shoulders and leveled his gaze at her as if she were a charging bull, and he had no intention of giving ground. "Is there anything else you wish? All my teeth? My first born? Or the skin off my back?"

"You can keep all of that," Darcy sniffed and laid the page on the counter but didn't relinquish it when he tried to pick it up. It was pinned it to the wood with two fingers. "Did you get everything I asked for?"

Pete looked as if he could spit in her face. "Yes, it's all there in backpacks." He nodded to five backpacks setting in a neat row on the edge of the counter. Folded on each one was a travel cloak with a hood.

"Good," Darcy said with a frosty stare. "We're leaving, which I'm sure you're pleased about, but before we go, I'm going to leave you something you don't deserve: a warning."

Darcy leaned forward, bringing her face within inches of Stinky Pete. "Open up your ears and listen good because this might save your life. Your working with bandits is done. You will not sell out your patrons to any criminals ever again. If I hear of any travelers being attacked or robbed near Spring Bell, I'm going to assume you had something to do with it and come back here and burn this place down with your sorry ass inside it. Do you understand?"

A trickle of sweat rolled down his pale brow, but he nodded slowly. "I do."

"Good." Darcy removed her hand and let Stinky Pete take the ledger page. She must have rolled well for her Intimidate. "We will be checking back to make sure you understand."

With that said, she turned away, and Tom followed her. Once they were out of earshot, he whispered, "Are we just going to let him get off easily? People have lost their lives because of him. My guards and valet, all good men, were killed."

Darcy glanced back to make sure Stinky Pete couldn't see and then reached into her armor and pulled out a few folded pages of the ledger. "I told him he could have that page. Not that he could have all the pages." She offered them to him. "You take them and make sure he pays for what he's done later."

***

The early morning air was cold and crisp and Sally could just make out the mist of her exhalations. Only the villages who tended their gardens and who were eager to begin their daily work were outside, starting their day. So the group only received a few glances as they left the village. Sally wasn't sad to see it fall behind them until it was out of sight.

"Sally, wear your hood." Darcy had been leading the party as they departed the village, but now she had fallen behind to speak with Sally.

"Why?"

"The reason why I wanted travel cloaks with hoods was so you can hide your ears," Darcy said, touching Sally's shoulder. "We're traveling through a part of the world that's racist against non-humans. It's better to avoid trouble as much as possible."

Sally lifted the hood over her head. It was comfortable, like wearing a hat that didn't pinch her forehead. "Good idea."

"It's two days' walk to the next village, River's Edge," Darcy told everyone once they were well outside the village. "It's a little bit of a detour, but we can spend the night the tavern and restock our supplies. Then we'll spend three days traveling to Everguard."

The next thing she did was made them throw out their rations. "I'm not putting anything from that man in my body. If he's willing to sell out his own customers, then he isn't above poisoning us for blackmailing him. Between Naomi and Mina, we should be able to scrounge enough food for us to eat along the way until we reach River's Edge."

Mina furrowed her brow. "Then why did you make him give us rations then?"

Darcy gave her a smug grin. "Because it cost that bastard. I hope someone tells him we threw them on the side of the road for the animals."

"Remind me not to get on your bad side," Mina muttered as she threw her ration bundles onto the grass.

Sally did the same, though with some doubt. It seemed pretty risky to rely solely on their survival skills for sustenance for two days. Darcy, however, was the closest thing they had to an expert this world and the System, so she likely knew what she was talking about.

Holding his rations in both hands, Tom gave Sally a questioning look that told her that he shared the same thoughts. Sally gave a shrug and an uneasy smile to indicate that she felt the same, but there was nothing she could or would do about it. With a sigh, he tossed his rations onto the ground too.

Then Darcy noticed something and furrowed her eyebrows. "Naomi, where are your shoes?"

The blonde girl blinked. "What shoes?"

"The ones I made Stinky Pete get for you. The ones I made you put on before we left. Where are they?"

"I left those behind. I don't need them," Naomi said with a casual shrug and wiggled her toes in the dirt. "I like going barefoot."

Darcy shook her head, "It's a long walk and your feet are going to get blistered, and we're in a hurry to get to Everguard for…reasons you know about."

"I don't need shoes," Naomi said stoutly.

"You're not a hobbit."

Sally interposed herself before this blew into a diatribe. "Darcy! I've seen her run barefoot through the forest and her feet were fine. If they do get hurt, she's small enough that one of us can carry her or you can use a heal spell on them."

The Cleric huffed at the thought of blowing a spell on a preventative problem like blistered feet, but relented with a stern warning. "The next time I blackmail someone for a pair of shoes, you're going to wear them, even if I have to nail your feet into them."

When they resumed their journey, Tom sidled next to Sally and whispered, "Your sister has some colorful threats."

Sally shrugged, "She gets it from her dad. He was always making threats that he wouldn't ever carry out. He once threatened to knock our teeth down our throats for talking back, but he'd never laid a hand on us."

"You have different mothers?"

"And fathers," Sally said. "Her father married my mother when we were kids."

"Was your mother an elf? Or was it your father?"

Sally skipped a step, mad at herself for not being on guard. "It was my father. He was the elf." She was going to have to tell Darcy, so she will give him the same story if he asked her the same questions.

"Her father didn't mind marrying a woman with a half-elven daughter?"

"He was open-minded," Sally replied.

They had to be with gamers for daughters and they met because of their daughters' hobby. When the Xbox 360s came out, both Darcy and Sally had dragged their parents to Gamestop to get their pre-ordered consoles. While both girls were eyeing people who were leaving the counter with newly purchased consoles, their parents had eyes for each other. Neither could understand the obsession their daughters had for something they had both sank several hundred dollars into and stood hours in line to collect. Maybe that was the common link between them that led to a romance that saw them marrying by the end of the following year.

Sally liked Darcy's father instantly as he didn't expect her to do girly things like hanging out at the mall or obsessing over celebrities and music idols. Likely because he knew what he was in for, as his own daughter pored over RPG gaming books and bought dice instead of shoes.

Their parents tried to get their daughters to bond over gaming, but their tastes in games were too drastically different. Sally had been into single-player console and PC gaming while Darcy was all about MMOs and tabletop. Sally thought Darcy was too loud, and Darcy thought Sally was a recluse. It wasn't until *Fallout 3* came out that they were forced game together. Though the girls had their own consoles, their parents saw no need to buy two copies of the same game.

"Unless one of you has fifty dollars hidden away, you can either play it together, or you can take turns with it," they said when Sally and Darcy each demanded their own copy.

The matter was settled with a coin toss that Darcy won, and Sally went to her room to sulk. Later, unable to help herself, Sally ventured into Darcy's room to watch her play the opening scenes and got sucked into the story and graphics. They both created the character together and made decisions through discussion and took turns playing the action scenes while exploring the apocalyptic Capital Wasteland together.

That was when Sally realized there was a kindred spirit in Darcy who understood the hold a game can have over someone. To fall in love with a digital world and the characters inside of it and to immerse yourself in the gameplay, the satisfaction of success, and the fury of failure. To pine for a delayed release only to be disappointed by the unfulfilled promises of the developers.

And here there was no screen in front of her nor a controller in her hand. She could imagine this was a dream for many people to be inside a fantasy realm straight out of a Tolkien or George R.R. Martin book, but the stakes were too real. Twice, Naomi had almost been killed, Mina and Darcy kidnapped, and she still felt the aches from fighting Cut Throats the day before.

Were they stuck here forever, or was there a way back home? These thoughts rolled through her mind over and over and she was certain the same question was troubling Darcy and Mina. Naomi, however, was too busy enjoying herself, actually skipping as if they were on the way to a merry picnic or festival.

Just as Darcy predicted, Mina and Naomi were adept at finding food. More than once, Naomi spotted some edible berries or wild fruit by walking a bit off the road and once Mina spotted a wild rabbit. Naomi ran it down with her high Monk speed, but it was a task to convince her to let them eat it for lunch. Mina, shocked at herself, set up the campfire and knew how to properly prepare and cook the rabbit on sticks leaning over the flames. Between the rabbit, berries, and wild fruit, there was just enough to ease their hunger pains for a while.

***

The more Tom traveled with these women, the more he knew they weren't from Farron or Saige nor anywhere that he knew of for that matter. Being a prince, he had been taught geography, culture, and been exposed to numerous foreigners and their customs, but these women were beyond his comprehension. The way they thought, spoke, acted, and saw the world was alien to him.

Darcy, the so-called cleric of Shantra, didn't know funeral rites and didn't pray over every meal, nor did she hold herself with a religious superiority he had come to attribute with that order. He would have believed her a fraud if it wasn't for the fact that he had seen her use divine magic, so she must have Shantra's favor despite her irreverent demeanor and lack of grace.

The barbarian woman wasn't like any tribesman he had ever seen, and he had met several during his travels. They spoke very little of the Common Tongue, if at all, and had an aversion of outsiders. The Tribespeople held their heads with strict pride in stoic silence, but Mina was the complete opposite. She doubted herself and wasn't ashamed to show discomfort, fear, or—what was most sinful in the eyes of her people—weakness.

Naomi, a girl who was almost a woman, acting with the spirit of someone years younger than herself; she fought with the skill of those from the east, but she lacked their discipline. Being nearly killed by a werewolf and fighting through a horde of bandits would leave its mark on any girl, but Naomi treated it like a tussle in the courtyard with a playmate. And she was ready for more with a ferocity that only the strongest of knights could hope to match.

And then there was Sally, the beautiful half-elf woman. He knew of half-elves living in the slums of the capital who joined gangs or bandits to eke out a living as poor souls who belong to neither world. The women were highly sought for bordellos or as mistresses for the nobility. Despite their elven blood, the pockets of elven communes in Saige had very little use or room for those who shared human blood. The half-elves were a sad, lonely race with no home that welcomed them.

But Sally was different: she often acted surprised when her background was mentioned, as if she had forgotten she was a half-elf. The relationship with her stepsister was warm and affectionate, with none of the shame most families would have for a member of non-human blood. They chatted freely, even laughed together, and teased each other, and it reminded him of the time he spent with Maureen.

Tom's sister had been a free-spirited girl who believed herself human until she turned eight. He was the only family she had, as Tom's father made no time for her and her mother had died in childbirth. Being the youngest of three sons of the king, with no prospects of inheriting the throne, Tom was set aside, almost discarded to his mother's estate. Maureen made life interesting with her games and imagination and when she died, it had been a wound that never healed. Perhaps, if she had been openly accepted, then she could have led a happier life or received more care when she became ill. Perhaps she would be alive now.

In honor of her memory, Tom had led the peace effort with Saige, a neighboring country that had an open acceptance of non-humans, even electing them to low positions of power. Many elves, dwarves, and halflings had made their home in Saige to enjoy the many freedoms and privileges denied them in Farron.

It would make sense to him if Sally had grown up in Saige, but according to Sally and her friends that wasn't the case. He didn't know what to make of the women until it came to him in an epiphany. They weren't what they appeared to be. In Mina, he saw a tribeswoman, but she didn't act like one. Darcy was far from being pious or religious. And Sally didn't have the defeat or anger of a shunned hybrid caste. None of them were what they appeared to be.

He thought back to when he tried to kiss Sally and regretted it. It had been the wine that lowered his inhibition. Being rejected stung, but he was most taken aback by the shock and confusion in her eyes. As if she were astounded that he wanted to kiss her and didn't know how to respond to it. A woman that beautiful must have been kissed a few times in her life.

Tom wasn't a man to force his attentions where they were not welcomed, yet, it was hard to fight the desire to be close to her. The sunlight played on hair that hung like a waterfall of gold on delicate shoulders. She moved with the grace of a dancer and had the courage of a warrior. Standing in the face of danger, Sally blocked McRando from retreating, determined to end the fight then and there, and she'd launched herself onto a werewolf, thrusting both blades into his hide over and over.

Tom admired the Rogue, and was growing fond of her. Maybe during the course of their journey together, she would lower her walls and become more open about herself.

***

"Do you think Mom and Dad are looking for us?" Sally asked. It was late in the day, the descending sun had nearly met the tree line of the horizon.

"Knowing them, they probably have an Amber Alert out for us even though we're in our twenties," Darcy said, but her expression held a twinge of sorrow at the thought of their parents worrying. "I'm worried about Gina. She was in the living room studying when I—I disappeared. It must have freaked her out."

"Knowing her, she's probably out looking for you," Sally said kindly, remembering the feisty redhead Darcy had moved in with last month.

"Let's focus on finding a good place to camp off the road," Darcy said shrugging off the brooding moment. "Can you go with Mina and find one while we take a rest?"

"You sure you want to make camp now? It's still daylight."

"It's going to take time to set up camp, and everyone is getting winded. The earlier we turn in, the earlier they can get going in the morning," Darcy said, shouldering her cloak. "Don't worry, we made excellent time today, and tomorrow we'll be at River's Edge. Why don't you go hunt with Mina? We don't have enough leftovers from lunch to make a decent dinner."

Sally arched a brow. "Wishing you hadn't made us throw out the rations?"

"No, wishing I had the create food and water spell," Darcy retorted.

Sally wasn't sure if she was being serious or joking. "Why not send Naomi and Mina together?"

"Because it's getting late and it's going to be dark soon and Mina doesn't have low-light vision."

"Ah, sure," Sally nodded and called Mina over, and they left the road together.

Mina was mindful of where she stepped, while Sally had Rogue's instinct of moving without sound. They moved silently among the trees that cast long dark shadows over them. Sally realized the sun was setting faster than she had expected, making Darcy's call to make camp so soon a valid one. Mina paused and held up a hand, stopping Sally and with one finger to her lips, she pointed upward at a large bird pecking away at foliage near a bush. Its dark feathers mingled so well with the background that Sally had missed it, even with her elven vision.

Slowly, Mina took a sling and stone from her hip. It had been part of the supply package Darcy had blackmailed from Smiley Pete. Upon receiving it, Mina declared she had no idea of how to use it until Darcy prompted her to take a few practice shots at some flying birds. She had missed each time but still had been surprised by how close she had come. Maybe with a bigger target and her Survival skill, she might pull this off.

Sally crouched low, fearful that her growling belly, triggered by the thought of cooked fowl, would alarm the bird. It kept pecking away at something in the grass, completely oblivious of them. Mina loaded the smooth stone into the sling, and after weighing it, began to swing it in a small loop above her head. Never taking her eyes off the bird, she let loose the rock. The bird died instantly as its small head was impacted by the missile and Sally whooped with arms in the air as if Mina had performed a touchdown.

"That was awesome!" Sally declared as she broke through the bushes to collect their dinner. It looked like a cross between a chicken and turkey with long tail feathers and large wings. "This should feed everyone."

"Thanks," Mina said, putting the sling back on her belt. "Three days ago, I was studying for a chemistry exam, and now I'm out here hunting wild birds for dinner. I never thought to ask, but what was your job before you got here?"

"Oh, me? I'm a freelance editor," Sally said, carefully picking up the heavy bird by the leg. "People send me editorials, college papers, and novels to proofread and edit. I also work part time as a secretary for my Dad's office. What were you studying to be?"

"A doctor," Mina replied, looking almost wistful. "I'm still in my first semester of medical school, so I don't know yet what kind of doctor I'll be. I'm thinking of either cardiologist or rheumatologist. My dad wants me to be a family doctor, but the real money is in being a specialist, especially cardiologist."

"Well, do what you think suits you best for you." Sally pushed through some bushes, the bird swinging from her hand. "Look over here. You think this is a good spot for a camp?"

It was a small glade with tall grass, but it was surrounded by a dense copse of trees that offered privacy. There was a tall gnarled tree with firm roots bursting from the earth, which were large enough to be used as seats.

"This is a good sp—" Mina went silent, her head raised and dark eyes scanning the trees.

Sally went still, holding her breath and looking about frantically. A chill was creeping down her spine. "What is it?"

"I…I thought I heard something. It must have been my imagination," Mina said slowly. She blinked, shaking her head to shake off the sudden alarm. "There's nothing out there, at least, I don't think so."

"Maybe we should find somewhere else?" Sally suggested, still eyeing the copse warily.

"We could, but it'll be dark soon," Mina said with a quick glance at the sky. "Then, it'll be harder to find another place, we might not find one at all."

"That's oddly brave of you…" Sally said.

"If there's something out there, I rather face it with the others and a campfire, instead of it coming across us alone in the dead of night."

"That makes sense," Sally admitted. She gave the area a quick scan but saw nothing worrying. Maybe whatever it was that alarmed them had left or, better yet, it was just their imagination fueled by being in this world.

She gave her log a quick glance.

Sneak Check: Success!

After doing a quick scan of the log, she noticed that now all the skills checks were listed. There was nothing for Perception, Charm, Deceit or Intimidate. So had she never used those skills? Wait, she intimidated the Cut Throat into telling them where the hideout was, but it wasn't listed. Odd. She'd have to ask Darcy about that later.

***

Night fell by the time they finished setting up camp. Mina cleaned the bird while Naomi and Darcy started the fire. There was no need for tinder as Darcy simply pointed two fingers at the pile of wood and cast Divine Flame. The wood burst into flames, much to Naomi's delight, and she kept the fire fed with twigs and chips until it lit up the camp.

Sally stretched out her bedroll, trying to ignore her hungry stomach. She never went long without something to eat as her pantry was always stocked with food, and delivery was just a phone call away. If Mina hadn't gotten the bird, then their dinner would have been a few slowly chewed mouthfuls. Sally missed the real world where food was readily available from the fridge, store, or restaurant and she had a greater appreciation of them now that she was living hand to mouth.

Once bellies were sated, mouths opened in yawns, Darcy asked who wanted to take the first watch. Since Naomi was already asleep, curled up on her bedroll like a kitten, she was out. Feeling that Mina had already done her part by getting the bird for supper, Sally volunteered.

Sally passed the time of her watch studying her character screen until she heard Tom calling her name. Dropping the screen, she looked over to where he was sitting up on his bedroll, an arm's length away. "What were you looking at?"

"The stars," she said dumbly. "What is it?"

"Just wanted to talk."

She stiffened, her hands tightening on her knees. Was he trying to come onto her again? "You should really go to sleep. Darcy is going to browbeat us hard to get to River's Edge tomorrow."

"Yes, you need to get to Everguard in time to cure Naomi before the full moon," She opened her mouth to protest, but he held up a gentle hand. "No, please, it's alright. I saw the girl get bit myself, and I assumed that was why you've all been giving her these worried looks since yesterday."

Since he already knew about it and didn't seem disturbed, she asked, "Is there a cleric there that can help her?"

"Yes, perhaps a dozen. Everguard is a large city with many temples for different faiths. Once we meet with my uncle, I can arrange for one to cure Naomi within the hour."

"That's kind of you," Sally said, realizing she didn't know what they would do after they cured Naomi and claimed Darcy's money. The plan was to look for other players, but how?

"My uncle's manor has plenty of rooms for everyone, so you'll be very comfortable," he continued.

It would make things easier to have a place waiting for them when they arrived. What if Darcy's money wasn't there after all? Where would they stay? She certainly didn't fancy sleeping in the streets of a crime-infested city.

"I'll have to talk to Darcy about it. She might already have plans for where we'll be staying," Sally said. "I appreciate your offer, though."

"It's the least I can do. I would still be in that cell were it not for you," Tom said, watching her carefully.

The fire had died down to embers, but with her low-light vision, she could easily see the affection in his eyes, and it troubled her. Was he offering them a place to stay to be close to her? Was he going to try something else now? Stop it, she told herself, she was being paranoid. Tom had been a gentleman since they first met, and they have been through so much together that she ought to trust him.

He was just a character in a game, a Wikipedia entry about *Shadow's Deep* lore. Yet, here he was talking to her, had befriended Naomi, took orders from Darcy graciously, and fought side by side with Mina. And he had almost kissed her last night.

Sally didn't know how to feel about that and wished it hadn't happened so she could be more relaxed around him now and not be looking for ulterior motives. She never had to be on guard around a guy before as boys had never been interested in her in high school or college. It was the tall, leggy pretty girls they were interested in, not the quiet wallflower chubby girl.

It's not me he wants. He's attracted to this shell I inhabit. If he saw the real me, he would run in the opposite direction. That's why I can't be attracted to him because I know he would have nothing to do with the real me.

"Saving you was an accident," Sally said, feeling a bit annoyed now. "I was trying to find Darcy and Mina."

He shrugged. "It was a happy accident."

If she could have, she would have stapled her mouth shut or kicked her own ass to keep the words from leaving her mouth. "Like your sister?"

God, why did I say that?

The silence filled the air between them, almost suffocating her as shame filled her throat.

"I'm sorry," Sally said, feeling tears prick her eyes. "I shouldn't have said that. You were trying to be kind, and I'm a bitch."

"Be quiet," he said harshly.

A tear rolled down her cheek. "I'm sorry."

"No, listen! Did you hear that?"

Sally pricked her ears and listened. At first, she heard nothing, and that was it. The crickets had stopped chirping, and the owl that had been asking its eternal question had gone silent. There was a stillness in the air, now charged with a kinetic energy that threatening to burst. Chills swept down between her shoulders, and she slowly drew her rapier and dagger.

"Darcy," she whispered in a low voice. Rising slowly to her feet, she stepped over the embers and scanned the edge of the glade. Nothing so far, but she felt it out there watching them. "Wake up."

Darcy curled up in her bedroll, but after a few prods with Sally's foot, she was awake. "What?"

"Something's out there," Sally repeated, lowering herself. "I don't know what it is, but it's watching us."

"Shit," Darcy hissed, rising to her feet. "Get the others up and get that fire burning. Maybe if it sees us all up, it'll go away."

Tom added kindling to the fire while Sally went to rouse Mina, who was already awake, as if she had sensed the danger in her sleep. It took Sally several prods to get Naomi up as the girl kept rolling away from her boot. Soon, all that could be heard was the fire crackling and their own hurried breathing and beating hearts. They stood in a circle facing outward with their backs to the fire, providing a wide swath of light. Their eyes searched the dark trees but could see nothing.

"Sally, do you see anything?" Darcy said in a low voice.

"No," she said, frantically looking. She could see several yards beyond the edge of the light, but there was nothing there. "Should we throw out a torch?"

"Yeah, we'll be able to see better in a forest fire," Mina muttered darkly.

"Stay on guard," Tom said. "If it wants to attack us, it has to come into the light first."

Not one second later, Tom was proven correct.

A streak of gray dashed between the trees like a missile towards Mina. She barely had time to step to the side as the snarling wolf's teeth grazed her leg. It could have been a severe injury if she hadn't reacted so quickly. The wolf snapped its jaws as if furious for missing and immediately lunged for Darcy with razor teeth and murder in its eyes. Before it could reach its mark, Naomi barreled into it from the side and both girl and wolf rolled away in a ball of flashing teeth and flying fists.

"Naomi!" Sally shrieked and her scream was echoed by the others.

A second wolf, black fur and amber eyes, cut through the darkness and caught Tom by the wrist. The prince howled, the blade fell from his nerveless fingers. Sally leaped over the fire, and as she landed on the other side, she shoved the rapier between the wolf's ribs. It crumbled and died with a choked yelped. Backing away, Tom held his wrist with one hand, using his sleeve to stave the bleeding.

A glance suggested he was okay, so Sally turned her attention to what was happening with Naomi, yet before she could help the Monk another wolf appeared, lips curled back revealing rows of sharp teeth. Sally positioned the dagger and rapier and waited. If it leaped at her, she would go low and cut open its belly. If it charged, she could sidestep it and get it from the side.

Neither happened, for when it charged her, a gout of flame appeared along its left flank, catching its fur on fire. It screamed as fur and flesh burned. It took off in a blur of light from the glade. Darcy was standing with two fingers pointed at where the wolf had charged, her mouth still forming the word of power used to utter the cantrip.

Screams drew their attention. Mina was standing over where Naomi and the wolf still fought. She had dropped the greataxe, and with both hands, she grabbed the wolf by the scruff and lifted it off the girl. Naomi was lying on her back, panting and bleeding from several places.

The wolf twisted, trying to flip over to tear into Mina's arm, but the Barbarian held it high above her head and heaved it across the glade. It smacked into a tree with a crack and landed on the ground with its back broken. Darcy put the creature out of its misery with a swing of her mace.

They all remained standing, too afraid to move or too shocked to do so. All of them looked about the trees, waiting for the next attack, but none came. Mina bent down to collect Naomi from the ground while Darcy hurried over to heal her. The girl's arms and shoulders were covered in scratches and bites with a gash above her right eye.

"Sweet Jesus, Naomi, you didn't have to fight a wolf with your bare hands," Darcy moaned, seeing the injuries.

"You didn't notice, but I bit off a chunk of its ear," Naomi said through bloody teeth.

"Just hold still," With a single spell, the Monk's injuries were healed, replaced with puffy pink skin. Then Darcy turned to Tom who was still holding his wrist. "How is it?"

"Deep and painful," Tom said as blood dotted the ground at his feet.

"C'mere and I'll take care of it for you." One healing spell later, Tom's wrist was tender, but no longer bleeding. "Sally, Mina, are you two okay?"

Sally checked herself and found no injuries. "I'm fine."

"Mina? Mina! Are you okay?" Darcy looked frantically at the Barbarian who was bent double panting.

Her broad shoulders heaved as she dragged in deep breaths, coming down from the Rage she entered moments earlier. "Just need a few moments to catch my breath…are they gone?"

"I think it's over," Sally scanned the trees but saw nothing. The tension in the air was gone with the danger. Relief eased the tension in her shoulders, and she almost sagged onto the ground. "God, I just want to sleep and never wake up."

Chapter 15

RiVER'S EDGE

The sun was just making its appearance when they broke camp and left the glade, eager to be on their way. There was no mention of breakfast, as none of them could find their appetites after the attack, and they wished to leave that place as quickly as possible.

Naomi was her usual merry self, as if she hadn't gotten into a dog fight with a wolf. Mina's injury was only the shallow cut on her leg, which had long since stopped bleeding. It didn't seem to trouble her, but she walked with a slight slump in her shoulders. Sally and Tom kept a careful watch as they left, no longer striding with cool confidence.

Yesterday had been more cheerful and easygoing, but today a cloud hung over them as they all scanned the forest for any wolves, and the slightest movement startled them. Everyone chastised Naomi from straying too far, and Mina didn't feel confident about leaving the road to search for food.

We had thought the dangers were over. Darcy thought as midday drew near. *We had dealt with the Cut Throats, and we let ourselves be lulled into a false sense of security, which the wolves tore to pieces. None of us are safe as long as we're in this world.*

Darcy was thinking of how she wanted to stop the group and give them a much-needed pep talk and tell them it was just a random encounter and praise them for handling it so well. They needed to know that everything was going to be okay.

Yet, her own hands were shaking. It was easier to believe all would be well when she was on the other end of the monitor or seeing everything through character sheets and miniatures. This was real, and they could be hurt or worse.

Sally walked up beside Darcy, shouldering her backpack and wearing her hood up. "There's something I noticed about the log."

"What?" Lord help if there was something else the System was doing to make their lives miserable.

"I notice that it'll tell if you failed succeed a Sneak or a Swim check and others, but it doesn't say anything about Perception checks. I'm sure I must have passed that skill check several times since the Incident...or at least failed it yesterday."

She told Darcy about the cold feeling she and Mina had experienced yesterday in the clearing. Darcy listened and nodded with her mouth set in a grim line. "I was afraid of that. I hate to say it, but the System is actually being a good Game Master."

"What do you mean by that?" Sally paused for a moment to check the forest to her left and when there was no sign of any wolf, she caught up to Darcy.

"Well, let me explain it like this," Darcy said, getting into her lecturing mode. "I'm running a game and the players are in a room. One of them wants to look for treasure or a secret room. I tell them to roll an Perception check and they roll it. If they roll high enough and there is a treasure or secret room, I tell them where it's located and what it looks like. However, if they roll the check and failed it, I wouldn't tell them they failed the roll, I'd say they didn't find anything."

"I see. You keep it ambiguous so they don't know whether there is something to find or not. Is it the same with Charm and Deceit?"

"Pretty close. Another example is a player trying to determine if an NPC is lying to them. They would roll a Perception check. They roll higher than the NPC's Deceit check, I'd tell them the NPC is trying to bullshit them. However, if they roll lower, then I'd say their character believes the NPC is telling the truth. I wouldn't advertise whether they failed or passed a social check because roleplaying is supposed to reflect real life," Darcy explained, looking ahead at the road, but not really seeing it.

"Think about the celebrities you and I liked until we heard they had harassed and assaulted women. They were so charming they fooled fans into thinking they were cool when they were really assholes. Remember in high school, when I had a crush on Beverly Kemp? I thought she was the coolest girl in school until I found out she was putting cigarettes out on the back of middle-schooler's necks between classes. Damn, I wished somebody told me I had failed my Perception check on her so I could have spared myself the heartbreak."

"Jesus, I remember that. Whatever happened to her after they expelled her?"

"She's shacked up in a trailer with more kids than she can afford and a boyfriend who is maybe the father of one or two of them," Darcy said, waving a hand to dismiss the memory of Beverly. "Back to the topic, the System will keep a log of checks that are clear cut about whether we failed or succeed like Climbing or Swimming, but anything that can be ambiguous will be left out."

They walked on in silence for a while. Darcy found herself missing her car. It'd be a tight squeeze, but all five of them could travel in it. She'd be sitting in the driver's seat, Mina would have to take the passenger side as she was so big. Then Tom, Sally, and Naomi could squeeze in together in the back. Then this five-day journey would be done within an hour, maybe two, tops.

"Then there would have to be a second log," Sally said, breaking up her fantasy.

"Sorry, pardon?" Darcy said, refocusing on Sally.

"Well, if there is a log that we can see, then there should be a second log with checks that we can't see."

"That's possible," Darcy said with a shrug.

"Then, my next question is, why keep a log, a recording of all our failures and successes? To go back and review later?"

Darcy pondered this for a moment. "I'm not sure what you're getting at."

"You said that an NPC rolls a Deceit check that the players have to roll against. Who's rolling for the NPC? Who determines how high the NPC's Deceit skill is?" Sally said, thin golden brows knitting in deep thought. "I don't think it's the System that needs a log, it's whoever is running the System that needs it."

"That's a plausible theory," Darcy said, getting tired thinking about it. "But we're just going around in circles with this. We just don't have enough information to come up with anything other than theories. Maybe other players can give us more details. Right now, let's focus on getting to Everguard. Later, you and I will sit down and have a really hard think about this."

"Oh, that reminds me. Tom said we could stay in his uncle's manor in Everguard."

Darcy perked up. "That's nice. We'll have a back-up if the money isn't there."

Sally grimaced and looked away. "But I think he might have changed his mind after last night."

"What? He thinks we summoned up the wolves?"

"No, I…I was kinda mean to him last night." Then she told Darcy what had happened before the wolves attacked.

Darcy stared at Sally appalled. "Why would you say such a shitty thing to him?"

"I don't know. It just came out."

"You need to go apologized to him right now."

"I did…just before the wolves attacked."

"Jesus Christ, Sally, I know you have bad social skills, but I thought you had better manners than that."

"I'm sorry. Tom makes me nervous, and you know how I get."

"Don't apologize to me," Darcy growled, glowering at Sally. "You need to go smooth things over. Don't burn bridges we might need later. We have no clue if we're ever going to get home again, and having a royal prince in our corner can make things a lot easier for us."

Darcy being angry with her hurt more than Sally would care to admit. "What do you want me to do? Hook up with him?"

"Why not?" the Cleric muttered. "It might do you some good."

Sally bright red, and it wasn't just from the anger. "He's not interested in me. He wants this!" She motioned at her body with both hands. "If he saw my real fat ass, he'd run in the opposite direction."

"What does it matter? It's not like he's going to follow you back into the real world," Darcy retorted. "Look, you have the body thousands of women have made themselves miserable to get, and you're not enjoying it? I'm not saying you should marry him or anything, but he seems like a nice guy. What's it going to hurt?"

"You mean to lead him on?" Sally couldn't believe what Darcy was suggesting.

"Set some boundaries first and tell him it's just for funsies. He's a prince of a kingdom that hates elves he would know it can't go any further than a fling."

"Okay, okay, sure, I'll go back there and fuck him dry, I just need one thing," Sally said before thrusting a hand out in front of Darcy.

Darcy looked down at the empty palm. "What?"

"A condom."

The Cleric's face went blank. Her mouth opened to speak, but no words came.

"That's right," Sally said, lowering her hand. "I don't know about you, but I don't want to get pregnant in a world where the number one cause of death for women is giving birth. And if this world is going to treat me, a half-elf, like shit, I don't think a quarter elf kid is going to have it any easier."

She had caught Darcy completely caught off guard, and Sally took some pleasure in that. It wasn't often that she could shake up Darcy.

"It might not work like that..."

"Why wouldn't it?" Sally said, not letting up. "All my other bodily functions work here. I've bled, cried, pissed, and sweated here as I did in the real world. I bet if we're here long enough, I'll have a period. Why wouldn't I get pregnant too? And since you're such an expert in this world, tell me, what sort of birth control do they have here? Other than the pull it out method?"

"Alright, alright, you have a point," Darcy conceded, but not to be put off too much, she insisted, "You still have to make things right with him."

"And I will," Sally promised.

They didn't stop long for a midday meal. Instead, Mina passed out what was left of the bird, which was just a few bites for everyone. They ate in silence, still watchful of the forest and the road while Sally stole glances at Tom, wondering how the hell she was going to apologize. Before, he had been the one to initiate conversations between them, but this time she knew she would have to be the one to do so, and she had no idea how. Should she walk beside him and say "hi"? Or just come right out with an apology? What should she say or do if he became angry? Maybe should she wait until it blew over?

The one thing she did decide was that whatever she said or did, it could wait until they arrived in River's Edge. Maybe by then, once they had a good meal in their bellies and some wine, he might be more malleable towards an apology than he would be on the road.

***

Naomi was becoming bored with the group who were all slouching about as if their mothers had just died. Sure, wolves attacked them, but that happened all the time in the game, and why should it be any different in this world? Even Tom seemed down. Naomi suspected that Sally had been mean to him again. What was wrong with Sally? Tom was cool and liked her, and she acted like he had cooties.

The one that seemed worst off was Mina. If she looked any lower, she would be dragging her belly on the ground. Naomi had no idea what was troubling her as she had been magnificent the previous night, tossing that wolf like it was a dirty dish towel, and she didn't even get hurt enough to warrant a healing spell from Darcy. Naomi hung back until she was walking side by side with Mina and then walked backwards so she could look into Mina's face. From their height difference, Naomi could look directly up at Mina's downcast face.

"Why so glum, chum?" Naomi asked. It was something she and her brother said when the other was sad.

Mina arched her eyebrows. "Naomi, you're going to trip if you do that."

Why did everyone have to scold her as if they were her mother?

Be careful, Naomi, or you'll hurt yourself.

Don't do that.

Watch what you're doing.

Would you listen to me?

"I'm not going to trip," Naomi said wryly. "And what about you? You're going to run into something if you keep your head down like that."

Mina rolled her eyes. "What do you want?"

"Just wanted to say you were awesome last night."

The Barbarian made a derisive noise through her teeth and looked away. "What I did was not awesome. I got pissed off and broke an animal's back. A freakin' wolf, for God's sake. They're a protected species."

Naomi considered this for only a few seconds. "I think that law only applies if you're hunting them, not if they're hunting you."

"That's not what I meant. I mean…I hate this Rage thing." Mina's face darkened as she remembered the sudden fury that overtook her when she saw Naomi wrestling with the wolf. "I didn't summon it or activate it. It just happened on its own."

"So? It's a Barbarian thing," Naomi said unconcerned. "I thought about taking a level in Barbarian so I could have Rage too, but the Monk gets something cool every level, so I decided to stick with it."

Mina shook her head and said nothing as she knew Naomi wouldn't understand. It wasn't Raging that scared her. It was what she wanted to do during under its effect: she wasn't just angry with the wolf for fighting with Naomi, but at Naomi for carelessly putting herself in danger. When she reached into the pile of fur and girl, she was going to tear apart whichever she grabbed first. In her red filled mind's eye, she saw herself lifting Naomi and breaking her across her knee like a stick. It had been sheer luck that it had been the wolf and not Naomi.

What happened if she should go into another Rage and this time, she injured someone in the party?

***

It was late afternoon by the time they came across the overturned cart and a dead horse on the side of the road. The horse's mangled legs were tangled in the reins, and its exposed flesh drew flies and carrion birds, hiding the body with their wings until they took flight. A terrible smell hung in the air, and they kept their distance with hands over their noses.

"What should we do?" Sally asked.

"There might be loot?" Naomi suggested.

This earned her several severe looks and Mina glowered at her. "We can't just loot it. It's not ours. It would be stealing."

"But it's not stealing if the owners are dead," Naomi said pointedly.

"We don't know that," Tom said. "Someone could be injured and needing help."

"I do need help!"

The voice was muffled, but loud enough to startle them. They looked around but still couldn't see anyone until Naomi took noticed of the scratching from beneath the cart. Together, Mina and Tom lifted it to reveal the man trapped beneath. He was an older man whose balding head was turning gray; he had a large bulbous nose set above thin lips. Once the man was clear of the cart, he laid on the road, panting, his ankle swollen so much his shoe was squeezing the skin.

"Thank the Gods, I thought I would die beneath that wretched thing," he moaned as Mina and Darcy helped him to his feet and wailed when he saw the dead horse. "Oh, no! Poor Shawn! For a good creature to have such a fate…"

There wasn't anything Darcy could do for the horse, but she could help the man with a healing spell. The swollen red skin reduced in size until it was back to normal. He tested it on the ground, giving it his full weight, and then he beamed in gratitude at Darcy. "Thank you, dear Sister. I'm as good as new and eager to be home before the wolves come back."

At the mention of wolves, Sally glanced around as if one would show up right then. "Is that what happened?"

"Aye, miss, wolves, and in broad daylight too."

The man introduced himself as Erns, a local merchant from River's Edge. The previous day he had been on his way to a nearby farm for produce when the wolves attacked the horse and cart. Shawn panicked and ran off the road which threw Erns from the buckboard and twisted his ankle when he landed. The cart overturned, taking Shawn with it, likely breaking a leg that prevented the horse from fleeing. Hearing the pursuing wolves coming closer and unable to run or defend himself, Erns crawled to the cart and managed to bring it down over him before they arrived. They ignored the upside-down cart in favor of the easy meal of a fallen horse.

"Poor horse," Naomi said sadly. Sally couldn't tell if she was sadder for the horse than she was for not getting to loot the cart.

"I spent the night and day beneath under there thinking this is where I would meet my end," Erns said, taking Darcy's hand in his to express his gratitude. "How can I repay you for saving my life?"

"We're on our way to River's Edge," Darcy told him, a bit embarrassed by the man's indebtedness. "If you can take us there, that will more than enough repayment."

"Take you to River's Edge? Of course! Of course! Follow me!"

***

Erns took them along a path that wasn't on the map. It branched off from the main road, having been created from many years of carts journeys and traveling villagers. Erns explained it was a shortcut that led directly to the village, cutting through the forest and along the river where the village had been settled (hence the name River's Edge). It was a fishing and farming community that used the river as a means to carry their goods to other villages downstream and, further along toward the sea, was Everguard. The path cut nearly an hour off their travel time, and the village was a welcome sight for all of them. Especially since Erns had been telling them about the trouble the village had been facing.

"Usually it's more lively than this," Erns told them as they neared the village. Only a few people were outside their homes doing necessary chores. They greeted Erns as he passed, but all the while, they looked around with nervous eyes. Their group drew some looks, but the people were more focused on the trees beyond the village.

"It started two days ago," he had told them. He spoke jovially as if they were his dearest friends of many years, but now his voice took on a worried edge. "We've had our usual share of trouble with wolves like any village. The occasional beast would steal a goat or a goose that strayed too far from the village, but since two days ago, they've been attacking people. They stole the Miller's son right from his mother's arms, killed all of Master Alveres's livestock, and chased children into their homes. Why, the night before a wolf even smashed through the blacksmith's window and would have savaged his wife if Smith had not his hammer in hand. And many have suffered injury defending their homes and families. The Mayor has sent word requesting the aid of the kingsmen, but I believe it would be better to hire hunters to rid us of the creatures."

"We were attacked by wolves last night," Naomi piped up, despite Darcy's to sign for Naomi to be quiet. "Three of them attacked us while we were camping, but we killed them before they could kill us."

Erns looked impressed. "Four women and a man camping alone in the woods. It seems strange, but you'll hear no more from me about it. As far as I am concerned, you are good folk who saved my life. And able to handle yourselves well, I see." He eyed their weapons and their armor of leather and metal.

Since her hood had been up when they came across Erns's cart, Sally intended to keep it over her head for as long as they were in River's Edge. Erns seemed friendly, but she had the feeling that his cordial manner would turn sour if he knew one of them was a half-elf.

"I'm sorry about the Miller's son," Darcy said. "Was anyone else killed?"

"Oh, yes! We have lost a few poor souls. Master Frest, the baker, was found dead along with his horses. The tavern keeper's brother, Den, has suffered such a severe mauling that he died yesterday morning. And Madame Senna was killed in her own home! The door was forced open, and her throat torn out. Gods above, I can only pray that it happened so quickly she didn't suffer."

Sally noticed Darcy's face tightening and could tell something was bothering her, and it wasn't just the loss of life. Now she had a sinking suspicion that the attack from last night was more than just a random encounter. Was this a questline they were walking into?

It was midday by the time they arrived at the tavern. Like Smiley Pete's tavern, it was two stories and made of stone rather than wood. There was, however, no warm smell of cooking food or spiced wine, which they all found themselves missing.

"Tell Master Benson I sent you to him, and he'll treat you right," Erns promised with a wink. "I'd take you to him myself, but my wife is home worrying for me, and I have to see about replacing my horse. Poor Shawn."

"We're sorry about the horse," Darcy said politely. "And thank you for bringing us here. It would have been a long trip without your help."

"Think nothing of it, my dear, it's a small price for saving my life."

There were only a few people inside drinking or eating: all eyes looked up as they entered, and curious stares followed them as they found a table. The man behind the bar, Master Benson, carried the usual weight attributed to all tavern owners, but he had far more hair than Pete and wore his weight well. When Darcy approached the bar, he regarded her with icy blue eyes that lacked the friendly warmth that Erns had carried for them.

"Hello," Darcy said, taking the friendly approach. "Master Erns sent us. We need some rooms."

Benson regarded her armor and face with an arched brow. "How many are some?"

"Two or three?" she said hopefully.

"You can have two," Benson said stoutly. "Four gold."

Darcy was impressed with herself for maintaining a calm face. Two gold a room was a bit pricier than she had anticipated. She was hoping to spend two to three gold, with enough for rations and meals. "We, uh, helped Master Erns after wolves attacked him."

The innkeeper raised his eyebrows. "You saved Erns?"

"Yes sir, we did," Darcy said, feeling a bit relieved.

Then his eyes narrowed. "I hate that bastard. He plowed my sister and wouldn't marry her. Six gold!"

Darcy kept her teeth set in a tight grimace. So Master Erns wasn't as popular as he had believed himself to be. "Surely we can work something out."

"What's there to work out? Six gold and the rooms are yours for the night."

Darcy sighed, "How about just one room and meals for five?"

She left the counter with one gold coin left. The meals had cost extra, also for the sin of saving Erns' life. When she sat down beside Sally, she was in a foul mood. "Bad news. Erns is an asshole, and the innkeeper is a bigger one. We have to cram into one room and enjoy dinner because it's going to be slim pickings from here on out. We only have one gold piece left."

Sally's eyes widen. "Holy shit, that's all of our money. How big is the room?"

"Some of us are sleeping on the floor regardless of how big it is," Darcy said dourly.

Tom's face hardened, and he started to rise. "Perhaps I should speak with him. He is intentionally overpricing us."

"No, don't do anything. You'll only make it worse, and Sally, please, keep that hood up, or the price will skyrocket."

Sally secured her hood, tugging it down until it almost hid her eyes. "Fine, I'll be careful."

A skinny waif of a girl brought them bowls of grayish soup with bits of meat floating in it. Instead of mulled wine or cider, she set a pitcher of lukewarm water on the counter as if it were a bucket of filth and walked away without a curtsy nor smile.

Mina stirred the soup with a wooden spoon in dismay. "I don't think this is safe for human consumption."

"What is this? Dirty dishwater?" Sally was staring at the concoction in horror. As much as she hated Stinky Pete, he had least provided good food in his tavern.

Only Naomi was brave enough to venture a taste. She licked her spoon and winced. "It tastes like nasty feet."

From the corner of her eye, Sally saw that Darcy was about to boil. She reached out to touch her hand just as she was standing. "Don't. It'll be fine..."

"Screw that! That asswipe back there price gouges me and makes me pay two gold for food I wouldn't feed to a dog," Darcy said as she wrenched her hand free from Sally's.

Tom stood with his hand held out a placating hand towards the wrathful Cleric. "Let me speak to him. You're too angry."

Darcy almost growled at him. "I'll take care of it."

Sally stood, catching Darcy's arm and turning her around. "Stop, just stop it. Let Tom handle it. You go over there, and you'll get us run out of town."

She nodded at Tom for him to leave before Darcy could get away from her. Sally coaxed her stepsister to sit down while maintaining a grip on her. Darcy sat down, but it was with an exasperated sigh.

"Alright, I'm fine. You can let go of me," Darcy muttered, flexing her hands as if she wanted to choke someone.

"I will when Tom comes back. Right now, calm down and breathe through your nose or something."

"Are all the taverns in this world run by assholes? Stinky Pete sells out his customers, and now Benson cheats them." Darcy moaned, raking both hands through hair as if she could pull it out by the root.

"Let us just see what Tom says when he comes back," Sally said as she looked over her shoulder to see the prince standing at the counter, having a serious discussion with Benson. The tavern owner was shaking his head and had his thick arms crossed over his chest. It didn't look promising.

Sally leaned in and whispered. "In the game, did the River's Edge have a wolf problem?"

Darcy momentarily distracted from her fury, blinked, taken aback by the sudden change in topic. "Uh, no. Wolves are common random encounters, but there was never a quest line specifically involving them."

Catching onto where Sally was going, Mina leaned in whispering, "Erns said the problem with the wolves started two days ago. We've been in this world for two days. Coincidence?"

Darcy looked between then, her mouth forming to say no, but stopped, thinking. "I don't know. It might be, or it could be one of the differences between the actual game and this world. Things aren't happening as they should be, and I don't know if it's because of us or something else…where's Naomi?"

The three of them looked to where Naomi had been sitting just moments ago. Now there was only an empty chair.

"Mina, why didn't you keep an eye on her?" Darcy rounded on the Barbarian.

"What? No one told me to be responsible for her!" Mina blurted out.

"Go look for her and find her before she causes trouble!" Darcy said, nearly standing to try to loom over Mina. It was a failed effort as even sitting down Mina was still almost eye level with a standing Darcy.

Red-faced, Mina stood up and stormed through the doors, muttering something about leashes and how she was not someone's mother. The door slammed shut behind her, nearly rattling on the hinges. Sally flinched at the slam and turned back to see Darcy with her head in both hands.

"God, everything was going right yesterday," she moaned into her palms. "We made such good time yesterday, and I thought we would be okay until we got to Everguard. Then the wolves attacked us, and River's Edge turns out to be a pimple on the ass-end of nowhere, and now Naomi pulls a runner when we need to keep low the most."

"It'll be alright. Naomi couldn't have gone far, and Tom is smoothing things over with the innkeeper," Sally said, rubbing Darcy's shoulder. "You've done great to get us this far, and surely you didn't think we wouldn't run into problems along the way? You do this to yourself sometimes. You get so worked up, and get mad when it doesn't go the way you planned. Remember when you threw your *Dungeon Master's Guide* at Larry's head?"

Darcy raised her head to give Sally a mournful look. "I'd been planning that campaign for months, and he ruined everything by killing off the NPC that was the linchpin in the whole plot. He had this shit-eating grin on his face because he knew what he was doing. I'm glad I knocked out his teeth."

"Yeah, but remember, Dad grounded you for a whole month, and you had to help pay that Larry's dental bill for a whole year?" Sally gently reminded her. "When you get worked up like this, you do and say things you regret later. Okay, here comes Tom. Maybe he has some good news for us."

Tom looked at the empty seats. "Where's Mina and Naomi?"

"Naomi ran off, and Mina went to go look for her. What did the tavern owner have to say?"

Tom sat down across from them and didn't appear to have better news. "He's a decent sort, though gruff. He told me there's nothing to be done about the food because of the wolves. They attack anyone who leaves the village, and no one is willing to leave their homes unprotected to fetch supplies."

"So he wasn't full of it," Darcy mumbled. "What did he say about the rooms?"

"He won't lower the price, but he's willing to let us have another room if we do some work for him. Such as clean his chimney, chopping wood, and tidy the pantry."

Darcy and Sally gave him blank looks. They had grown up in the modern age with electric conveniences such as dishwashers, laundry machines, and vacuum cleaners and were blessed to have been born to families with disposable income that could hire home cleaners. The hard work that Tom was mentioning was inconceivable for them.

"How do you tidy a pantry?" Darcy asked dumbly. "I can wipe down counters and sweep the floor."

"I don't know how to chop wood," Sally said a bit stunned.

"And do chimneys really need cleaning? I thought it all turned into smoke and floated away," Darcy added.

Tom looked between the two of them and leaned in close. "I was hoping you knew. I'm a prince, remember? I had over a hundred servants clean for me."

Darcy rubbed her temples, thinking. "Let's wait until Mina and Naomi come back. Mina can handle the firewood, and didn't they have little boys go up the chimney and scrub them with soap and water? Naomi's little, she'll fit up there."

"But wasn't that unhealthy?" Sally seemed to recall there was a poem from William Blake about it. Something about coffins and angels, if she recalled correctly.

Darcy shrugged dismissively. "The girl survived being nearly bitten in half by a werewolf and being mauled by an angry wolf. I think she can handle some soot in her lungs."

***

The few people who were brave enough to go outdoors were giving Mina a generous berth, and that was just fine with her. She wasn't interested in interacting with the local populace any more than she absolutely had to. Right now, she wanted to find Naomi and wring her neck for running off.

No, no, no! She pushed the anger down, refusing to let it take hold. What if she Raged and went on a rampage like that giant green monster from the comics?

This wasn't her; she was not an angry person. She hated confrontations and always avoided conflict and drama. Her parents had taught her violence was never the solution and to compromise instead. And here she was in a magical world where she had to be violent to survive. Worse, it was expected of her because of her stupid class. The sooner they returned home, the better.

"Naomi! Where are you? Get out here now!" she called in a low growl. It was the tone of voice a person would use when they were angry with their dog. "If you don't get out here right now, I'm going to…to…put you in a time out."

She rounded a bend in the path between two buildings and saw a construction site. It was like someone was set up the frames of a building, but got bored and left to go do something else. The sides had been planked with lumber, and atop of it was the wooden frame of a tall steeple held up by a single pillar.

The structure creaked ominously as Mina drew closer and stared at it, taking in the means of construction. It had been thrown together through lackluster carpentry and barely supported itself. Her insight was odd as she never had any interest in architecture or house repair, so why was she seeing and noticing this at all? Damn, it was the game again. It had to be her Perception, but it was low with only plus one, probably Darcy would tell her that she had "rolled high."

A man was sitting on a stack of lumber, smoking a pipe, with a tool kit sitting discarded by his feet. Mina didn't see anyone else working on the construction, nor were there any barriers to tell people to keep their distance. What had drawn her attention, other than the evident construction hazards were the children playing within the empty husk. They were climbing through the windows and chasing each other in and out through the main doorway. Some of them were drawing on the wood with bits of charcoal, and a group of little girls were playing house with handmade dolls.

"Should those kids be playing in there?" Mina asked the man with the pipe.

He barely glanced at the kids. "They're not hurting anything. I'll paint over the drawings with fresh paint."

"It doesn't look sound enough for them to be crawling all over it like that," Mina ventured.

The man gave her a hard gaze with grey eyes set beneath bushy brows. "My family built all the houses in this village for the last five generations, and not one building has collapsed yet."

"Then you better go get them to fix this mess," Mina said, pointing at the frame. "It's swaying in the wind! It's a sneeze away from falling on those kids."

The man took his pipe from his mouth and spat on the ground. "I don't need a tribeswoman, whose people build their homes from mud and sticks, to tell me about my craft. If you think you can do better, then, by all means, the wood and my tools are over there. Show me how it's done." He kicked the box of tools towards her, and they scattered across the grass. The sound was loud enough to draw the attention of the kids who stopped playing to watch.

Mina stepped back, holding up her hands. "You don't have to be rude about it. I'll just go."

"You do that," the man snarled.

Mina turned on her heel and marched off. Her face was burning in embarrassment and anger. No, not anger, just humiliation. She wasn't angry at all. What was it to her if digital kids got crushed in a digital building built by some cranky old digital man.

And where the hell was Naomi?

At last, Mina saw Naomi knocking on the door of a large house at the far end of the street. Striding forward, Mina kept her hands from curling into fists and pushed away the images of wringing Naomi's neck.

"Naomi!" She said sternly as she approached the front steps.

Naomi looked over her shoulder with a hand still raised in a knocking motion when the door opened. A woman with graying, dark hair peered through the crack in the door. "Yes?"

Ignoring Mina, Naomi turned to the woman. "Is the mayor here, ma'am?"

"My husband is resting," the woman said, eyeing Naomi's scruffy appearance, and then she noticed Mina standing behind her. Her eyes widened, and she slightly closed the door a touch more. "What need have you of my husband?"

"I want to offer him our services as hunters," Naomi said.

The woman looked surprised, and she opened the door a bit more. "Are you hunters?"

"We killed some wolves last night on our way to River's Edge, and we heard they were causing problems for you."

Mina had no idea of what she could do to keep Naomi silent short of grabbing her and slapping a hand across her mouth. She hissed Naomi's name several times, but the girl kept plodding along.

"If I could have a few minutes of his time?"

The woman considered this for several moments. "One moment while I fetch my husband. Wait a moment, please."

The door closed, and they heard footsteps hurrying away. Mina bent down to speak into Naomi's ear. "What are you doing?"

"We need money. Darcy said we don't have enough money for rations to get us to Everguard. If we take on a quest, we'll get paid, and we might find some good loot." Naomi said back with a conspiratorial wink.

"You haven't had your fill of wolves after last night?" Mina hissed in disbelief. "You want to go looking for more?"

"It's part of the game. You go to a village, they got a problem that you have to solve, and they reward you with money or loot."

Wringing her hands, Mina said, "Naomi, this isn't a game. I mean…it is, but it doesn't work like that anymore. And you can't make decisions like this without talking to the others. Just tell the woman you made a mistake, and let's go back to the tavern."

The door burst open, and a bearded man leaned out from the door frame. "You're hunters? Genuine wolf hunters? Thank the gods that you've come. Please, come inside. There is much we must discuss."

***

"They better have been kidnapped, chopped up, and buried somewhere to be gone for so long," Darcy muttered, glaring into her soup as if she was holding it responsible.

Sally spooned some gruel into her mouth and grimaced. "Don't be like that. They'll come back soon." She was reassuring herself as much as she was Darcy. What if something had happened to them? What if they never came back?

It didn't seem as though Tom was enjoying his soup either. He ate each spoonful gracefully, but Sally noticed that he waited a bit between each swallow as if bracing himself. "We can go look for them if they don't come back soon."

And she still had to apologize to Tom for last night. Now she had even less of an appetite, and it had nothing to do with the food. Maybe she should talk to him now while Darcy looked for Mina and Naomi. Before she could make that suggestion, the door opened, and Naomi was practically skipping in while Mina trudged in behind her with a stricken look. Naomi was happy about something while Mina was upset about something. That didn't bode well.

Darcy was on her feet as if she would lunge for their throats. "Where the hell have you two been?"

"Naomi got us jobs hunting wolves," Mina said dourly. "Don't look at me! It was her idea! I didn't get there in time to stop her."

Naomi sat down as pleased as a cat bringing its owner a dead mouse. "It'll solve our money problems."

"Are you freakin' serious?" Sally burst out. "I don't care if I never see a wolf again in my life."

"How much are they offering?" Darcy asked.

Both Sally and Mina looked at Darcy with raised eyebrows.

Naomi settled into her chair and said, "He was offering twenty gold per wolf tail, but I told him we'd do it for five gold per wolf tail instead. We're doing it for the good of the village after all."

Darcy's eyes narrowed. "Remind me to slap you later. Did you ask about an advance?"

Sally became alarmed as Darcy developed a very familiar thoughtful look. "Darcy, you aren't seriously considering…"

"We could use the money."

"What about Naomi? We're on a time limit," Sally hissed in a low voice, bewildered by the sudden change in plans. "We don't have time to traipse after wolves."

"We made good time getting here," Darcy said with her brows knitted. "And we don't have to go after them. They said the wolves regularly attack the village from the north. We'll wait until they attack and kill enough of them to put money in our pockets."

Mina wrung her hands in a near panic. "But look at what happened last night."

"They took us by surprise," Darcy stated wisely. "This time, we'll know they're coming and be ready for them."

Shaking her head, Mina said in a pang voice, "I think we should just stick with the plan and leave in the morning..."

Sally knew that Mina's pleas would fall on deaf ears. Once Darcy made up her mind, nothing short of winning the lottery or death would change her plans. Naomi was practically squirming in anticipation of them taking on a quest. Sally turned to Tom, wondering what he thought of this.

She caught his eyes, and he gave her a small shrug. What did that mean? Was he on board with Darcy, or was this his way of saying "don't look at me, I'm not talking to you?" Dammit, she needed to find a good time to apologize.

Chapter 16

THE JOB

It was decided that they would patrol the village in two groups. Mina and Naomi would partner up since—as Darcy sardonically put it—they seemed to work so well together. After rolling her eyes, Mina led Naomi away towards the east side of the village while Darcy, Sally, and Tom set off for the other side. Word had passed quickly among the village inhabitants, as it would in small towns, of the mayor hiring hunters to solve the wolf crisis. More people ventured to leave their homes, and some even waved gratefully at them as they walked by.

Oddly enough, Sally found herself raising a hand in greeting. There was something infectious about a simple nod and salute of acknowledgment from the villagers. The greetings seemed more earnest than they did back home when people did it as a second thought or to appear polite.

"Keep your hood up," Darcy whispered in a harsh hiss. "Those happy grins will turn into hisses and boos if they see you're a half-elf."

"Thanks for the reminder," Sally said sourly but gave her hood a sharp tug to ensure it was in place.

From the edge of the cowl, she noticed an unhappy look on Tom's face. She assumed it was meant for her until he drew close, and she could see the regret lining his face.

"I hope to change how people perceive elves in the kingdom someday," he said. "I want to make it safe for all people to live in these lands without fear of being assaulted without repercussions or driven from their homes. To make it safe for you, Sally."

She looked away in shame. Was he the sort of person who's really nice to the offender to make them feel like shit? God, if he was, then he was succeeding. She needed to apologize, but what would she say? Sorry, I was a bitch, and I didn't mean what I said about your sister? That would be a good start. Okay, first, she needed to ask Darcy to give them some time. But before she could ask, Darcy spoke.

"Tom, could you give us some space? I need to speak with my sister for a minute or two," Darcy said with a polite smile.

Tom gave her a scrutinizing look. "More secret talk?"

It was to Darcy's credit that she didn't react, but instead said sweetly, "Just personal family business."

Tom acquiesce with a short sigh, "Very well, but one day you're going to have to share your secrets with me. Especially since we're traveling companions."

Sally couldn't prevent herself from wincing. He wouldn't want to know the truth that his world and life were fiction written up by writers in a video game studio, that he was just a character animated by pixels and given voice by an actor. And he wasn't even a character on the box cover of the game.

"Maybe," Darcy said with the same polite smile. "We'll only be a minute or two."

With a playful bow, he trotted ahead with a hand on his shortsword to keep it from hitting his legs. Once he was several houses ahead of then, Darcy sidled close to Sally and whispered, "You must think I'm crazy in making us take this quest, but there's a method to my madness."

"I kinda figured there was something else going on than just the money," Sally said sourly.

"The money will help, but I'm we need to level up as quickly as possible. Check your log. We've gained XP since Spring Bell."

Sally brought up her character screen and swiped over to the log. It took a few scans, but three lines caught her attention.

50 XP for rescuing trapped villager

Successful Encounter: 30 XP

100 XP for Confronting Corrupt Innkeeper

Checking her leveling bar, Sally saw it had increased to 797 of 900. She was little more than 100 points away from leveling up.

"Darcy, I am so close to leveling up," Sally said, suddenly so excited it was a struggle not to pump her fist.

Darcy gently took Sally's arm to draw her closer and lowered her voice to a near whisper. "That's good because we need to level up as much as possible before we get to Everguard. Players are not supposed to get there until level 5, and three of us are below that. Everguard is technically a safe place in the game, but some areas have random encounters. Now there's no telling what's waiting for us there."

"Hopefully, more players who know what the hell is going on," Sally muttered.

Darcy nodded and continued. "And I need to level up so I can learn third level spells. Then if somebody gets killed, I can resurrect them."

Sally drew in a long breath, her eyes widening. "Do you think you'll need it?"

"We almost needed it for Naomi couple of times," Darcy grimaced at the memory of the girl nearly bleeding to death on a table. "If she had died, I doubted she would have resurrected at the graveyard."

"We...We don't know that," Sally said weakly. "It's possible..."

"I can still smell the blood and how warm it was on my hands," Darcy said, raising a hand and stared at it as if was still stained. "When this was just an MMO, the dungeon would reset for the next group of players. Cut Throats would resume lurking in the halls, and McRando and Wolfe would be available for the next boss fights. If we went back there, they'd still be dead and rotting where we left them. I believe that if we die in the game, we won't respawn in a graveyard. We'll just be dead."

"If you believe that, then what makes you think you can keep us from dying?" Talking about this was freaking Sally out, but she needed to know what Darcy believed.

"Because magic works in this world. I've healed almost everyone several times since this started. If this world follows the same rules of magic as the game does, then I'm pretty sure that it can bring back the dead."

Exasperated, Sally flung out a hand towards the surrounding houses. "If it worked like that, then this world would have a huge overpopulation problem. If people just have to say an incantation and bring back poor dead mom and pop, then why are there graveyards? Why didn't the Cut Throats have a mage bringing them back from the dead?"

Darcy shook her head with an amused smile. "It doesn't work like you're thinking. Only fifth level clerics of good alignment can cast resurrection spells and those only work within limits. The spell I can get at fifth level can only revive someone who's been dead less than a minute per level and didn't die of old age. And it can't regrow lost limbs. So you can forget about it if that person died of decapitation. On top of it all, I can only cast it twice a day."

"Oh, I guess that makes more sense now," Sally admitted, but it disturbed her no less. "How much do you lack before you level up?"

"A lot, about two thousand more XP, but hopefully we can at least get you and Mina to level three by the end of the day," Darcy said giving Sally a pat on the back. "You two will become stronger and the party will be a bit more balanced."

"I think we've done okay so far," Sally replied. They had managed to overcome bandits, werewolves, and asshole innkeepers together, so maybe they were ready for whatever was waiting for them in Everguard.

Then Sally's confidence waned when she recalled the name Riker who was in Everguard and might have good reason to be unhappy with them. Then again, maybe gaining a level before arriving in Everguard might not be a bad idea.

Focusing on the quest at hand, Sally asked, "Darcy, do you have any idea why the wolves are so aggressive? Is there something that would make animals crazy?"

Shifting her weight on her boots with a hand on one hip, Darcy took on a thoughtful stance. "Yeah, there are a few things. Maybe a Druid got pissed off at the village, or maybe there's a curse disturbing the wolves. We don't have time to find the cause of the problem, but maybe killing enough of them will get the pack to leave the village alone."

Sally glanced up at the noon sky and wondered if the skies back home were this bright blue. There was no pollution in this world; no factories pumping the air full of smog and chemicals; no planes crossing the sky; nor drones hovering overhead. Nor was it too hot either, not as she would have expected at home with climate change. Then again, who was she, a shut-in, to judge? She hated being outdoors in the cancerous sunlight and sweat-inducing heat. If it weren't for going out to visit her parents, she would be content to live every day of her life indoors. Being outside now, however, in this world, wasn't too bad at all.

"Tom's waving at us," Darcy murmured, breaking through her thoughts.

"Think he saw something?"

"Let's go find out."

At their approach, Tom led them to an overgrown bramble patch near a fence bordering a garden of tiny sprouts. He pointed at a clump of matted fur caught in the bush. "Wolf hair. They came through here." He pointed at the edge of the forest just yards away from the house. "Possibly two or more."

Sally arched an eyebrow. "How do you know?"

Tom knelt onto the ground and pointed at obscure markings in the earth. "A few people come through here, but I can still make out the paw prints. One set is bigger than the other, so there was more than one."

"They teach you how to hunt wolves as part of your princely duties?" Darcy inquired, eyeing the tracks herself.

"Why, yes," Tom said blankly. "My family goes on regular hunting parties with the nobles. Mostly we hunt stags and boars, and the occasional wolf if we come across one."

"Good work, Tom," Darcy said with a slight nod. "You and Sally stay here. I'm going to check on Mina and Naomi and see if they found anything. I'll bring them right back."

Sally did not want to be left alone with Tom. It was true that she still had to apologize, and perhaps Darcy was giving her the chance to do so now. As much as she wanted to do so, to bring it up was a daunting prospect. What he if refused to accept her apology? What if he wanted to make a scene about it without Darcy here to intervene on her behalf?

No, she resolutely refused to address it until the wolf situation had been handled. She reasoned that they needed to be on guard. After what happened last night and from the stories they'd been hearing, the wolves were dangerous, and since Darcy didn't have the means to resurrect anyone yet, then they had to be doubly careful. Though her logic was sound, she still felt guilty for yet again putting off what her conscience told her she should be doing.

Tom, however, didn't seem to mind being alone with her. He gave Darcy an amused smile and nodded. "We'll keep watch until you return."

"Don't have too much fun without me," she said with a backward wave as she departed.

Once she well out of earshot, Tom turned to Sally and casually said, "I know I said this before, but your sister has unusual behavior for a cleric of Shantra."

Sally could only give him a wordless shrug. She hoped he wasn't going to try to pry into their background again. In a moment of inspiration, she turned the questioning round on him. "Do you get along with your dad and brothers?"

"Dad?" He quirked an eyebrow.

Dammit, she misspoke again. "Father, I mean."

"Ah, I'm not sure how to answer that question," Tom said, furrowing his brow. "To get along with him would mean we are like commoner families. I'm the third born son, so there wasn't much use for me at the castle. My eldest brother, Cedric, is the crown prince: being the heir to the throne, his favor is the most coveted in the royal court so most of his time is spent on official business for my father across the kingdom. My second brother, Daniver, is a warrior born; if he isn't sparring in the training grounds, he's off leading soldiers in skirmishes against Saige."

"Then he must not be happy about you seeking peace with them," Sally said. She wondered if Daniver and Cedric had character profiles from the game and if what Tom was telling her matched what was in their wiki pages.

Tom released a tired sigh. "He was quite vocal against what he perceived as letting the enemy believe we're spineless cowards. Cedric wasn't as angry as Daniver, but he too voiced his objections. Thankfully, my father supported peace, and I volunteered to go."

Sally walked over to the fence, and, after testing her weight on it, she climbed up and perched on the top railing. In her real body, she wouldn't dare sit on the fence, much less lean on it. It was almost liberating, like she had one less worry in the world. Well, actually more so. It seemed that diabetes and heart disease didn't feature as a grim future for her anymore. It felt nice not to be so self-conscious about her body or weight, but it was an otherworldly feeling that kept reminding her that this body was not hers.

"Your father must be a nice man if he wants to make peace with Saige," she said. She peered down the path to see if Darcy was on her way back with the others. The path remained empty, with only the wind stirring the grass on either side.

"One would think," Tom said with reluctance. "My father is not a cruel man, but he is pragmatic. He sees that a continued war with Saige would not serve our kingdom well, and losing a third-born son will not harm his lineage."

"I wouldn't think he'd want anything to happen to you," Sally said gently. "I can't imagine a parent being happy about losing a child. And if he's a king, then he would have plenty of diplomats and officials he could have sent, but he decided to have you go instead. So that must mean that he has confidence in you. Maybe he's worried since he hasn't heard from you yet."

Tom raised his eyebrows and broke into a smile. "My Lady, I do believe this is the most you have ever said to me without a scowl."

Sally looked down at her knees, feeling awkward. Now was as good a time as any to apologize.

"Tom, I want to say..."

"Sir! Miss!"

A young girl was running towards them. Her gray, homespun dress flapped around her knees, and hair—tied back in a long dark braid—flew behind her like a flag. Sally scooted off the fence and landed on her feet, knowing something was wrong from how panic was etched in the girl's face.

The girl stopped, almost bent double to catch her breath. She couldn't be any older than twelve or thirteen. Tom lowered onto one knee to look up into the girl's face. "What's wrong, child? Is it the wolves?"

"My brother!" she gasped, her eyes wide and fearful. "Mother and I told him it was too dangerous to go into the forest to check his snares. But we can't find him, and we're afraid he went anyway. The mayor said you could help!"

"Oh no," Sally moaned and looked down the path. Surely Darcy would be back by now and not leave her alone with this mess.

"How long ago did he disappear?" Tom asked, taking on a severe look.

"An hour ago, we think."

"No, no, no, no, no," Sally groaned, dropping her face into her hands. She knew where this was going, and she wondered if it was possible to hold onto the fence to prevent it from happening.

"Where are his snares?" Tom rose to his feet, looking into the forest.

"Two miles west, sir," the girl said tearfully. "He's only six years old! Please, you have to bring him home before the wolves get him."

"God help me, I don't wanna go into those woods," Sally prayed. From Tom's offended look, she said quickly, "not without the others."

"We cannot wait for them," Tom said firmly, "The lad has been gone for too long. The longer we wait, the more peril he could be in."

"Please, miss, please help my brother." The girl had her hands clasped together in a desperate plea.

"Goddammit," Sally hissed and looked down the path. Nope, no Darcy. Nor Naomi or Mina. "Shit. Okay, kid, stay here and tell my friends we went ahead to find your brother. Tom, let's go before I change my mind."

Tom gave her a look of immense gratitude and took her hand. "Yes."

Sally didn't see sense in him leading her by the hand. She had already said she would go against her better judgment. Yet, feeling his hand pushed back some of her fear. With one last glance over her shoulder at the empty path, she followed Tom into the scary forest to save some stupid little kid from the crazed wolves.

***

"Gol-lee! I gotta pee!" Naomi said, dancing in an indication of her dilemma.

"You should have gone at the inn," Mina muttered, shooting the Monk annoyed glare. "Stop doing that. What are you? Four?"

"No!" Naomi snapped. "Are there any bushes?"

"Oh. My. God. You can't use the bathroom outside! You're a girl!" Mina said in a hiss, frantically looking around to make sure no one heard. The villagers kept a wide berth from the Barbarian and the bizarre girl in white clothing so no one was around to hear or witness them.

"Girls can go potty outside. We just have to do it differently from guys. Think I can go over there?" She pointed at bushes at the edge of a garden.

"That's next to someone's house!"

"It looks like it needs watering."

"Go back to the inn and pee." Mina threw a thumb back the way they had come.

"That will take too long! All I need is a couple of minutes."

Mina looked around, and there was no one around. The paths were empty, and no one was watching from the windows. With a groan, she said, "Hurry before someone sees."

Mina turned her back to Naomi and the bush and waited. The bush rustled, and Naomi complained about the leaves being scratchy.

"If you don't hurry up, a wolf is going to bite you in the ass…again." Mina retorted nastily.

"I'm not worried," Naomi declared amid more rustling. "I know you'll pull it off me and throw it like a Nerf ball."

Mina made a face at the thought of a repeat of last night, but there was no use in trying to explain that to Naomi, though. They were wasting time hunting wolves when they should be figuring out how to get home or finding other players who might know the way back.

She never thought she'd miss her cramp old dorm room so much or her own body for that matter. This one was just too big to be real and she had to handle everything with care for fear of breaking what she held into several pieces. If she had to come to this world, then why couldn't she have gotten a gorgeous figure like Sally's? Sally drew stares wherever she went but had no idea of what to do with it. Mina drew stares too, but more cautious looks than of those of admiration.

"Are you done yet?" Mina barked over her shoulder.

"I'm trying to figure out how to do this without getting pee on my pants. Should I take them off?"

"No, just squat with your feet apart and lean forward, so your ass sticks out away from your pants. It helps to pull your pants forward if you can, to be sure it's out of the way. It might be better to lean against something like a tree."

"Really?" Naomi said, and there was more rustling. "Did you pee outside a lot?"

"No," Mina sighed. "It's this stupid Survival skill. It just told me how to pee in the woods."

"Have it tell you what leaves are good to wipe with."

"Gross," Mina shuddered when the knowledge came to her. "The leaves on that bush are okay to use."

"Thanks!" This was followed by telltale plucking noise.

Within minutes, a sated Naomi was strutting alongside Mina as they continued their patrol, waving at every person they passed. Some people waved back, and others just stared nonplussed. Mina wanted to tell Naomi to quit acting like some cartoon but didn't believe she would understand what she meant by acting normal. Nothing that Naomi had done since they had met was normal. Mina was almost happy to see Darcy when she appeared so that she wasn't alone with the hyperactive girl.

"Please, tell me that you have already taken care of the wolves, and we can go back to the inn."

Darcy shook her head. "Nope. We just got a bead on where they're coming from. Did you find anything?"

"Other than a good bush to piss behind, nope," Mina replied.

"That's useful," Darcy said, rolling her eyes and waving them along. "C'mon, we might as well check out the lead we found."

The Cleric led them in a westerly direction. Mina groaned at her Survival skill that would not stop feeding information into her head. If she wanted to know which way was north, then she should look at a compass and not at the sun or shadows. Naomi cartwheel forward and then rolled to her feet like a professional acrobat, much to the delight of some small children watching from a yard. They waved back in response to Naomi's eager greetings but cringed when Mina looked in their direction. God, she hated this body so much, she thought as she quickened her pace to walk beside Darcy. It was simple enough with her long legs.

"Maybe we should give them some time alone," Mina said as casually as possible to Darcy. "Tom does like Sally…"

"I know," Darcy replied, almost miserably. "Much to his misfortune. Sally doesn't date, and unless they have role playing dialogue options, she doesn't know what to say."

It was galling that the wallflower got the supermodel body and attracted a prince while Mina, who had dieted, exercised, and spent hundreds on beauty products, was the one who got the behemoth body for trying to impress a guy who didn't even rank with Tom. God, the unfairness of it all rankled. The skin between her eyebrows was beginning to knit when she forced herself to relax.

No, no, no, don't get angry. Do not get mad, do not Rage.

"Admit it," Darcy said, cutting into her concentration. "You're hoping we don't find any wolves."

Mina made an indistinguishable noise through her nose. "I just don't see why this problem has to be our problem."

"For reasons I don't want to get into in public, trust me when I say that we have to do this."

Trust you? How? You're leading us into danger, and you're acting like it's a detour on some road trip. How can you be so calm about this? Mina said none of this, keeping it bottled away. She wanted to pick up Darcy and give her a good shaking until she made sense, but no, she would not do that because she wasn't that sort of person.

A loud crash halted them in their tracks. It sounded like hundreds planks of wood being broken at once and a cloud of dust rose over the roofs like a plume of smoke. Then the screams started ringing out across the village, both frighten and mournful.

"Is it the wolves?" Darcy looked around with her mace in hand.

"I don't hear any howling," Naomi said for once, not fidgeting in place.

"Oh no," Mina moaned, her bronze countenance turning several shades paler. "No, no, no, no!"

Darcy and Naomi looked at the Barbarian and before either one could ask what she was talking about, Mina sprinted down the path. Her legs pumped as she ran faster than she ever could have managed in her old body. She was barely winded when she arrived at her destination and looked on in horror at the disaster.

The rickety building had collapsed into a pile of broken wood. Dust filled the air causing the people around the pile to move like shadows in a brown fog. A woman was on her knees, wailing while men struggled to dig through the wreckage. There were high-pitched screams and crying coming from beneath the mound of broken wood.

"Oh, God." Mina scanned the growing crowd and saw the builder staring at what his poor carpentry had wrought with a white face.

First Naomi appeared at her side, barely panting and then Darcy, who gasped and bent over to catch her breath. When she was able to breathe, she said, "What...happened?"

"It fell," Mina said. "I told the carpenter it could fall and he didn't listen. He was letting the kids play in that death trap and now..."

More screams of fear and pain came from the pile of rubble, and Darcy's face went white. "Oh God! There's kids under there?"

In a blur of white, Naomi ran past the men struggling to lift the wood and seized one of the larger pieces and red-faced with exertion, tried to move it. When it didn't budge, she tried again, digging her feet into the grass and tried again to lift a pillar of wood that was many times her weight.

"She's going to end up hurting herself," Darcy said, taking a few steps towards Naomi and stopping. "We...we should help too...but I...I don't know how."

Mina felt the same. In their world, helping would consist of calling Nine One One or the police and standing out of the way as rescue crews went in. Or recording the disaster on your phone. In this world, there was no rescue team, cops, or ambulances coming. It was just desperate parents trying to save their children.

Naomi noticed them standing there and stopped struggling with the wood and ran back to them. Her tear-stained face was red with a fury they'd never associated with her. With her fists clenched at her sides, Naomi shouted, "Are you going to stand here and do nothing while kids are dying?"

Both of them faltered, uncertain of how to respond to Naomi's accusation. Finally, it was Darcy who said, "We don't know how we can help."

Then Naomi looked as if she could fly at them in a rage worthy of a Barbarian. "What kind of heroes are you!? Darcy, you can heal people! Mina, you're strong enough to move mountains! If you don't help th- then I don't want to be in your party anymore!"

Darcy flinched from the vehemence of her yell, which drew the attention of villagers from their concerns for the children. The villager's stares made Darcy feel put on the spot, as if an interrogation light was shining on her face. Darcy looked away from Naomi's tearful face and saw the desperation with which the men dug through the wood with bare hands. In their world, cranes and trucks would have been called in to help remove the debris. Here, though, at this rate, the men would still be clearing the mess by this time tomorrow. By then, it could be too late for the children.

Broken ribs, contusions, fractured skull, broken limbs, and internal bleeding were all possibilities from being crushed by a fallen building. The ones crying and screaming were the ones that were awake; there was no telling how many others were under there, unable to cry or beg for their parents to save them.

"Mina, c'mon." Darcy began walking forward.

Mina sank her teeth into her lower lip, but followed Darcy as if they were going to their execution. People parted, giving them a way through. An old woman had her hands clasped before her in a prayer to Shantra, but Darcy refused to look at them. There was enough pressure to be had with saving lives without having to answer prayers.

Darcy surveyed the piles of wood: the large pieces were jumbled together like a jigsaw puzzle dumped from its boxed. Spotting what she was looking for, she motioned for all the men to get clear and took care not to trip. Waving Mina over, she pointed at a pillar that lay half-buried under the rubble.

"This pillar is at the bottom. If you can lift it up, there should be enough space beneath it for Naomi to crawl under. She can get the kids out while you hold it up."

The pillar was almost as big as she with a massive amount of rubble on top of it. Mina shook her head. "Jesus, Darcy, I'm strong, I get that, but I'm not that strong. I can't lift that!"

"You have to try," Darcy said firmly. "And I can help you. I have a cantrip that will give you a bonus to your Strength check."

"I—I still don't know…" Mina said, shaking her head.

"You're the only one that can do this!" Darcy barked as she wretched Mina down to her eye level by the front of her leathers. "Stop doubting yourself and help us! Blessing will give you a plus one and bring your Strength up to plus four, that's more than enough to lift this."

With that said, Darcy gave her a rough pat on the cheek and spoke a word of power before turning to Naomi. "I can't cast Blessing on you, but I think with your level you can manage on your own. If they aren't awake, check their pulse at the neck or wrist and bring out only the ones you know are alive. Don't waste time on the ones that we're too late to save."

With a white face, Naomi nodded. "I'll get them out."

"And I know you don't want to hurt them, but do what you have to get them out." Darcy laid a hand on Naomi's shoulder and squeezed it. "If Mina fails her Strength check while you're under there, you might get crushed too."

If the notion of sharing the children's fate frightened her, Naomi didn't show it. She nodded and got down on the ground in a crouch position, ready to dive in. Darcy noticed for the first time that a small group of villagers were gathering near them. Anxious and teary eyes watched them with a hopeful gaze that made her feel all the more the pressure of what was at stake.

Darcy pointed at a man who had been trying to move the rubble, earlier. "Does this village have a healer?"

"Yes, Mistress," the man said, standing straighter as if being addressed by a superior. He probably thought he was. "She's tending to the ones who didn't get trapped."

"Tell her she's about to get more patients in critical condition." Darcy spotted a nearby cottage and pointed at it. "Have her set up a hospital in that house and give her whatever she needs. Hot water, blankets, medicine; if she asks for it, give it to her."

"Yes, Mistress!" The man took off at a full sprint, nearly knocking an observer out of his way.

Darcy looked at the other observers. "All of you be ready to take the wounded to the house and stay out of the way."

The people gave their affirmation in earnest nods and hands raised in prayers. The Cleric looked between the quaking Barbarian and to the determined Monk. "Alright, let's do this."

Mina resigned herself to the task and wrapped her thick arms around the pillar. Her cheek where Darcy had patted her still tingled, but from it, she felt a sense of strength running through her bones. Was this the Blessing cantrip?

Bracing her feet on the ground, Mina drew a deep breath and, with her eyes squeezed shut, put all her strength into lifting. The wood groaned and creaked, dust rose, and chips fell, but slowly the rubble rose, levered up by the pillar. As soon as a large enough space formed, Naomi darted inside without a word or hesitation. Darcy looked between the hole and Mina, who held the pillar with quivering arms. A minute passed and then another. Sweat beaded on the Cleric's dark brow as her eyes kept switching between the post and the hole.

"Naomi?" Darcy called, kneeling by the hole. "What's going on?"

Naomi emerged so fast that her head nearly knocked Darcy on the chin. She pressed a sobbing child into Darcy's chest and disappeared into the hole. Darcy transferred the child into a waiting villager's arms, and a cheer went up from the villagers. A woman, likely the child's mother, followed them to the house, weeping and praising Shantra all the way.

Soon Naomi emerged with another child, a little boy bleeding from the arm, and this one was transferred to a waiting villager and then another. Each time a child was brought out, Darcy recast the cantrip on Mina again, giving her the Strength bonus she needed to keep the pillar up.

Mina tried to focus, but her mind kept asking how much longer? How many kids had Naomi hauled out? How many were left? Her palms began to ache, and sweat rolled into her eyes and her back was hurting, and her arms were going numb...she needed a break.

"How are you holding up there, Mina?" Darcy said.

"Don't. Talk. To. Me," Mina groused.

Darcy touched her arm, granting her another bonus to her Strength. "Just stay in there. You're doing great."

To the narrow, dusty opening Naomi brought an unconscious little girl with a streamer of blood running down the side of her face and across an ear. The blood shone brightly in the afternoon sun that it cast an after image in Mina's eyes. How much longer? How many more?

To her horror, the pillar nearly slipped from her hands. Villagers cried out in fear, but she managed to grab it in time. The rubble cracked, and terrified screams erupted from within. Mina almost broke her back, trying to get part of her body beneath the wood and lift up. Darcy patted her arm, casting another cantrip, and the pillar was easier to lift again.

Darcy knelt by the hole again and yelled, "Naomi! You got to hurry! Mina almost failed a Strength check!"

Naomi emerged, her face and hair covered with dust and dirt. Her eyes were red and streaming from the grit in them. "There's three more, but I have to dig them out or break boards to free them. I'm going as fast as I can."

"You're gonna have to go faster! Any second, Mina can fail her Strength check and if that happens…"

"Can she lift it higher? If she can lift it higher, it'll give me enough room to get them out faster!"

Mina wasn't sure if she had heard correctly. There was no way Naomi had suggested she lift this damn pillar higher! It was all she could do to keep from dropping it on her head!

Much to Mina's horror, Darcy nodded. "Be ready."

Naomi disappeared like a rabbit into a burrow, and Darcy stood and turned to her with a determined look. Maybe she had another spell that could help her along with the cantrip.

"Mina, you have to Rage."

Oh no. "I'm. Not. Fighting." Mina groused out.

"You don't have to be in combat to Rage," Darcy said. "It'll give you a plus two bonus to your Strength, and coupled with a plus one from Blessing, it'll bring your total to plus six. It should be more than enough."

"I. Can't."

Darcy's face turned stormy. "Not can't. You won't because you're too damn afraid of Raging, but you need to be afraid for those kids and Naomi. You and I both know she won't come out without them."

This was so unfair! How could they expect her to get angry when she was so scared! Why did this have to happen? How the hell did she get into a situation like this?

Over Darcy's shoulder and through the crowd, she spotted the carpenter. He was the reason this was happening to her! She warned him this could happen, and he insulted her.

Fire filled her vision, and the adrenaline surged.

He called her a tribeswoman! Well, tribe people probably knew how to build better houses with their mud and sticks than he did with his wood and tools. A two-year-old with Playschool Lego could make a sturdier construction than that jackass.

"Mina! You're doing it! Keep going!"

Screw him and this world too! She was in medical school for God's sake! She was supposed to be in class, attending a lecture or in her dorm studying. Not in some magical fantasy world where bandits kidnap you, and wolves try to bite you in the ass.

The pillar was above her head with both hands propping it up. Then she was walking forward, her boots treading on wood and dirt, hefting the post up higher and higher. The rubble seemed to roll back from her in a wave of wood, throwing up clouds of dust and dirt. Shifting her shoulder against it, she pushed with all her might and fury until the pillar was nearly upright. Behind her, huddled together, was Naomi with three children with tear-streaked faces.

After bunching her shoulders and drawing her Strength for one last endeavor, Mina pushed the pillar with all her might. It stood erect for a moment, swaying to and fro, before falling away and crashed through the roof of a house. Shattered glass sprayed from the windows, and splintered wood rained on the heads of fleeing villagers. A cry of dismay went up from the crowd as the carpenter shoved himself to the front.

"That's my house!" he shouted, pulling at his hair with both hands.

Villagers surged into what remained of the wreckage, gathering the children who were whisked away to the makeshift hospital. Naomi was thanked and kissed as she was practically carried from the rubble. Darcy was at Mina's side in time to catch her before she could fall, despite Mina nearly bowling her down as her body slumped.

"You did good," Darcy said, patting Mina on the shoulder. "You were awesome."

Her lungs felt like they were going to pop out from her chest. Mina heaved in deep breaths while Darcy led her to a clear spot on the grass and lowered her to sit down. When she was able to, she wheezed, "Who's that yelling?"

"The carpenter. The pillar landed on his house."

"Good," she muttered and was surprised at herself. Her father would be shocked by the pleasure she felt at another's misfortune. Maybe she should feel wrong about his house being smashed, but it felt good to see karma at work. "Did we save them all?"

"Yes, by some miracle they all survived a building landing on their heads, but I don't know how they'll do afterward." Darcy looked almost as tired as she felt. "I hope to God that healer knows how to disinfect wounds."

Mina grimaced at the thought of how, after their efforts into saving the kids, they might die of blood poisoning or infection due to the medieval version of medical care. Back then, people died of infection or lost limbs to gangrene because wounds weren't correctly cleaned or dressed, or the healer didn't bother to wash their hands or tools before tending to the injured.

"We need to go help her," Mina said. "You have healing spells, and I have some medical training. Maybe between the healer and us, we can still keep some kids alive."

"It's gonna delay our wolf hunt, but we have some time to spare on this. I'll send Naomi to get Tom and Sally." Then Darcy furrowed her brows and searched the crowd. "You'd think they'd have heard about what was happening by now."

Mina scanned the area but didn't see the tall Tom nor Sally's hooded head. When the building fell, it was loud enough to rattle her teeth so there was no way they could have failed to have heard it and not come to investigate.

As if on cue, a little dark-haired girl wearing a homespun dress shyly approached them. "Are you talking about your friends? The tall, dark haired man and the lady in the hood?"

Both Mina and Darcy looked at her, becoming apprehensive. Darcy said, "Yes, do you know where they are?"

"Yes ma'am, they went into the forest to find my little brother. They told me to wait until you came and tell you where they were going, but then the building fell and..."

Darcy's eyes went wide, and she got to her feet in a rush. "How long ago?"

"I don't know..." the girl said regretfully. "Before the building fell."

"Shit!" Darcy hissed. "They went in thinking we'd be right behind them, and we've been here the whole time! We gotta go!"

Mina's legs ached, but she stood up all the same and checked her battleax. "You have to go heal those kids. Naomi and I will go after Tom and Sally."

For the first time, Mina didn't feel nervous or agitated. She was calm and held her battleax, not as if it was some distasteful object, but something that belonged to her and only she could use.

"Are you sure you can handle this?" asked Darcy.

"No, but I know this is how it has to be." Mina tucked the ax behind her back. "Those kids need you. We'll help Tom and Sally and bring them back safely."

As much as Darcy didn't want to shatter this newfound confidence of Mina's, she couldn't let her go without warning. "I won't be there to heal you, and if I spend all my spells healing the kids, it's going to take an eight-hour rest before I can cast more spells."

What Darcy meant was that they were going into a dangerous situation without a healer backing them, and they shouldn't expect any healing spells if they returned injured. Mina drew a deep breath, not liking the situation, but knew what had to be done. "We'll be fine."

Then the world darkened and for several terrifying moments, Mina believed she was passing out, until a familiar sight glowed before her eyes.

YOU HAVE LEVELED UP!

A smile so big, it hurt her cheeks, spread across Mina's face. And for the first time since she logged onto *Shadow's Deep*, she knew the satisfaction of being a gamer.

Would you like to continue leveling up in the Barbarian Class? Yes/No?

There was some hesitation, but Mina selected "yes." As Darcy had told her, it wasn't possible for her to multiclass and somehow, that didn't bother her anymore.

You have gained the Reckless Attack ability. You may add +1 to your Strength for attacks, but must take a -2 penalty to your Armor Class until your next turn.

Well, that didn't seem like a fun ability to have. She'd rather have it the other way around: -1 to her Strength in exchange for +2 to her Armor Class.

Then she got her allotment of four skill points. Where should she put them this time? Well, Darcy wanted her to add some in Climb and Swim and that would take half of her points. So where should she put the other two?

Healing wasn't a class skill so putting that to a +2 would take up the last two points. She could use Healing to help Darcy with the kids, but then on second thoughts, she and Naomi were about to go into a forest infested with wolves to find three missing people. No, the last two points should go into Perception to give her a better chance of finding them. Thus her Perception skill went up from +1 to +2.

When the skill faded away, she could see Darcy still standing before her and giving her a concerned look. Then she gave Mina an encouraging smile and said, "Alright, good luck."

Wait, did leveling up only take a second? Or did time stop? Was that possible? How could she question time manipulation when she was transported into a game world with magic and werewolves? Anything was possible now.

She would need to tell Darcy that she had leveled up, but that could wait until they returned with the others.

Chapter 17

ENCOUNTER

Sweat rolled down her neck and back and tickled her spine. Sally had no idea how long they had been trekking through the woods. In her previous body, one minute of physical exertion was too long, but now with this one being more fit, she could go on like this for hours.

"He couldn't have gone far," Tom said from ahead. He was standing atop of tall protruding roots of a tree and scanning the foliage. "A child wouldn't have laid traps too far from the village."

She looked around and saw only trees and, try as she might, she couldn't see the signs that Tom could perceive with a passing glance. He pointed out minuscule broken twigs and imperceptible marks in the earth. It was likely because her Survival skill was just a +2. She could only trust that he knew which way they were going and while he tracked the boy she kept an eye out for wolves.

Thus far, nothing lunged from the bushes for their throats. The rays of sunlight piercing the forest canopy provided plenty of light. If it wasn't for the circumstances of wolves and being trapped in a fantasy world, Sally could imagine this to be what a forest like would be like in the real world. Years of playing narrative video games, watching movies and TV shows, however, had taught her to see the signs of a false sense of security.

Any second, something is going to happen. Maybe Tom will get yanked into the bushes by something big and mean, and then I'll end up as the Last Girl, running through the forest screaming.

She was so tense that she nearly jumped when Tom called her name. "Sally, this way. We're getting close."

"Good. Let's find him so we can get back," Sally said.

She looked over her shoulder in a forlorn hope that Darcy and the others would appear right behind them. With it being just the two of them—a Rogue and an NPC Fighter—the situation was dangerous and she'd feel safer if they had Darcy with them, not only for her healing spells but for the leadership and mettle she provided. And she would know the most reliable and efficient way to accomplish this task. Not to mention that having Mina and Naomi around to help fight and act as extra pairs of eyes would be most welcome. Maybe her friends would catch up before anything happened?

Tom stepped over a large rock and froze. "Damn."

"What is it?" She paused behind him, her heart skipping a beat as she didn't like the sound of his voice.

"Look here."

She looked but still couldn't see what he was pointing at. "You're going to have to explain what I'm looking at because all I see is grass and dirt."

"The lad was chased by a wolf." Tom pointed at the mark on the ground as he explained. "The heel is heavier so he was running and along his tracks are paw prints and these aren't old at all. They just came through here."

Tom took off in the direction of the tracks, and Sally followed, her heart pounding, though it had nothing to do with exertion. They went only a few yards before she heard a noise and grabbed Tom's arm, shushing him before he could speak.

"Listen!"

It was a keening wail that carried on the wind. Drawing back her hood to remove any barrier between her ears and the sound, she listened carefully. The sound of crying was coming from ahead, and something else was there: growling, from multiple throats.

"He's ahead, and there's more than one wolf."

"Damn," Tom said again. "How many?"

She took a moment to concentrate, even cupping her hands behind her ears to catch the sounds. "I want to say three, but I can't be sure."

"There's no superior hearing than that of elven ears," Tom said with an admiring smile for her. Then he knelt and grabbed a long stick.

"Wouldn't your sword be a better weapon?" Sally said, watching him tear off his shirt sleeve. "What are you doing?"

"Wolves fear fire," he said, wrapping the cloth around one end of the stick.

"That didn't stop them from attacking us when we were around a campfire last night," she pointed out. Now that she thought about it, it did seem strange for wild wolves to attack people so close to a fire.

"True, but I don't think they'll enjoy having it smacked over their heads." He took a tinderbox from his pocket and looked at her. "You wouldn't happen to have some oil?"

"I actually do!" Thank God for Rogues having hidden pockets that could contain small items like thieves' tools and little pouches of oil.

With oil drizzled over the cloth, it only took two strikes with the tinderbox to ignite it. Tom lifted the torch in his offhand and drew his sword. "This won't last long, so let's hurry."

She would have asked Tom to make one for herself, but she already had the rapier and dagger. They were more familiar to her hands than any torch. Without a signal, they both charged through the brush, Tom keeping the makeshift torch raised high to avoid setting the foliage on fire.

As before, Sally continued to be amazed by the dexterity of this body. If she had tried running in the forest in the real world, she would have tripped over every root and fallen into every hole. Sally trotted over uneven terrain, her feet finding the right place to step off to propel her forward. It was exhilarating to be able to go so fast, and she even had to slow down for Tom to keep up.

They broke into a clearing where three wolves gathered at the foot of a large tree. A weeping child was clinging to the trunk, one hand holding onto a low branch while the other grasped the edge of a knothole. A wolf took a running leap, and its teeth just barely missed the boy's ankle. It landed on the ground whipping around as if it would make another try and the terrified screams from the boy were deafening.

Upon first glance, Sally wondered why the kid didn't just climb up the tree and out of reach, but then noticed the white arrow pinning the boy's leg to the trunk. A streamer of blood oozed down his ankle and dropped off the toe of his shoe and a wolf was lapping at the blood as it fell on the ground, saliva dripping hungrily from its maw. The boy was trapped where he clung, with his blood keeping the wolves interested and hungry.

Tom roared and rushed the animals and bashed the torch into the side of a startled wolf. The smell of singed fur filled the air along with the painful yelps in a replay of the previous night. Before the wolves could turn on Tom, Sally jabbed the rapier tip into the heart of one, ending its life. The third wolf howled bitterly and took off with its tail tucked between its legs, followed by its still smoking fellow.

Tom dropped the torch and kicked dirt over it to douse the flames before heading to the tree where the boy was still screaming. Being tall, he could reach the boy's lower half and touched the arrow, causing the boy to shriek.

"Easy! Easy, lad, we're here to help you," Tom said, inspecting the arrow and grimacing at what he saw. "Sally, it went through his leg and into the tree."

Not since Darcy was kidnapped had Sally so wished for her presence now. She would know what to do or cast a spell on the injury. "Should we leave the arrow in? In his leg, I mean. It'll keep him from losing more blood than he has already."

"Yes, but we have to him free him from this tree, or he'll fall and cause more harm to his leg. Here, can you hold him while I pull the arrow free?"

"What if you cut the arrow near the head? That way, you won't risk hurting him." She stepped up close to where Tom was supporting the weeping child who let go of his death grip on the tree.

His small hands were raw and bleeding from continually trying to pull himself up onto the branch and away from the snapping jaws of wolves. How long had this kid been trapped like this? Terrified and in pain with death below, waiting for him to lose his strength and fall.

Tom took a knife and tried to cut through the arrow, but the blade couldn't make a mark on the white wood. To Sally's eyes, the wood seemed to have the smooth surface of plastic with the durability of metal. Sally swallowed a lump in her throat when she recognized it as a mastercraft arrow. A white mastercraft arrow...

They had no choice but to pull it free. Sally braced the boy while Tom took a firm grip on the leg and arrow. He didn't bother counting, as doing so would make the boy anticipate the pain so with a dull crack, the shaft was jerked free. The boy made no noise and shuddered in Sally's arms as she lowered him onto the ground. For a moment, she believed he had passed out until she saw his pale face with large eyes staring at her.

As Tom bound the wound, Sally comforted the boy in the only way she was sure of. She held his hand and patted his head until Tom finished tying off a cloth around the ankle to keep the arrow in place until they returned him to the village. By then, the boy had calmed down enough to tell them his name was Mikel.

"Mikel," Tom said gently, "if it doesn't frighten you, will you tell us what happened?"

As his sister had said, he had gone into the forest to check his snares. Mikel didn't believe the wolves would attack in daylight, despite the warnings. When the wolves broke through the bushes, he ran to the nearest tree to seek refuge in the boughs, but searing pain lanced through his leg, and he couldn't move. Each time he tried to move his leg, agony shot up it. It was all he could do to cling to the tree, just out of reach of the wolves.

"It's alright, lad, we'll get you safely home," Tom promised.

Silently, Sally stared at the white arrow as her stomach filled with dread. Seeing it brought chills down her spine, and she looked around in the trees furtively for a figure watching them from the dark boughs. It was too much of a coincidence for this not to be connected to whoever killed the captured Cut Throat and was attacking caravans. And whoever it was might still be close by.

"Mikel, your sister sent us to find you. Once you're rested, my friend and I will take you home."

"You're friends with an elf?"

Sally blinked, realizing that her hood was still down. She jerked it up over her head, hoping that Tom will take the hint to deny she was an elf.

"She's a half-elf," Tom said firmly, much to her horror. "And she's also a brave young woman who risked herself to save you, a stranger she had never met. Her name is Sally."

It was all she could do to keep from groaning. Dammit, now the whole village was going to know about her race. Hopefully, the adventurers would leave before the villagers decided to chase them out.

"I won't tell anyone," Mikel said meekly. "She helped me!"

"Good, remember that whenever you meet another elf."

Jeez, Tom, you don't have to keep lobbying for elf rights, Sally thought then froze when a noise reached her ears.

"Mikel, I'm going to carry you home. It might hurt your leg, but there's a Cleric that can help you…"

"Tom, get him back up the tree, now." Sally unsheathed her rapier and dagger.

"What?"

“Something’s coming.” She could hear the bushes being disturbed and the sound of heavy breathing coming closer and closer. “This was a trap!”

She was so stupid! She was a Rogue, and didn’t realize this was all a trap until it was too late. It was too perfect! The boy was bait, but not for the wolves.

“He can’t climb with his leg like this!” Tom stood with Mikel in his arms. The boy’s face was white, either from pain or terror, Sally couldn’t possibly tell.

Her heart began to race as they came closer. Yes, *they*. She could hear several large animals cutting through the thick verdure towards them. “Then take him back to the village while I hold them off.”

“I can’t leave you alone…”

“Dammit! Then do whatever you want, but hurry up and decide!” Sally snapped.

To keep herself from panicking, she went over the advantages she had in a fight. She had a high Dex of +4, two weapons meant she had two attacks each turn, and she was level two. And being a Rogue granted her a higher chance of dealing a critical strike. The disadvantages, however, still flooded her mind. She only had 18 HP, and if her attacks weren’t critical, they dealt little damage. The reason she had just killed the wolf so quickly was her Sneak Attack bonus to damage. By themselves, Rogues were mediocre fighters and served better fighting in a group, particularly backing up front line fighters like Tom or Mina or even Naomi.

She needed Tom with her if she was going to have a chance, but the reason they came out here was to save the kid. The boy had to come first, and that meant Tom had to get him to safety while she fended off their attackers. Was it selfish of her that she rather he protect her than the boy? No, just cowardly.

“How many?” Tom asked from her right.

She looked at him, stunned. In any TV show, movie, or video game, someone always took the wounded to safety while the hero stayed behind to ensure their escape. What was going on? “What about the kid?”

“I helped him onto one of the lower branches. He’s safely out of the way.”

“No, you need to get him away from here.”

“I’d rather take both of you away from here,” Tom said firmly. “How many are coming?”

She barely felt any shame at being relieved and happy that he chose to stay. Without any further thought of the boy, she focused on what lay before them. "I think there's five, but something pretty big coming with them. It's bigger than a wolf."

"A person?"

"No, not a person. Something bigger."

Within seconds, they got their answer. They came from the shadow as if molded from it. Four wolves with bared white teeth served as entourage for a wolf the size of a pony with fur white as snow and eyes like black coals that gleamed with malice.

From the corner of her eye, she saw Tom's face go several shades pale, and he drew an unconscious step backward. "A dire wolf."

"Oh God," Sally breathed, knowing they were not going to get out of this alive. Four wolves and this monstrosity was too much for a Fighter and Rogue alone. This must be a boss fight they'd stumbled into.

Dammit, they should have both taken Mikel and ran. The more pragmatic part of her said that outrunning the dire wolf would have been impossible. And what about the owner of the white arrows? Arrows might have perforated them before they had a chance to clear the forest.

With a vicious snarl, the dire wolf charged. It barreled at them with the ferocity of a speeding train. Sally and Tom split apart, and the monstrosity cut through where they had stood together moments ago; it spun in place, unable to decide which of them to go for, until it settled on Sally.

As if predicting its intentions, Sally backpedaled as it lunged. Swinging the rapier, she nicked its snout with the rapier's tip and blood bloomed across its ebony nose, but it kept coming, fangs wet, and glistening snapping the air.

From behind it, Tom swung his sword in a wide arc and caught the monster along the side. The cut wasn't deep as the thick fur offered natural armor and it seemed only to serve to make the dire wolf angrier. It whipped around so fast it was a blur, and Tom barely ducked its snapping jaws. At its back, Sally was in her element as a Rogue and she thrust forward and would have found her mark if it wasn't for the searing pain lancing up her leg.

Damn, they had forgotten the other wolves. One was now tearing into her leg, and after a downward thrust through the throat with the rapier, it let go. Tom was holding his own against the dire wolf, giving ground while standing close enough to return attacks. Sally spotted another wolf about to take a bite out of Tom's leg, and she sprinted towards it.

Her boot had protected her from most of the damage, but it still hurt to run on her leg. Zipping past the dire wolf before it had a chance to notice her, she shoved the rapier between the encroaching wolf's ribs and straight into the heart. It died on her blade, and she pulled it free just as the dire wolf, angered by the death of a pack member, attacked her. Teeth snapped inches from her elbow, and she returned with a dagger aimed for its eye. She missed but slashed along the long muzzle. The cut wasn't deep, but it was enough to make it back away, shaking its head and howling. The last two wolves were stalking forward to avenge their fallen.

"Sally, can you take care of the wolves if I keep their leader off your back?" Tom asked, adjusting his grip on the sword.

"Yeah, I think so," she said, breathing hard. The pain in her ankle had lessened, maybe from the adrenaline.

Tom hollered, waving an arm to get the dire wolf's attention and moved in a broad circle to draw it away. The monster stalked after Tom with murderous intent, lunging for him again. Tom danced backward just in time, but it was a close call.

How long could Tom handle that beast on his own? She needed to kill the wolves quickly and help him as soon as possible.

As if sensing they were being paired off, the wolves parted to flank her. Maintaining her stance, her eyes switched between them. If she attacked one, then the other would jump on her. If one of them attacked, she could counter it with a thrust of the rapier and a slash from the dagger. But if they both attacked her at once...

As if reading her mind, they went for her, one immediately after the other. She pivoted to the left and then to the right, ducking one and then the other. With a twist at the hips, she retaliated with a long swing. The tip of the rapier bit into the dirt, leaving a short, shallow trench no wider than her small finger before it arced upward and caught the wolf's flank.

Damn, the cut wasn't deep enough to kill the wolf, but it was enough to make it retreat. The creature crouched with its tail tucked growling menacingly. The other wolf wasn't dissuaded by its companion's injury and went for her uninjured leg. Sally danced backward, slashing the rapier back and forth, but missing the mark each swing.

The back of her foot hit a root, and losing her balance, she fell on her ass. The wolf took advantage of this opportunity, but Sally was faster. Her dagger caught it in the throat just when its snout was less than an inch from her face. It collapsed, eyes still open and tongue lolling as if it were an affectionate dog resting its head on her lap.

She kicked it off and got to her feet and checked for the other wolf. It had vanished, likely fleeing when its partner was killed. Tom was still facing off with the dire wolf. Its bloody side revealed that he had managed to score some hits on it, but not enough to warrant severe damage.

With Tom drawing the dire wolf's attention, she could get a sneak attack and if not kill it outright, at least deal some critical damage. They might actually get out of this alive. The thought hadn't fully formed in her head when a flash of white left the highest boughs. The arrow hit Tom in the shoulder so hard his body twisted from the impact creating an opening for the dire wolf to act. Its jaws locked across Tom's chest and torso and began to savage him like a chew toy. Blood spurted, spraying across the grass and dotting the tree.

"No!" Sally churned up dried leaves in her mad dash. Sheathing her dagger, she gripped the rapier with both hands intending to shove straight deep into the dire wolf's heart.

Then the monster wrenched Tom around, putting him between Sally and itself and she came to such a sudden halt that her boots left skid marks in the dirt. Tom's face was contorted in agony, but he still held onto his sword and lifting it in one hand, he brought it down across the head of the beast. The strike had more impetus from gravity than from any strength behind it, but it was enough to shear off an ear.

The dire wolf howled, dropping Tom onto the grass and it began rubbing its head with a forepaw as if it were a cat. Sally didn't dare let herself look at Tom, who had fallen in a bloody heap on the ground. As long as the dire wolf still stood, it was a danger to them.

The dire wolf raised its head, blood streaming down its face from its cut ear and it looked at her with the evident intention of tearing her violently to ribbons. Sally was impressed that her rapier wasn't quivering in her shaking hands. If it lunged at her, she only had one shot to stab it in the throat.

A shrill whistle cut the air like a siren. Instantly, the dire wolf drew back and sat down on its haunches. Its enormous maw opened with a pant like a dog who had just enjoyed a day outside playing catch. For Sally, it was surreal to see the animal take a long yawn and then lope lazily through the trees.

Was it over? Just like that?

A choking noise from Tom drew her attention and she rushed to his side, dropping the rapier and looked over his injuries. His shirt was soaked in crimson and had to be cut off him with the dagger. A large half-ring of deep punctures all seeped blood, spurting at each breath he took. This was more than she could handle with basic first aid, and she didn't even have so much as a Band-Aid. This would require cleaning and suturing, that is if he hadn't suffered some internal damage. He needed a health potion or a spell to survive the next few minutes.

Tom's face was turning a sickening shade of white. He was going to die, and she had not apologized to him yet. It was stupid to worry about, but it seemed like the most important thing in the world since he was bleeding out before her.

Something sailed through the air and landed next to her. She drew away, fearful it was another attack, but then stare in stunned silence at the large bottle with a golden clasp filled with red liquid.

"It's a high-level health potion. Pour it over the wounds, and they'll close up," said a woman's voice from the boughs.

Sally couldn't see the source of the voice. "Who's there?"

"You gonna worry about me or you gonna worry about your pet NPC?" a sarcastic voice said. "He's lost about two liters of blood, give or take. Hurry before he exsanguinates."

What if this was poison? Yet, what did Tom have to lose? His blood was staining her knees and the grass around him. The potion had a thicker consistency than the smaller potions she had seen. It was like thin syrup that almost glittered in the sunlight and like syrup, when she poured it across Tom's chest, it drizzled. Slowly, as it mixed with the blood and was absorbed into the skin the wounds stopped bleeding, and the flesh molded back together. She could be mistaken, but it seemed some of the color was returning to his face. The arrow was still in his shoulder, and she pulled it out before the flesh could close around the head. The action barely drew any blood. The hole closed without leaving a mark.

Sally turned her gaze back to the boughs. "That dire wolf...it's your animal, isn't it? And you were the one who shot Tom!"

"I couldn't let him hurt my dog," the voice replied wryly.

The word dog was pronounced "dawg."

"And you were the one who shot the kid and trapped him against the tree! You sick freak!"

"Careful," the voice said with a warning edge. "Your tone is pissing me off, and, honey, I promise you that ain't a smart thing to do right now."

Sally could imagine the stranger whistling for the dire wolf to return or just putting an arrow between her eyes. Taking a deep breath, she spoke slowly, "You're the reason why the wolves have been attacking people."

"After my dog killed the pack leaders all the wolves fell in line behind him. I wanted to see what they could do, but they only understand basic commands. Go here and attack these people or go over there and attack those people. I've gotten bored with it, so we'll be moving on."

All of this was done for fun? Sally felt her stomach heaving, but swallowed it back. "You've been attacking caravans too."

"I'm just playing the game."

"You're killing people."

"Oh Christ, of all the other players I could have run into, I come across one with a bleeding heart." Sally could hear the eye roll behind those words. "They're not real. They are not people. They're NPCs. You know what an NPC is, right?"

"Yeah," Sally replied, turning her gaze back to Tom. His chest rose and fell, and she could still smell the blood congealing on her hands. Since she met him, she had seen him laugh, eat, drink, and even try to kiss her. "But it's no longer that simple anymore."

"I'll grant you that," the voice agreed. "I guess that's what makes it all the more fun."

I don't know what her stats are, but if she can kill an entire caravan of people then they must be pretty high. She could be moving all around me and she's high level enough that her Sneak outclasses my Perception. And my Armor Class is probably nothing to her.

A wave of helpless anger rolled over Sally, and her hands clenched uselessly on her knees. This is where she should shout that it wasn't right! That NPCs were people too! It was wrong to kill them for fun. Yet, Sally was too afraid of an arrow in her gut or being mauled to say anything like that. Instead, she said, "Do you have any idea of how this happened?"

"Nope, none. Just glad that it did, and I hope it lasts forever." The voice sounded further away. "I'm going now. You can go collect whatever reward you'll get for saving the boy. And you can untwist your panties about the village. The wolves won't bother it anymore."

Sally watched the boughs with eyes squinted against the light penetrating the canopy. Something white moved from branch to branch like it had wings. When she blinked, it was gone. Perhaps in that moment, Sally's Perception check was high while the stranger's Sneak check had been low. That was how she could explain it.

YOU HAVE LEVELED UP!

Her world darkened save for the hot glow of letters. Before, she would have been happy to see them, but she felt only defeated. She had gained level three, but she would still be completely outstripped by the stranger.

Would you like to continue leveling up in the Rogue Class? Yes/No?

Could she afford to multiclass? What would be her options? She selected "no" and a list of classes appeared before her.

Bard

Cleric

Druid

Fighter

Monk

Ranger

Sorcerer

Wizard

This was a bigger selection than that which was offered to Mina. Which one? She wasn't sure what Bard or Druid meant. It'd be nice to learn spells like a Sorcerer or Wizard, maybe get some healing spells from Cleric. Monk or Fighter would make her a stronger fighter.

It was tempting, but something in her heart told her that she should remain as a Rogue. Darcy had said that each of them should embrace their roles in a party and so far, being a Rogue had served her and her party well. She dismissed the list and selected "yes."

Your Sneak Attack damage has increased!

Now for her ten skill points. It was pretty cut and dry. One point to Sneak (+9) and one to Perception (+5). Legerdemain might come in handy in a city like Everguard, so two points to it (+9). Darcy did say not to ignore her social skills…so a point in each. Charm (+7). Deceit (+7). Intimidate (+6).

In order to finish up, she put the last point gain into Climb (+7) and Evaluate (+3). Highlighting Evaluate told her it allowed her to appraise an item and determine the identity of an item and its worth. Might be useful, might not be.

"Are they gone?"

She blinked, her eyes adjusting to the light after the level up screen had faded. Wow, being so enthralled with leveling had made her forget about the boy.

"Yes, they're not coming back. It's safe to come down if you're able to." How much did the kid hear? What exactly did they say? Had he been watching her stare at nothing for several minutes? Her mind was drawing blanks, and she could only focus on one thing at a time.

"Is Tom alive?" The white face was looking at Tom's prone body.

"I think he's going to be alright, but we need to get him back to the village." Tom didn't seem to be in danger, but she wouldn't feel sure about this until Darcy looked him over.

Yet, how were they going to get him back? Her Strength bonus was 0, so there was no chance of her carrying an unconscious man as tall as Tom and a lame boy too. Maybe she could cobble together a stretcher and drag him behind her with the kid on her back.

Then she heard rustling from nearby. Before she knew it, the rapier and dagger were back in her hands. Of course, the sicko wasn't done playing games with them. She had come back to finish them off. Then Sally recognized the voices, and lowered the weapons and nearly fell against the tree in relief.

Naomi appeared from the thicket and upon seeing Sally, her face lit up in a bright smile, and she flung herself at the Rogue in a tight squeeze. "I found her! Mina! She's here and so is…Tom! What happened to Tom?"

"He's alright. We just had a run-in with the wolves. Where's Darcy?" Her eyes were welling with tears, but she held them back. If she started crying now, she might not stop for a long while.

"Back at the village. A building fell on some kids, and we saved them. She stayed behind to heal them, and we came looking for you."

Well, that made sense of why it took them so long to catch up. "Wait, do you mean you and Mina? Did you run into any trouble?"

"Yeah, but Mina took care of it," Naomi stepped back and noticed the boy in the tree and waved. "Hey there!"

Mina took care of it? What did she do? Faint and fall on the wolves?

Then Mina finally made her appearance, and Sally barely recognized her. There was still a frantic energy about her, but it wasn't the usual nervous wreck sort that Sally had associated with her. Mina held a great blood-stained ax expertly with both hands, which gave her a grim appearance. If Sally hadn't come to know her so well, then Mina would have certainly looked the part of a Barbarian who had just left the battlefield.

"Mina? Are you okay?"

Mina put away the ax on her back and nodded. "Yeah, I'm fine, but I'm more worried about you and Tom. What happened?"

"We found out what was causing the wolves to be aggressive, and it kicked our asses."

Chapter 18

THE AFTERMATH

With Mina carrying Tom and the boy on Sally's back and Naomi scouting ahead, they made it back to the village without incident. They went straight to the makeshift hospital, where Darcy was working tirelessly with the healer. Most of the kids were out of danger, but there were a few that would need to be watched throughout the night.

Sally made sure to pull her hood up to hide her ears. Though Mikel seemed willing to accept her, she didn't want to risk it with the villagers. She noticed Mina watching her, and she received a nod from the Barbarian, indicating she shared the same thoughts.

The main room's furniture had been moved, and cots were set up for the wounded. Thankfully, some were minor injuries that only needed their wounds cleaned and bandaged and those children were able to go home with their parents. The healer, a small older woman who looked like she could be Methuselah's great-grandmother, knew how to clean wounds and to use clean bandages. Leaving the superficial injuries to the healer, Darcy cast healing spells on those in more serious condition.

By the time they brought Tom in, she had used the last of her healing spells to stabilize a little girl who lost too much blood. When she saw his condition, she went pale. "What happened to him?"

"I'll explain later," Sally said she set Mikel on a cot. "This one needs help too."

"Aw Jesus, I'm fresh out of spells. Let me get the healer for the boy, and I'll see what I can do for Tom. Is anyone else hurt?"

"No, we're all fine."

Mina laid Tom down on an empty cot, and he appeared to be resting peacefully. "I don't think he's in any danger. I'm not sure what happened to him, but whatever it was, he's recovering from it."

"Good, because we're stretched thin as it is," Darcy said, looking at the rest of the injured. "Since I ran out of spells, we can only do so much with what we have."

"What about this?" Sally unhooked the large potion bottle's clasp from her belt and held it up. It was still a quarter full, and the thick liquid clung to the inside of the glass as it balanced in her hand.

Darcy's eyes went wide as she took the bottle from Sally and held it up to the light to stare at it in shock. "Where did you get this?"

"What is it?" Mina said, peering at the bottle. "It looks like strawberry syrup."

"It's a potion of Supreme Healing," Darcy said, almost entranced by the bottle. "Or what's left of it. It's the most powerful healing potion that you can get. How did you find this?"

"I didn't find it. It was given to me." Sally sighed. "I know everyone has a lot of questions right now, but it's not something we should discuss around...other people." She made a pointed look at the parents who were staying at their children's bedside and the healer puttering about tending to them.

Nodding in understanding, Darcy gave the bottle her full attention. "There isn't enough to go around, but we can water it down, maybe brew it into a tea."

Mina furrowed her brow. "Will that work? Is it that strong?"

"Yes! One dose of this can restore over a hundred hit points. A watered-down version could do half of that, more than enough for NPC kids."

"How can you be so sure?" Mina said firmly. "If a dosage is too weak, then it won't do anything. Too strong, and you'll end up causing more harm."

Darcy tapped her temple. "I have a Healing skill of plus nine, so I know what I'm talking about. The healer and I can take it from here, you three can go to the inn and rest. The mayor had a talk with the innkeeper, and he's letting us stay in two rooms free of charge until we take care of the wolf problem."

Sally gave her a tired sardonic smile. "Already taken care of. No more wolf problem for the village."

Darcy's eyebrows went up. "What? How did...never mind, you'll tell me about it later. Go get something to eat and rest."

***

The innkeeper was in better spirits and gave them plates with actual food on them. Freshly baked bread, roasted chicken, tender roast, fried fish, and candied apples. It was a beautiful sight to behold.

"Where was this yesterday?" Mina groused, giving the innkeeper a narrowed look.

"It ain't mine to give," the man said. "It's from the parents of those children you saved. They brought it over and said to make sure you ate like kings tonight."

Sally didn't have it in her to give him any grief over how he treated them earlier. The smell was mouth-watering, and her stomach reminded her that it had been a while since their last good meal. With a small thanks, she helped herself and ate until she was full, while both Mina and Naomi followed her example. Before long, Naomi was asleep with her head on the table and a drumstick in hand.

Mina gently picked her up to take her upstairs to bed, but Sally touched her arm before she could head up and said, "Don't go to bed yet. When Darcy comes in, the three of us have to talk."

Mina checked to make sure Naomi was asleep before she whispered, "Alright, I'll put her in a room, and we'll wait for Darcy in the other one."

There was change about Mina that was hard to put her finger on, but the Barbarian stood with her back straight instead of her usual slouch as if she were trying to retain her original height. And she didn't complain anymore nor seemed to be near a panic attack either.

She can handle what I have to tell them, Sally thought. Naomi will want to go after the stranger, but Mina will see the sense of staying away from her without breaking down into hysterics. She's grown up or has come to terms with being in this world. I actually envy she has something figured while I feel like I'm drowning.

Sally asked the innkeeper for a pot of coffee and cups to take upstairs.

"Will there be anything else, milady?" he asked politely, which was a far different attitude than before.

Since they were considered heroes of the village, the people had been bowing and addressing them as such. As if they were knights from a storybook or heroes instead of people that were hired to deal with wolves and got roped into helping the kids because of bad carpentry.

"No, just tell the Cleric when she shows up we're waiting upstairs with coffee."

The room was narrow with two beds, similar to the inn in Spring Bell. Against the wall, between the two beds was a small table where she set the tray. The smell of coffee was so tempting that she helped herself to a cup while she waited.

Mina came in a few minutes later and poured herself one too. After taking a long sip, she said, "How old do you think Naomi is?"

Surprised by the sudden question, Sally paused in raising the mug to her lips. "I don't know. Sixteen, maybe fifteen? Why?"

"I don't know. She's spunky for a teenager, is all." Mina took another pull from her coffee and set it on the tray. "I guess I better tell you what happened in the village."

"Naomi said a building fell on the kids."

"That sums it up, and then I had to lift it off of them." Mina gave her a wry smile. "I wasn't strong enough to do it myself, not until I…Raged."

Sally raised an eyebrow and said, "I thought you could only do that when you fight."

"No, I can do it anytime I need it. I just have to get angry for it to kick in. I got pissed off at the carpenter for not listening to me when I warned against letting kids play in a construction site."

"What did the villagers do to him once everything was over?"

"I don't know what they're going to do with him, but I did drop the pillar on his house, so I guess it'll even out."

Sally laughed and slapped her knee, "Seriously? You dropped a pillar on his house?"

"Not on purpose!" Mina said quickly. "I didn't know it was his house when it fell. Only after he started shouting, "That's my house!"

Sally sniggered. "Serves him right. So are you…are you okay with Raging now?"

Mina's smile faded, and looking away, she picked up her coffee mug, took another drink from it, and held it between her large hands. It was like a small egg in her thick fingers. "Yes and no. It still scares me, but I don't see it as something bad anymore. I'll never enjoy fighting, but I'm not going to wuss out of it. If I'm needed at the front, then that's where I'll be."

"Wow, Mina, that's...that's great. At least you have your shit together. That more than I can say for myself."

Mina raised her eyes to Sally, "What do you mean?"

Sally rubbed the back of her head and wished she hadn't said anything. "I'm a mess. Tom almost got killed on my watch."

"I still don't know what happened out there, but I wouldn't believe it was your fault. You led the rescue mission to save Darcy and me from the Cut Throats."

"That was me following Naomi's lead."

"No, I think it was more than that. Do you honestly believe that Naomi could engineer a rescue on her own? I like the kid and everything, but she's not...I don't think she's playing with a full deck sometimes." Mina said with a shrug. "And you managed to save Tom too."

"That's another thing." Sally looked down at her hands. The fingers were long and thin with fingernails perfect crescents. "I know that Tom likes me, but he likes this hot supermodel that isn't me. The real me is an overweight couch potato who can eat a large cheese pizza and drink a two-liter Coke by herself."

"I think he admires you more than being attracted to you physically," Mina said with a gentle smile. "But I guess the bigger question is, do you like him back? I mean, setting aside the fact you aren't in your real body."

"I...I don't know...I don't think so, but I never really liked anyone before." Most of her school life had been spent studying and reading books, and she avoided social gatherings like the plague. The first person she ever opened up to was Darcy, and that had taken living under the same roof for a while to happen.

"It's okay if you're...ya know..." Mina looked uncomfortable but kind. "An Ace?"

Sally shook her head, her cheeks turning pink. "It's not like that. I just...don't think I'm something anyone would want."

It was at that moment Darcy finally came inside, halting anything that Mina would have said to Sally's comment. The Cleric was carrying a demijohn under one arm, and several cups hooked over her fingers. "The innkeeper said we could have this."

Pleased to have an awkward conversation interrupted, Sally jumped up to help Darcy with the cups. "I got coffee on the table over there if you need it."

Darcy looked as if she could use some. There were dark circles beneath her eyes, and she looked as if she would fall asleep as soon as she lay down.

Her eyes brightened when she spotted the coffee pot, and Darcy handed the demijohn to Mina. "The kids are going to be alright and I don't think they'll be in any hurry to play around unfinished buildings again. Tom's going to make a full recovery, but the healer says he's going to be weak for a few days due to blood loss. I suspect that he took serious Constitution damage, but I'll try a heal spell on him in the morning to see if that helps."

Then Darcy looked pointedly at Sally and said firmly, "You need to go see him first thing in the morning. When he woke up, he was afraid for you and tried to get out of bed to find you, but I told him that you were alright. The healer insisted that he go back to sleep and gave him a tea that helped him to relax. Knowing you, you still need to apologize to him."

Sally hung her head. "I give you my word that I will apologize to him before I do anything else tomorrow."

"Good, now let me at the coffee before I fall asleep on my feet." After draining a cup, she turned to Sally and said, "Alright, what happened out there?"

Then Sally told them everything: from finding Mikel pinned to a tree with an arrow, to the dire world attacking, and then about the stranger. Mina listened in silent horror while Darcy only interrupted her to ask questions. What color was the direwolf? Did she catch a glimpse of the stranger?

"I did, but barely for a second, she was so fast I couldn't catch any detail about her except that she was wearing white."

Sally noticed that Darcy didn't seem tired anymore and her dark complexion looked almost pallid. "You said she. Are you sure it was a woman?"

"It sounded like a woman, and she had a southern accent too."

"Shit," Darcy moaned, rubbing a face over her face. "Oh, dear Lord, no, no, not this. Anything, but this."

Both Sally and Mina stared at her in unsettling silence. They had seen her upset and afraid before, but not like this. Even Sally had never seen her sister so frightened as if she was about to piss herself.

It was Mina who broke the silence. "Do you know who she is?"

"I, unfortunately, do," Darcy said, wringing her hands. "White arrows, white direwolf, and white clothing, it matches what I've heard about her. Goddammit...of all the people to be trapped in this world with..."

"Darcy, don't keep us in suspense," Sally said, getting impatient and more scared by Darcy's reaction. "Who are we dealing with?"

"Lemme correct you right there." Darcy held up a finger and wagged it Sally's face. "We aren't dealing with this woman at all. We are staying as far away from her as possible."

"Okay, we get it. We understand," Mina said, exasperated. "This isn't someone we want to mess with. So please tell us who it is we don't want to mess with."

Darcy pinched the bridge of her nose, looking haggard and so very tired. "I don't know her name, but I do know she's a PK."

Sally and Mina had different reactions. The Rogue's jaw dropped open, and her eyes went wide with fear. Mina looked between the sisters, confused and afraid. "What's a PK?"

"It means Player Killer," Sally said. Even though she was a single-player gamer, she had heard the phrase tossed around in the gaming community more than once. "It means she goes around killing other players for fun."

Mina's dark eyebrows arched upward. "The game allows you to do that?"

"There were some servers that are non-PK, but the more popular ones are not," Darcy said, eyeing the demijohn longingly, but changed her mind and looked way. "And guess which one Aslan Twenty-Five is?"

"Shit," Sally moaned, also eyeing the demijohn.

Darcy wasn't finished with the bad news yet. "There's this group that call themselves the Hunters. They ambush players for fun, but they don't pick up their fallen items. They'll leave them as bait for other players and kill them too."

"So, she's one of these Hunters?" Sally said, tempted to take a swig of wine too.

"She'd have to be one of them to be their leader," Darcy said and let that hang in the air over them.

"If it's just one person..." Mina started.

"Let me stop you right there," Darcy said with a sharp motion. "The Hunters are high-level players. They all have twenty levels in one class and several levels in others. The last time their leader posted her stats online, she was a level twenty Ranger with five levels in Rogue and Fighter. Not only that, the Hunters all have top tier equipment and items. If you swing at her with your ax and manage to somehow, someway land a hit, it'll just bounce off her masterwork enchanted leather armor like a Nerf bat."

There was a long silence as Sally drew a slow breath and Mina sat stoically, but even she could see beads of sweat forming on her brow.

"What about the direwolf? How does she have control over it?" Mina asked, breaking the silence.

"Rangers can get an animal companion," Darcy explained. "It levels up with the player and changes into stronger forms. Hers would have started out a small dog and eventually become a direwolf. What's more, animal companions have an empathetic link with their masters so they can follow complex commands and report whatever they see. And it knows when its master is in danger, so even if we by some divine intervention, manage to get the upper hand over her, it'll come charging in to save her."

"She had it take over the wolf packs to see what she could make them do," Sally said, looking haunted. "She's been terrorizing the village and killing caravans for fun."

Shaking her head, Mina stood to her full height. "I just can't believe that someone would do that! She's...she's like a mass shooter or a terrorist!"

Darcy gave her a sad look and touched her arm in a comforting pat. "You're not a gamer, so you haven't seen the toxic side of gaming. Some gamers can be complete and utter assholes just for laughs and the Hunters are the worst."

"She doesn't see the NPCs as people," Sally said, her voice started weak and scared, but it rose to a firm tone as she drilled into Mina all that she had learned. "She sees them as playthings, people she can kill and hurt without consequences. She loves being in this world because no one can touch her."

"I can see how she would see NPCs as toys, but she knows we're players too, right? She gave Sally a potion and didn't attack her." Mina was looking between them almost desperately.

"Don't fool yourself into believing it was out of any kindness," Darcy said hotly. "It's possible we may be the first players she's come across, but that could mean anything. She might want an audience for her atrocities, or hasn't decided what she wants to do to us yet."

"Then how did she get so strong?" Mina demanded as she rounded on Darcy. "You said this was a new server! We all had to make new characters…"

"You can transfer a character to a new server by paying a fee," Darcy groaned. "That's what makes the Hunters so dangerous. They either have a rich member that can pay for all of them to change servers so often or they're all wealthy enough to afford it. They don't stay in one server for long so you never know when they'll show up. One week, they had a genocide contest where each member killed off players of different races and our friend in the forest won that contest."

Sally hung her head, hating this conversation with a passion. The more she learned about the Hunter, the more frightened she became. "So what can we do? Since we can't fight, can we at least hide from her?"

"Everguard is our best bet," Darcy said with a stiff nod. "The game developers didn't want to take away options from players, but they did install serious consequences for causing trouble in a city. If you attack an NPC or they see you stealing, then all the guards converge on your location. They aren't as high level as our Hunter, but there's a lot of them so they might be able to overwhelm her."

Mina sat down while Darcy was talking and looked a bit more at ease. "How big is Everguard?"

"Pretty big," Darcy replied. "There'll be enough people there that she'll think twice before going there to start trouble."

Mina nodded, "Good and we'll find other players. As scary as this is, this proves we're not alone."

"And don't forget, we got Naomi's lycanthropy to cure too," Sally reminded them. "We lost a whole day and if your heal spell doesn't help Tom, then we're going to be slowed."

"Ah, no worries," Darcy said breaking into a bright grin that she could bring some bit of good news. "I talked to the mayor and he says that since the wolf problem is gone they'll start sending rafts up to Everguard and we'll be there by tomorrow afternoon."

"Oh, thank God," Mina praised, relieved by the notion they wouldn't have to do any more walking or camping.

Darcy gave a long jaw popping yawn. "Let's get some rest. We'll have plenty of time to plan tomorrow morning."

"One more thing before we go to bed," Sally said. "I leveled up."

Mina grinned, a smile clearing away the fear and dread that had darkened her face. "So have I. Level three."

"When did that happen?" Darcy asked, looking between the two of them with large eyes.

"It happened after we saved the kids. Just before I left to go find Tom and Sally. Didn't you see me just standing there and poking the air?"

"Uh, no, you just said you were going to find them and left. That's when you leveled up? Why didn't you say anything?"

"I don't know," Mina said, shrugging. "I think...maybe this is going to sound weird, but I think time stops when we level up."

"What do you mean?" Sally asked, leaning forward with her hands clasped together before her.

"Well, when I first leveled up, I didn't know what I was doing so it took at least ten minutes. It would have been more if I had more skill points."

"Wait, but you were right behind us," Darcy said.

"I was, and that confused me. At first, I thought you two had waited for me despite what happened to Naomi. I just haven't had a chance to speak about it until now."

"Mina, did you feel rejuvenated after you leveled up?" Sally said, touching her chin in a resemblance of Darcy in deep thought.

"Ah, yeah, like I just drank a Red Bull."

"The first time I leveled up," Sally said, taking off her boots. "I broke my leg fighting the werewolf. It healed when I leveled up." She stretched her legs out for them to see. They were whole and solid without a mark or bruise. "And earlier, when Tom and I were fighting the wolves, one of them bit me here."

She touched her ankle where a wolf had sank its fangs into her boot. "It hurt like a sprain, but the pain went away when I leveled up. Darcy, does the game heal restore all hit points when you level up?"

"Yeah, it does," Darcy said. "It's convenient when you're low on hit points and out of health items. I had no idea whether that would remain the same in this world or not."

"It'll be useful one day," Mina said with an ominous air. Then she gave a long jaw popping yawn.

This was contagious, as Sally followed Mina's example and yawned too. "Are we forgetting anything? Is there anything else we need to talk about before going to bed?"

It was the Cleric's turn to yawn and began removing her armor. "No, I don't think so. Unless you can think of something."

Considering it for a moment, Sally shook her head. "I'm too tired to think. Maybe it'll come to me in the morning."

Without another word other than a brief goodnight, the women retired to bed. Mina and Darcy stayed in the room, and since Sally had the highest Sneak skill of +9, she crept into the next room to share with Naomi. As she undressed, she watched the Monk sleep. She was spread almost eagle spread across the bed with one arm curled above her head and one leg hanging off the edge.

Sally remembered Mina questioning how old Naomi was and now Sally was seeing something that Mina had noticed…but couldn't put her finger on what it was.

Well, it was too late to care about it now. It could wait until morning.

Chapter 19

INNPEASEA

It was hours before the sun would rise, but Tom didn't believe he could sleep for another moment as his body was still bruised and painful from the attack. He remembered the wolf biting him: the smell of his blood and the pain of almost being ripped apart. Then there was darkness. When the light returned it revealed Darcy bending over him and a cup of oddly sweetened tea pressed to his lips.

He had seized her wrist and demanded where Sally was or if she still lived. Darcy gave him a wry smile and assured him she was safe and the direwolf was gone, and with it, the village's wolf problem.

Reflecting on the events, he was content that they had done well. They saved a boy's life, rescued children, and aided a village in their time of need. They had accomplished so much, and done so much good.

"I did more for my people in one day than I ever had in my whole life," he said to the ceiling as it was his only listener. "And I did it outside the safety of the castle with my own two hands…and with companions."

He couldn't have done it alone without Sally and her friends. This must be what it meant to travel with companions and see the world and have adventures. It was childish to think such things, but it was there all the same.

There was an unsteady movement outside the door and it opened slowly. He expected it to be Darcy or Sally coming to see him, but instead, it was the boy, Mikel, who peered at him from the door.

"Lad? Are you alright?" Tom sat up despite the ache in his chest and back.

"Aye, I'm fine, but the healer said I shouldn't walk or climb trees for several weeks." The boy edged into the room on a crutch. The ankle that had been pierced by the arrow was bandaged. The skin at the edges was red and swollen.

"You shouldn't be on that ankle, boy," Tom said firmly. "You'll likely hurt yourself again or do more damage than what the healer can mend."

"Can the cleric woman heal me again? So I can run and climb again?" Mikel asked, hopefully.

"I shall ask her on your behalf," Tom promised. "Now, go you to bed before you're caught out of it."

Mikel started back through the door, paused, and then turned back. "Did they catch the woman who shot me?"

Tom blinked for several long moments. "It was a woman who shot you? You never said anything about it being a woman."

Mikel shivered and looked very small and frightened. "I didn't know it at first. Not until your elf friend spoke to her."

"What do you mean?" Was the lad dreaming up such things?

"It was after the large wolf near killed you. I was so certain you were dead, sir. There was blood everywhere, and your elf friend was trying to rouse you, but you wouldn't wake up."

Tom touched his shoulder, just above his armpit. A forgotten memory of a white missile and sudden pain in his shoulder returned to him. "I was shot with a white arrow…white arrows…"

How could he have forgotten about finding the man dead with arrows in his back? Or the news of the caravan of the dead, all killed by white arrows. Whoever was responsible had been there, had tried to kill him.

"What happened? Was Sally hurt?"

"No, she wasn't hurt, but she talked to the woman." The room was dim, with only the light of the moon coming through the window. Mikel's face almost glowed in the dark, making his eyes larger and skin white, like a ghost. "I never saw the archer because she was talking from the trees. High up, higher than anybody should be able to climb, sir. And when she spoke, I almost made water on myself. It was like she was talking from all around us."

"What did she and Sally say?" Tom felt his throat going dry.

"I don't know. I was so afraid I was going to be shot too and what I did hear I don't understand," Mikel said. "I can tell that you that Sally was scared too, and was angry. And the woman…the woman called you a…something strange."

"Strange?" Did she know about his being a prince? Did Sally tell her?

"It was a foreign word. I don't know what it means. She called you a-a," Mikel struggled with the word, "innpeasea."

"Innpeasea? Are you sure that's what she said?"

"Yes. I think so…your friend knew what it meant. Is it an elven word?"

"Not one that I had ever heard of," Tom said. The elven word for humans was Drikens, a word originally meant for short-lived little devils, but now more suited for the humans who had usurped the elves' rule over the continent.

"Mikel, have you spoken of this to anyone?"

"No, only to you."

"My friends and I will take care of this woman, so you need not speak of it again. Go back to bed and rest. I'm sure Sister Darcy will heal your leg before we leave."

Relieved, Mikel's face brightened, and he nodded, "Yes sir, I like her. She's not as strict as any other cleric I've met. I didn't have to pray at all while she was helping me."

"Yes, she is an odd one."

Tom wished he was as confident as he sounded for the boy. When the door closed, he lay his head on the pillow and could not rest because his mind was full of too many questions, not enough answers. Yet again, Sally and her companions presented another mystery.

When they had seen the dead bandit, they had been horrified: innocent Naomi had been in tears. And when they heard of the caravans, they had been equally concerned. Unless they were all good actors, which he doubted, they knew how to feign shock and sadness well.

Naomi was too open to hide any ulterior motives, and Mina's emotions were too visible for any deception. He couldn't say the same for Darcy nor Sally, however. If any one of their group could lie or deceive, then it would be them. They were the ones who spoke in hushed whispers, and more than once he saw them exchange a communicative look when they thought he wasn't observing them.

Though he welcomed their lax treatment of him, it was still bewildered him. They treated him as an equal, as if his station was no higher than theirs. There was no servitude, reverence, nor admiration in how they acted around him. Sometimes he felt ignored and out of place.

Who were they? The way they spoke, their mannerisms, and even how they interact with everything around them was queer. And worst of all, they were somehow familiar with the white arrow culprit.

What was their connection to that fiend?

***

"Sally! Get up! Now, please!"

Sally moaned into the pillow and tried to return to that warm, wonderful place where she didn't have to wake up, but a rude prodding at her side wouldn't let her do that. Her eyes reluctantly opened to see Darcy bending over her.

"Five more minutes?" Sally pleaded meekly.

"You said that twenty minutes ago. Get up, or I'll have Naomi come up here and get you up. And she suggested a bucket of cold water."

Sally didn't start to wake up until she was halfway downstairs, and the pleasant smell of fresh coffee hit her nose. She hurried down to the table where Naomi was having a grand old time recounting the tale of Mina single-handedly lifting the pillar to save the children. A few early risers were listening intently and cheering at the right moments, and Mina was trying to hide her red face in her coffee mug.

Sally drained a mug of coffee and grabbed a piece of toast to eat on the way. Darcy led them across the yard and past a well that reminded Sally of a wishing well. Unaccustomed to being outside so early in the morning, Sally marveled at how the chill air seemed to fill her chest. It gathered up into a tight achy ball beneath her sternum until she exhaled in a long rush of breath.

Warmth welcomed her as she quietly opened the door and stepped into the house filled with the scent of tea and herbs. Children were still sleeping, squeezed between their parents. The ones who could fit in the cot, slept on the floor beside their child, their hand grasping the tiny one above their head.

Moving carefully to prevent disturbing parents or children was easy with Sally's Sneak of +9; she moved without sound, nor even disturbed the flames of candles as she passed them. Darcy, however, had to take pains not to trip over legs or a blanket left forgotten on the floor with her paltry Sneak of +2.

When they arrived at Tom's door, Darcy peeked inside.

"Tom? Hey, you're awake? Sally is here to see you." Darcy stepped back and waved Sally inside.

Why did it feel it feel so grave? Like she was visiting someone at death's door? She knew the answer: it was because she was dreading apologizing to him. If she had any guts, then she would have done this long before now, before Mikel's sister ran to them for help. No use in putting it off any longer. The man had gotten hurt on her account, and she should be hurrying in there to see him.

Tom was sitting up in bed and looked better than he had yesterday. He smiled at her and she found herself smiling back. Any trepidation she felt about seeing him fell away, like a shroud being lifted.

"Darcy told me you were alright, but I couldn't stop worrying until I saw you for myself," Tom said as she crossed the room. Darcy quietly closed the door, leaving them alone.

"I'm fine," she said. Hearing Tom talk after watching him having been nearly ripped apart gave her profound relief. The healing magic in this world was phenomenal. In the real world, Tom would be in the hospital room on a ventilator and receiving blood transfusions. Now he was able to sit up in bed as if he had gotten over a bad cold.

If she didn't do it now, then something catastrophic would happen to delay it like the building catching on fire or another kid getting lost in the woods.

"Tom, I'm sorry about what I said about your sister." She spoke quickly to get it over with...

He stared at her, his brows knitted in confusion. "What did you say about her? And when?"

Had he already forgotten? A lot had happened since then, so she supposed it might have slipped his mind. And here she was reminding him of it. "You don't remember?"

With eyebrows raised, he shook his head. "No. What did you say?"

"Remember when we were camping before the wolves attacked? We were talking, and I said that rescuing you was an accident and you said it was a happy accident and I..." She sighed, hating herself all over again for her crassness. "And I said 'like your sister.' I am so sorry I said that."

Instead of becoming angry or offended, Tom threw his head back and laughed. Sally stared at him, uncertain if she should be happy or disturbed that he wasn't yelling at her. When he stopped laughing, he wiped away a tear and said in a jovial tone, "She was a happy accident."

Sally confused as she thought that Tom cherished his sister. "I don't understand."

"As in most cases with men of power, my father never intended to have a child with his mistress," Tom said with a soft smile. "And his mistress certainly didn't sleep with him to bear him children. So what you said is correct, she was an accident for them, but she made me very happy. After my mother died, she was the only person I could call family without duty and honor linked to it. I don't know how my life would have been if my father and his mistress did not have their 'happy accident.'"

Dumbstruck, Sally couldn't believe she had been sweating this whole time over something Tom wasn't even offended by in the first place. Then, slowly, a grin spread across her face, and she broke into a laugh. Tom joined her and their laughter mingled between them and until they were almost in tears.

Sally wiped her eyes and shook her head, so happy to have that off her chest. "So we're good? I mean, we're on good terms?"

"Yes! I never saw us anything else than on good terms," Tom said. His smile faltered at the edges until it diminished.

Sally noticed the sudden change in his mood, and her jovial mood faded too. "Is something wrong?"

"I...I heard a strange word," Tom said slowly. "I was wondering if you knew what it meant."

He touched her hand for a moment before curling his fingers around it. Sally was surprised by the tight grip as if he was hanging from the edge of a cliff. "What's wrong, Tom?"

"Nothing. Just curious over this word I heard. Innpeasea? Have you heard of it?"

Confused Sally mouthed the word to herself. "I never heard of it. What does it mean?"

"I don't know. I was hoping you would."

"Innpeasea? Am I saying that, right? Sorry, but I have no idea," Sally said, shaking her head.

"Please, think about it." His eyes were on her face, watching her eyes and mouth.

Why was he so insistent that she knew what this strange word meant? Darcy might know. She was so familiar with this world she ought to recognize any unusual names or labels. Sally took a moment to think about it. Innpeasea? It sounded like three words put together. Separated, they sounded like Inn. Pae. Sea.

Inn. Pea. Sea. Her blood chilled in her veins. It wasn't three words. It was three letters. NPC. Where the hell did he hear NPC?

Maybe it was fast thinking, maybe she had rolled high on her Intelligence score of +2, but she suddenly realized where he had heard it and she now understood why she felt something niggling at the back of her mind. Mikel had listened to her conversation with the Hunter. How could she forgotten that? Did she just assumed in that he wouldn't have understood anything they had said?

Unless an NPC was essential to a quest, a fan favorite, or served as a love interest, then they were pretty much ignored. She was still thinking as if she were sitting in front of a monitor playing a game, not in a fantasy word.

Now Tom was looking at her, waiting for her answer. What should she do? What could she say? Her Charm was a +7 so she should be able to convince him it meant nothing. She raised a shoulder in a shrug and offered an offhand smile. "I have no idea. It sounds like a silly word to me. Like something a child would make up for a game."

Slowly, Tom removed his hand from hers and laid it on his lap. Drawing a deep breath, he slowly released it through his nose, his eyes never leaving hers. "I suppose you're right. It is a silly word, isn't it?"

Did he believe her? Best to change the subject, so he didn't have time to dwell on it. Babbling, she said, "Do you need Darcy to heal you? I can go get her. Did she tell you we're leaving for Everguard by boat? We'll be there before tonight."

"I'm sure you're quite eager to get there," Tom said, following her lead into another subject. A smile softened the hard expression giving her cause to relax. "To cure Naomi."

"Yeah, the last thing we need is another wolf problem to deal with," Sally said with humorous candor. "We really don't need Naomi sprouting fur and howling at the moon."

"Well, I believe she would make an adorable werewolf," Tom said. "I can see Mina walking her on a leash like one of the noblewomen with their little dogs."

"It would take Mina to hold that girl's leash," Sally replied, quite pleased they had left the uncomfortable topic of NPC behind them.

Chewing his lower lip, Tom looked at her again, this time with a silent plea. "Sally, I know I've said this before, but I shall say it as many times as it takes for you to trust me. I have come to adore all of you. From the endearing Naomi, to the cautious Mina, to the resilient Darcy, and you, the beautiful Sally. If you're in peril or fleeing from it, I can help you, but you have to trust me with the truth."

Damn, he didn't buy it and worse, he was more confident that they had something to hide than before. She must have failed her Charm check, or maybe he had passed his Perception check? How was she supposed to handle this? Darcy would know what to do, but it would seem suspicious if she excused herself to get her now.

"Tom, we like you too, but I don't know what to say," she said evenly. "I'm sorry if we come across suspicious to you, but I promise you we're not bad people."

"Then why hide the truth?" There was accusation in his voice.

Anger pulsed in her temples, and her eyes narrowed. His suspicion actually hurt, and this time she was in the right for being offended.

"You don't trust us?" she said, surprised by how much his distrust stung. "If it weren't for us, you'd still be in a cell waiting for a rescue that probably wasn't ever coming. The Cut Throats would still be terrorizing the countryside with that asshole innkeeper sending them new victims. This village would still have a wolf problem with a bunch of kids trapped under a building, and Mikel would have been supper for the wolves. Let's not forget that for the second time we saved your life after a direwolf almost took your damn head off. I would think we've more than proven ourselves, but if that's not enough for you, then maybe we should part ways once we reach Everguard."

She rose from the chair and walked away, not caring to hear whatever he would say. It felt good to speak up for the group, but now she felt hurt, tired, and just unhappy in general.

Darcy met her in the hall with an expectant look. "Did you…"

"Yes, I apologized, and he accepted, but we have a bigger problem now," Sally said as she took her arm and towed her outside.

Darcy went along with her in silent worry until they were outside and well away from anyone overhearing them. They stood by a well near the well they had passed earlier, the one that looked like a wishing well. Being outside made her feel better, but Sally still felt on edge.

"What is it this time?" Darcy asked, looking exasperated.

"Tom just asked me if I knew what NPC meant," Sally said, looking down into the well. It was a dark tunnel with a minimum of sunlight glinting on the water's surface.

"Are you sure?" Darcy moaned, leaning against the edge of the well beside her.

"Yes, I'm sure. He pronounced it as Innpeasea, but separate the words you get NPC." The well was deeper than Sally would have expected. She could see how someone could die or drown falling into a well. "It was Mikel. The kid must have overheard the Hunter and me talking."

"How much did he tell Tom? How much did the kid overhear?" Darcy said, getting more riled.

"I don't know. But if Mikel told him about NPC and the rest of the conversation, then it's possible that Tom assumes we have something in common with the Hunter." Sally looked around for a rock to drop in the well but decided against it as that could be an unhygienic thing to do.

"So...What did he say? What did you say?"

"I tried to play it off like something silly a kid would make up, but he didn't buy it. Said he wanted us to trust him so he could help us." Sally looked away from the well's depths and locked her gaze with Darcy. "I said that if he didn't trust us after all the good we've done, then we should part ways in Everguard."

Darcy closed her eyes and sighed, shaking her head. "Oh, Sally..."

"No, Darcy, I'm serious. If he feels that way, then we need to cut him loose. Let him take the first boat to Everguard, and we'll wait for the next one."

"Good luck explaining that to Naomi," Darcy muttered.

"If she's so in love with him, then she can go off with him into the sunset."

"C'mon, don't be that way," Darcy said. "Naomi's okay, even if she can be annoying sometimes."

"I know...I'm not mad at her, I'm just irritated with everyone right now," Sally said, hanging her head. "You know how I am."

"Yeah, I do," Darcy sighed. "C'mon, let's go eat and let things cool down. We'll see what Tom wants to do later."

When they returned to the inn, Mina was sitting alone at a table with Naomi nowhere in sight. At the sight of them, the Barbarian stood up so fast she shifted the table and almost tipped over the mug she had been nursing. She stalked towards them with urgent energy and grabbed their wrists with both hands. "You need to come upstairs with me right now."

"What's wrong?" Sally heard herself asking and wondered how many times had that question been asked in the last twenty-four hours?

"Goddamn, it's just one thing after another," Darcy muttered to herself. "When it is going to stop?"

Mina didn't speak as she took them upstairs and into one of the rooms. Naomi was sitting on the bed, staring out the window in sullen silence. She almost sagged into a puddle when they came inside. "Am I in trouble?"

Mina let go of Sally and Darcy and shut the door behind them. "Just tell them what you told me."

"I didn't do anything," Naomi whined.

"Naomi," Mina said a stern voice that Sally or Darcy had never heard her use. "Tell them how old you are." Naomi's lips tighten in a thin line with obstinance. Mina's eyes darkened as she glared at the girl. "Either you tell them, or I'll tell them. They'll find out regardless."

Naomi made a noise between a grunt and a snort, then mumbled something.

Darcy stepped forward, crossing her arms. "A little louder, honey, we can't hear you. How old are you?"

Naomi's face turned red as she glowered. "I'll be…I'll be ten in two months."

There was a long moment in which Sally's world shattered. She stared at the girl who couldn't look any younger than sixteen with a developed body and voice to match. It couldn't be true, but then…remembering back to Naomi's behavior…

Sally whistled aloud. "This explains things a bit."

"If you're going to turn ten in two months, then that means you're nine years old!" Darcy snapped, jabbing a finger at the teenage girl who was actually a young girl.

"Almost ten!" Naomi yelled.

Mina cut her off with a sharp motion. "Keep your voice down, or the NPCs are going to wonder what we're doing. Darcy, how did this happen?"

"How do you think? Remember, these aren't our real bodies! My hair isn't this long, Sally isn't this thin, and you're not that tall. And now Naomi isn't this old either."

"This certainly explains why she can't take anything seriously," Sally said, sitting down on the opposite bed. So much of it was making sense now. Naomi's intense morality, her attachment to Tom, and why she was so eager to "play the game." She was living out a kid's fantasy of being transported to a magical world and becoming a hero.

"This is bad," Mina moaned, shaking her head. "This means we can't leave her alone for a second."

"Mina, c'mon, it's bad, but it's not..." Darcy started.

"It's very serious. She's a kid, but everyone is going to see her as a young woman. They'll take whatever she says seriously and expect her to understand things a kid wouldn't."

"I think we were already treating her as a kid from the beginning," Sally said, interposing herself between Mina and Darcy in case it became another row. "Let's be honest with ourselves. We've been treating her differently because we instinctively knew she was different, that her packaging didn't match what was inside. We'll have to keep an eye on her."

Mina gave Sally a deadpan look. "I agree but it won't be easy because she's gone. Right out the window."

***

Tom stared up at his dutiful companion, the ceiling. Over and over, his exchange with Sally played in his mind's eye. That could have gone better, he could have chosen his words more carefully, or said nothing at all.

The women fascinated him, but maybe it was because they let him feel a part of their group. Being the third-born prince with radical ideas of equality among the races never warranted much popularity in court. Just that of sycophants who orbited him in hopes of currying favor from the royal family. And the daughters of nobility who sought to seduce him so that they could be married into royalty. There was never anyone who wished for his presence because of who he was: they were only socializing with him for what he could grant them. In Sally and her party, he understood for the first time what it was to travel with companions, friends.

So deep was he in his thoughts that he didn't hear the window opening until a voice piped, "Morning!"

His ribs jolted in pain when he jerked around to the source of the voice. "Naomi? Why are you here?"

"To see you!" she said as she climbed inside without ceremony. As if it were the most natural thing to climb through a window. "And to get away from the others because they're jerks. And buttheads. Jerky buttheads."

"That's a colorful term for your friends," he said blankly.

She perched on the edge of the bed in a huff. "They're not acting like friends. They started talking about me as if I wasn't there and I hate that! Like I'm furniture that can't hear what they're saying."

"I know that feeling," Tom sympathized. How often did he overhear a conversation about him only a few steps away in the court or ballroom? "Did something happen?"

"No!" Naomi said in a confessional quickness to indicate that something did happen, but she wasn't going to tell him what. "They're jerks, and I hate them." After a moment of reflection, she admitted, "No, I don't hate them, but I hate that they're jerks."

"What are they being 'jerks' about?" Tom ventured.

"They think because I'm a kid, I can't do anything," Naomi said, bringing her legs up to her chest and hugged them. "Even my parents don't think I can do anything for myself."

"Parents tend to be overprotective of young daughters," Tom told her gently. "I have to admit that I'm surprised your parents let you wander alone unchaperoned."

"My parents don't know I'm here," Naomi muttered into her knees.

Tom leaned forward, concerned, "Did you run away from home?"

"I don't wanna go back home," Naomi grumbled. "I'm having too much fun. Getting bit by wolves is no fun, but it's part of having an adventure."

So, Naomi had run away from home to find adventure. When Tom was her age, he had entertained such notions, to pick up a sword and a backpack of supplies and just take to the road for a life of traveling and adventure. As tempting as that sounded, he was wise enough to remain in the castle where he was safe, and his sister needed him.

"My sister wanted to go adventuring too," he said fondly. "It was part of our games. I was always the bandit or monster while she was the adventurer on her way to fulfill a quest or destiny like in her favorite storybooks. You might have become friends. No, I know the two of you would have been terrific friends."

"I'm sorry she died," Naomi said solemnly. "I wish I could have met her too."

Whatever it was that Sally and Darcy were hiding, Naomi was innocent of it. How had they come to travel together? When he first met them, the only two who were familiar with each other were Sally and Darcy. Naomi and Mina were almost strangers to each other and the sisters. Despite their awkwardness, however, they put themselves in danger to save the others.

Sally had thrown herself at the werewolf with a vengeance after seeing it savage Naomi. Darcy came up with a cunning battle plan against the Cut Throats and used her spells to fight their foes. And Mina and Naomi came into a forest full of dangerous wolves to find Sally and him. The women had their secrets, but they were good people and that mattered most.

"Naomi, do the others know where you are?"

"No," Naomi muttered.

"They're probably worried and looking for you."

"They can keep looking."

"Naomi," Tom said, taking on the elder brother tone he used with his sister when she was having one her childish fits. "You mustn't make them needlessly worry for you. What if something should happen to you and they don't bother looking because they believe it's you being angry. In Everguard, the unwary can go missing and never seen again. They're going to need you to watch over them. Especially Sally..."

It was like a hand had squeezed his heart. Sally would be in more danger in Everguard than any of them. A beautiful half-elf was highly sought to fill brothels and prized as a mistress. In most cases, the women had no say in the matter and that wasn't touching upon the underground slave ring. Darcy could use the Divine Power and wore the armor of a cleric of Shantra, but she didn't uphold their rituals or prayers. Would that draw the ire of the Church? And soft-hearted Mina's visible Strength could make her a target for the Everguard's dark underbelly. Were the women aware of the danger that Everguard would hold for them?

And thinking of dangers, there was one looming over them in the form of white arrows. Was it possible this monster was a threat to them too? Was that why they were going to Everguard? For safety?

“I want to protect them. Will you help me do that, Naomi?” Tom said firmly.

Naomi’s bright grin filled her face. “Yeah! I can do that! Are you coming with us? That’s great! I’ll go tell them!”

Then she was out the window before he had a chance to speak another word.

Chapter 20
THE GAMERS

Darcy used two healing spells before they finally left the village. One to heal Mikel's ankle and the other for Tom. Mikel was able to walk without a crutch but was firmly ordered by both the healer and Darcy to take care as he could easily injure himself again. Tom felt better, no longer in pain, but he still felt quite weak.

"You must have taken some Constitution damage," Darcy muttered to herself as she looked him over. "I think you're fit to travel, but I wouldn't be getting into any more fights if I were you. You should be back to normal by tomorrow if you get plenty of rest."

"There will be plenty of time for rest on the boat," Tom promised, his eyes meeting hers. "And you'll be there to ensure I do rest."

Darcy gave him a pleased smile. "I was actually hoping we'd travel a little further together."

"Have you decided what you are going to do in Everguard?" he asked.

Darcy said. "I have some money saved in the Royal Bank. It'll be enough for us to find lodgings."

"My invitation still stands. My uncle's estate has plenty of room for all of you."

"That's a very kind offer, but I'll have to talk about it with the others," Darcy said politely. "We'll let you know where we'll be staying so we can keep in touch."

While Darcy was tending to Tom and Mikel, the others were waiting by the river, watching the men prepare the boat for departure. It wasn't a large craft, as it was meant for cargo instead of passengers. It functioned like a raft with barrels of goods tied together in groups of five and secured to the wooden floor.

"So, what's the plan for Everguard?" Mina asked Sally as she shielded her eyes from the morning sun. It was casting a long blade of light over the trees and made the water flash and sparkle.

"We'll have to go to the bank," Sally said. Her hood kept the sun from her eyes, so she was able to enjoy the morning air. "Hopefully, there's a fortune waiting for us there. We can find a place to stay, get Naomi cured of lycanthropy, and then look for other players."

"Do you think they'll know what's going on?" Mina asked, looking down the river in the direction of Everguard.

"Maybe," Sally sighed with a shrug. "It's the only plan we have, so I'm good with it."

A fish flipped from the water in a wet arch before plopping down in the water. Both of them cried out in surprise as the small dark shape disappeared beneath the water. The men working with the lines shook their heads at the women in bemusement.

"I heard of fish doing that, but never saw it for myself," Sally said, watching the water for another fish to leap.

"I'm a New Yorker. The only fish I see are in aquariums or grocery stores," Mina replied. "Naomi? Did you see the fish?"

The girl was sitting at the edge of the dock with her feet in the water. With her hands braced behind her on the wood, she leaned back to regard them. "No, I was busy thinking."

"Oh, Lord, save us," Sally sighed. "What were you thinking about?"

"We gotta have a name," Naomi insisted as she got to her feet. She left wet footprints on the dock. "All the best groups have names. Like the Avengers, Justice League, Team Avatar, the Ghostbusters, and Fellowship of the Ring all have names. We should have one too!"

"Oookay, so what name should we have?" Mina glanced at Sally with almost fear in her eyes. What name could Naomi have come up with?

"We should be called," Naomi paused for a dramatic effect which only served to annoy Sally. "...The Gamers."

"Gamers?" Mina said.

"The Gamers!" Naomi emphasized on "the." "That's what we are. Aren't we?"

"I never considered myself a gamer," Mina replied, looking between Sally and Naomi. "But, I guess most people who play this game would."

"I like it," Sally said. "It makes sense. Anyone from our world who hears it will recognize it. NPCs won't know what it means and it'll help us find other players."

"In that case, it sounds like a solid idea," Mina said with a nod. "We could say it's a club name?"

"More like a mercenary group name," Sally said.

"No, we're a band of heroes," Naomi said solemnly. "We help people like we helped this village."

Mina and Sally exchanged a look over Naomi's head. If Darcy's money fell through and they didn't return home soon, they were going to need a way to support themselves. And in any RPG world, the best way to make money was taking on sidequests or jobs. Also, calling themselves The Gamers felt right. It would remind them that they weren't of this world and that they had a life in the real one.

Sally watched the last of the cargo being loaded onto the boat and knew it was time to depart for the next part of their grand adventure within the world of *Shadow's Deep.*

***

His eyes scanned the trees despite knowing the futility of it. He wouldn't see her until she wanted to be seen. She was a ghost that could materialize out of the air and move as silent as the shadow of a predator.

The sun was high in the sky, but he didn't feel its warmth. Shivers crawled down his spine as he continued to search the boughs. How much longer would she make him wait? Was she watching him from the canopy now? With an arrow nocked?

No, she wouldn't kill him. He had done as she had asked. It took nearly two days, but he had managed to collect a sizable group of men, the remnants of the Cut Throats, and had them make camp in the deepest part of the forest, far from roads or villages. Most of the men assumed he was going to take over the gang while others were giving him a critical eye, knowing as well as he that the Cut Throats were no more without McRando to lead them. He promised them he had the coin for them to start over, and they assumed correctly that he was talking about the treasure he looted from McRando's treasury. What he didn't tell them was the gold was being held by someone to whom he answered. That was something he kept to himself under her orders.

The thought of fleeing and going it alone came to him. It would hurt to leave behind the gold, but it would be worth the price not to see those eyes again or hear that strange sing-song voice.

Yet, he didn't dare. He remembered all too well her warning.

"If you try to run away and hide, just remember," she had said sweetly as a lover. "I'll find you. You can swim across the widest ocean. Climb the tallest mountain. Or hide in the largest city. It doesn't matter because I'll find you and make you pay for making me look for you."

The eyes gleamed at him like the sharp edge of a blade at a throat. A shiver went down his spine, and he rechecked the trees. Damn her. She was out there watching him sweat and taking joy in it.

"Boo," a voice whispered an inch from his ear.

From years of living on the streets among scum who'd as soon slit your throat as look at you, with a practiced motion, he drew his knife and spun in a wide arc. The blade cut nothing but the empty air and a giggle to his right drew his attention.

Upon first glance, he thought her beautiful, but this beauty had dangerous thorns that would tear him apart. Her clothing was white as falling snow, which made her long black hair stand out in contrast. Long elven ears were angled backward along with the dark tresses. It was the first time he had seen an elf walk so freely without a hood to hide their race. She didn't act like any elf he had ever met before. They were aloof around humans, ancient with an air of superiority that could piss someone off. This woman was a contradiction. One minute, she was like a child with a new friend, playful and grinning, and then the next second, she was more lethal than an angry viper.

"Relax, Sikes Kites," she teased. "I was just playing around with you."

If he had been a bit quicker, he could have slashed her throat. He could watch her bleed out on her grass and be done with her once and for all. No, he was only fooling himself. She teased him because she knew he could never match her speed. Blink once, she was gone, blink again, and she was in front of you, staring with cold blue eyes.

"I did as you asked," he said, sheathing the knife. It wouldn't serve him against her anyway. "I have them gathered three miles south from here."

"Good, good," she said, walking a circle around him with her hands behind her back like a churlish maiden. "Did you tell them about me?"

"No, no, I told them nothing about you," he promised. A bead of sweat was rolling down the back of his neck. "Most of them think I'm running things now."

"Most?" She paused, tilting her head at a slight angle.

He swallowed as more sweat slipped down his temple. "Some of them don't think I can lead the gang because I'm not McRando."

Casually, she drew an arrow from the quiver across her back. The arrow as white as a fang and she brought a fingertip along with the head. "Are they going to be a problem?"

"No, mistress, I can handle them," Sikes said quickly. "They'll come around, I…I need to know…what I'm going to tell them…"

"You're going to Everguard, of course," she turned to him with a beaming smile.

"Everguard?" He stared blankly. "To hide?"

"No!" she said with a shake of her head. "Hide from what? Is someone looking for you? Are they looking for me?" The pitch of her voice dropped a few octaves as she leveled her gaze at him.

"No, mistress, but…I don't understand. What are we going to do in Everguard?"

"Take it over," she said.

He blinked. "The smuggling ring? But Riker runs that." Were they about to get into a gang war with Riker? Of all people? He didn't doubt her abilities, but by the gods, they weren't even a quarter of what they were under McRando's rule.

"Don't worry about Riker," she said. "Did you do that other thing I told you to do?"

"Yes, mistress," Sikes said. As distasteful as it was, he had spread the word that the four women had been the ones to cut down McRando. "I made certain everyone will know that it was the half-elf who killed him."

"Good, good." The elf's grin was malicious as she put the arrow away. "Riker is going to be too busy dealing with that issue to figure out what we'll be up to."

"I still don't understand," Sikes said in an almost a plea. "We're taking over Riker's turf?"

"Yeah, I guess you could say that. We're taking over Riker's turf, the other gangs' turf, and the whole goddamn city."

"We're going to become a syndicate?"

"You're thinking too small. I'm talking about Everguard itself. I want the whole goddamn city. Not just the criminal underbelly, not just the gangs, but all of it. I want it all."

Sikes stared at her, unable to comprehend her words. A gang war was one thing, but she was talking about...A rebellion against the city's lords, the nobility and the king!

"We—we can't do that! It's impossible...to topple Everguard..." Sikes whispered.

"Honey, I know that city better than your dick knows your right hand," the elf said with the finality of death. "You do as I say, and I'm going to take you places you've only dreamed of. Consider me your personal angel, Sikes Kites. If you're a good boy and obey me in all things, I'll take you to Heaven. But if you're a bad boy, disobey me or try to fuck me over, I'll send you to Hell."

He believed in her threat as he believed in the ground beneath his feet. And he also believed that her aspirations of taking over the city of Everguard weren't merely a grand illusion. He had seen madmen before, even had done a few jobs for them. This elf, though dangerous and violent, didn't speak like an insane person. This was a woman with enough foresight to know that the men would never follow the lead of an elven woman and had him take on the appearance of leadership. And she had something that Sikes lacked, but McRando and Riker had in spades. An instinct for leadership and a ruthless edge.

"Yes, Mistress, I swear I will obey without question."

"Good boy," she said. For a few seconds, he believed she was going to pat him on the head. "Wait until night and have your men move to the Wester's woods, about five miles from the city. Let no one see you. Make camp and have some men go into the city for news. I'll be along shortly to tell you what to do next."

Sikes couldn't stop himself from asking, "What will you be doing, mistress?"

A grin stretched her lips as she caressed the wooden limb of her bow. "I'm a Hunter, Sikes Kites. I'm going hunting."

About the Author

Cambry Varner has been an avid gamer since the moment she first picked up an Original Nintendo controller. From then, she could measure stretches of her life in console generations from Dreamcast to GameCube, and then to Xbox and Playstation. Between these bouts of gaming, and because school is a play for growth and education, she read epic fantasy novels between classes.

By her late twenties, she fell in love with Dungeons and Dragons and met her first real friends outside of a video game. And somehow, between her life investments, she graduated from Straughn Highschool and obtained a Bachelor's Degree at Troy University. Then she decided to take her dedication to gaming and great storytelling and crafted her own world of fiction in *Gamers*.

Cambry welcomes feedback from readers, feel free to get in touch: cjvgamers01@gmail.com.

For more Level Up titles visit www.levelup.pub/books

There you can sign up to be an ARC reader for our books, find out about new releases, or learn about special offers for Level Up titles.

Other LitRPG communities include:
www.reddit.com/r/litrpg/
www.facebook.com/litrpgreads/
www.facebook.com/groups/litrpgforum/ (highly recommended)
www.facebook.com/groups/LitRPG.books/
www.facebook.com/groups/GameLitSociety/

and for authors (including aspirant authors)
www.facebook.com/groups/LitRPGAuthorsGuild/